WHAT THE CRITICS SAY ABOUT *OJ'S K*

"*OJ's Knife* is an inventive tale, a wry comment on celebrity and it weaves fiction into real history very well. Gibson was a TV journalist so he knows whereof he speaks."—Paul Burke, *Crime Fiction Lover*

"In this comedic novel set in the mid-1990's, a fictionalized free-for-all centers around the titular object… it's a wackily endearing tale, though the real-life saga turned out to be far more twisty than any self-aware work of fiction could be."
—Chris Chan, *The Strand Magazine*

"[Gibson] creates believable characters, put into unusual situations, ties them together for a fun read that keeps you guessing till the end. Reminds me of Carl Hiaasen....I am ready for another one."
—*Amazon.com*

"It's a hell of an entertaining ride."
—Melodie Johnson Howe,
author of the Diana Poole novels

"Gibson shows a talent for character description and plot development. These, along with the well-known events of the arrest and trail, are what capture and maintain our interest."—Alan Cranis, *Bookgasm*

"...a raw, bare knuckled, gritty, nail biting page turner that will keep you breathless and awake long into the night."— Judge Andrew P. Napolitano

"In this rollicking, vividly entertaining book, John expands the world we knew and the one we suspected."—Geraldo Rivera

DEATH IN THE REEDS

A MICKEY JUDGE MYSTERY

by John Gibson

Stark House Press • Eureka California

DEATH IN THE REEDS

Published by Stark House Press
1315 H Street
Eureka, CA 95501, USA
griffinskye3@sbcglobal.net
www.starkhousepress.com

ISBN: 978-1-951473-85-3

Book design by Mark Shepard, shepgraphics.com
Cover photo by Aaron Lau
Proofreading by Bill Kelly

First Stark House Press Edition: September 2022

TO BE NOTED:

One of British archeologist Max Mallowan's great achievements—not counting his marriage to the famous crime novelist Agatha Christie—was his 1952 discovery of a series of ivories buried in the wreckage of a palace in the ancient Mesopotamian capital of Nimrud.

At the bottom of a well, preserved in a blanket of sludge, were two almost identical small plaques that depicted the death of a young boy in the jaws of a lioness that caught the boy in a field of reeds. The plaques have been known by various names, including The Lioness and The Nubian Boy, and occasionally Death in the Reeds.

Rendered by an unknown Phoenician artist some three thousand years ago the plaques are premier examples of representational art created at the dawn of recorded time, approximately 900 B.C.

Owing to their age and their exquisite beauty the value of both plaques is incalculable, beyond any sum of gold, silver, or dollars.

One plaque is in the British Museum. The other was in the Iraq Museum until the start of the Iraq War launched by President George W. Bush in 2003.

1

In the late evening hours of March 19, 2003 in Baghdad, Wajahat Zardari waited for George W. Bush to keep his word.

The American President promised military action against Saddam Hussein if the dictator did not leave Iraq within 48 hours. As midnight approached, time was running out. Saddam had not abandoned his country.

The American bombing was certain to start soon. In Baghdad people huddled in their homes expecting the worst.

This was the moment Wajahat Zardari put his audacious plan into action.

At 10 o'clock in the evening Zardari used a slim-jim to pop open the driver's door of a 1990 Mercedes belonging to a minor Saddam regime figure. Wajahat had been watching the man for weeks because he had an automobile ripe for the taking. Once inside Wajahat had no trouble defeating the ignition lock. The thirteen-year-old car started instantly and purred softly.

The minor regime official was sloppy securing his vehicle, and equally inattentive about the weapons he kept under a blanket on the floor of the back seat. Wajahat checked the AK-47. Seemed standard. Alongside it lay a Stechkin machine pistol, a personal defense weapon the Soviets sprinkled like rainwater throughout the Eastern Bloc and the Middle East for years. Zardari had seen the Stechkin everywhere he'd traveled. Heavy, dependable, fully automatic if the shooter chose. "These will do," he muttered to himself.

He slipped the Stechkin and an extra magazine into a jacket pocket on his left side, counterbalancing a stolen .22 Ruger in the opposite pocket.

In the throes of grunting sex with a woman not his wife the regime official didn't notice his prized Mercedes 300 SL easing away over crunchy gravel into the Baghdad night.

Just a few minutes later Wajahat Zardari pulled into a small parking lot of a hairdressing shop in the Al Bustan district not far from the Mosul Road. It was the meeting spot picked by his accomplice, a fellow janitor at the Iraq National Museum. The young man was central to Wajahat's plans: he was entrusted with the keys to an array of heavy locks securing the Museum.

"You did it!" Mustafa Hajj exclaimed as soon as he slammed the door, tossing a battered backpack into the back seat. The backpack contained a change of clothes, a bottle of musk aftershave, a toothbrush, and a photo album of his best poses. All he would need for his escape. "You got the car I wanted! Thank you, thank you," the beautiful young man enthused, running his soft hands over the leather seat, his dancing eyes taking in the details of the luxurious interior. "This is the life I deserve."

A thirteen-year-old Mercedes? Wajahat marveled at the third world innocence of the boy.

Mustafa Hajj was twenty years old, an impossibly beautiful man-child, the kind pederasts gamble their lives and reputations to have. He touched the faux wood paneling of the dashboard with delicate fingers. "At last! I've so dreamed of a Mercedes."

Wajahat nodded yes. "We will arrive in Beirut on your magic carpet as you asked."

Mustafa's smile radiated self-satisfaction. He was desperate to get out of Baghdad. Obsessed with the stylish life pictured in smuggled Western magazines, once he agreed to Wajahat's plan to escape Baghdad he insisted—badgered might be a better word—for a "proper" automobile for their escape. He loathed Wajahat's beat-up Toyota. He called it a humiliating Baghdad wreck. Wajahat didn't quibble; the boy's description was not far off.

Mustafa flipped down the mirror on the visor to check his hair. Mustafa Hajj was certain his beauty was wasted in Baghdad and while he wanted out, he wanted to arrive at his destination—Beirut—in style. "Admit it, Hamid. Don't you much prefer the Mercedes?"

In Iraq Wajahat's fellow workers and employers knew him by his father's name, Hamid, as he used his father's Pakistani passport, the photograph and birthdate altered.

"You'll be dancing on the tables in the most fabulous clubs the Middle East has to offer," Wajahat said, ignoring the boy's question. He laid a reassuring hand on the boy's thigh. "You will arrive in a manner suitable for the most beautiful young man in the Middle East."

Mustafa's brown eyes danced with excitement. "Inshahlah." God willing. "I have waited for this moment my entire life." Ecstatic, he gripped Wajahat's hand. "Thank you for saving me. If I stay I know I will die."

Wajahat Zardari returned a kindly smile. He had been grooming the young Hajj for weeks. Promising the excitement the beautiful boy craved, out of the reach of the homophobic terror of Saddam's Iraq. Wajahat led Mustafa on, firing the boy's imagination with overblown tales of the glamor and the sexual freedoms of the outside world. Mostly exaggerations, or outright lies, of course. But Mustafa was transfixed.

Wajahat understood the boy. Wajahat was empathetic and supportive. He didn't judge. The boy yearned for acceptance. Wajahat's soft touch was entirely unlike Hajj's fist wielding father, petrified his feminized son would be exposed as a homosexual, and humiliate the family.

An odd couple, they needed each other. Mustafa needed to escape. He fell hard for the promise he'd be dancing on the Beirut Corniche in two days.

Wajahat Zardari needed Mustafa Hajj for one reason: the young man carried the keys to the Iraq National Museum, Zardari's target tonight.

In ordinary circumstances a man as young and inexperienced as Mustafa Hajj would not be entrusted with the keys to an institution like the Iraq Museum. But Mustafa's father was the personal assistant to a ranking officer of Saddam's military, and therefore his son pulled rank, even on a lowly janitorial staff. Improbably, young Mustafa was the chief of the Museum janitorial crew.

Careful to conceal his true feelings, Wajahat secretly scorned the boy. An escape requires a Mercedes, Wajahat thought to himself. What utter nonsense. It was for the keys that Wajahat played the role of an older gay man. It was for easy access to the Museum that Wajahat put up with the emotionally unstable and needy boy.

Wajahat Zardari was a wiry, muscular man of forty. He was a little under six feet tall, a slim hundred seventy pounds. He wore a closely cropped beard showing flecks of gray. His hair was cut short, and he had a circle of bald on the crown of his head. His eyes were brown, intense and wary. He had a pointed chin in gray stubble, a hatchet nose, and flappy ears.

Zardari was not gay. But he's lived among gays growing up in the San Francisco Bay area, and he knew how to lead the boy on, how to prey on the boy's sexual repression and paranoia and weakness.

Engine off. Seated in the Mercedes in a dusty Baghdad alley behind the Babylon Mall in the Mansour district. The two men waited for the war to begin. Wajahat expected the Americans might bomb bridges over the river, perhaps on purpose, perhaps by accident. Therefore he was careful to stay on the west side of the Tigris fairly close to the Museum.

They waited for the action.

"If the Americans don't attack, what are we going to do?" Mustafa asked. His secret lust for men compelled him to take risks to flee Iraq, but the exhilaration of escape faded as the decisive moment grew near. He reeked of nerves.

"They will. Bush will do what he said he'd do," Zardari replied softly.

"But what if they don't?"

Wajahat didn't answer. He didn't have an answer. If dawn arrived without an American attack Wajahat's plan would have to be scuttled. In that event he knew Mustafa might break, turn in Wajahat, reveal the older man's scheme. Either out of bitter disappointment or to save himself. And even if all went as Wajahat planned he knew the fragile Mustafa could never be trusted to keep his secrets.

Any way you cut it, Wajahat concluded, the beautiful young Mustafa Hajj was a dead man the moment he got in the car.

The waiting was agony. In the gloom of a pitch-black night Wajahat had just about given up hope. Mustafa dozed off. Even Wajahat caught himself drooping his eyes.

But sudden explosions startled the two men upright. The American bombing of Baghdad—later known as the Shock and Awe campaign—kicked off in the stealth friendly darkness of four in the morning. As the first thundering, reverberating explosions rattled windows, Wajahat Zardari breathed a sigh of relief.

Quietly Wajahat reveled in the shaking ground and the night lit orange. He delighted in the strobe effect of multiple missiles striking a mere instant apart.

But the deafening bursts frightened young Mustafa to his core. "The bombs are so close!" he whispered in the hoarse voice of fear.

"There's more coming," Wajahat whispered back.

There was a pause and then another round of thundering reverberations.

The next detonations came in a roaring wave, like a string of firecrackers on an ear-shattering massive scale. Zippers of explosions bubbled the boy's natural cowardice to the surface.

"I changed my mind. Take me home," the boy whimpered. "Please."

Iraqi gunners filled the night sky with panicky and useless tracer fire.

"I can't do this," Mustafa wailed.

"Too late to back out now," Wajahat Zardari said, pulling Mustafa Hajj close. A firm hand clutching his neck.

The missiles were finding their targets; the explosions lit up the sky like high noon. Pieces of buildings whirled into billowing orange air, like autumn leaves that somehow defied gravity, falling upward into the dark sky.

His fingers dug into the boy's neck. "I already stole the car. You defied your father when you sneaked out of his house. You want to quit now? The Mukh will come for you." There was nothing more threatening than Saddam's secret police, the Mukhabarat, especially for a boy who loved boys. The girlishly thin Mustafa Hajj retreated from Wajahat's grip, huddled in the passenger seat bathed in the cold sweat of fear.

Scared, quivering Mustafa was useless except for the key ring in his pocket. Wajahat knew it might have been easier to kill the boy and take the keys. Now he wondered why he hadn't.

No looking back, he thought. Wajahat fired up the stolen car, and slipped into the night. The Mercedes aroused neither notice nor suspicion as it sped past anti-aircraft emplacements lighting up the night with tracer fire. Gunnery crews assumed the driver of such a prestigious vehicle was an important figure and had good reason to be tooling around in the onslaught.

On the ground in Baghdad the booming detonations rattled the speeding car, shaking a driver's grip on the wheel. At half past 4 o'clock in the morning, under the cover of the American attack, the stolen Mercedes glided past the grand entrance to the National Museum of Iraq. Wajahat turned into the employee parking lot at the backside of the campus and pulled the automobile to a stop in the shadow of the building near the unmarked employee entrance.

Booming shock waves shook the car. In the passenger seat Mustafa Hajj was trembling like a leaf in a windstorm. "I didn't know it would be like this," he squealed. His lower lip quivered. "The bombs are coming close. Please let me go home. Please."

"The Americans won't attack the museum. Don't be a girl. We're perfectly safe." Now that they were on the move Wajahat was past concealing his disgust with the boy.

In the night sky a roaring pyrotechnic light show transfixed television viewers around the world. But Wajahat was right about his confidence in the Americans: their high-tech missiles were extremely accurate. And they were not targeting the Museum or its immediate surroundings.

Wajahat had to pull the boy out of the car. He grabbed the AK-47 from the back seat, shoved it into Mustafa's hands. "What am I supposed to do with this?" Mustafa objected, squealing.

"You never know," Wajahat said, pushing him forward. He hoped the gun would rouse sleeping courage.

While the sky lit up in strobing flashes Mustafa fumbled with his keys. The staff door was rigged with multiple locks. Mustafa's nervous fingers slowed progress. The last lock open, rusted hinges creaked a pained squeal.

Wajahat signaled for Mustafa to walk in front. He didn't trust a man with a gun behind his back, even a quaking flower like Mustafa. Tapping him on the shoulder to indicate where to turn, Wajahat led from behind, the beam of a flashlight illuminating the way along a maze of corridors and hallways, through one locked door after another. It was slow going. The boy janitor struggled with hands shaking so badly he could hardly fit a key into its slot.

As they proceeded through the darkened hallways Mustafa Hajj wondered where exactly the older man wanted to go. He had the sense they must be getting close because they were entering rooms with shelves of ancient objects, some thousands of years old. Yet Wajahat bypassed these treasures.

They arrived at what turned out to be a final door. After Mustafa keyed the door open, Wajahat held him back. "Wait here," he said in a whisper and pushed by him.

This was a room Wajahat Zardari knew well. During his late night janitorial rounds he had determined the exact location of the object he intended to take. Now he was about to betray his employers. He was here to steal one of the most valuable and irreplaceable objects the Museum owned.

He went directly to a certain drawer and pried the lock off with a heavy military knife. The drawer slid open, revealing a steel box with yet another lock. Zardari popped it off with the knife and slowly opened the lid.

Inside ... the object he came for.

It was a four-inch by four-inch plaque. Almost three thousand years old, carved ivory, covered in gold leaf, inlaid with rubies. It depicted a scene in the reeds and rushes of the Babylonian-era marshlands south of Baghdad. It was a scene of breathtaking and heartbreaking violence: a lioness on top of a boy, one paw on the boy's chest holding him down, the other paw under his neck, the lioness' jaws biting down on the boy's neck. The moment of death.

In the world of antiquities the piece was known by several names, but often called Death in the Reeds. It was thought to have once decorated the throne of King Ashurnasirpal about 850 B.C. in Nimrud, thirty miles south of Mosul. Wajahat first saw its identical twin in the British Museum a dozen years earlier. Enthralled with the beauty of the piece, he'd planned this raid for years.

Mustafa was behind him. "Is that thing killing that boy?" he asked.

Startled, Wajahat swung around pointing the Russian pistol at Mustafa's chest. "I told you to wait." The boy retreated two steps in horror at the sight of the gun. "Now stay there."

Wajahat slipped a backpack off, unzipped the cover. Inside was a small metal case. Inside foam padding had been cut to the exact size of the plaque. He slid the delicate Lioness plaque into the foam cutout. He snapped the case closed, slipped it into the backpack. He seethed at Mustafa. "Don't be an idiot anymore," he whispered.

"Sorry," Mustafa said, hurt. The older man was suddenly sounding like his father—abrupt, mean.

"Let's go."

"We're not taking anything else?" Mustafa asked, glancing around at the shelves of precious antiquities.

"We got what we came for. Go," Wajahat said, pushing him forward. "Just be ready to shoot if someone gets in our way."

But there was no one. The city was cowering under the American assault. No one was coming to save the National Museum of Iraq from the first of what became a flood of looters.

Back in the stolen Mercedes, Wajahat wheeled the big sedan through Baghdad streets, dodging the Americans' exploding raindrops. He had a hunch which buildings would be targeted. Military and government buildings were the ones to avoid.

This was a bold and daring plan. Patient and meticulous, he put the pieces of his operation together despite very long odds of success. Wajahat sacrificed personal pleasures. He damaged relationships, especially with his family. He prepared for years with a single mindedness. He never gave in to the temptation to opt out for a normal life.

Now success. Now the precious antiquity was in his hands. Now his escape.

Yes, he would bask in the sublime beauty of the ancient piece of art. But he had not gone to all this trouble simply to luxuriate in a private museum. The value of the piece was straightforward: it would set him up for life. Some billionaire somewhere—some Russian oligarch, some Saudi prince, some technology robber baron—was going to pay many millions for it.

There were still obstacles to overcome and total getaway was not complete, but he knew the road out, and he had plans.

He couldn't suppress a smile. It was the longest of long shots. Some might have said impossible. But the American President had given him the opportunity, and he had taken it.

Death in the Reeds was his.

2

The Empire News Network stood astride the national media in a glass and concrete monolith on Sixth Avenue in New York City.

On the ground floor an elevator opened and Mickey Judge bounced out, headed for the glass doors that led to the studios. His hit time was right after the break.

The guard pulled the door open and gave him a friendly nod. Mick quick stepped down a narrow hall past makeup rooms, through a heavy sound proof door into Studio A.

Careful to avoid tripping on cables, fastidious about not making any distracting sounds, Mick took the on-deck spot in the dark watching anchor Martha Molloy wrapping a segment, heading into a break.

Martha Molloy was done up in the manner the makeup ladies of The Empire News Network were famous for: blonde hair inflated as if by compressed air, shimmering lip gloss, long lash extensions, rosy cheeks, flashing eyes. Martha was a natural beauty, but the makeup department supercharged her look.

She said "back after this," throwing to the break. The floor monitor went to black, signaling the network was in commercial. Studio speakers popped on, and the floor director, a young woman, shouted "Clear." Mick headed for the second seat on the anchor set.

"Hey Mick," Martha said, greeting him with a smile. "Making the competition bow down today?"

"Last American to speak with Saddam Hussein. Got it to ourselves," he said, smiling back. Martha Molloy was one of his favorite anchors. Not only glamorous, but smart, and read-in. She knew what she was talking about.

"The New York Times guy?"

"Uh huh," Mick mumbled.

"I was surprised to hear it in the meeting," she said. "Isn't he on the forbidden list?"

"He is a New York Times reporter, so I'd say he's on the suspect list," Mick said. "But he's a big get. I'll take my chances with The Beast."

Mick opened his jacket to let the audio guy drop a wire down the back, hook an IFB pack on his belt, a lav mic on his jacket lapel. A scrunchy with an earpiece was clipped to his collar.

The crew in the studio consisted of four camera operators and an audio person. Tucked away in the darkness were operators of the teleprompter and the lighting grid.

Mick glanced around at three cameras, winking hi to the guys. A woman was behind them operating the jib, a long pole with a camera for sweeping bumper shots.

"I told him it was for your show," he continued to Martha. "Said the Times wouldn't allow him to go on with our prime-time guys. Called them wankers. I thought that was a little harsh," he said with a mirthless grin.

Martha pretended not to hear. She knew better than to be seen or heard agreeing that her colleagues in prime time, the opinion hosts, were wankers.

A pair of women, makeup and hair stylists, hovered nearby. "You never come sit in the chair," one scolded, spraying his hair, putting fly-aways in place. Her partner dabbed his face with powder. "It's always hurry up with you."

Mick made kissy lips and winked at her. He heard the senior producer in his ear. "Sixty," meaning a minute to air. "And double check your role cue, please."

"It's ... 'Last American to interview Saddam Hussein,'" Mick said.

"Got it," the voice in his ear said. "Back in forty-five."

The whole process was calm and coordinated. These were the routines the crew executed over and over every day.

The floor director shouted out, "Back in thirty."

"How are you?" Mick asked Martha, to be courteous. He was a guest in her house.

"Couldn't be better," she smiled. "Did Rod clear your guy?" she asked with an arched eyebrow. Meaning Rod Wings, the founder and CEO of The Empire News Network.

Mick shrugged. He knew what she meant. The interview subject was John Hearns, the Middle East correspondent for The New York Times. The Times and The Empire News Network were sworn enemies.

"Rod told me to get the good stuff even if I have to walk on people," Mick whispered.

She grimaced. As they came out of the break she transitioned to her on-air face.

Staring into the lights and the glass face of the camera, Mick kept an eye on the air monitor as it popped from black to the bright colors and swooshing images of a "WAR IN IRAQ" animation. A music bed composed specially for the impending war coverage, which the young men and women on the crew acidly referred to as the "war boogie."

Out of the video, the bumper to the studio was a diving jib shot that settled on Martha.

Sitting at her elbow, Mick watched as Martha Molloy read the prompter copy flawlessly and with authority. Her toss to Mick was a simple "TENN's Mickey Judge has more."

At this point the gig was pretty easy. All the hard work went into building the package. Once on the set, Mick read his lead, not more than twenty seconds of copy, and the control room rolled his package. Today the interview with John Hearns was long, two and a half minutes. While it rolled he and the anchor didn't talk. The New York Times' John Hearns related what Saddam Hussein told him, described the defiance in his attitude, concluded that war was inevitable. Martha listened closely.

When he came back on camera for a wrap and a toss back to her, Martha Molloy asked a question: With all his experience in Iraq and the Middle East, did John Hearns think Saddam would back down before the invasion was launched?

Mick said John Hearns believed Saddam would not.

It was a big story, a big get. Nobody else on television at one minute after 5 pm ET had it. The segment would rate.

In the next break the audio guy pulled Mick's mic, Martha gave him a knowing look, covered her own mic with her hand and said, "Good luck with her."

Of course, he knew what she meant. He'd committed a borderline offense with the Vice President of Public Relations. She famously had an ongoing battle with The New York Times. Mick saw no reason he should participate in her private war. So it was not a surprise when he walked out of the studio he found a breathless intern arrive at a run with a message. He was summoned to see The Beast: Elaine Constantine, the head of The Empire News Network's public relations department.

Mickey and the PR Vice President had a relationship that was dismissive on Mick's end and openly hostile on hers. She felt entitled to issue orders to reporters and anchors and most of Mick's colleagues were afraid to stand up to her. Those who did often found their name appearing in a gossip column somewhere hinting at terrible things the TENN star might have done. She was a fixture in the senior executive meetings with Rod Wings, and she left everyone the impression he gave her free rein to do whatever she wanted. To Mick and other reporters there was no logical explanation for her power. It wasn't as though she and the founder had a personal relationship, such as secret lovers. No one could imagine Rod Wings' taste in women had sunk that low. Instead, it evidently was some corporate voodoo that Mick just could never understand. His way of dealing with her was to ignore her.

Which had the effect of infuriating her.

On the 18th floor Mickey marched down a long hallway. Executive offices on his left, assistant pods on his right. Smiles and hellos from the assistants, many of whom he knew from the smoking and gossip area down on the street.

Dressed in a navy blazer, pressed jeans, a light blue dress shirt, his tie loose at his neck, he strode forward in a hurry, annoyance and determination on his face.

Mickey Judge was a decent looking man closing in on forty, shocking white hair, usually mussed, lively gray eyes, a long narrow nose, a dimpled chin and thin lips. He was a correspondent known around the building as a voluble type, friendly, talkative, quick to argue, certain he was right. Which sometimes led to trouble. Like today.

He swung into the office of Elaine Constantine without breaking stride and stood in front of her desk, hands on hips in a pose of unmistakable defiance.

"What's up?" he asked. "I have a flight to Kuwait," he added impatiently. Mick was an embed with the 10th Mountain Division out of Fort Drum, New York. He would be in Kuwait in less than 24 hours.

"Sit down," she said.

He shook his head no. "I don't have time. If you were watching our air you might have noticed a war is about to start."

Elaine Constantine's nose scrunched a sneer at the insult. She was in her mid-thirties, dark hair, her skin the deathly pallor of New York's office dwellers. She was also conspicuously overweight. She wore thousand-dollar plus-size pant suits that projected power and dominance. Today's color was brush fire reddish orange. She looked like a flaming log sitting in a thousand-dollar C-suite executive chair.

Completing her impeccably curated wardrobe, she wore a hitman's mean face of pleasure from causing hurt. Behind her back she was called the head bitch in charge. She did not discourage the description.

"You don't seem to understand that when I issue an order I expect it to be followed," she said slowly in the soft voice of a corporate cobra. "I've told everyone that people from The New York Times are not allowed on our air."

The slight cock of Mick's head projected resistance and insolence. "I heard something about your ban. But I didn't get an email."

She scowled. "Right. You'd love me to commit instructions to writing so you could leak it to your hack media friends who hate TENN."

The accusation jerked Mick to attention. "I don't leak," Mick shot back. "I'm loyal to Rod and he knows it."

"Your loyalty is highly suspect."

"If you mean I'm not loyal to you, bingo. You're the public relations gal," he said, emphasizing the diminutive gal. "You are not Rod Wings. Huge difference," he said, spreading his arms wide miming a fatso.

Reacting to the insult she arched in her chair to raise herself to command height.

"I speak for Rod. You need to get that straight."

Mick shook his head. "Rod speaks directly to me. He told me my job is to hunt down the good stuff and drag it onto the air 'over corpses of the defeated.' Direct quote. Beat the competition. My loyalty to him is following his instructions."

Her face flushed in anger. She hated that some people got direct orders from the founder of The Empire News Network.

"Rod approved my ban on New York Times reporters."

"He didn't tell me that."

"He didn't have to. When it comes to the ban I speak for him."

"Then you should tell him to tell me personally to obey your insane ban."

She doubled her sneer. "It's not insane. The Times attacks us every day. We don't promote them when all they do is crap on us."

Mick rolled his eyes. "It's your job to conduct that war. My job is reporting and today it was John Hearns' interview with Saddam Hussein."

Elaine Constantine swiveled in her chair like a cat swishes its tail. "Even if by some stretch of the imagination we needed to hear from the Times reporter, you lied to the producer about what was in your package."

Oh that. Mick wouldn't call it a lie. It was a petty offense. He neglected to enter a script in the computer system that was exactly the script that went on the air. A little fudging, changes on the fly in the edit room under deadline pressure. Nothing he and other reporters hadn't done before. Many times before.

But a lie? Not really. "What's that?"

Constantine stood up, her hands flat on her desk, leaning forward like a pitbull straining at the leash. "You put the Times guy in your script as a ten-second bite wrapped by your narration."

"The narration was junk. I dumped it."

"What aired was an extended interview with Hearns, over two minutes. Big blocks of narration replaced by long sound bites with the guy I ordered to never appear on our air."

Mickey Judge wrinkled his face. In disbelief. "John Hearns was the last person to speak to Saddam Hussein. He had quotes from Saddam nobody has heard. It's what we call an exclusive."

Exasperated, she squeezed her eyes into angry slits. "The rule is 'no Times people.' Not two seconds, not ten seconds. And a minute forty-five of someone forbidden is not what we call a scoop or an exclusive." she said. "It's what we call insubordination."

"A ratings block buster exclusive?" He laughed in her face. "That's insubordination?"

She narrowed a withering glare at her quarry. "Take my word for it."

Mick snorted a guffaw again. "No way."

She recoiled at his defiance. "The order was clear. You need to show respect to your superior."

Mickey's eyes flashed. "There it is. 'I'm your boss.' No, you definitely are not."

"Try obedience, Mr. Judge."

"No. You want to make reporting a public relations thing. It is not. It's what gets the huge ratings that make us number one. Which is the reason you can throw your weight around."

That gratuitous reference to "weight" was meant to sting and it did.

Her fury flushed her cheeks a deep shade of red. It was well known that joking about her weight brought vicious reprisals. "I told you not to do it." She spoke the words slowly, as if he were too thick to comprehend their meaning.

It wasn't that Mick didn't know this woman was dangerous. He'd seen her handiwork on people he knew. Her favorite garotte was planting an item that her target of the day was under investigation for sexual assault. She did not mind doing it to TENN people who crossed her.

But he was confident she was overstepping her bounds. "I am a reporter. I don't take orders from the Vice President of Public Relations. That would make me a flack and I certainly am not that," he insisted. Mick threw his arms in the air in exasperation. "I work for the Vice President of News. I don't answer to you."

She raised herself to her full height of five foot one inch plus spike heels. "Let me make clear your position in this company. You follow orders. Think of yourself as a servant in the basement waiting for instructions from your betters upstairs."

Mick laughed instantly. "Now you sink to insults," he said. He sighed and shook his head. "Know what?" He mouthed the words "go fuck yourself," without saying them out loud.

"What did you say?" Not that she hadn't seen "go fuck yourself" on his lips. She dared him to say it.

"I said I don't work for you."

"No. The quiet part. The insubordinate part. The part that shows you can't stand working for a woman. The misogyny part. Say that part like you were on television, you coward."

"You're baiting me now. Time to go."

"You're a pussy," she seethed. "You tell me to go fuck myself but you haven't got the guts to say it out loud."

Turning back, pointing his index finger at her, he let caution slip away. "You've always been a bully," he said, "You just love pushing people around. You're addicted to scaring people. You really ought to see a shrink."

Mick turned to walk out.

"Hold on," Constantine said.

Mick stopped. "I got a plane to catch," he said, dismissing her.

"You're fired," she said. Hurried, she wanted it said before he went through the door.

The words were spoken as Mick's back was to her. "Oh, for fuck's sake."

"I'm not mouthing the words," she barked. "I'm saying it for you to hear. You are fired."

Mickey Judge snorted. He turned back. "You can't fire me."

"You are fired," she repeated, emphasizing are. "Go to your office. Security will be there in five minutes to escort you out. Now get out and don't hide from security."

Mick glared. "Now you really can just go fuck yourself. Go. Fuck. Yourself," he said emphasizing each word.

And Mickey stormed out.

He headed for his office to grab his go-bag and the big suitcase. Passport, tickets, various electronics. He was ready for Kuwait and then on to Iraq.

An hour later Mickey Judge walked out of the building onto 6th Avenue.

He was dragging his rolling bag, but it was not headed to the invasion force. The Beast had won. He was fired.

He'd been called to the office of his immediate boss, the Vice President of News. As far as John Goode was concerned there was no coming back from "doctoring your script to conceal the contents of your report from the senior producer, much less telling a Vice

President to go fuck herself."

"John, she was giving orders as if she had your job."

Goode rolled his eyes. "You should have come to me before telling her to fuck off. At this point there's no going back."

More or less the same routine when Mick barged into Rod Wings' office. Rod was meeting with his secretary about his calendar. He shooshed her out. "Sorry, Mick. Loyalty can't abide telling a Vice President to go fuck herself. What were you thinking?"

"I was thinking I don't take orders from the PR girl and you'd stand behind me."

Rod puckered his lips in annoyance at the "girl" jab. "I regret to say this, but not this time," the fat man said, shaking his head. "I am your biggest fan in this building. I'm the reason you've been on the air. I've had to fight my own executives over you."

"Cowards who go limp at the first complaint."

Rod Wings shook his head. "You were scheduled for Kuwait, right?"

"Wheels up in three hours."

"Yeah, well that's done."

Mick's face sagged. "Are you serious?"

Wings nodded. "Yes."

What? No war? All that work to get embedded and poof? Gone? "You're joking. Right?"

"Look. I brought you in because you had brass balls. But you have to check your balls at the door. I can't have my Vice Presidents defied."

"She wanted me to gut a story that is going to be a ratings hit when you see the numbers tomorrow."

Rod Wings glanced at him with hard eyes then looked away. "I have two attack dogs. You and her. I love 'em both. Don't want to lose either."

"Good. You can work it out with her."

"Actually no. She'll walk if I don't back her."

"Don't let her push you around."

"Somebody has to go."

"Sounds like she's volunteering."

"No. It's got to be you."

Mick recoiled. What? "Why me?"

Wings shook his head, his jowls flopping. "She knows too much. She goes across the street or to the Times, I'm fucked. The network is fucked."

Mick's eyes widened. Cornered. No way out.

"Hate to do it, but the firing sticks."

Rod Wings stood up, signaling the meeting was over. "Sorry, buddy. Good luck."

In less than an hour it was over. Mick was fired. Confirmed at every step all the way to the top.

He was escorted out the door dragging his suitcase, his go-bag slung over a shoulder. A security guard named Greg, a pleasant young black man, walked beside him.

Mick stopped to watch the crowd gazing up at the screen on the side of the building just below Rod Wings' second floor office. The war was starting, on live television. Bombs would begin falling on Baghdad any minute.

Humiliated. Embarrassed. Mickey Judge was thinking, Jesus, Rod how could you let her do that?

Greg, the security guard, said, "Have to walk you all the way to the sidewalk Mick. Sorry. You gotta be off Empire property."

Mick nodded. Right.

"Yeah. Sorry, Greg," he said and continued shuffling until he was on a New York City sidewalk. He fished in his pocket for a pack of cigarettes. He lit one, inhaled deeply, and exhaled a cloud of smoke. He watched the television on the wall. American jets were launching off an aircraft carrier, file tape showed American Tomahawk missiles blasting out of tubes on American warships. A war would soon be underway.

And it was going to happen without Mickey Judge. He was fired.

He looked up. A silhouette appeared in Rod Wings' second floor window. The Beast staring down on him. The image of Muhammad Ali standing over a flattened Sonny Liston flashed before his eyes. "Jesus. Rod fucking Wings how could you let her do this?" he mumbled to himself.

He looked away.

The sidewalk in front of The Empire News Network—TENN as it was known in the trade—was always jammed with pedestrians. There were tourists by the hundreds, plus the thousands of workaday New Yorkers who toiled in the neighborhood of 49th street and 6th Avenue. They all seemed to be streaming around Mickey Judge at this moment. He was an obstruction to traffic. They jostled each other to get around him. He didn't care. He stood stolid and un-movable, smoking, watching the war that would proceed without him. Fuck, he thought. Fuck!

"What you gonna do now?" The voice came from behind. Mick turned. His friend David Stork, the weekend executive producer.

"You heard already?" Mick asked.

"Dude. She put out a press release," David said, holding up his Blackberry. "Mickey Judge separated from Empire News."

"Bitch," Mickey mumbled.

"Jesus, man, what'd you do?"

"We had a major fight. I told her to go fuck herself." Mick shot his friend a grim grin.

David Stork laughed. "You told Elaine Constantine to fuck herself? What were you thinking?"

"That's what Rod asked. She was telling me who I couldn't interview. I told her I worked for John."

"What'd John say?"

Mick sighed. "He said I hid what was in the package from the senior producer. I let some bites go long, dropped narration blocks. He played stickler. The senior should have seen what was really going to air. Therefore he had to go along with her."

"As a senior producer I must say I'd be pissed if you did that to me," Stork shook his head, and let a small laugh sneak out again. "Believe it or not she likes her nickname. Helps her scare people."

Mick pinched his face in confusion. "I never really got it. Why does she have so much power? It's baffling."

Stork laughed. "I know why. I've been in the meetings. She brags about bullying the media when they start digging around about Rod. She protects him, and he gives her a lot of leeway. Plus she knows the state secrets, if you know what I mean."

"Yeah, that's what Rod said. 'She knows too much.'" Mick stamped out his cigarette. And he reached for another.

They both noticed Martha Molloy coming their way. Her face was stripped of the TENN makeup, and she was wearing her street clothes, jeans and a light sweater. "Mick, I was searching all over for you. I'm so sorry. I should have killed the piece this morning in the meeting."

Mick was flattered she cared enough to search him out. "It's not your fault, Martha. The Beast and I have been on collision course for a while. This isn't the first time I didn't follow her orders."

"Did you really tell her to fuck herself?"

"The accurate quote would be 'go fuck yourself.'" Mick grimaced. "Heat of the moment."

She laughed. "That might make Page Six." She shook her head with that what-are-we-going-to-do-with-you expression, and took his face in two hands. "Part of your charm is that incorrigible thing. But this is not fair and a real loss for us. I'm going to tell Rod what I think." She gave him a hug. "We're all going to miss you."

David Stork stood aside so Mick could have his moment with a pleasant and intelligent woman who just happened to be one of the hottest anchors in the building.

She gave him a little kiss on the cheek, and turned away.

Mick watched her cross 48th street toward the parking garage and her white Range Rover.

"Don't fantasize," David Stork scolded him. "Wishful thinking is a waste of time."

"Let me bask in her warm glow for a moment or two," Mick mumbled.

"Why don't we get out of the traffic?" David asked, annoyed at the bumping he was taking on the sidewalk.

"Can't be on Empire property," Mick said.

"What you doing now? Do you know?"

Mick sighed. "I'm picking up my bags, walking over to Langan's. I'll take a booth, get an Absolut and soda."

"I meant what are you thinking about working?"

Mick grimaced. "See the agent tomorrow, I guess. I'd like him to get to Rod and back this up. I don't want to leave."

Stork shook his head no. "Usually doesn't work that way."

Mick nodded. He knew that was true. He was being optimistic. Unwarranted optimism, but it was his last hope. When the Empire News Network fired you, you stayed fired. Not like NBC. He'd worked for them too. They fired him, hired him back and fired him again. He liked to say he held a firing record.

David Stork slapped Mick on the back. "Sorry bud. I'll try to get over there later," he said, meaning the bar.

Mick shook his hand but he knew David wasn't going to show. A fired anchor or correspondent was radioactive, especially on the day of firing. "If you got time I'm sure I'll be there."

A crowd was gathering around the TENN big screen. Something about a faraway war that brings people out.

Mick was profoundly sorry he'd not be covering the war.

"She can still go fuck herself," he said to himself.

He slung his go-bag over his shoulder, grabbed the rolling bag and headed down to 47th street to Langan's.

3

Wajahat wasn't out of Baghdad yet. He needed to put the rest of his plan into action.

Soon he would head west into Anbar province, through the tough towns of Fallujah and Ramadi. But first the Mercedes needed to be dumped. No point in standing out in the rush of refugees. He calculated people in Anbar would be so distracted by the American attack he could slip by without problems. As long as he was not driving a rob-me-at-gunpoint German luxury car.

However, there was still the issue of Mustafa. Wajahat Zardari told the boy many lies to secure his cooperation for the keys. The boy didn't care what Wajahat took from the museum. He only cared about escaping Baghdad. He had been promised his face would be celebrated on magazine covers, that his beauty would make him rich, that in the coming days he'd be the star attraction of nightlife in the world's most exotic resorts.

Had the boy shown some courage, some poise, perhaps Wajahat could have seen a way for him to complete the tricky journey across Iraq and Syria and Lebanon to the Mediterranean. But the boy was a weakling, gutless, and entirely untrustworthy. How would he do under questioning by a hostile and suspicious border guard? Wajahat knew in his heart the boy would collapse, and doubtless he would confess.

The Mercedes glided to a stop behind Wajahat's battered Camry in a neighborhood of poor Sunnis where the older man occupied a small room.

"What are we doing?" the boy asked.

"I want you to drive," Wajahat answered.

"Me? Drive this car?" The boy perked up.

Wajahat and Mustafa exchanged places. The boy was visibly thrilled to be behind the wheel. Once again he ran his soft hands over the instrument panel, the steering wheel, the gear shift. He smiled at the older man. "Can I drive all the way to Beirut?"

"You certainly may," Wajahat lied

The boy pulled on the seat belt. "Straight out on Highway One?" he asked.

But everything changed in an instant.

Wajahat knew this was the moment to rid himself of a problem.

Reality raised its ugly head. Mustafa felt the cold metal of a gun barrel against his temple. A .22 Ruger pistol Wajahat stole for just this moment. "What are you doing?" he squealed. His eyes darting sideways in a panic.

"I'm sorry it's come to this," Wajahat answered.

The boy eyes widened. He pissed his pants.

"Oh, you spoiled the leather," Wajahat said. He pulled the trigger. A cracking reverberation in the car. Crashing glass. A bloody jagged hole in the driver's window. Blowback of blood on Wajahat's face and jacket.

To the people in the surrounding apartments and houses, just another strange noise in the night of a violent American assault.

The dead boy slumped over the steering wheel. Wajahat put the gun in the boy's hand.

He popped the trunk of the bashed Camry. First thing, a bottle of water and a rag to wash the blood off his face. He peeled off the bloody jacket and shirt, put on a clean shirt and jacket. All the bloody stuff in a plastic bag on the passenger side floor, to be dumped on the road out of town.

Then he removed two five-gallon gas cans. He threw back the trunk carpet. He reached inside the tail light assembly, and yanked a wire which released the lid of a hidden compartment. It fit the case with the stolen Death in the Reeds perfectly. Wajahat carefully placed the case in the hiding spot. He snapped the lid closed, replaced the carpet. Gas cans back in.

Now he was ready to make his escape. He had one of the most valuable antiquities in all of the Middle East. He'd rid himself of a problem accomplice. He was in an anonymous poor man's vehicle. He would be just another frightened Iraqi running from the American onslaught. Perfect cover for his getaway.

Even as he started the long drive to the border Wajahat's chest swelled with pride. It was a daring foray into Iraq from the beginning. Posing as a poor Sunni laborer in Aqaba, Jordan, Wajahat was taken on by an Iraqi big rig driver, a fellow Sunni who wanted help at the wheel on the thirteen-hour return run to Baghdad. His father's Pakistani passport with his father's picture replaced by Wajahat's own got him past the Jordan-Iraq border check. It showed Hamid Zardari was from Balochistan, one of Pakistan's most fundamentalist and militant provinces. An Iraqi border lieutenant let him pass because he admired Balochis, along with many men in Saddam's military. The mastermind of 9/11 was a Balochi.

In Baghdad he was known by his passport name, Hamid. He worked mopping floors and washing dishes in a street café. He visited the Museum, enthralled with the treasures. He caught his first glimpses of Death in the Reeds. He learned the layout of the city. He planned.

Alert to any favorable possibility he spotted Mustafa Hajj holding forth in a café with friends. He immediately recognized the beautiful boy was gay. Curious how that worked in officially homophobic Iraq, he chatted the boy up. He was pleasantly surprised to learn the boy was the head of the janitorial crew at the Museum. Wajahat played the worldly gay man and the deception worked: the boy liked him. The boy could hire him.

A couple months sweeping floors and cleaning toilets at the Museum and Bush got serious with his war drums. Wajahat saw his opportunity coming.

Now he was on his way. Once Wajahat Zardari sped through Ramadi, his tension eased. It was open road for a couple hundred miles to the split in the highway, left to Amman, veer right for Damascus.

Wajahat relaxed a bit, at least more than the first few miles out of Baghdad. In those tense minutes his senses were attuned to danger, the possibility anything could happen, an obstacle or enemy could pop up at any point. Now, clear of the towns that could have been hazardous, headed west, a silent sigh of relief.

Knowing that one day he'd make an escape out of Iraq he took a few small steps to be ready. He brought a stash of dinars he knew he'd need to buy a used car. He stole a set of Lebanese license plates he thought he might need on the trip out. And as a plan formed around using young Mustafa he seized an opportunity to steal a .22 pistol from a drunk in a café.

But beyond those simple measures his getaway plan was never set in stone. Bush's war presented an obvious opportunity. As that fateful day approached, Wajahat figured refugees would be streaming west into Jordan or Syria. Many Iraqis thought of

Jordan as their escape valve, at least the Sunni Iraqis. The Shia, of course, tried to go east to Iran if they wanted out. Syria was a little less traveled, but it was the route Wajahat preferred.

He had given Jordan a lot of thought, but problems were quickly obvious. Following that route he would have to go through Amman, south to Aqaba and across to Sharm El Sheikh in Egypt and then on to Cairo. All that trouble in order to arrive at the Med and then find a ship that would take him back to Beirut. That was a long trek. He couldn't take the shortcut straight across Israel, because his Pakistani passport was not good for Israel. But most important, he had to get to Beirut.

So Jordan was out.

That meant he had to go through Syria across the mountains to Lebanon, and downhill into Beirut.

Wajahat knew it was doable. He had crossed Syria a few times; he was familiar with the ways of the Syrians. He'd been saving an expensive European watch for just this problem. The Syrians were addicted to bribery.

On the highway west Zardari blended in with other escapees. Traffic was picking up. People were starting to leave Baghdad while they could. The bombing announced by the Americans were coming. Everybody knew they were poised to invade from Kuwait, and now it would begin. It would take two weeks to claw their way north to Baghdad, but judging from the traffic headed west Wajahat saw people were getting out while the getting was good.

Short of the Syrian border he stopped to change license plates. His set of stolen Lebanese plates was hidden behind the back seat.

At the Iraq-Syria border Wajahat had to wait a few hours to be checked through by Syrian guards, as well as pay a hefty bribe with a stack of worthless Iraqi dinars.

Zardari had his Pakistani passport, and his story. He played the simpleton: he was a common laborer. He worked in Baghdad at menial jobs reserved for simpletons. Until the Americans started bombing. Then he fled, headed anywhere he thought he might find safety. Border agents pestered him about his story, shook him down for cash. Treated him like a harmless idiot. The Bulgari watch was the final bauble that turned the trick. But not before the officer whose eyes danced at the sight of it pestered him about how he got it. The poor Sunni laborer admitted he stole it from the home of a rich man. To the Syrian the story made sense. The only way a man such as Wajahat could obtain such a treasure was thievery.

He was allowed to pass through.

Wajahat Zardari's Iraqi accented Arabic was flawless. The best the American military's language school in Monterey, California could produce. No one in Baghdad nor at any check point on his infiltration into Iraq or his escape ever suspected he was in reality an American.

He pressed on. The dangers of the road out of Iraq and across Syria were many and potentially harrowing, but he needed to take chances. He had to get to Beirut because his U.S. passport was in his apartment there. He was going to need that passport to complete his escape with his prize.

4

The day after he was fired, Mickey walked into a high rise at 53rd Street and 7th Avenue to meet his agent.

Jimmy O'Neal wore a two-thousand-dollar black Armani suit, a five-hundred-dollar silk shirt the shade of pearls, and a three-hundred-dollar scarlet tie. Mick didn't like face to face meetings with his agent. He always left wondering if it was the ten percent of his salary that dressed Jimmy so well.

The office commanded a view of Manhattan to the south. When Mick first began doing business with Jimmy the view of the World Trade Center towers was perfect. Now they were gone.

As a young man Jimmy O'Neal was an aspiring jockey at Belmont Park who never got beyond breezing horses for trainers. His first clients were fellow jocks who needed representation with the trainers Jimmy worked for. Now he represented some of the biggest stars in television, much bigger than Mickey Judge. In the two decades since his first fifty-dollar jockey commission Jimmy O'Neal had done well for himself.

Jimmy's red hair was going white, but his eyes sparkled blue, and he always seemed to have a smile on his lips. Dwarfed by an enormous desk chair, he pulled an ashtray close and lit up a Marlboro Light. Mick flipped one from his pack and lit up with his Zippo.

"Only got two more weeks and then we have to go outside to smoke," Jimmy said.

"Fucking Bloomberg," Mick said, sullen.

"Hey perk up, sunshine," Jimmy said. "I got some good news."

Mickey gave him a side eye. "Yeah, you talk to Rod? Get me back in?"

"Well, no. I talked to Rod and found you are definitely out." He took a drag and exhaled dragon smoke. "What were you doing pissing off a Vice President? That really doesn't play."

"It was an argument. I got hot. Big deal."

"Yeah, actually it was a big deal."

"What's the hold she's got on him, anyway? The PR mook is somebody you kick around like your poodle. How can she can fire me?"

Jimmy sighed. "You're actually lucky she only fired you. Rod told her to back off. If he hadn't stopped her she would have gone rogue. Dropped items all over the media that would make you look like a child molester, a drunk, a deadbeat, a sexual predator. That's how she rolls. You actually got off easy. You just lost the job. Your character was saved. You can thank Rod for pulling back on the reins."

Mick was not mollified. "Two can play that game. I'm sure she doesn't want the world to know she's the tail that wags the dog."

"What's that mean?"

"She gives orders to reporters and anchors and producers and bookers. That gets out, it's a serious problem."

Jimmy raised his hand to stop his client. "Really not a good plan."

Mick sulked. "Now I'm missing a war. Because that bitch is power mad."

There was an uncomfortable silence. Yes, his agent knew Mick fucked up, but it wasn't good for an agent to rub it in. Only a few moments later, however, Jimmy couldn't contain himself. "You didn't ask me the good news."

Mick snorted a small laugh. "I thought my character saved from a cannibal was the good news."

The agent shook his head no. "I got you three choices on your next job."

Staring out the window at the Manhattan panorama, Mick turned back to him. "Where?"

Jimmy beamed. "Chicago. Boston. San Francisco. Your choice. But I think the best one is KBAY in San Francisco."

"Why?"

"Chicago and Boston are both street reporter gigs, some weekend anchoring. The GM at both places were like 'yeah, he's good' but they didn't seem in love, if you know what I mean."

"Chicago is brutal for a street reporter. Out in subzero half the year?"

Jimmy nodded. "I didn't think you'd jump at that one."

"Boston is okay I guess," Mick said. "But still cold."

"About the same as New York."

"Worse," Mick said. "What about San Francisco?"

"It's an investigative unit. It's your hometown, and wait for it ... fifty K more."

Mick whistled. "Fifty K more than what?"

"More than you're making now."

"For a job in local?" Mick scrunched his face at his agent. "What kind of job is it? Blowin' the boss?"

Now Jimmy was a little insulted. "C'mon, man. I score some things for you before you're fired a whole day, and you get all crusty on me? What the fuck?"

Mick held up his hands to take it back. "Sorry, but before you go on, I'm really going to miss the war?" Mick said. "You sure you can't get me back in? There's nothing at CNN?"

Jimmy scowled and shook his head. "You're radioactive at CNN because you're coming from TENN. They hate every one of you, which you already know. And MSNBC just laughed at me when I called."

Reluctantly, Mick nodded that he understood. Fired by NBC twice. And the pretty boy Nightly News anchor hated him—the very one who once popped out of his office during a break in Mick's live show waving a birthday cake knife and shrieking at Mick "shut up, shut up, shut up." Evidently he didn't like Mick relentlessly badgering lying guests, and his general loudmouth style. That place might as well be Chernobyl as far as Mickey Judge was concerned. A complete no-go zone.

"So what's the job at KBAY?" he asked.

"The GM loves you. He jumped at the chance. Bang, I want him, he said. So I mentioned Chicago and Boston were interested and went to the money. He bumped you up. I told him done deal."

"What's the job?"

"Do you even listen to me? Investigative team. Good gig."

"Is there a team?"

"No. It'll be just you. He'll get you a producer. He's got some fakakta name for it. The A Team or something. Who cares? Good gig. Back to your home town."

Mick thought about it. Yeah. Back to my hometown. Back to where I started over twenty years ago. Not exactly what I had in mind. But Jimmy is right. A job.

"What's this GM's name?"

"Don Saracenetti. Been around a few places. New Orleans. Sacramento. Orlando. San Francisco is a big gig for him. O and O." Meaning a station owned and operated by the network. "Corporate. He'll move up. Stay cool and he'll take you along."

Returning to his home town hadn't occurred to Mick until now. Upside? Aside from not even a single week of unemployment there was a load of personal pluses. His late father's house was sitting vacant, the renters just moved out. Dad's car was in storage there, along with some furniture. Yeah, it was convenient.

God, I hate missing the war, he thought.

"Think he'd let me go cover the war?" Mick asked.

"No, I brought that up," Jimmy said. "Told him you were all teed up, embedded already. What was it?"

"The 10th Mountain Division. Fort Drum."

"Yeah. Told him that. Be the perfect fit for him. He said New York would say absolutely not. He'd have to take network reports."

"What about Chicago and Boston?"

"Same thing. Bow down to the net."

Not a shocker, Mick thought. Networks tended to not like the locals invading their turf. And a war was definitely network turf.

"If you can't do the war, got something else in mind?" Jimmy asked. "Something to hit the ground running?"

Mick shrugged. "A corrupt politician I've been following since Dad was killed."

The agent ignored the "killed" word. His client made no secret of his belief that his police detective father was murdered, despite indications it was suicide. "In San Francisco?"

Mick nodded yes. "The District Attorney there. Black, gay, got her eye on the White House."

What he didn't say was the black, gay super ambitious empty suit politician was also married to a woman who was a might-have-been girlfriend from long ago.

The agent laughed. "Okay, so you're going to go after a possible President? Buddy, be sure you take her down. Shoot and miss and she makes it to the White House? You'll have so much shit raining down you'll wish you were back in the claws of the bitch at The Empire News Network."

Mick shrugged. "If that doesn't work out, something will happen. There's always a fuse burning somewhere."

But he was thinking something else. Cassandra Papadopolous, now known as Cassie Papadop, two decades ago the temptress he briefly wanted to fall in bed with, now the wife of the corrupt politician he had in his crosshairs.

"Okay," Mick said. "Tell him I'll be there Monday."

"Best decision you've made all day," Jimmy said.

Right, Mick thought. San Francisco. Hometown. Familiar turf. Closer to his girlfriend and daughter, both in L.A. Could be worse.

Plus a juicy investigative target in that DA woman.

It promised to be an interesting homecoming.

5

Wajahat Zardari drove all the way across Syria, to the Lebanese border and the gateway to Beirut. Of all the suspicions he might have raised with border guards and soldiers at checkpoints, his U.S. citizenship was not one.

Except for being shaken down for yet another bribe at the Syria-Lebanon crossing and the inevitable hours lost while being made to wait, the journey was as smooth as one would expect crossing Middle East borders.

In Beirut Wajahat drove to his apartment in the Badaro district. He parked the wreck on the street and removed the antiquity from its hidey hole in the trunk.

Paid for a year in advance, he had no worries about leaving the apartment for an extended stay. It was as he left it: musty and hot. He fired up the air conditioner in the bedroom, opened the living room windows to let in some fresh air. He was exhausted but he'd left clean sheets on the bed. The precious antiquity safely tucked away in his small living quarters, he finally got a relaxing night's rest.

He dozed off thinking of the millions of dollars his prize would bring.

Meanwhile, Wajahat Zardari wasn't the only man targeting the antiquities of the Iraq Museum. In the first moments after the American bombing in Baghdad ceased, but before the invading troops arrived, looters rushed the Museum.

A crew of professional thieves arrived in a swarm of Russian attack helicopters. The military choppers set down in the employee parking lot of the museum. A couple of dozen Russian soldiers spread out forming a protective perimeter. The choppers idled in place, rotors churning slowly.

An extensively armed group headed for the entrance to the museum. A swarthy man, dressed in ballistic black, a SR-2 Veresk Russian submachine gun slung over his shoulder and accompanied by black clad commandos, he was followed by a frightened young man who had been conscripted to be the guide. They stormed into the museum teeming with small time looters grabbing anything they could.

The leader of this raiding party was Pete Grand, a six-foot five-inch, two hundred fifty-pound package of angry muscle and raw determination. At the moment he was extremely annoyed to find so many amateurs in his way. He and his men fired into the ceiling, scattered the roaches, and pressed on, following their frightened guide.

They first went to the basement. "It's where the gold is," the young man promised. But the basement was flooded. Pete Grand stood at the top of a staircase that disappeared into black water. Judging by the stench he realized it was probably sewage from a line ruptured somewhere by American bombs. If the gold was there, it was under fifteen feet, perhaps twenty feet of raw sewage packed with god knows what diseases. If it was there—and he couldn't be certain—there was no way he and his raiders could retrieve it. The lake in the basement would have to be pumped dry and there was neither time nor gear for that.

There were other items on the raiders' list. Pete Grand turned away from the basement and sent a team to gather up what had been ordered.

Pete Grand took it upon himself to secure one important item from the list. "Death in the Reeds. Where?" he barked.

The youth led on.

They arrived in the right room, and at the right drawer, but they found The Reeds was already gone.

"Fuck fuck fuck!" Pete Grand screamed like a wounded animal, echoing off the stone walls. He punched a number into his satellite phone.

"Gold impossible. Got most of the rest of the list. The Lioness gone already."

On the other end of the call a Russian named Gennady Markov grimaced. He was a handsome Slavic man with a shock of gray hair, and the cold eyes of a predator. He sat in a throne-like chair before a comforting fire. The walls of dark wood were hung with art stolen from museums around the world and lined with bookshelves bulging with leather bound volumes. He smoked a cigar, a tumbler of whiskey in one hand. He was dressed in a light green silk shirt, black wool and cashmere slacks and Italian shoes, all of which cost a Lamborghini payment.

"The boss isn't going to like this," he said.

"Don't lay this off on me," the team leader in Baghdad barked into the phone. "I'm getting whatever we can. No time to drain the basement and the other thing is gone already. These are things I can't control. Somehow I got in here without getting my ass blown up. The idea of going in while the Americans are bombing was crazy. Way more dangerous than I signed up for."

Pete Grand waited. There was more silence coming back over the phone than he liked.

"Collect what you can. See me when you get back," Markov said. And he clicked off the phone.

Pete Grand dropped the phone into a pocket. "Asshole," he muttered.

6

San Francisco's glitterati swarmed a billionaire's house near the corner of Broadway and Lyon.

The occasion was a fund raiser for the rehabilitation of the War Memorial Opera House, just next to Davies Symphony Hall on Van Ness Avenue behind City Hall, in a stretch of San Francisco called Culture Gulch.

The War Memorial Opera House was the venue for the birth of the League of Nations in 1946, which eventually became the

United Nations. For decades it served as one of San Francisco's high society haunts. Sad to say, the old Opera House was in need of very expensive repairs and the city's open checkbook crowd gathered to make certain one of the country's premier see-and-be-seen venues remained standing.

The host of the party was a fifty-year-old socialite and old money heir named Phinias "Finn" Armistead. He billed himself as an "entrepreneur" and "investor" but in reality he did nothing but spend the money his grandfather had earned. Finn Armistead's wife decorated their home in a style she called eclectic, but which seemed to be little more than putting jarring colors together in the same room with lots of curious odds and ends on the walls and table tops.

Finn Armistead's face reminded people of a cartoon: round like a ball, a squiggly line that passed for an aristocrat's smile, bugged out green eyes, and ears that seemed to be competing with the other for just the right elevation on the sides of Finn's bald head.

For Finn Armistead and his color blind society wife Maxine Itchy Armistead, the Itchy's Soup heir, the fund raiser for the ancient Opera House was merely an excuse to gather San Francisco society. The real reason was to hoover up checks for the campaign committee of District Attorney Jean Washington. Ms. Washington was said to have her pick of whatever political position she wanted next: Attorney General, Senator, Governor. The reason was simple: Jean Washington was everything San Francisco wanted in a politician. She was a gonzo liberal, reflecting the liberal city's values. And part of those "values" was the person herself: she was African-American and Punjabi Indian, gay, and in a gay marriage. She checked all the boxes.

Plus she was beautiful: tall, elegantly slim, a regal bearing, possessed of a luminous smile (or on occasion a withering glare), and importantly, skin not too dark.

Wealthy San Franciscans thought she was Presidential material. She did not discourage their assessment.

Finn Armistead was one of those who saw President Jean Washington in San Francisco's future and he wanted in on the ground floor. He had dreams of an ambassadorship somewhere, anything that would give him the credibility he'd long sought and always seemed to elude him.

In his peculiar quaking voice, Finn pointed guests through the foyer, his oddly busy hands betraying nerves. "Careful of the TV cables. Jean is being interviewed," he cautioned. "Sky's the limit for her," he whispered in each passing ear. "And when it comes to the checks she has the memory of an elephant."

In the living room a television interview wrapped up and the evening's "it" couple was posing for the photographers with wide and gleaming smiles. Jean Washington, the District Attorney for the City and County of San Francisco, stood arm in arm with her wife, Cassandra Papadop, one of San Francisco's most popular and famous television anchors. Neither was as rich as the guests, but if one set aside "generational" wealth like Finn Armistead's, the "it" couple had all the right stuff: glamor, fame, and power. With her popular television program "More Money Than God" Papadop had the power to sprinkle the fairy dust of fame on the super-rich women and men desperate to be recognized everywhere in town. Her wife, the District Attorney, had the power to prosecute and jail. San Francisco was mesmerized by the magical power couple.

Jean Washington was certainly the most glamorous and attractive of California's crowd of bland and often shabby politicians. She stood just a hair under six feet tall, willowy slim. Tonight she was in a sea foam green body sleeve that was so form fitting it appeared to be sprayed on. She had a long neck and elegant facial features that one writer declared was "Nefertiti brought to life." She was keenly aware sex sells.

Her wife, the television star Cassie Papadop, was a Greek beauty: hazel eyes, copper skin, bronzed hair. She had a beaming smile and a flash in the eye that both men and women found beguiling and personal.

Finn dragged over a late arriving television crew to interview the District Attorney. Cass Papadop stepped away, ceding the spotlight to her wife.

Papadop spotted an acquaintance and walked a few feet to say hello.

The Mayor of San Francisco was with his wife. Betty "Tina" Vargas-Watson was confined to a wheelchair and uncomfortable with the flurry of activity that surrounded her. Her husband Mayor Bobby Vargas-Watson looked pained to be here.

He knew his presence was essentially in support of a woman who just might decide to take his job first, before moving on to higher, then highest office. But Finn Armistead billed the gathering as a fund raiser for the old Opera House, so his attendance was required.

Robert Vargas-Watson won the mayor's office after a thirty-year career as the city's most popular and successful television news anchorman. Silver hair, tall, broad shouldered, the smoldering good looks of a Latin movie star, he grimaced as Cass Papadop shook hands with his incapacitated wife and made lady to lady small talk.

Bobby Vargas-Watson and Cass Papadop were having an affair. And the painful reality that Papadop, the love of his life, was in a phony gay marriage with his most serious political opponent was excruciating. Not only did Jean Washington have his one and only love as an official "wife," but Mayor Vargas-Watson was pinned down with a wife suffering from the incapacitating nervous system condition called Yakov-Gutberg disease, a form of nerve cancer. In California politics, a husband could get a divorce, but not if the wife was confined to a wheelchair and obviously suffering.

To make matters worse, the Mayor was trapped in a political duel to the death with DA Washington. She might just take him on in an upcoming Mayoral election. Not that she wanted to be Mayor. She just wanted to knock Bobby Watson-Vargas out of the running for the next election on the calendar, the Governor's office.

Cass Papadop retreated a few steps as another television crew asked for a few words from the Mayor while they wanted their turn with DA Washington. Bobby Vargas-Watson seethed at the obvious second place, but he said the things a mayor is supposed to say about a cause such as this. "The War Memorial Opera House is one of San Francisco's treasures, and I am grateful to the generous people here tonight who will make it possible for the city to quickly make the repairs so urgently required."

A nurse standing by took control of Mrs. Vargas-Watson's wheelchair. "She's exhausted," the nurse whispered to the Mayor. "It's about time I got her home."

Inside the green and pink and lavender living room a crowd of toadies pressed close to the District Attorney. Jean Washington had a reputation for an icy personality, and she tried to warm up on these occasions. But she was afraid to laugh because when she did pundits jumped on the chance to mock the DA's "cackle."

Those pundits also mocked her start in politics as the girlfriend of a powerful politician. Even then she knew she was gay, but if sex with a man was part of the deal, she would suffer both the sexual ordeal and the critics.

She was beautiful and successful and she absolutely despised being mocked. Consequently she tended toward cool and aloof, and tried to keep conversation on "issues." She could regurgitate the talking points her advisers set on her desk each morning with studied ease.

Her wife, Cass Papadop, had no such restraint. She was boisterous, laughed a lot and laughed loud. People naturally gravitated to her.

Jean Washington was a gay woman, but Cass Papadop was not. Their "marriage" was for the notoriety, for the attention, for the admiration of self-important people anxious to be on the cutting edge of social consciousness and to be close to such a powerful couple. They had an understanding they each could go her own way, as long as discretion was foremost. Jean Washington knew Cass would never share her bed, and she knew Cass and Bobby Vargas-Watson were in a tempestuous off again, on again affair. Whatever Jean Washington could do to fracture that relationship she would do. So when a piece of salacious information crossed her desk, she made sure it was leaked to the papers. News broke suddenly that police were investigating a report the Mayor had visited a brothel in the Mission District. No matter that a brothel in the Mission District could operate under the nose of the SFPD and the DA's office, embarrassment for the Mayor was more important.

Cornered in a stultifying conversation about "unconscionable" right wing political figures, the District Attorney's gaze wandered. She noticed the Mayor take two drinks from the tray of a passing waiter, and offer one to Cass Papadop. She kept an eye on the secret couple, silently mesmerized to see the Mayor have a few whispered words with her wife. She knew she had caused trouble.

Across the room the whispering between Cass Papadop and Bobby Vargas-Watson was unfolding as the District Attorney hoped.

"What the hell were you doing there?" Cass whispered.

Bobby Vargas-Watson glanced over at the DA. "She must be ecstatic. She smears me in the papers and gets you pissed off. It's a twofer. The bitch."

Cass kept the smile wide and her voice low. "Were you there or not? Is it true?"

"Of course I went there. To see if it was true. A brothel, a whorehouse in this city in the twenty-first century? And the woman who is supposed to make certain there are no whorehouses in the city plans to run against me? I had to see it for myself."

Cass arched her eyebrows. "You were an investigative reporter again? That's your story?"

"Yes, dammit. That's not just my story. It's the truth. And by the way, you could ask your wife why she hadn't shut it down."

"So now you're blaming her for not busting the place before you could get there?" Cass tilted her head and gave him blinking eyes.

"That's turning the story on its head."

Cass grinned, but it was not a smiley grin. It was the kind that says something hurts. "You know what? I think it's time we took a break."

"A break? Why?"

She looked over both shoulders to make sure she wasn't overheard. "Because I don't tolerate whoring. Cheating on your seriously ill wife with me? That's one thing. But if you're going to cheat on both her and me in a whorehouse, we just might be at the end of the road."

"You know it's your so-called wife who invented the whole thing. She's not doing it just to show me up with voters. The bitch is doing it to break us up."

"She doesn't care who my boyfriend is as long as he's quiet about it and he doesn't get caught in a whorehouse."

"Oh, for gawdsakes, Cass …"

She interrupted. "Let's just see how wifey's investigation shakes out. Until then you're on hold."

She turned her back on him and walked away.

Across the room Jean Washington felt a glow in her chest. It was so great fucking over Bobby Vargas-Watson. The wild man reprobate Mayor had a long run of carefree misbehavior owing to his decades-long popularity with television viewers. They became his voting base, and they would forgive anything. Correction: almost anything. A whorehouse was pushing the envelope.

"It's time he pays," she smiled to herself.

Finn Armistead's annoying floral cologne announced his arrival at her elbow. "The Mayor looks a little perturbed. Your investigation going to wrap up soon?"

"Oh no," she smiled. "I'd say it will be bubbling along until about two weeks before election day."

Finn grinned. "I like a woman who's good with a dagger," he said. "Let's move you along to that Oval Office as quick as we can."

"All good things in good time," she said. "Meanwhile we need to bury a few bodies. Starting with the hizzonor the Mayor."

7

Less than a week after being fired—how many firings was this?—Mick deplaned from American Airlines flight 76 at SFO at 9:30 in the morning. He was still a little shaky from his escape from New York. True to his promise, the night TENN fired him he hadn't left Langan's until owner Des O'Dowd was locking the door. And the hangover lasted through his meeting with the agent the next day and into the day after as he packed his bags, shipped what wouldn't fit in suitcases, and cleared out of the one good perk in his TENN contract: a corporate apartment in midtown.

Mick was not all that sorry to be leaving New York City. It was too easy to spend too many hours in bars. And being on the opposite end of the country strained his relationship with the two women in his life who lived on the West Coast—his longtime girlfriend and his teenage daughter.

While there was upside in going west, he brooded in first class, stewing about his situation the entire six-hour flight. Missing the war was bad. And it was a strange way to get a new job. Somebody leaping at the chance to hire him. It made him suspicious but he couldn't quite put his finger on why. Maybe the guy was a fan from a distance. It wasn't impossible. But he didn't like to flatter himself.

His dad's house was waiting for him, but getting in turned out to be a problem. The renters had recently moved out, and he was still considering offers when he got himself blown up at TENN. At SFO he called Mark Barasch, an old friend, and his real estate guy. "Forget new renters. I'm moving in."

"Welcome back, man, but come on. Let me list it. You can get over a mil!"

Mick said no, he wasn't selling the place. It was a nice little house on a street called Paramount Terrace just off Stanyan Street near the University of San Francisco. He was actually looking forward to living there. His daughter would have a room for visits.

His off-again and on-again girlfriend Gracie would love it, though he doubted he could pry her out of L.A. on a permanent basis. It was a good place for him to settle in. And he owned it outright. "Hard to beat no mortgage," he said to his real estate pal.

He got to the house about noon but he didn't have a key. The real estate guy was in Marin and Mick didn't want to wait. So he broke a window in the downstairs door, the one that led to a bedroom his old man had kept as an office. There was a hidden key in the office.

A neighbor heard the noise, called the cops. Mick had to explain who he was. It took invoking his father's name—the late homicide Inspector Nicholas Judge—that finally sent the uniforms on their way.

He spent the rest of the day calling movers to get his possessions out of storage and moved into the house. He took a cab to the garage where he had his dad's car on blocks. The tires were low, but drivable. After checking the oil and coolant, and reconnecting the battery, he fired it up. The nineteen-year-old '84 Mustang convertible—five-liter V-8, midnight blue, with baby blue interior and dark blue rag top—roared to life right away. He got the jack out, lifted the car off the blocks, and drove it home. He pulled it into the garage where his dad kept the car and promised himself he'd get a beater right away. His dad's car was the old man's pride and joy, kept in perfect shape. Mick couldn't bring himself to put it through everyday driving.

He took his clothes out of the bags and hung them up. He walked a couple blocks to drop a suit at the cleaners, asked for a pressing only. He'd need it the next day to go see the new boss.

He sat on a lawn chair in the living room looking out the window on Stanyan Street traffic and called Grace Russell in L.A.

"I'm in my dad's house in the city," he said when she answered.

"The Eagle has landed. Congratulations on another excellent firing."

It wasn't so excellent to Mick, but he knew what she meant: he was much closer now.

"You coming up?"

"I'll come up but not until you get furniture."

"But you will visit, right?"

"You are my longtime lover whose wandering from job to job is exasperating, but I love you. So of course. Haven't I always?"

"Yes, but occasionally you say you never will again."

"Just when you've been an ass." She was quiet for a long moment. "But I do miss you. So yes, I'll come up. Call me when you're settled in."

"Just a few days. Count on it."

That was it. Tentative, a little jab about wandering, referring to his bouncing from job to job. But not the worst.

"One more thing," she said. "Call your daughter."

Right. "Okay. Good idea."

Tammy Judge answered on the first ring. "Did you get fired again, Dad?" Tam was fifteen and way past the age of being unaware.

"Honey, I did. But I was standing up to a bully."

"Mom said you have a new job in San Francisco."

"I do. Want to come up?"

"Yes, but it will have to wait till school's out. I have swim team on weekends."

They ended their call with "love you, love you." Then the quiet descended on him. The house was spooky when empty. He thought about sleeping on the floor, but quickly realized that wasn't going to work. Mick walked over to Geary Blvd. and found a motel. At least he could sleep in a bed and have towels for the shower.

In the morning he picked up his suit and hustled back to the house, got dressed to meet the new boss. He called a cab. "386 Golden Gate," he told the cabbie, "corner of Hyde."

Mickey Judge knew the KBAY building well. He'd worked there as a street reporter for three years before L.A. and New York.

Not much had changed. It was still the gloomy concrete structure in the shadow of Hastings Law School at the corner of Hyde and Golden Gate just off Civic Center.

Mickey paid the driver and popped out of the blue and white DeSoto cab at the curb. Across the street was the Studio Café, a coffee and burger joint run by surly Greek brothers. Mick estimated he must have guzzled a tank car of the coffee from that place, not to mention a monster pile of burgers he'd either consumed himself or picked up for others in the newsroom.

While he was away the other stations in town—KPIX and KRON and some others—had moved down to the Embarcadero. Fancier digs, but nothing compared to the funk and the incipient danger of the Tenderloin. Mick had to admire KBAY for hanging on in the tough side of town.

He walked into the KBAY lobby and first thing he noticed—which anybody would notice—was the lineup of on-air talent. Large portraits of each man and woman lined the lobby, illuminated by special lighting, and arranged by rank. The lead anchors first—Mick didn't know them—then the reporters. One caught his eye. Cassandra Papadopolous, the Greek beauty. He had to smile to himself. He'd known her years ago when they were both in first jobs in the city. Now she was a star. She certainly was beautiful enough to be a star. Always had been. "Avoid temptation," he said to himself.

The security guard already had a name tag made out, and was expecting him. Mick was more than a little surprised. "Third floor, sir," the man said.

Mick got off on the third floor and was greeted by a lovely young woman. "Mr. Judge? Welcome. Come with me."

He was ushered into the office of Don Saracenetti, the General Manager of KBAY-TV, Channel 8. The office was on the corner of the building, windows with a view up Golden Gate Avenue toward the Federal Building. It was large—there was a couch and coffee table arrangement on one side—and the man's military and television career documented in framed pictures and awards crowded the walls.

Mick didn't have time for a close look. The man was on him in an instant.

"Fantastic!" he almost shouted, as he leapt to his feet from behind his desk. He came around to shake Mick's hand. "I have so been looking forward to this moment."

Don Saracenetti was close to sixty, just under six feet tall, trim, dressed in a gray suit and a pale blue shirt—what the professionals called "TV white"—and a dark blue tie. His graying hair was cut short, clinging to his head like a cap. He had a strong jaw, creases in his cheeks, a good looking nose and mouth, and bright green eyes. He was a handsome man.

"Sit sit sit," he said, pointing to the couch. He took the chair opposite. "You happy to be back home?"

Mick smiled. "Yes, of course. The house is empty. The movers might be able to get my things out of storage in a few days."

"Who are the movers?"

Mick reacted with confusion and an embarrassed smile. "I think the name is O'Connor. Why?"

"Bernadette," Don Saracenetti shouted to his assistant. She stuck her head in the door. "Call O'Connor Movers. Tell that fuckhead I need a favor. Get Mickey Judge's job moved up to like tomorrow at the latest."

Mick objected, but he was actually pleased, of course. "That's very kind of you, but don't put yourself out."

"No problem. I drink with that guy. He'll do it for me." He smiled at Mick, an engaging, charming smile. "I want you to feel welcome. This city was your home. You were born here. You went to high school here, Lowell. Which means you were smart. You went to college at USF, walking distance from your house. You got married," and here he paused, gave Mick a twinkly wink, "for the first time. And it was here that you dealt with sorrow as you buried your beloved father."

Mick was flattered. Don Saracenetti had done his homework. He had the broad outlines of Mick's early life pretty close to dead on. It had been a long time—maybe never—that Mick was treated this way. He didn't know what to think.

"I want you to feel welcomed, welcomed back."

"Look, I really appreciate this, Mr. Saracenetti ..."

"Call me Don. People around here actually call me The Don." There was that smile again. It seemed to sparkle.

Mick continued, smiling himself. "I appreciate the job. It came so quickly. I am flattered by your confidence in me. But to be honest I really don't get it. What do you want with me?"

"You're right," Saracenetti nodded in vigorous agreement. "I'm rolling out the red carpet. And you're smart to want to know why."

Don Saracenetti turned serious. "First off, you don't work for that wimpy prick down in the newsroom who thinks he's the news director. He sends teenage reporters out to hold microphones so politicians and gang-bangers and so-called community leaders can lie to the public on my air. Pisses me off, really pisses me off." He paused for effect. Then shrugged. "But it's the way of the world. Daily news is generally vapid, and sorry to say, rarely true."

Mick smiled, but not too broadly. He knew exactly what the man was talking about.

"You work for me," Saracenetti continued. "I don't even want you in the newsroom. I know you'll go down there and introduce yourself and see how things run. You'll pay your respects. Good to keep the troops on your side."

"I know Danny Fuller. He still here?"

"Sure is. Assignment editor. He'll be news director someday. Good thing you know him. You're new to most everybody else. Having a friend like Danny will help a lot."

Mick nodded. Sure. Got it.

The Don continued. "I got an office for you across the street. We'll get you a producer in a couple weeks."

Mick nodded. He hoped that promise was good.

Saracenetti wasn't through. "I used to be a news director and what I've learned over the years is that anchors and reporters are vital, but what really brings in the numbers is a balls-out guy—or woman—who can do the stories that light up the town. People call them investigative reporters, which seems redundant to me, but what the fuck, self-aggrandizing titles are the nature of our business these days."

He paused to see if Mick got it. "Like these assholes calling themselves 'journalists' as if 'reporter' isn't good enough. Bunch of puffed-up megalomaniacs."

Mick nodded. He'd nursed a similar grudge for years.

"I want you to go find stuff that punches through the screen," Saracenetti continued. "I want people sitting upright, saying 'holy crap look at this.' And I have known for a long time you're the kind of reporter who can do it."

Mick sat back amazed. He'd never got a vote of confidence like this from a news exec.

"Plus," Saracenetti continued, pointing his index finger for emphasis, "I've watched you at Empire, and I knew it was a bad situation there for you. I was waiting for the thing to blow up."

Mick popped a nervous snort. "You knew about that bitch I told to fuck off?"

"Is that what you did?" Saracenetti laughed with gusto. "I knew it would be something. I also know it's going to get ugly there someday. The two boys hate Rod. They'll blow him up eventually, so I can promise you it was good to get out."

Mick was impressed. The new boss knew about the two sons of the media mogul who founded The Empire News Network, TENN. The two spoiled rich kids despised Rod, even though he made them a billion in profit every year.

"You watch," he said. "It will be some blond back stabber who brings him down."

Mick sat back. No doubt. He could think of a couple so-so anchors who were probably waiting for an opportunity to gut him and get a go-away check.

"You think?"

"Absolutely. He has a weakness for the type. If he hires a hundred of them chances are at least one will be willing to knife him."

Mick exhaled. Okay. The guy was dead on. This was starting to feel comfortable. He liked the guy.

Saracenetti leaned back in his chair. "I'll be honest. To light up the town, I've got to have a kick-ass reporter with kick-ass stories. I had one of those types, but she decided to go a different direction."

"Who was that?"

"Papadop. You know her?"

Mick nodded yes, reluctantly. "A little," he fudged. "Years ago. I was working the street. She was a radio reporter."

Saracenetti continued. "Then you know. Very hot. But went soft on me. She still does excellent television, which is good. But she's doing 'personality pieces' now," here he made air quotes. "Basically sucking up to the rich assholes in Pacific Heights and in Silicon Valley."

"Does she rate?"

"Oh, hell yeah. Ratings like gangbusters. So it's not that I'm complaining, but you know, we kind of lost some ..."

"I get it," Mick interjected. "You want bite."

Saracenetti nodded yes, "'Bite,' exactly."

Mick nodded. He'd seen it before. Reporters get good at something then decide they want to do something else. Usually something they're not nearly as good at.

"And then she went and married the DA. The female DA ..." He trailed off.

Mick's eyebrows dipped, his brow furrowed. He'd heard, of course. "So Cassie is a lesbian?"

Saracenetti frowned. "Bullshit. She's straight as you or me. She went through with a same sex marriage because it was the thing to do in this town, and she always likes to make headlines."

"But you're happy with her work?"

Saracenetti made the waggly hand motion, meaning yes and no. "She does stuff people like, biography kinds of things, personality interviews. Gets rich guys to talk about their divorces and sex lives, that sort of thing. So, yeah. As I said, she pulls numbers,"—meaning the ratings—"just not to my taste. I like stuff that has, as you put it, bite."

Mick's mind was elsewhere. His former not girlfriend was married to a woman. Not just any woman but the very one Mick had been gathering string on. He'd planned to do an investigation of the black lesbian San Francisco DA with Presidential ambitions for TENN. But things went south before he could get to it.

"I forget now, isn't she some kind of racial mix?"

"Yes. Black and Indian. Dot—not feather."

"That's solid gold political correctness."

Saracenetti gave Mick a wink, pleased his new guy got it. The Don didn't like the cascade of political correctness one damn bit. "Yeah, it's best I keep my snark to myself."

Changing the subject, Mick asked, "Got any preference on what you'd like me to work on?"

"Something will come up," Saracenetti grinned. "I've watched you a long time. You got that special something." He pointed at Mick's chest, as if he were pointing at his heart.

Mick was confused. "What's that?"

"You ain't afraid of getting in over your head," he said. "You ain't afraid going to a place where you've never been and where you don't really know what you're doing, but you struggle through, you fight. And that's when you hit paydirt, when you get the good shit. You, my friend, are not afraid of getting in way way over your head."

Mick tried to hold his surprise inside. That's the reason he got this job? The reason he was being treated like royalty?

He wasn't afraid of getting in over his head?

What did this guy expect him to do? Push the envelope to the point he could get killed?

At that moment his questions went unasked and unanswered. Mick and the boss were interrupted.

The door flung open. A human whirlwind named Cassandra Papadopoulos blew in.

"Honey bunny," she squealed. "Welcome home, baby!" She threw her arms open, her smile wide as the Golden Gate, her eyes flashing with delight.

Mick stood to greet her, uncertain how this was going to go with his new employer.

With mincing tip-toe steps she ran across the room and threw her arms around him. "Holy crap you're really here!" She kissed him full on the lips and gave him another vertebrae crunching hug.

Saracenetti blinked, forced a smile. "You two are close?" The boss looked confused.

"Are we close?" she squealed. "You didn't tell him we almost were a thing?"

Mick shrugged. "Didn't mention that. In consideration of your reputation."

The jab earned him a punch on the shoulder and a booming laugh. "Oh, for Chrissakes you didn't reveal I almost succumbed to your famous charms?" she scolded. "Hiding the good stuff from the boss?"

Cassie Papadop had a smile like marquee lights. Her face was classic Greek beauty, high cheekbones, electric hazel eyes, narrow nose, sharp chin, lips like rose petals and gleaming white teeth that burst through her smile. Her hair was bronze with golden highlights. She was shapely and sexy and she loved to flaunt it.

"You never should have left. They've been mean to you everywhere you went," she scolded. "This was always the place for you."

She whirled around and gave Saracenetti a hug he wasn't expecting. "The Don came through for me. I didn't even have to ask. How'd you know I wanted you to get him?" she demanded, taking his face in her hands and playfully bouncing his head side to side.

Saracenetti laughed self-consciously. "I had no idea."

Mick shrugged again. "History," he said. "We have a little."

"A little?" she shrieked. "History in volumes! Shelves. A wing at the library. Oh my god we have to talk. The Don is the best. Love him." Turning to Saracenetti. "You done with him for now? Can I take him to lunch?"

The Don—Mick picked up that this was really was what he was called—shrugged okay. "Yeah, I guess." He picked up a key from his desk, handed it to Mick. "This opens your new office. I guess Cassie will show you where it is." He smiled sheepishly. One of his reporters had hijacked his very first meeting with his new hire. "It's across the street. We'll talk later. There's some paperwork to fill out."

"Of course." Mick shook his hand. "Thanks again, Mr. Saracenetti." He gestured to Cassie. "I guess I've got a date for lunch."

"Call me Don. And we need to finish our conversation, okay?"

Cassie practically dragged him into the elevator and out onto the street. Her new Audi convertible—silver with a black top—was parked at the yellow curb. A ticket was on the windshield. "This is a joke," she said, stuffing it into her purse. "The wifey will fix this."

Mick slid into the front seat, and she pulled away headed down Golden Gate with a jerk and a squeal of tires. She said something Mick couldn't make out.

"Wind and the traffic," he shouted.

She pushed a button and the convertible top came up from its hiding place at the rear, then came down with a thump and locked itself in position. "I said we're going to Tadich. Doing 'classic' to welcome you back."

Mickey nodded his approval. Tadich Grill was one of his favorites.

"So how many divorces since you left town?" she needled.

"Just the one."

"Still got that girlfriend?"

"Hope so," Mick nodded. "Getting blown up in New York might be good. Maybe things with Grace will work out better now that I'm not on the East Coast."

"You still hear from your ex?"

"Just whatever involves the daughter."

"Oh right," she said. "Almost forgot. How old is she now?"

"Tam is fifteen," Mick said. He yanked his seat belt on. Her swerving style reminded him he should.

He was proud of his daughter, but it was long distance parenthood and he didn't want to get into it with Cass Papadop. He changed the subject "So what's with your gay marriage?"

She brightened. "Yeah. I was a little hurt I never got a wedding gift from you," she scolded.

"I had no idea what to give a double vagina marriage."

She snorted a laugh. "You got to catch up. It's the thing now. Girl on girl is mega. Hollywood, Silicon Valley. Movies, music, tech."

"So you've gone lesbian?"

"You know how I am about being cutting edge," she grinned.

"Yeah, but for real?"

"Just for show," she shifted to a mock scowl. "God, how could you think I play for the other team?" She slipped the Audi around a Muni bus, and turned onto Taylor at the Golden Gate Theater.

"Truth is it means a lot in the social circles in this town. You should see me now. All the first nights. Symphony. Opera. Hanging with the Pacific Heights folks." She grinned and punched Mick on the shoulder. "Gordon Getty just loves loves loves me."

Mick gave her a side eye. "So you're pretending to be a lesbian.

What about the wife?"

"Oh her?" Another burst of raucous laughter. "Total muff chomper. She has her little girlfriends from time to time. Latest one a cop. A little on the dykey side. But nice. Wifey and I do the showboat stuff, get dressed up in gowns, go to the fancy parties, get in the society mags, it's that kind of thing."

"I get it. You're just using her, so what does she get out of it?"

She reacted with theatrical horror. "She's using me! I'm the famous one around here. I'm the one on television. She gets a lot more media action married to me than to some dweeby guy, believe me."

"And what do you get out of it?"

Now it was her turn to shrug off the question. "To be honest, just more attention. In my new line of work attention gets more action. It's a trend thing, riding the wave of the zeitgeist."

"So are you still ...?"

"With a man?" she interrupted him. "Sleeping with somebody? Banging somebody? Doing the nasty? Like you were aiming for?" Her laugh could shatter glass. "Yeah, Jane Fonda said she's closed for business down there. Not me, not yet. A girl best keep a few on the line, but I got a regular."

"So who's the victim?"

She shrieked again. "You asshole! He's not a fucking victim. He's the luckiest bastard in town."

Mick made the get-on-with-it gesture, rolling his finger.

"Well, if you must know. Remember Bobby Vargas-Watson? He's the Mayor now. Did you know that?"

"I did." Mick could feel a migraine coming on. "He's asked me to be his press guy a couple times. I passed."

Bobby Vargas-Watson. The big anchorman from a while back. Silver hair, jut jaw, deep voice, half Hispanic, half Gringo. All the right stuff for the anchor chair.

"Probably best you didn't," she said absently, flooring it, running a yellow light. "Thinks he's going to be governor or Senator or something. Going to be weird. He'll probably run against my wife," she said, taking her hands off the wheel to make two fingered air quotes over "wife."

"I would think that the business of the brothel would upset his plans," Mick said.

"I am super pissed about that," she snorted "But he swore he was just 'investigating' rumors there was a whorehouse there. Duty of being the mayor, blah blah blah. Swore up and down to me he was not screwing the girls."

"Sticking with him?"

She shrugged. "I'm on a break. Wifey's always got investigations going. I'm sure she'd love to catch him lying. Help her campaign. I'm waiting to see what develops."

"She can probably get the hookers to say anything." Mick caught himself almost revealing his working theory that the DA coerced and bribed testimony she needed to run up her conviction score.

"I know. At the moment I'm open to believing any evidence against him will be phony, cooked up just to help her campaign."

"Sounds like you're kinda sticking with him."

"Kinda," she agreed. "We'll see. I sure as hell won't be putting up with whoring."

She jammed across Pine Street, straight up Taylor, one of Mick's favorite scary vertical hills. Taylor between Pine and California is so steep that headed uphill all you see out the windshield is blue sky. She paused at the top, kitty corner from Grace Cathedral, ignored the red light, and flipped a right turn on California Street at the Huntington Hotel. "Crap," she said, glancing back at the Huntington, "maybe we shoulda done the Big Four."

Mick knew what that would mean. Sitting all afternoon at that great bar getting shitfaced, eating appetizers.

But she headed down hill to Tadich. Founded in 1849. Calls itself "The Original Cold Day Restaurant."

"It's kinda off and on with him anyway," she continued. "You probably wouldn't guess considering this whorehouse thing hanging over his head, but he's crazy jealous."

"Of your wife?"

"No. He knows that's for show. It's guys that make him crazy. I like to move around, maybe have drinks with a good-looking guy. Maybe a little more. And Bobby's still married. So it can be annoying as fuck the way he demands exclusivity. Crowds me. Double standard stuff. Sometimes I just get sick of it."

Mick thought, yeah he's a macho guy. The whorehouse thing is probably true. And for sure he doesn't like her bedding a sudden interest. "What else is new? You always make your boyfriends insane with jealousy."

"How come you never got jealous?" she asked, with a twinkle in the eye.

"Luckily I didn't catch the fever," he said. "Who you were banging didn't bother me."

"You missed out."

Maybe, he thought. But he swore off tumultuous women years ago. That rule improved life dramatically.

"What about these things you're doing for air?" he said, meaning her television work.

Her face lit up. "Oh that's the shit, let me tell you." She eased the Audi through the Powell Street light, scooched around a cable car unloading tourists, inching through a small crowd waiting to board.

The California Street downhill run stretched before them, Chinatown on the left, the silver cables and spires of the Bay Bridge framed by the financial district towers. A postcard day. Hills, cable cars, high rises set against a blue sky dotted by puffs of white clouds.

"I'll tell you all about it inside. Let me get parked," she said as they zipped past the Bank of America building. Mick glanced at the polished black stone sculpture in the plaza. A banker's heart, people called it.

On the flats of California Street, she hung a U-ey in front of Tadich, just behind a passing cable car. She wasn't even close to getting to the curb for the valet. A beer truck laid on the horn behind her. She got out, showing plenty of leg and smiled at the driver. His face lit up, and he waved.

"You are shameless," Mick said, shaking his head.

She grinned. "Welcome back to town, honey bunny. Things only got better since you left."

A booth was waiting. Along with two vodka martinis, a basket of sourdough, and Dungeness crab cake appetizers.

"I called ahead," she said as she slid into the booth. "They love me here."

Tadich was old San Francisco. Polished dark wood, green shade lighting, elderly waiters in white aprons and a patient manner.

Mickey ordered sand dabs. She had the cioppino. They both had two vodka martinis. And she told him all about her new gig interviewing billionaires, how several were her new best friends, and how the thrill of money—of so much money—was better than any orgasm she'd ever had.

"You know, when I did the gay marriage thing, it was because it was going to lead to something big. Jean is the toast of the town. Black, Indian, female, lesbian, all the right stuff. A bit of a lightweight in the smarts department, if you know what I mean …"

"I've heard," Mick said.

"But around here they're convinced she's going to be President one day."

Mick arched his eyebrows. San Franciscans lived in such a bubble.

"And she may be," Cass added quickly. "Knows she isn't the sharpest knife in the drawer, but makes up for it with a mean streak. Ambitious as fuck. Ruthless. Was banging Lonnie Black to get into politics."

The one-time Speaker of the Assembly, Mick reminded himself.

"Plus five years or so as a prosecutor," she continued, "and a couple years as counsel for a venture capital firm where she did nothing but make a shitload of cash, then ran for DA."

Talking fast. The way people do when they say more than they should.

"So she got some money. Not enough, but bank. Put some in tax free munis, kicking off income. Bought a nice house in Presidio Terrace. Melvin Belli's old house. Remember it?"

Mick certainly did. It was a monster. Probably the best house in the gated, most exclusive enclave in the city.

"Anyway, I live there in a kick-ass suite. Her lawyers made me sign a pre-nup. Protects her house or money. It's okay. I still have my apartment, you remember," she prodded.

"999 Green?"

"Yeah, that one. Love the view," she added.

Mick agreed. Her place was on a floor in the twenties, floor to ceiling glass, looking out to the Golden Gate. You felt like you could see Diamond Head in Honolulu.

"I like staying at the big house. The suite is awesome. She may seem dumb as a rock but she's smart enough to not bother me. And I'm meeting the people who really do have the money and the power. I got The Don to let me do this series on billionaires. I call it 'More Money Than God', which works in the promos like you can't imagine. I interview 'em, give 'em some strokes on the air. Other billionaires see their friends or rivals, they want to be done themselves. Works good. I got a contact list …" she held up her Blackberry … "that's totally awesome. I'm gonna get something good soon. Don't know what exactly, but that's my plot."

"Jesus, Cass. You must make a ton of money now. What's the problem?"

Now she got serious. "Buddy, you have no idea. I have plenty of friends with five mil in the bank. They feel broke, like it's nothing."

Mick arched his eyebrows.

She saw he didn't believe it. "Think about it. Conservatively five mil kicks off five percent, two fifty K a year. In California you see about half of that. You're fucked and you got five mil in the bank."

"Surely you can do better than five percent."

"Yeah, if you want to ride herd on a wealth management guy all day."

"Still, five percent is solid."

"If you got twenty mil you're looking at about a mil a year income, which is five hundred clear, depending on whatever tax scams you can work. That's doing okay. Far as I'm concerned twenty mil in the bank is the absolute minimum."

Mick must have looked gobsmacked. But she was dead serious. "Do the math for yourself. You'll see these jobs we have are crap."

Things had changed with his old friend. She was still selling sizzle, sex appeal. But the television job was now just a launch pad.

She pointed a polished nail at Mick. "Buddy, I shit you not. Silicon Valley is pouring money into the City. It's a flood. It's sweeping everything out to sea that isn't nailed down. Only reason this place is still open is they own the building. Same with the Buena Vista and Scoma's. Otherwise they'd be gone. I see it happening and I know I've got to find a way to score. And I'm going to fucking do it, I promise you."

Mick didn't know what to say, except something bland. "Good luck to you."

"Thanks," she said absently. "And you?" she asked like she really wanted to know, but she didn't.

My "crap" job, Mick thought. That's all I got going.

Of course, this was definitely not the time to bring up his plans for his first investigation. It was on wifey, the very ambitious District Attorney Jean Washington. The one who did not discourage rumors that she was Presidential material. The one who was using the DA's office to step up to Governor, or maybe Senator, with her eye set on the biggest prize of all.

Mick heard stories. She was running people into prison on a conveyor belt, guilty or not. All for her re-elect scorecard. Basically corrupt as hell, and for Mick a super-hot story. There would be an Emmy in it, possibly, and maybe a book deal if it all panned out. But it certainly was not going to load up his bank account the way she was talking.

Didn't matter anyway. Within seconds Papadop was back describing how she was going to score. Stuff about a start-up, stock, options, an exit strategy. Things Mick didn't understand.

What he did understand was simple: Cassie Papadop was on the hunt for big money. She didn't know how it was going to come, but Mick saw that flash of determination from the old days. He could see she wouldn't rest until she scored.

8

Wajahat Zardari had many names. At home in Badaro, his Beirut neighborhood, Wajahat Zardari was known by the false name on his counterfeit Lebanese passport, Hassan Shaloub. Mr. Shaloub had been away for a while, but nothing unusual there. He was often away on business for weeks at a time, though not many of his café acquaintances would have been able to describe what his business was. The few who could just repeat his lies. Nobody knew he lived on a U.S. Army pension routed through a bank in Cyprus. Dollars converted to Lebanese pounds went far.

In the small apartment he roused himself from a long nap. He rooted around some cabinets, found a towel and soap, showered, got into fresh clothes, and went for a walk. He'd been away for a few months—how many was it? Three? No four. Whatever. The neighborhood seemed fresh all over again. The sweet smells of orange and lemon and pomegranate trees always relaxed him. The vaguely familiar faces in the cafés and small markets. But traffic on narrow residential streets seemed crazier than he remembered. Maybe it was the war two countries to the east. War in your backyard tended to be unsettling.

On foot he headed for Charles Malek Highway, and the O Monot Hotel. As far as hotels were concerned, he much preferred the Albergo and its cozy bar on Rue Abdel Wahab El Inglizi. It was much more typical of the Beirut he loved. But the O Monot catered to European visitors, it was modern, and it was more likely than the Albergo to have today's foreign newspapers.

Yesterday's would do as well. He just needed something to date his possession of The Reeds for a picture.

At the O Monot he took coffee and breakfast at the street level café, and picked up two out of town newspapers. The Paris Match, and the USA Today.

Concluding breakfast with a smile and generous tip, Hassan Shaloub walked back to his rooms. He gently removed Death in the Reeds from its protective case and placed it on the coffee table, on top of a copy of the USA Today newspaper. He chose the American paper because it was in hotels almost anywhere in the world, and there was no chance it would give away his location.

With his Canon Sure Shot digital camera Wajahat carefully photographed the plaque on top of the newspaper, clearly showing the headline and main photograph of the day as well as the publication date.

He stopped to admire the small plaque again. The scene was in the tall reeds of the Iraqi marshland, he assumed near what was now Basra, where the marsh Arabs lived before Saddam drained the swamps in one of his many purges of opposition Iraqis. The reeds were the background. In the foreground, the lioness, the hapless boy, the end of a young life. The animal had the boy in a death grip, its teeth already sunk into the tender flesh of the boy's neck. The boy's serene expression seeming to accept his fate. If it were a video, in the next instant blood would gush. It was such violent image, and yet exquisitely beautiful. The lioness rendered with grace, the boy shaped by the loving hands of a person who felt profound empathy for the young man's short life and tragic end.

Wajahat wondered about the king. Did he have just the two plaques on his throne? The one in Britain, and this one? Or were there more? Certainly others had not emerged in almost three thousand years. There were just two. And he had one.

The computer and printer were dusty from months of disuse. Wajahat wiped down both, then successfully tried a test print. He loaded The Reeds photo into the picture file, then printed two copies. He carefully inspected the prints. They showed Death in the Reeds in perfect focus, and the newspaper behind, slightly softer focus but clear enough to see the date.

He drove his battered Iraq Toyota to the offices of DHL. He sent away two envelopes. One was addressed to Winslow Sampson, an antiquities dealer in London who went by the nickname Pippy. The other to Wajahat's brother Ali Zardari in Fremont, California, across the bay from San Francisco. Fremontistan, as his brother called his hometown.

There was no need to write anything to go along with the photos. The picture proved the object was in his hands.

Before he infiltrated Iraq, Wajahat sent Sampson an anonymous note, an alert that a priceless antiquity would be available soon. He suggested Sampson solicit possible buyers discreetly, quietly. Quickly.

Wajahat and Pippy Sampson were not acquainted, but he had faith the art dealer's greed would open doors.

The picture sent to brother Ali conveyed the same message. Ali was in the middle of a surprising and rapidly rising class of young billionaires in Silicon Valley. The young inventors and investors there had created an explosion of world changing technology and with it a tidal surge of riches.

The brothers had quietly discussed Wajahat's plans on his last visit home a year or so earlier. Ali Zardari knew the significance of his brother's scheme and insisted he be allowed to offer the object. "I'm sitting on an ocean of money," he reminded his older brother. "A lot has changed since you went away."

Wajahat reluctantly agreed—Ali was his brother after all—but Wajahat was quite certain his brother would never come up with a serious buyer. By that he meant a buyer willing to spend enough to match the recent sale by The Winslow Sampson Gallery. One of Pippy Sampson's recent scores was the sale of a purported Michelangelo to a Saudi prince for a reported $400 million. By Wajahat's reasoning, The Reeds should bring more. A Michelangelo was only five hundred years old, while The Reeds was close to three thousand years old, and every bit a masterpiece. In Wajahat's opinion on that count alone it should surpass the value of the Italian master.

Wajahat fully expected the Sampson Gallery of London would place the object with a suitable buyer. When that moment arrived, Wajahat would hand carry the treasure to the buyer.

The plan from this point on was simple. He would board a cargo ship in Beirut Harbor in three days as Hassan Shaloub, Lebanese national. The Argonaut was a bulk carrier that traversed the Mediterranean, and carried a few passengers for whom speed was not an issue. The voyage was nine days to Gibraltar, and another six days to South Hampton. He would disembark in London's port two weeks later, take a cab to Heathrow Airport, board a United Airlines flight on his U.S. passport under the name Wajahat Zardari. He would fly directly to San Francisco International. Death in the Reeds would be wrapped in tissue paper imprinted with the logo of a gift shop in the Louvre in Paris. He carried a receipt for a relatively cheap tourist souvenir. The typical U.S. Customs inspector would see the item as just another small trinket tourists brought home every day.

That was the plan. The bookings were in place. The passage on the Argonaut and the ticket to SFO already paid for.

Hassan Shaloub was set to disappear, to become a ghost in just a couple days.

Like everything up to this point Wajahat Zardari's planning was perfect, and the raid on the National Museum of Iraq had come off without any of the problems he anticipated might arise.

But fate lay in wait for Wajahat Zardari. He would not make the ship. He would not make the flight to SFO.

On his early morning drive to the port of Beirut to meet the Argonaut Wajahat Zardari ran into trouble. Five young Lebanese thieves bent on carjacking lay in wait.

Wajahat Zardari had lived in Beirut long enough to know driving without a gun was crazy. He dumped the Iraqi AK-47 from the Mercedes in a wadi alongside the highway before entering Syria. But he managed to hide the Russian machine pistol from the Baghdad Mercedes. Plus he had an old Smith and Wesson .38 Special he kept in his apartment.

Car hijackings were all too common, and this morning he could spot the ambush from a block away. Five young men, Palestinian toughs, were lounging on a car they pulled across the road blocking traffic. They either wanted a "toll," or they wanted his car.

Wajahat rolled to a stop and extended an American $100 bill out the window. The "toll." The leader of the gang had a three-day beard, bad body odor and stinking breath. He laughed at him, and put a gun in his face. "We want the car old man," he said.

The Reeds was tucked away in the secret compartment under the floor of the trunk. There was no way he was giving up the car.

Wajajat offered another five American 100s.

The gunman sneered in his face. "The car. Now."

Wajahat held the Russian machine pistol across his lap out of sight of the tough guy.

"I have a few more of these American 100s," he said to the man. "You won't get much for this wreck."

"Cars are valuable in Beirut right now. Your offer is nice, but no thanks." The carjacker's mocking tone exasperated Wajahat.

"I'm trying to make you a deal that will make both of us happy," he said.

"I don't care about you being happy." The man's nasty teeth peeked through his mean smile.

Wajahat gave up being reasonable. "Have it your way," he said. He shot the guy through the door panel. The gunman threw his arms out and toppled backward like falling into a swimming pool.

Startled, his four compatriots hesitated before raising their guns. By then it was too late. The Stechkin spit out rounds in jarring pops and metallic clanking, instantly emptying the magazine. Wajahat sprayed the group, left to right, downing one, then the second. The other two turned to escape, but not nearly fast enough. They both caught rounds in the back and they fell on the pavement face first.

The full-auto spray from the Stechkin exhausted the clip. Wajahat threw it on the passenger seat, and pulled out his .38.

He let his temper get the best of him, a release of tension from the long escape from Iraq. He was angry, insulted these young men would dare. Wajahat should have driven off, but his pride wouldn't let him.

Five men lay bleeding on the road. He threw open the door and stepped out of the car to finish them off.

He walked among them firing coup de grâce shots to the head with the .38. His back was turned to the two men face down on the pavement. They had been motionless. No one stirred. But one of the men wasn't quite dead. He rolled on his side, raised his weapon and fired once before he lost consciousness.

That last shot caught Wajahat in the back of the head. Wajahat's face disintegrated in a cloud of bloody mist. He toppled like a tree.

On a pleasant dawn beside the blue Mediterranean Sea the meticulously planned and flawlessly executed raid on the Baghdad Museum came to an end.

Officers from the Wadi Abou Jmil police station near the port were the first to arrive. The scene was odd, difficult to sort out. To the street cops one of the dead seemed to be the intended victim. The officers knew right away the Beirut Internal Security Forces inspectors would be taking this case.

Wajahat lay dead. The priceless antiquity known as Death in the Reeds remained hidden in the secret hiding place beneath the trunk of a Baghdad wreck. Now it would be carried along on the wings of chance.

9

The Italian tomb robber—a tomborolo—called Pietro Granatelli anglicized his name to Peter Grand when he landed in a new life in London.

Pietro Granatelli didn't want to give up his previous life. Raiding tombs for valuable antiquities was steady and rewarding work for many years. But he saw the end coming. New antiquity laws outlawed trafficking in ancient artifacts and put him out of business.

He'd spent all of his life in the fields of Tuscany and Greece and Turkey probing suspicious mounds with a long thin steel pole, learning to feel for a grave, or a trove of broken pottery. He learned from his father, who learned from his father, and young Pietro was good at the work. He was big and strong, able to push a probe deep into the ground and dig great piles of dirt and rock. When he was just a boy, he accompanied his father and grandfather on their explorations and listened to the two men argue about whether a particular bump in the earth could contain a find. As a result of their schooling he seemed to have a sixth sense for antiquities. He had an eye for the spots where the ancients might have lived, where they left behind treasures. He wandered Italy and Greece and Turkey over shepherds' fields and crop lands searching for the places where riches lay hidden beneath the ground.

When Pietro Granatelli exhumed long-buried artifacts they usually came to light in a confusing jumble of broken pottery or if he was lucky, busted statuary. He learned to sort through the pieces, finding those that fit together like a puzzle. He had a feel for ancient times and habits of ancient peoples. Some of the greatest finds of Pietro Granatelli's lifetime were his very own finds. In Greece the wine mixing bowls called kraters, along with kouros, statues of young men. Roman funeral busts in Tuscany and Campagna and Sicily. Troves of coins and jewelry in Turkey.

It was an excellent business. Granatelli brought cardboard boxes of dirty pot shards to a duty-free zone in Switzerland. Antiquity smugglers kept repair workshops busy. The ancient finds were carefully cleaned, glued together, and sold for fortunes to the most prestigious museums in the world. Sometimes the lesser pieces went to individual collectors. It was a good business and while Pietro Granatelli was never a truly happy man, he was satisfied with the work and content to spend his life in the fields.

The end came slowly and painfully. Antiquities police began to close in on the tomboroli and one by one they were put out of business.

Granatelli held on longer than most. But his anger grew and his methods became more aggressive. He threatened property owners in order to gain access to fields. Once he shot and killed a man who refused permission and caught Granatelli illegally searching his property. Then he had to murder a witness who was set to testify against him.

That case taught Pietro Granatelli an important lesson. Police investigators could corner a killer with evidence and gain a conviction in almost any kind of murder that involved knife, gun, poisoning or strangulation. But one type of killing frustrated police and almost always went unsolved if the killer was careful. That was the murder of a victim who fell from a high place.

Such a death was almost always attributed to an accidental fall, or a suicide.

A large, strong man such as Pietro Granatelli could pick up a man and throw him from a cliff, or a building top, or from the high floor of an apartment. If someone saw him, that would be a problem. But fingerprints from the fabric of a shirt or a coat or pants were not yet retrievable. Consequently, as long as no one observed the large man throwing the smaller man over the edge, there was no way to turn a suicide or an accident into a murder.

Pietro Granatelli saw the danger of a coming proliferation of security cameras. If dirty work was required he patiently waited for an unobserved place and moment.

But a habit was set. Throwing people into thin air was Pietro Granatelli's preferred method of solving a problem when simple threats failed. Yes, it was murder. He realized that. Consequently, when it came to such a situation, he was very careful. He learned well the hard lesson of that close call with the law which he only escaped by throwing a witness over an Aegean cliff.

However even with increasingly brutal and remorseless methods the end came for all tomboroli, including Pietro Granatelli.

The museums would no longer buy the 'dirty pots' fearing antiquity authorities. Individual collectors shut their checkbooks when they saw friends go to jail and their collections confiscated.

Tomb robbing was over. Granatelli had to reinvent himself. The easiest and most convenient new career was an aspect of his old career: hired muscle.

Pietro Granatelli became Peter Grand and offered his services to people who needed a brute. Threatening, and following through with his fists became his new profession. It wasn't work he truly liked, but he had no choice. He really had no other skill than bending people to his will.

His face seemed to be in a permanent scowl. His eyebrows, black and bushy, angled down to the bridge of his nose giving his countenance a demonic cast. His fist-shaped nose sat on his face a little out of center owing to a long-ago street brawl. His brown eyes were heavily lidded but his expression was of a man always on alert. He had a scar that ran from just under his left eye to his jaw line, across the corner of his mouth. He wore his beard in a careless scraggle. He really didn't care much about his appearance.

Pete Grand, professional thug, had a meeting on this breezy London morning with his most important client. His relationship with Gennady Markov was not perfect. Markov was imperious, condescending and cold. But his money was good, and he kept Pete Grand busy.

In order to have this meeting Pete Grand had to squeeze his many pounds of muscle and six-foot five frame into a proper black suit. Accustomed to digging up ancient graves in boots and muddy jeans and a padded work jacket, the civilized clothing of city people made him feel uncomfortable and out of place.

But he had to adjust. In his new life he was hired muscle. He was exquisitely suited to the job.

He strode into The Arts Club on Dover Street in London, glancing around the reception area as if it were nothing more than a filthy latrine. His expression was a lava glower.

A pretty girl, the receptionist, asked if she could help.

"Yeah, Gennady fucking Markov. Where is he?" His English bore a distinct Italian accent.

The girl's sunny expression wilted. She directed him to a private suite where Mr. Markov said he'd be receiving guests.

Peter Grand stalked through the halls and rooms where hung artwork of the famous and revered. The pictures and sculpture meant nothing to him.

He found Gennady Markov beneath a canopy on an outside courtyard under gloomy London skies. Markov was a dapper dresser. He wore "smart" jeans, black and pressed with a razor crease. A tan blazer and an open-collar red silk shirt. His was a sharp Slavic face, with triangular high cheekbones, an unsmiling mouth and slate gray eyes. He had a three-day growth of white beard.

Markov was holding a lit cigar, trailing smoke. He had a cocktail glass with three fingers of amber liquid. At the sight of Pete Grand, he signaled a passing waiter. "Please get this man a whiskey," he said in a slight Russian accent.

Pete Grand sank into his chair. "The shit you have me do," he said, opening with a gripe.

"Come on," Markov said. "I got you choppered in. No easy thing. Had to tell the Americans it was an evacuation of Russian nationals."

"They didn't believe that, did they?"

Markov shook his head. "Not after you landed at the Museum. But by then it was too late for them to do anything. They certainly weren't going to fire on a Russian military unit."

Pete was still pissed. "I don't do wars. I dig things up. I deal with people who dig things up. I threaten dealers to do what I want. I don't do wars."

"Oh, for god's sakes," Markov snarled. "For one thing, your days of digging up pots are over. For another, I sent a Spetsnatz team with you. You had the best protection the Russian Federation could buy."

"Which made me all the more a target!" Pete hissed. "American jets shadowed us the whole way. Might have put one up my ass at any moment."

Markov waved him off. The waiter returned with a drink for Pete Grand. Markov offered to clink glasses. "Let's drink to a semi-successful trip."

"Only semi?" Pete asked, tapping his glass on Markov's. "I got you everything you wanted that I could get. The gold was impossible and that other thing was gone."

Markov nodded. Yes, the gold was impossible, and liberating the Treasures of Ur would probably have caused endless trouble, anyway. On the other hand, Death in the Reeds was something that shouldn't have got away.

Pete Grand slugged down half his drink. "You're supposed to sip," Markov said.

Pete grunted, glancing around. "What is this fucking place, anyway?"

"It's a club. 1800s. Mr. Dickens one of the first members. Name familiar?"

Pete grunted again. "No. Why?"

Markov shook his head and sipped his drink.

"Why are you in this club? You're a fucking Russian spy or an arms dealer or some shit."

Markov gave Pete a sharp glance. He took a drag on his cigar and whooshed a purposely annoying cloud of smoke in Pete's direction. "To these people I'm the representative of the Hermitage Museum, one of the great museums of the world, as I'm sure you've heard."

"Yeah, but why are we here? Shouldn't we be in your fancy mansion?"

"We're here because I have to meet art people. You're the first on my schedule." And he added, almost under his breath, "And because Boodie's and White's won't let me in just yet."

"Who?"

"Never mind," Markov said. No point in trying to explain to Pete Grand the social standing of the two oldest gentlemen's clubs in London. He would just grunt his ignorance.

Markov sipped in silence for a minute. Grand stared at his empty glass. "What do I have to do to get another?"

Markov ignored the request. "We want you to keep looking for The Reeds."

Pete snorted a laugh. "How am I going to do that? There must have been a thousand looters in that place. Looked like an American mall at Christmas."

"Hmmmm," Markov mumbled, reaching into his jacket pocket. "Look at these."

Pete took the sheets of paper. The first one was black, except for a bright spot in the middle. "What is this? A joke?"

Markov shook his head. "That's who took The Reeds. That's the heat register of a car parked outside the museum while the Americans were bombing, six or seven hours before you arrived."

"I can't see a car."

"Doesn't matter what you can see. That's what it is. These images come from satellites. So that's the first image. Then look at the second."

Pete shuffled the papers. "Okay, what?"

"See that? It's an older Mercedes. The same car at the museum in the previous picture. Abandoned. It's parked right behind a battered Jap car of some kind."

"How do you know it's the same?"

Markov nodded. Fair question. "Look at the next one."

Pete stared at the third sheet with renewed interest. It showed the battered car on the open road. "What's this?"

Markov set his cigar on the glass ashtray. "If you were able to make out the detail our experts see, you would see that's the same beat-up car that was in the previous picture."

Pete nodded in agreement. "Okay, and?"

Markov took the sheets back. "What we've learned from our friends in Baghdad is the first car was discovered with a body in it. A young man who worked as a janitor in the Iraq museum. Appears he shot himself."

"Okay, so?"

"It also appears the man in the Mercedes at the Museum changed cars. We believe he was at the wheel of the … whatever that older car is, escaping Baghdad with The Reeds."

"Got anything more? Who he is? Where'd he go?"

"Our people on the ground there think he was a co-worker. Might be a Baluchi named Zardari. He's also suddenly missing. We think he headed west, Damascus, maybe Beirut. We're trying to find him, but he's not a guy who checks into hotels or rents cars or cashes checks. Hard to locate someone who operates close to the ground like that."

"So you may or may not find him. What am I supposed to do?"

"We have to assume the thief is going to try to sell the object. Here are a couple names …" Markov handed another sheet of paper to Pete Grand. "These are the dealers here in London and New York most likely to be contacted about the object. You should go around to these fellows and impress upon them that you are the buyer who is first in line."

"Do I use your name?"

"Best not. I'm known to be close to the boss. So just impress them, employing your many charms, that you expect to be contacted first when the thief begins, shall we say, his marketing campaign."

Pete nodded that he understood. Markov meant he was to beat people up if he suspected they weren't agreeable to his demand. He scanned the list. One dealer in London. One in New York. "This is it? Two guys?"

Markov shrugged. "That first one is here in London. He's the guy who got some Arab to pay four hundred million for a Michelangelo that was probably a fake. Every reason to believe anyone screwing around in the antiquities world would go to him first. So start there."

"And the New Yorker?"

"Interesting guy, that one. He's a collector who made a stupid mistake and had almost all of his collection seized and returned to countries of origin. You tombaroli all know that guy. He bought a lot of your dirty pots."

"Oh yeah," Pete said, studying the sheet of paper. "Irwin Feinstein. I remember him. He got busted, right?"

"Yes. Schmuck. Had one of your dug-up pieces in his bathroom. Let a magazine run a feature on his apartment. Cops saw the pot in pictures."

That didn't seem right to Pete Grand. "What cop would recognize the kind of thing we dug up?"

Markov nodded in agreement. "Ordinary cop wouldn't. This cop is called Bart Trappani, a U.S. prosecutor. Bad luck for Feinstein. Trappani happens to be an expert in antiquities. He seized virtually all of Feinstein's collection."

"So why am I going to see this guy? He's a dumbshit."

Gennady Markov shook his head no. "Reason is that he might be contacted to authenticate it. He's one of the world's most famous experts."

"Famous?"

Markov made a waggling motion with his hand. "Famous in a small circle. Antiquity experts."

"How do you know these are the only two who might get a contact?"

"I don't," Markov quickly interjected. "This is a start. I may learn more as you go along. Maybe." He shrugged, "But maybe not. We'll see." He picked up his cigar and lit it again. "Start with the dealer here in London. He's an annoying little gay guy named Pippy Sampson."

Pete Grand's face squeezed tight like he smelled a fart. "Fucking Brits. What kind of name is Pippy?"

"The kind of name with a gay bodyguard in his bed. But that's not your concern. The deal is he handles old masters, contemporary shit, and the occasional antiquity. He can move anything, so he's scary because we don't want him selling The Reeds to anybody but us. And he shouldn't get the idea he can use his contacts to jack us up. You should convince him that he will make a nice profit but he's not going to gouge the boss. I'm sure you can impress upon him that you need to get the first call and there will be no dickering. We'll pay what we'll pay."

"And how much is that?"

"You don't need to know. That's the boss's business."

Pete Grand shrugged okay. He folded the paper, slipped it in his jacket pocket. He stood, slurped down the last drop of his drink. "This place sucks, by the way. It's not up to your standards."

Markov smiled, grim. "Make the boss happy and the circumstances for both of us will improve. Fail him, and things get ugly fast."

Pete grunted. "Bosses are all the same."

10

Exhausted, Mickey Judge stumbled through his door at midnight, headed straight for bed. He'd driven from Vacaville State prison after a long bureaucratic wait to do a quick get-to-know-you interview with a key witness in his investigation of DA Jean Washington. It was a guy who traded testimony—doubtless lies—for a prison assignment where he might not get killed. One of many in Jean Washington's snitch racket.

The phone rang before he could sling his jacket over the back of a chair. He listened. He looked at his watch and sighed.

"Sure, no problem," he said.

Now it was the early morning hours, and Mick was running on three hours sleep, just a tad late. He pushed the '99 Honda down Market Street as fast as the four-banger hamster wheel could muster. He had bought the car the previous week, something to run around town. He was surprised how gutless it was.

This morning's gig came in a midnight call from the KBAY assignment editor, Danny Fuller, a guy Mick knew for years and happened to like. As a special favor could he do a live shot in the morning? The regular reporter called out sick and Fuller was desperate. Mick said sure. He was new. Didn't hurt to do the newsroom a favor.

The live shot was about a story that had transfixed the city for a couple days: a young woman shot and killed while strolling on a tourist pier with her father. An illegal immigrant was under arrest.

Mick was aware of the details of the story. Like everybody else in the news, he kept up with developments, so he felt comfortable doing a live shot.

Even as he drove to the location, he mulled where he was on the Jean Washington story. He'd been to Vacaville State Prison to contact a man who snitched his way out of the very scary Pelican Bay prison, California's gang killer supermax. But it was going to take a couple more trips, a couple more cartons of Marlboros to convince the guy to talk on the record. Meantime Mick was stalling anybody at the station who asked what he was working on.

To others Mick was in a period which looked like he had nothing happening. The News Director kept badgering him about when his "investigation" would be ready for air. If for no other reason than to get the News Director off his ass. he figured it wouldn't hurt to show his face on television. Saracenetti had warned him about the shithead on day one. Mick could already tell the guy despised him. For no apparent reason, other than he wasn't consulted on Mick's hiring. Mick agreed to do the morning live shot figuring a few suck-up points couldn't hurt.

Zipping down Market Street felt like the old days, when you could move around the city with speed. In San Francisco these days nobody drove fast anymore. The streets were gridlocked all day and late into the night. But this was very early, a live shot for the pre-Today Show morning news. He was alone on Market Street, except for the occasional staggering shambolic shape of a homeless person on the edge of his headlights.

He hung a sliding left on Embarcadero, and pulled to a stop opposite Pier 7, the tourist walk that thrust into the bay. It was the pier for tourists to get the perfect shot of themselves in front of the

Oakland Bay Bridge.

Across the street the crews were set up and ready for air. Checking his watch, Mick slowed himself down. He still had ten minutes. Plenty of time.

A rather typical foggy morning. The lights of the Bay Bridge hazy through the mist. The television news crews bathed in a pool of TV lights, lined up like ducks. Mick's cameraman stood closest to the street, checking his watch, undoubtedly wondering where Mick was. Stretched to his right were crews from all the English language stations—plus the two Spanish language stations. It was a full turnout because the story involved an illegal alien shooter. In these times an illegal Hispanic shooting a white girl automatically goes national. Not only would the reporters do a shot for the local audience, but the networks would take a shot for their morning shows.

He walked up to the cameraman, gave him a nudge with his elbow. Spike Snyder turned and grinned. "Hey welcome back."

Mick and Snyder had worked together many years ago. This was the first time they'd seen each other since he'd been back.

"Sorry you're missing the war."

"Trying to forget that. Evidently I fucked up."

Spike handed him his stick mic. "Whatever. Just stand over there. We're about five minutes out."

"Got it," Mick said. "First let me say hi to my new colleagues." Mick walked down the line of reporters, introducing himself, and saying hello to the camera people, several of whom he knew from way back. Three of the air talent were stunning young women, the others athletic looking young men. At the end of the line he said hello to the security guard. "I'm Mickey Judge," he said, shaking the big black man's hand.

"Nice to meet you. I'm Otis Moore." The big man had a nice smile.

Mick hustled back to place, standing next to Spike. "It's only courteous to introduce myself."

"You dog. You just wanted to meet the cuties."

Mick shrugged. "Can't hurt. One or two of them might need advice."

"You're twice their age."

"And that would be wrong," Mick admitted. "But it's not quite twice."

Spike suddenly broke it off, clutching his right hand to his ear piece. "They're calling. We're up."

Mick stood in front of the camera, giving a countdown mic check. It'd been years since he did this kind of work, and in a way he missed it. Street reporters went out to do their story, cut a package of voice-over and video, stood in front of a camera for a live shot, then they went home. Or to the bar. At the end of each day it was over till the next day.

Mick, on the other hand, carried a story around with him for weeks, sometimes months, until it was ready for air. Sometimes he wondered if the day-of people had it better. Their stories were often mindless, but at the end of every day it was done. And the next day it was new again.

On yet another hand, he knew he couldn't go back to that work. A street reporter gig was for young people. It was run run run, get it on the air, run run run to the next thing.

He was done with that.

Otis Moore gave him a smile from the other end of the line of cameras. Seemed like a nice guy. There'd been a spike in robberies in the last year of crews in the field. Now a security guard on live shots was standard.

As if on a common cue, the other reporters in the row brightened and began speaking. They were all leading their shows. KBAY led with the war. Mick was second story in, about two minutes after the top of the hour.

Mick was concentrating on the live read he would do while video rolled. He was called out too late to cut a proper package so Fuller had the overnight editor put together voice-over video Mick could narrate live.

But something behind Spike caught his attention. He heard an almost imperceptible screech. It sounded like tires on the wet pavement. He focused past Spike. Between the line of live trucks parked at the curb a car stopped. And then the passenger door opened. And then a man emerged.

Mick focused, brow knitted. This wasn't right. The man—a kid, really—was thin, wearing black jeans and a dark hoodie. He walked quickly between the live trucks and made straight for Otis, who was not paying attention to the street. He was watching the reporters do their live shots, leaning on the pier railing.

Mick felt a buzz of alarm.

The man in the hoodie was holding a gun at his side. It was a black pistol. Mick recognized it as a Glock or something similar that his father used to carry.

The guy was making a beeline straight for Otis, the security guard. Otis didn't see him coming.

He was raising the gun!

Mick didn't hesitate. He bolted straight down the line of live shots between the cameras and the reporters. He screamed, "Otis, gun! Gun! Gun! Gun!"

Otis reacted in confusion. Startled, staring at Mick running at him instead of turning, he was trying to make out what Mick was shouting. He was a sitting duck.

Mick had no choice but to launch himself at the man with the gun. The guy's peripheral vision was blocked by his hoodie, but he could hear Mick. He was starting to turn toward the commotion.

But he didn't see Mick flying at him until it was too late. Mick knocked into light stands, his shoulder banged the last camera in the row, and he flew into the gunman in an open field tackle.

Now pandemonium. Light stands crashing, reporters screaming, the camera crews trying to figure out what was going on.

Mick was on top of the gunman, struggling with his arm for control of the gun. Then …

Booom!

One shot went off. Straight up in the air. Startled, the shooter hesitated for an instant. Mick seized the opening. He cracked him across the face with his elbow. He wrestled the pistol out of his grip.

Big Otis flopped on top of the shooter instantly, smothering him like a three-hundred-pound blanket. Mick was on his knees, breathing hard, holding the pistol. He knew how to use it, but it didn't seem necessary now. Otis had the skinny kid wrapped up.

Somebody yelled, "Gun! Gun!"

Mick turned. He saw a second man coming through an opening between the live trucks. "Shit!" Mick thought. The guy was raising an assault rifle, one of those nasty black things with a big magazine sticking out of the bottom.

Mick splayed on the ground facing the second guy, pointing the gun he'd just wrestled away from the first guy. He knew that assault rifle could kill them all. He didn't wait. Mick started pulling the trigger.

Boom! Boom! Boom! Boom!

It sounded like a cannon crashing against his ears. But Mick kept firing, pulling the trigger over and over. He watched the second man stagger back and collapse. But he kept firing until the gun would fire no more.

Then it was very quiet. A shocked silence.

Otis quick-stepped over to the downed man and kicked the rifle away. Mick glanced sideways, noticed the first man starting to rise again. Mick scrambled to his feet and whipped the pistol across the kid's face. This time the first guy went down for good.

Then the pandemonium started again. Reporters talking at once in excited voices, one or two of the women near hysterical. Mick could feel the camera lights on him. He steadied himself on his feet and walked over to Otis. The security guard was kneeling beside the downed man, his finger on his neck. "No pulse," he said to Mick. "Dead."

Otis stood up and hugged Mick. "You saved my life," he said, tears forming in his big eyes. "You saved my fuckin' life, man."

Mick nodded. He didn't know what to say. He was still holding the pistol at his side. He noticed the gun, and dropped it. The cameras followed the gun to the ground.

Then there was a cascade of voices. Questions, near as Mick could tell. Questions mixed in with narrative. Reporters excitedly relating what they'd seen. Mick felt the camera lights go off him, over to the dead body, then turn back abruptly. Of course: dead people not allowed on television.

Mick and Otis held on to each other and staggered to the railing for something to lean against. Reporters were firing questions at them both. Mick didn't answer. He didn't know what to say. Otis was talking. "Mickey Judge, he save my life, he save my fuckin' life, man. That boy gonna shoot me down and Mickey Judge fly outta the sky like an angel and he save my life ..." Otis went on this way, tears streaming down his cheeks, clutching Mickey like a rag doll.

"Where are the cops?" Mickey thought. Then he realized it was too soon. The whole episode had taken seconds. There wasn't time for cops to arrive. Yet.

He felt naked. The cameras were pointed at him. The reporters were asking questions, he was shaking his head, saying some words, but he knew they didn't make sense.

A KBAY colleague suddenly appeared looking disheveled, like she just rolled out of bed. She pushed her way to the front. Carol

Stein. Mick knew her ever so slightly. She was still in slippers and pajama bottoms, but she had a blazer on and her hair under a KBAY ballcap. She must live in those high rises across the street, Mick thought.

"Mick, just tell us what you saw."

The other reporters went quiet. Six cameras pointed at him, camera ops peeking around the view finders nodding at him, "Go ahead Mick, talk now." He was on all six Bay Area stations at once.

Mick began. "I was getting ready for my shot. I heard a car squeak to a stop. I saw a guy coming at Otis with a gun …"

And on he went recounting the last few minutes best he could remember.

11

After his meeting with Markov, Pete Grand followed through on the order the boss gave him. He studied the sheet of paper from Markov. The Pippy Sampson Gallery on Grafton Street was the only location in London. There was another name in New York, but that was obviously for later.

It was pouring rain in London. On the street Pete popped open an umbrella, and squinted through the rain at oncoming traffic for a taxi. He spotted one, but it had the occupied light on. Pete stepped in the street and held up his hand—stop! The black cab slid to a stop inches from his knees.

"What the hell are you doing?" the cabbie screamed at him through the window.

Pete stepped to the passenger door, pulled it open. He yanked a middle-aged man out by his collar. Pete Grand had a knack for lifting people off their feet. The gentleman's eyes widened as he felt himself sliding out of the cab in the clutch of a huge hand. "How dare you. What do you think you're doing?"—various futile objections. Pete put some cash in his hand, along with the umbrella. "Get another cab and sod off," he said.

He folded his huge body into the back seat. "Keep the meter running, go here," he said, shoving the paper through the security opening. Gape-mouthed the cabbie instantly realized it would be a mistake to object. He glanced at the address. "You realize this is only three blocks away, right?"

Of course Pete didn't. "Just fucking go there. It's raining."

The cabbie lurched forward into traffic, his former fare standing in the gutter wondering what just happened.

The Pippy Sampson Gallery was a four-story Georgian building, wedged shoulder to shoulder with houses of questionable fashion and restaurants that served small dishes at gasping prices. Pete threw cash at the driver and jumped out without a further word.

A formidable door painted a glossy black greeted him. He pushed his way through. He found himself in a gallery room that extended the depth of the building. The walls painted bright white, the floors black tile. On the walls contemporary art, the stuff Pete Grand hated: "Retarded kid shit." He walked the length of the gallery, swiveling his head left and right giving the art cursory inspection. At the far end a young woman dressed in black pants and a black turtleneck sweater. She had red hair, green eyes, and a restrained smile. "Sir, may I help you?"

"Pippy Sampson. Where is he?"

Now her smile turned to mild amusement. "Do you have an appointment?"

"It'll only be a minute. Over there?" he mumbled, glancing around for the staircase to the floors above. It was to his right.

He immediately turned to the staircase, ignoring the young woman asking him to please stop. He heard her pick up the phone, say something. Didn't matter what she said, far as he was concerned.

At the top of the stairs the person she had called was rushing over to intercept him. He looked like some kind of junior grade assistant, an art student type. Pete blew past him with a forearm shove. There was a door at the end of the room, behind which it seemed there must be offices that looked out on the backs of buildings lining Albemarle Street. Pete strode toward that door, paying no attention to the Dutch Masters discreetly lit on the walls to his left and right.

Peter Grand pushed the door open, banging it on the wall. He encountered what seemed to him to be a personal security man. He was dressed like the woman downstairs. Black pants, black shirt buttoned tight at the throat, biceps bulging through the sleeves, stomach flat, a tree trunk neck. He had a goatee beard, and an earring in his left ear. "Hold on there, pal," he said, putting his hands up to Pete's chest.

"It's alright mate," Pete said. "Just here to see Pippy Sampson."

The man laughed as if Pete didn't understand how wrong he was. "He's a busy guy. You got to make an appointment, pal." The guy was an American, Pete thought. Brits didn't say 'pal,' they said 'mate.'

"Look, I walk in all nice. Dressed nice. Being polite," Pete said, thrusting his face close. "Got some important business with Mr. Pippy. Will just take a second." Pete stepped around the guy.

The security guy stepped back in his way. "Listen. I told you once. You can't see him now. Go back downstairs and make an appointment."

Pete was taller by several inches. He looked down on the guy contemptuously. "He ain't too busy for me."

"Damn sure is."

"You got no fucking idea."

"Course I do. He's busy. I know that for a fact." The guy was smiling at Pete as if to say "you may be bigger but I can take you down."

His attitude annoyed Peter Grand. "Fuck off," he sneered, and stepped around the man again.

This time the guy put his hands on Pete's chest. "Just stop, pal. Turn around and leave." He put some muscle behind his hands, pushing Pete back a step.

Pete cocked his head, and glanced down at the hands on his chest. "Oh yeah?" he said. He jabbed the man in the throat with an open hand, his fingers stiff as nails. Doubled him over clutching his neck. Pete picked him up, one hand on his collar, the other on his belt. Spinning like a discus thrower, he launched the man through the doorway. As if he were a bowling ball, the man slid across the polished floor about thirty feet before thudding into the pedestal of a marble bust. The pedestal tilted, the bust cocked sideways, the pedestal rocked, the bust fell, hit the floor in a crash and pieces scattered across the room.

Pete stood looking, making sure the guy wasn't getting up again. "Idiot," he mumbled and he turned back to the offices. He walked past the ones that seemed small, headed for another door that felt like it might be the boss' spot.

"Are you Pippy Sampson?" he asked a startled man sitting behind a large desk.

Pippy Sampson looked like his name. The first name. He was smallish, Pete guessed five foot four. He weighed perhaps one fifty, if you counted his shoes and clothes and his mobile phone. His face was round, puffy cheeks and a flat nose, slightly piggish. His skin was pink and his eyes were watercolor blue. He was wearing a sea foam green sweater vest, over a pink Oxford shirt, and white boating pants. "You might be the most ridiculous man I've ever seen," Pete said, blurting out the first thing that came to mind.

"Who the fuck are you?" Pippy Sampson asked. Indignant. Rising voice. "And did you just break something?" He came around his desk, walking in short steps past Pete to look out the door. "Oh my god, that's a Brancusi." He turned to Pete, color flushing his face. "You smashed a fucking Brancusi. Who the fuck are you?" he repeated. Not waiting for an answer, he shouted to his assistant. "Is Lenny okay? My god, he's not moving. Call an ambulance and call the police."

Pete took him by the neck and stood in the doorway so the assistant could see he had the boss in the grip of his huge hand. "Go ahead with the ambulance but do not call the police," he said, lifting a squirming Pippy Sampson like a rag doll. "It won't go well in here if you do."

Peter Grand slammed the office door shut and shoved Pippy Sampson back toward his desk.

Gasping for breath, Sampson clutched his neck as if that would help. His mouth was hanging open, he was breathing heavily, and his eyes were wide and disbelieving. He had never been manhandled like this and he didn't like it one damn bit.

"Who the fuck are you?" he stammered, "and what the fuck do you want?"

"Sit down," Pete said, taking a seat for himself in front of Sampson's desk. "We have some business to discuss." Pete flipped a business card onto the desk. "That's me."

Sampson walked to his chair with his hands on the desk to steady himself. He collapsed in the chair staring at Peter Grand in disbelief. He picked up the card. "Peter Grand and a phone number. What is this?"

"That's how to reach me. You'll need to do that."

Sampson sat back in his chair, shifting his eyes from the card to Pete and back again. "What is this? Are you a blackmailer? Nobody cares that I'm gay, if that's what you think you got on me"

"I don't care if you like dick."

"Then what the fuck do you want?"

Pete leaned over the desk into Sampson's space. "There's a certain item that will soon be offered to you to sell. I want it to come to me. You are not to offer it to anyone else."

Sampson reacted in both surprise and confusion. "What item?"

"A certain antiquity. Recently stolen. From Iraq. You'll know it when you see it. The thief will soon put it out there. It may be offered to you. That's because you get very high prices for things. I want you to understand when you are offered this piece, you will call me. I will come to pick it up and I will pay you. But no games. No bidding wars. You won't offer it to anyone else."

Sampson was barely listening. He didn't care about the item, whatever it was, or the order he was to follow. Instead, being manhandled and threatened raised his notorious temper to fury.

"I have no idea what you're talking about. You need to get out of my office and never ever come back," he said. "I know people in this town and I can make you very sorry. Get the fuck out now."

Pete laughed. "You? Threatening me? Midgetman, I break things much larger than you. Shut your mouth and do as you're told."

"Don't think you can order me around," Sampson said heatedly, emphasizing the word me. He picked up a letter opener to defend himself. Pippy Sampson found courage in defiance.

Pete Grand laughed again. "I am ordering you around. You have my number. When the item is offered to you, call me. If you don't, that thing won't help."

He kicked the chair back as he stood. On his way out, he gave a disinterested glance at the EMTs who were attending the injuries of Pippy Sampson's security guy. It looked like maybe a broken arm, not that Pete Grand cared.

The young lady assistant was standing over the scene, eyes wide, still aghast, not quite sure what happened.

Pippy Sampson quickstepped out of his office to survey the damage. "How bad is it Lenny?" he asked, still seething.

"Fucked me up pretty good," Lenny said, gritting his teeth in pain.

"Should I call the police?" the girl asked.

Pippy Sampson shook his head. "No. I'll take care of this." And he retreated to his office in his mincing step. "Nobody pushes me around like this," he shouted to his quavering staff. "Nobody."

At his desk he found his phone, scrolled through some numbers, punched one. "Alfie it's Pippy. Come see me."

He listened for a moment. "Whatever it is, drop it and get over here. Somebody needs to just fucking die."

Pippy Sampson clicked off the call and threw the phone at the wall. "Nobody pushes me around like that," he steamed. He plopped back down in his chair mumbling bitter threats.

This was the nightmare Pippy Sampson had spent a lifetime amassing money, status, and security to insulate himself from. This was the dreaded moment: the fact that a small weak man was always at the mercy of a large strong man, a reality he both loathed and feared.

After a lifelong quest to build a protective wall of intimidation and fear all his efforts were shattered in less than five minutes. Until now people just did not fuck with Pippy Sampson. He was powerful. He was ruthless. He had lawyers who could rain lawsuits down on enemies in a torrential storm. He had people who could make other people hurt.

Pippy Sampson seethed. It was galling that one man could burst through his door and effortlessly knock down all the walls he'd built up over a lifetime of work.

He fingered the card. Peter Grand. A phone number.

Fuck.

Pippy Sampson's anger was both volcanic and bottled up. He wanted revenge now. The idea that revenge should be served cold was abhorrent to him. Blood rose in his eyes. His fury consumed him.

Wielding his letter opener like a gutting knife he slit open envelopes from the stack of mail on his desk.

A yellow and red DHL envelope caught his attention. He sliced through the clear tape, and pulled out a single sheet of paper.

What's this? Pippy Sampson thought. He examined the picture closely. It tripped a memory. Was this the thing he'd received a message about a while back? That cryptic message that something big was coming?

Pippy inspected the photograph closely with a gilt handled magnifying glass. It looked like a piece he'd seen at the British Museum. A slow recognition crossed his face: this was the companion piece that was at the Iraq Museum.

Then he realized it wasn't in the Iraq Museum any longer.

He picked up Pete Grand's card again.

Could it be? he asked himself. Could this be the piece that would both bring him many millions and serve as the perfect bait to bring that goon to meet the fate he deserved?

Oh Pippy, you mean little shit, he thought to himself. "Payback," he said out loud. "I'm going to fuck you up, big boy."

12

Ali Zardari, the earnest and studious son of Pakistani immigrants, lived in the South Asian diaspora city of Fremont, California, known among the young locals as Fremontistan. Ali was 22 years old, occupying a spacious room in his parents' house. They supported themselves and their son in a mom-and-pop halal market serving south Asian immigrants. Ali worked hard on his studies directly across the bay at Stanford University. Computer sciences.

Ali was a handsome young man. He was tall, broad shouldered, athletic. His thatch of thick hair was jet black. His eyes were dark, shadowed by a heavy brow that lent his appearance an air of sympathy and concern. His jaw was firm and strong, his smile effortless and charming. Unassuming, and humble, he was only barely aware how his stunning good looks affected women. The young kufr women who were his classmates wondered how he would kiss. Sexually alert women in their thirties and forties pondered the possibilities.

His parents, Hamid and Nazia Zardari, the halal grocers, were intent on his success at university. They had lost one son to the American military, followed by an urge to wander. He said in search of his Islamic roots. That older son Wajahat seldom made it home. They desperately hoped second son Ali would complete his studies, become employed, find a good Muslim girl from a good Pakistani family, marry and bring them grandchildren and happiness.

Ali was aware of his parents' wishes. He did not want to disappoint his parents. He loved them. He revered them.

But he also worshipped his older brother. He longed to live the life of his brother Wajahat. He yearned to travel, to see the places of his heritage, to study archaeology and art. His older brother Wajahat told him "All the good stuff came before Mohammed." The antiquities.

Computer sciences were interesting, occasionally fascinating, but the allure of the highly lucrative tech world belied a reality he found daunting: so many students, so much competition, so many ideas, so many failures. The blind optimism of many of his fellow tech students left Ali Zardari skeptical, frustrated. "You must fail to succeed," they told themselves. Ali didn't see the wisdom of failure.

But even big brother Wajahat pressed him to focus and push forward. "Stay in school," he would say. "These countries of our ancestors are barbaric shitholes."

"But the fabulous art of the ancients!"

"Buried beneath shitholes. Take my word for it. I will be home soon."

Discouraged, but Ali kept a secret. His brother's secret. He knew his brother Wajahat was going to liberate—yes, steal—a highly valuable antiquity. His brother had confided his plans during his last visit a year earlier.

The American bombing of Baghdad seemed the perfect cover. Ali had no way of knowing for certain—Wajahat's communications were few and far between—but this opportunity made sense.

After all, big brother Wajahat had been in the American invading force that liberated Kuwait from the Iraqis. He was fluent in colloquial Arabic, he was a native speaker of Urdu, he moved freely as a Muslim in Muslim countries. Wajahat had a residence in Beirut. He traveled between Lebanon and Cyprus and Egypt and sometimes even Syria. He slipped in and out of identities and local accents like a ghost. Ali knew Wajahat's plan for slipping into Iraq. He would pose as a common laborer from Baluchistan seeking work.

Ali had helped. He secretly sent Wajahat their father's Pakistani passport. At the time it was issued the Pakistani government had not yet transitioned to modern passports and it was easy for Wajahat to change one digit of the birthdate and substitute a picture of himself. Ali carefully sliced out the page that showed a United States entry stamp.

Ali knew Wajahat traveled to Aqaba in Jordan on that passport looking for work. As Aqaba was a principal port supplying Baghdad, Wajahat intended to somehow hitch a ride on a freight truck into Baghdad.

Silence followed. That either meant Wajahat was in Iraq and unable to communicate, working on carrying out his plan. Or it could have meant some terrible fate had befallen Wajahat. Ali had enough faith in his brother to believe it was the former, not the latter.

This particular morning Ali was up early. The time difference between Baghdad and the west coast of the U.S. meant that the network morning shows had the latest video on the American invasion of Iraq. He tuned in Channel 8, his favorite station. He favored the local station over cable news networks mostly because he liked an exotic, transfixing woman who did interviews of famous people.

Her name was Cassie Papadop. He knew the name was Greek, not Arab. But she had the look he liked. Olive skin, bronze hair, high cheekbones, flashing Mediterranean eyes that seemed to call his name. He was slightly ashamed of himself for giving in to the temptation to stalk her online. But he did it anyway. He knew where she lived. He knew her details. He had her email address, her phone number, her calendar. He fought the urge to contact her, at least until he had a solid plan.

It was six in the morning when he got a bowl of Cheerios with milk and a banana from the kitchen, and set himself up at his desk in his room. He put on a headset to listen to his bedroom television without waking his parents.

He knew his favorite television personality wasn't on the air this early. He tuned in to Channel 8 looking for Baghdad video.

There was something weird on the television. Something chaotic. He heard a gunshot, and screaming, and the camera waved around like a loose garden hose. Then the picture became clear. There was a shooting; a black man went down. He seemed to be carrying a combat rifle. Then there was a reporter guy being pestered with questions. Then the whole thing was replayed. And replayed again, and over and over. Evidently a reporter from Channel 8 shot somebody who was coming to rob the camera crews and reporters who were on the Embarcadero for some reason.

Ali Zardari was annoyed there were no pictures from Baghdad. What was this shooting on the Embarcadero in San Francisco compared with half a million American troops invading yet another Muslim country? What was the matter with these people?

It was a question he would love to ask Ms. Papadop. Ali didn't actually know Cassie Papadop, of course, he just thought he knew her. He thought about her a lot. He realized he had a boyish crush on her, and while that was embarrassing, he also harbored a daydream that luck would show the way for his crush to become something more.

Ali removed a yellow DHL envelope out of the top drawer of his desk. He slipped the sheet of paper out and laid it on the desk to inspect it again, for maybe the hundredth time.

He looked at it closely. It was an object lying on a copy of the American newspaper USA Today. When it arrived a week earlier it took him a moment, but he soon recognized the piece in the picture. It was the very object Wajahat told him he was going to capture one day. It was called Death in the Reeds. It was one of two in the world. It was three thousand years old. It was priceless.

Again, as he had several times since the DHL envelope arrived, Ali Zardari held the sheet of paper in his hands as if it were a message that had dropped down from heaven. It meant his brother had succeeded, it meant his brother had survived the harrowing journey in and out of Baghdad, it meant his brother had the object. It meant total victory. It meant when Wajahat Zardari stepped off the plane with the object in his bag the family would be set for life. The pressure to create a breakthrough tech idea, raising money, shepherding a startup and selling out for millions—all that soul crushing anxiety would be bypassed.

The sheet of paper also meant it was time for Ali Zardari to take action. He'd promised his brother he would find a buyer. A "buyer" meaning one of the billionaires or multi-millionaires who actually lived in close proximity, who could afford such an object and who had the education to know how valuable it was.

Straight across the Dumbarton Bridge to Palo Alto. The billionaires' headquarters were in Menlo Park, in Los Gatos, in Mountain View, in Cupertino. Their mansions were in Atherton and Woodside in the hills. All he had to do was get to them.

Ali had thought about this extensively. He couldn't just walk up to a billionaire's house, or barge into his or her office.

Weeks ago he had realized he needed the help of someone who was already in touch with these people.

That's when he thought of the woman he so admired on television. She interviewed these billionaires at least once a week. She lived among them. She had contacts "out the ass," as his rude American classmates would say.

He needed to get in touch with Cassie Papadop of Channel 8.

Since he'd already tracked her using his online skills he knew where to find her. He had her online calendar. He knew when she went to the gym. He knew which hairdressing salon she used. He knew the nail salon she patronized. He knew her restaurants, her bars, the people she called and emailed. He knew she was seeing a man from time to time. He was noted on her calendar as "VW." Ali was jealous of this man.

He practiced how he would interest her in his proposal. He'd refined his pitch. Now he just had to do it. He rejected a "chance" meeting in person because that might blow up in failure. What would she think of him if she could see him? It would be better to just be a voice. A voice with an intriguing promise of riches. He had to call her.

Cassie Papadop would be the one who could be the bridge between the Zardari brothers, and the men or women who had the vast fortunes it would take to possess the object.

Channel 8 seemed to be chaotic this morning, owing to that shooting, but he knew this was the time to call. He knew this was the hour she readied herself for the gym. This was the hour she was least likely to blow him off.

Ali punched the number into his phone. He listened as it rang somewhere across the bay.

Cassie Papadop answered. "Hello?"

Ali Zardari took a deep breath and began. "Miz Papadop you don't know me. I have a priceless piece of art looking for a new home. You can make millions for yourself if you can connect me with a buyer."

Ali waited for a response.

She asked his name. "Ali," he said softly.

He heard her press the phone to her body while she shouted something to someone else. He could hear her come back on the phone. He waited. He could hear the television in the background. Maybe she was watching. It seemed to take forever.

"Sorry," she said after a few moments. "I'm listening. Please go on."

13

First light cast a soft spread of morning glow over the large and lovingly kept homes of Presidio Terrace. Hydrangeas and rhododendrons and roses. Blooms opening to morning light.

Presidio Terrace. The pinnacle of San Francisco exclusivity. Massive iron gates, homes of only the wealthiest. The ones who quietly scorn wealthy friends who felt they must have a view of the bay.

Through the gates, take a gentle turn to the right. There a hulking home of big shoulders seemed to intimidate its neighbors.

A second-floor bedroom suite. Dripping water, a tall black woman stepped out of an Italian marble walk-in shower. She started to wrap her body in a luxurious fluffy white towel, but paused to admire herself in the mirror. Skin like coffee and cream, narrow waist, not too wide hips, cupcake breasts, long runner's legs all the way up to "a booty to die for."

I do look good, Jean Washington thought. Ever been a President who looked this good? No. Damn right. No.

On a small television in a corner of the bathroom a chaotic scene on the waterfront was unspooling. The sound was down. District Attorney Jean Washington did not notice the mayhem playing out on the screen.

She ran a hand over her long delicate neck, turned her head, checked her profile. Her face was perfect, in her own estimation. A thin nose, actual cheekbones, gently pointed chin, and full lips that did not require a puff up job at the dermatologist. Most of all, those killer gray green eyes. Jean Washington could make them bore a hole through a person. Devil eyes, her critics said. Damn right! she thought.

District Attorney Jean Washington wrapped the towel tight over the top of her breasts, took another towel for her hair. She was giving her head a vigorous rubbing when something on the bathroom television caught her eye.

It was chaos exploding on the screen. She squinted at the screen, reached for her glasses. She made out the waterfront.

Oh. It's the pier where the white girl got her snotty ass shot.

Jean Washington's eyes darted over the screen, puzzling out the words at the bottom, the headline—Just Now—at the top, and the scene itself, people tumbling over, a fight on the ground, gunshots.

Holy fucking shit, she thought. She whispered to herself softly. "It's that son of a bitch."

Now the District Attorney didn't hesitate. She dropped the towels and walked quickly out of the bathroom bare naked to the nightstand on the near side of the bed. She picked up her phone and punched a redial.

"That little son of a bitch just shot some kid dead on the Embarcadero. You need to get to him now." She listened for a second.

"Who? The one scheming on gutting me," she interrupted. "Just get him in an interrogation room. Make him slip up."

She disconnected the call and set the phone down.

She turned on the television in the bedroom and stood staring in stunned silence. The video of the incident kept replaying. A first viewing left the impression of a jumble of violence unfolding at such speed it was hard to comprehend. But by the fourth or fifth replay, Jean Washington could clearly see the face of Mickey Judge, the son of a bitch who was trying to derail her career. The Governor's office practically had her name on it. Maybe a Senate seat. Definitely a Presidential run, and this little shit was trying to scuttle it all. Fuck him. The son of the dead detective Nicholas Judge, who also tried the same stunt before he ended up with a bullet in the temple.

"Son of a bitch," she mumbled to herself.

Breasts bouncing Jean Washington padded barefoot down a long hallway to another bedroom door at the far end of the second floor.

She knocked hard on the door. "Cassie we need to talk right now," she said through the door in her boss voice.

Sitting at her dressing table in gym clothes doing her makeup, Cassie Papadop was holding her cell phone to her ear listening to someone intently. "Hold on," she said. She pressed the phone against her chest, turned and shouted back at the door, "I'm on the phone."

Outside Jean Washington's face twisted in disbelief. On the phone at this hour? This was the time she normally dressed for the gym. The incessant phone calls didn't usually begin until later. "Your old friend is in big trouble. Turn on the TV." And she turned and headed back to her suite. "Now I know why men get divorces," she thought to herself.

In her suite of luxuriously furnished rooms in the Jean Washington mansion, Cassie Papadop pushed the power button on the television remote.

"What was your name again? Ali? Okay, Ali."

The television picture came on, the chaotic scene distracting her slightly. Squinting at the television, she thought Holy crap. It's

Mick.

After a few moments taking in the scene on television, she said to her caller, "I'm listening. Please go on."

14

Not more than a couple miles as the sea gull flies from the District Attorney's mansion on the edge of the Presidio, stood a modest house with a pale green stucco exterior, attached to its neighbors. An unmarked SFPD Crown Victoria was nudged into the curb. In a darkened bedroom a man was up on one elbow, a put-upon expression on his face. With a pudgy index finger he punched the end button on his phone. His wife rose from the covers beside him.

"That the bitch again?"

"The boss again," he said, a mock correction.

"She's calling at this time of the morning?"

"I was getting up anyway," he said, rising slowly. He walked to the living room, clicked on the television. It took him only one play to recognize the scene. "Jesus," he said to himself, hurrying back to the bedroom for his clothes.

Bone Hendrix was out the door, talking on his phone as he walked quickly to his car. "Be outside in five," he said. He listened, interrupted. "No time. We gotta go."

The unmarked Crown Vic screeched on the fog wet pavement. Hendrix gunned it over the gloomy early morning streets of Miraloma Park, passing pleasant pastel stucco attached houses same as his own. He came to a stop sign at Portola, the street that winds over Mt. Sutro and drops down into San Francisco's Sunset District, where Irish and Italian and Polish families raised kids. Fully enrolled Catholic schools dotted the Sunset District.

Hendrix took the opposite direction, down Market Street toward downtown. He wheeled the Crown Vic into the Western Addition, an older neighborhood of not yet gentrified Victorians. He pulled up in front of a small blue house with white trim. A man popped out of a door, skittered down the steps, and jumped into the passenger side.

"I saw the TV," Billy Norton said to his partner. He had a plastic travel cup. Hendrix could see the steam rising.

"Coffee?" Hendrix asked, accusation in his voice.

"Instant and hot tap water," Norton said, defensively.

Bone Hendrix snorted, not mollified in the least. He wanted coffee.

Hendrix hit the flashing blue and red lights. They sped toward the foot of Market Street, and the piers.

"This is the guy who's been working up a hit job on the boss?"

"The very one," Bone replied. "No idea why he thinks she wouldn't hear what he was up to."

At the waterfront it was a scene of panic and confusion and relief. The reporters and crews who were involved in the shooting were busy retelling the story, and capturing video of one man sitting on the pavement, hands zip-tied behind him, nasty gashes across his cheek and forehead. A second man lay dead a few feet away, Otis' jacket covering his face. Cops everywhere, taping off the area, scooting the reporters out of their crime scene, taking over.

Mick was left alone for a moment. He wanted to walk away, catch his breath. Stand alone. Think.

No such luck.

Two SFPD Inspectors stood in his path, both flashing the seven-point SFPD police star.

Mick recognized them both immediately. Bonaparte Hendrix IV —known as Bone, sometimes Bone Four—a tall, imposing black man who seemed to have been born with a scowl. His partner stood alongside—a younger white guy named Billy Norton, nicknamed Billy Bob owing to his taste in footwear—various outlandish cowboy boots. He had the gray snakeskins on today.

Mickey expected to be talking to the cops. But not these two. Mick had a couple unpleasant encounters with Bone Hendrix when he started his career in San Francisco. The detective looked older but even after all these years every bit as suspicious and hostile.

Hendrix had been avoiding Mick's phone calls for months, even before Mick's return to San Francisco. The detective thought Mick wanted to press him about the death of SFPD Homicide Inspector Nicholas Judge, Mick's father. Mick was certain it was an unsolved murder. He never believed his father would kill himself, but the SFPD said he did.

While the murder of his father was important to Mick, the recent calls to Bone Hendrix were about something else. Mick's investigation of the District Attorney turned up hints the police were involved in her prosecutorial scam. It was Mick's working theory that she was running a snitch factory at the County Jail. A snitch factory was an illegal scheme whereby cops and prosecutors obtained phony testimony from jailhouse snitches to gain an indictment—sometimes a snitch proved good enough for a conviction. False testimony from a cellmate was almost impossible to impeach if the snitch was a confident liar.

Only two years earlier the entire Baker County DA's office had been banned by the Attorney General from prosecuting murder cases after an investigation by a local paper and later by the State Supreme Court revealed a snitch scandal that called hundreds of convictions into question.

As bad as the embarrassment was for the DA's office, the DA there was not considered a candidate for Governor or Senator or President. The outsized ambitions of the San Francisco District Attorney elevated such a scandal to career ending.

It appeared to Mickey Judge the Baker County news was repeating itself in San Francisco and like the previous scandal the only way the scheme worked was if police were involved. Mick figured it possible Bone Hendrix was up to his nipples in the DA's illegal snitch operation.

Bonaparte Hendrix IV was a senior homicide detective—Inspector in SFPD parlance—and one of the smartest. He was also the son of a former SFPD homicide inspector by the same name—Bonaparte Hendrix III.

Two sons of SFPD homicide detectives, one on the job, and the other adopting the profession most if not all cops hated—a reporter.

Hendrix motioned Mickey over to his car. "You should have stayed in New York."

"I think I saved some lives." Mick glanced back at the scene behind him. "I hope you'll be at my commendation ceremony."

Bone Hendrix smirked. He raised a lit cigar to his mouth and took a drag. Smoke trailed from his nostrils. He pointed the cigar at Mick. "You gonna run on me?" he asked in a low voice.

Mick shook his head, no. "Mind if I just stand here?"

Bone Hendrix waved over a uniformed officer. "Just make sure this guy don't wander off," he said. The cop nodded he understood.

Mick shook a cigarette out of a crushed pack. He noticed his hand was shaking when he flicked the lighter.

He stood leaning against Bone's unmarked detective car, smoking a cigarette, watching Bone and Billy Bob talking to the reporters and the crew folks, scribbling down notes. He glanced around at the gathering crowd of emergency vehicles, and onlookers behind the yellow tape. He noticed his car, the Honda he bought just a couple days ago. Side windows shot out, holes in the door panels. It had been directly behind the gunman Mick shot dead. With all the damage to his car Mick was amazed he'd managed to hit the guy.

His phone was buzzing. Saracenetti.

"I'm fine. Thanks for your concern," Mick said, skipping a greeting.

"I need you back here pronto. New York is up my ass."

"New York will have to wait. The cops have me."

"Christ. We got a shitstorm. Escape them as soon as you can. Lawyers want to talk to you ASAP."

"Wait. Do I get an attaboy? I think I saved some lives."

He could hear Saracenetti sigh. "Sure. Way to go. You'll get a parade. Meantime we got fires to put out. Get back here soon as you can break free."

"Maybe one of those lawyers could come get me. Evidently I'll be at the PD."

"I'll see what I can do," Saracenetti said and hung up.

Mick was left with the impression he'd just been blown off.

That's not right, he said to himself. Shouldn't the boss have been asking if he was okay? Shouldn't the station be rushing to his rescue?

Mick couldn't dwell on the troubling call. Bone and Billy Bob returned. Bone motioned for Mick to get in the backseat, and he scooched in beside him.

They headed toward the new SFPD headquarters on Third Street at China Basin in Mission Bay. Billy Bob was at the wheel. Bone Four was clearly not going to open a conversation.

Mick made the first move. "Inspector Hendrix, you must have noticed all those messages from me."

No response.

"I thought the son of a homicide inspector calling another son of a homicide inspector would rate a call back."

Bone Four took another drag on his cigar, rolled down the window to exhale a stream of smoke into the outside air. "You come around, start digging into court records, pestering cops, calls to their homes. I get it. You didn't believe he would kill himself. The ME's report says he did. When you don't believe the official report it means you think the cops are lying. Why would I talk to you if you think I'm lying?"

"I wanted to talk about something else."

Bone paid no attention to Mick's claim. "My Dad ate piles of barbecue and biscuits with half a stick of butter dripping down his chin. He killed himself that way. Your dad picked another way. I didn't come whinin' to you about why my daddy died. So why you doin' me like that?"

Bone turned to stare straight into Mick's gaze. "About those calls. You a reporter. I don't talk to reporters. Honestly don't know why you daddy didn't disown you. Bad deal what happened to your Pops. Guys in the department liked him. Felt bad about it. But facts is facts, and the forensics said he did himself. The investigation said he did himself. Sorry. All of us is sorry. I didn't return your calls because I could see you was gonna try to make it something else and all of us on the job got enough trouble."

Bone turned away. He'd made his point.

"Not what I was calling about," Mickey ignored Bone's reproach. "What do you know about the snitch factory over at county?" he asked. The City and County of San Francisco jail.

In the front seat, Billy Bob jerked his head toward the rearview mirror.

Bone's eyes widened. "See? That's how you assholes work. Come up with some sensation shit like a 'snitch factory.' What that supposed to mean? Forget your fucking questions right now. You damn well better have answers. You just shot someone dead."

Mick rolled his eyes. "Not feeling great about that. I just defended myself."

Bone continued. "You don't seem to realize what you done. Have you noticed dirt and blood on your clothes? You got all those reporters and camera crews tied up in a crime scene. Forget about your 'snitch factory', whatever the fuck that is. You just killed some kid on live damn teevee!"

In only a few seconds Bone got himself worked up. His head bobbing on his neck as he jabbed his cigar toward Mick. "Why the hell you get your sorry ass fired in New York? Big money, big time. Should be covering that war right now. Instead, you get fired. You turn up back here."

Silence followed Bone's outburst. "I like it here," Mick said, eventually. "Already done L.A. once, and nobody invited me back there anyway."

"Well, you shoulda liked L.A. twice. What's not to like? Beaches, bitches, riches. L.A. got you written all over it."

"I want to talk snitches."

"I don't know what the fuck you talking about and I really don't care."

"You ought to. Your boss is in trouble."

"Who?"

"Jean Washington."

"She ain't my fuckin' boss. She the damn DA. I work for the chief of the fucking police," Bone said in a loud voice meant to end the conversation. He pronounced 'police' ghetto style: Po-leece.

"Hey hey hey, settle down," Billy Bob interrupted, his eyes on the road. "We got business to do. Just sit tight and shut up, the both of you."

Bone Four glared at Mick, then turned and faced forward. "Fucking daddy issues," he grumbled.

"Evidently you got 'em too," Mick mumbled back.

Bone turned and glared at him again.

"Dammit, I said settle down!" Billy Bob shouted.

They rode on in silence.

The new SFPD headquarters on Third Street in Mission Bay was a concrete and glass box rising out of the bay mud next to a restored 1928 brick and red tile roof firehouse. The new building was designed to withstand both a massive earthquake and a siege of rioters. Bone and Billy Bob walked Mick in and took him directly to an interrogation room. It still had that new house smell, fresh paint, fresh carpet. A table, three chairs. Bone pointed at the suspect's chair. "You there," he said.

They sat. Bone and Mick stared at each other in silence while Billy Bob went off, came back with vending machine coffee.

Mick sipped at the coffee. "Sucks," he mumbled.

"This ain't no fuckin' Starbucks," Bone mumbled back.

They started off with Bone telling Mick to run down what happened.

Despite the tension in the room, Mick calmly went through the chain of events, best he could remember. They both stopped him a couple times to get details clear. As he talked, they nodded, watched him closely, both took notes. Mick assumed he was being recorded.

When Mick finished Hendrix had a series of questions. He asked if Mick made eye contact with the man in the hoodie? No. Did he know or recognize the man in the hoodie? No. Did he know or recognize the man in the car who emerged with the rifle? Assault rifle, Mick corrected. But, no.

At any point did he think he could have stopped the robbery—assuming it was a robbery, Bone noted—without shooting the guy holding the gun? "I only fired that pistol because I saw the assault rifle that could have killed everybody," Mick answered.

Did you order the man to drop his weapon? "No. I saw him raising the gun in our direction. I didn't wait for him to shoot. I fired first."

Did you sincerely believe your life and the lives of others were in danger? "Yes, of course."

Did you consider any other option than firing the weapon? "No. There wasn't any option."

How does it happen you knew how to aim and fire the weapon you took off the first kid? Mick took some pleasure in his answer: "My Dad used to take me to the shooting club at Lake Merced. I learned to handle a gun from him."

Considering their earlier argument, it seemed to Mick that was a question that didn't need to be asked, but he knew they had to get his answers on tape. Lock him down.

Bone Hendrix got up from his chair, nodded to Billy Bob to follow. "Sit tight," he said to Mick.

The detectives walked out the door, closing it tight behind them. They walked through another door immediately adjacent and into the observation room that had a view of the interrogation through a one-way mirror.

District Attorney Jean Washington stood staring at Mickey Judge in the darkened room.

"Billy Bob, go get more coffee," she said in a low voice. The junior detective got it: she wanted to speak to his partner privately. He left quickly.

"The son of a bitch was coming for me. He's been asking around. Showed up at Vacaville," she said, meaning the state prison. "He thinks people don't give me a call," she added.

"What's the shit he's talking about a snitch factory?"

"Oh forcrissakes, who knows? These goons make things up," she said, exasperated. "What can you do with him?"

"Doesn't look like much. One kid has a pistol, evidently intent to rob maybe murder. The other has assault rifle. This mook shoots one dead. He's probably going to be a city hero for saving the lives of all those shit heel reporters."

Jean Washington let out a snort and shook her head. "How'd he wind up back here with us?"

Bone shrugged. "New York papers said he told off the boss."

She grunted her disapproval. "See if you can find a reason to charge him. Like if he knew either one of those kids. Way things are these days white guy shoots a black kid could be a problem for the white guy."

"You mean like murder?"

She scrunched her nose. "Probably not Murder One. Pre-med probably a stretch." She shrugged. "I don't know exactly. But find something."

"You want to just dirty him up or actually stick him in prison?"

She had been watching Mick like a predator watching the next meal. She turned to Bone. "There are elections coming up. I do not need this guy digging around in my garden. See what you can do."

Bone grimaced. She wasn't his boss but she didn't seem to realize it. Jean Washington walked out of the observation room.

Bone returned to the interrogation room. Shortly Billy Bob showed up with three coffees.

The two detectives sat down. Bone slid a coffee across the table to Mick.

They sat looking at each other, sipping coffee.

"We gonna to do this all day?" Mick asked.

"Let's go over it one more time," Bone said. And they did. Mick felt like he told the same story over and over. Eventually Bone and Billy Bob decided they had him locked in on his story. They could cut him loose and see what developed. If facts or witnesses or evidence should emerge to contradict Mick, they'd drag him back in.

"Can you guys give me a ride back to my car?"

Bone snorted. "That's what DeSoto cabs are for. But you can't have your car yet anyway. They still digging bullets out of it."

Billy Bob spoke up. "You did manage to hit that kid but your shooting is crap. Thirteen shots, ten rounds tore up your car."

Bone interrupted. "It's been towed to the impound lot. Forensics has to pull the slugs out of the upholstery and door panels. Probably be a week till you can pick it up. And it won't be drivable."

"Why not?"

"Bullet holes. Windows shot out. Junk the damn thing."

Mick was out on Third Street in front of the new police HQ building an hour after he arrived, his head spinning.

He'd ignored his phone buzzing during the "interview" with Hendrix, and now his phone was buzzing again. He saw it was Grace Russell down in L.A. Again. He punched talk.

"I'm fine. I know it doesn't look like it, but I am."

"Jesus, Mick. It's all over the news down here."

"My guess it's news everywhere."

"Are you okay? My heart stopped."

"I'm tired. I'm not hurt if that's what you're asking."

"No. I'm asking if you're okay. You killed somebody."

Mick took a deep breath. "If something happens to you when you kill someone who was trying to kill you, it hasn't hit me yet. I'm a little annoyed that the cops are treating me like I did something wrong."

"Do I need to come up right away?"

"You do need to come up. I'd say you don't have to rush to the airport."

"You sure?"

"Look, great if you'll come up soon. But you may want to wait a few days until the dust settles."

"Okay," she said, reluctantly. "I will."

"I'll call you later. I'm sure they want to talk to me back at the station."

There was another silence. "I swear, Mick, I just don't know how you do it."

"Do what?"

"Always find a way to get in deep shit."

"Love, love," he said. "Gotta go."

"Try not to make it worse, okay?"

"I'll try."

He punched off the phone. Now what? A cab? Walk? As he was gathering his thoughts, he heard a horn honking insistently. "Mick! Mick! Over here!"

It was Cass Papadopoulos in her silver Audi convertible. Her hair was windblown, she had her big smile beaming at him, she waved him over. "Get in the damn car, you idiot," she shouted.

He slid in, slammed the door. "You need a drink," she said.

"Jesus, Cass, it's not even nine."

"Yeah, well Saracenetti wants you in his office and I'm telling you we need to get you a drink before you go in there."

She smiled. He grinned back though it almost hurt. "Thanks for thinking of me."

"Who loves you, baby?" she beamed, flashing those gleaming whites and hazel eyes sparkling. She leaned over, her sweater falling away, she shook her cleavage at him, her boobs bouncing under cashmere. "The one who got away loves you, that's who," she said laughing.

Ten minutes later they were in the basement of the most famous restaurant in North Beach, just off Columbus Avenue. The owner, Lorenzo DiCiara, opened the door personally for her, and brought a bottle of grappa down. Mick begged off. "Not that, Lorenzo. Can I just have a vodka and orange juice?"

Lorenzo shook his head. "It's my best stuff."

"I'll be stinking drunk and I need to go see the boss pretty soon."

"As you wish," the restaurant owner said, "but I think anybody should understand after what you been through."

He returned in a moment with four drinks. "Your seconds are already here," he said.

Cassie clinked his glass. "Holy crap Mickey. You need to decompress, baby. That was some show you put on."

He clinked back. He was ignoring his phone buzzing. Whoever it was could wait. The adrenaline was ebbing away. He was aching. He was starting to realize what just happened. "Thanks for getting me. I couldn't face The Don right this second."

"Oh, I know that babycakes," she said, running her hand through her mane of bronze hair. She grinned at him. "I wasn't going to let that happen. You just showed the whole town who the stud is. They be bowing down. Who got the swag now?" she said, affecting her hip hop voice. "But I'm not going to let them eat you up until you get your strength back," she said, rubbing his thigh. "You my boy!"

He hoped she meant it like a sister, not a lover. Women like Cass Papadop intrigued Mick in the past, but not now.

"Besides," she said, pursing her lips and flashing her eyes, "I got something big to tell you."

"Oh?" he replied cautiously. "What?"

She began to talk. Cassandra style. Rapid fire. Disjointed. Digressing. Doubling back. Confusing. As always, it takes her a long time to get to the point, but when she did, he had to whistle.

She'd been told there was a picture. Of an extremely rare antiquity. There was a guy who wanted to sell it. He wanted Cass to tap into her list of billionaires. She saw a big score for herself, a finder's fee in the millions. It was big for sure. And it sounded way out of her league.

"I want you to give me a hand."

Uh oh. "How?"

"After you decompress a little. Take a little time to rest. But when you got your sea legs back, I'd just love it if you'd run over to Fremont and check this guy out for me."

Fremontistan. Afghans, Pakis, Bangladeshis, a regular stewpot of post 9/11 weirdness and probably plenty pissed off over the Iraq invasion. Mickey didn't feel like agreeing to anything at the moment. And certainly not something that could turn out to be yet another Cassie Papadop wild goose chase into Indian country. Obviously, there was a reason she didn't want to go herself. Send someone in first and see if he comes out alive. "We'll see," he said. "I'll think on it."

"That's my baby," she gushed. "I knew I could count on you."

15

Only a few blocks from the restaurant where Cass brought Mickey Judge to bamboozle him into her scheme her on-again, off-again boyfriend was holding an important meeting.

The Buena Vista Café at the foot of Hyde Street boasts a spectacular view of the Golden Gate Bridge and the wind-whipped waters of the Bay. Tourists flock there for the whiskey based Irish Coffee, the breakfast of corned beef hash, sourdough toast, and the view.

This particular morning there was a butt on every stool at the counter, and every table was full, strangers sharing the larger tables. People stood outside in the fog, waiting for a vacancy inside. A few griped about the wait, wondering why the back room was closed off.

The reason was the Mayor of the City and County of San Francisco, Bobby Vargas-Watson. He commandeered the entire room to conduct a very private meeting with two political advisers. They were a husband-and-wife LLC called Snippen and Cohen

Campaigns. Willis Snippen was a Democrat, wife Marge Cohen a Republican They sold their services on the pitch they covered both sides of the track.

The three people sat at a long table, their backs to the window. Their voices couldn't be heard, their lips couldn't be read.

Bobby Vargas-Watson, His Honor the Mayor, shifted his stare side to side, from one to the other. "I don't know if you two are up for this job," he said as he sipped at the whipped cream topping of his Irish Coffee.

Willis Snippen was a rail-thin marathon runner who had elected a Democrat President. His Republican wife Marge Cohen wasn't a runner, but she kept herself thin and fit for television appearances. They picked up work such as Mayor Vargas-Watson's campaign for the money and to kill time until the next Presidential cycle kicked off.

"Why do you say that?" the woman asked.

"Your last two campaigns. Both guys lost huge."

"Extenuating circumstances," the man said. "People in our business can't be responsible for stupid candidates."

"We learned a lot that will apply to your campaign," she added.

"Like what?" Bobby Vargas-Watson wanted a cigarette bad. But the damn window. And judgmental voters passing by.

"Don't ignore scandal," Marge said.

"Here we go," Bobby Vargas-Watson said. "Somebody always bringing up my little bumps in the road. Wimps and pussies petrified by the mere whisper of scandal. You guys need to toughen up."

Willis and Marge smiled but the smiles were so phony they might have been painful.

"We're not afraid, Mr. Mayor," Willis said. "You can blow us off and move on to someone else. No skin off my teeth."

What's the word for that, Bobby thought. "Malaprop," he said out loud.

Willis shrugged. "Whatever."

Marge didn't want to lose the account. She hurried to soften her husband's brusque attitude. "We've just learned there has to be a strategy."

The Mayor was bluffing. Bobby Vargas-Watson didn't want to lose these two. They were ranked among the most powerful and clever political advisers and he had to pony up a huge stack of cash to get them. "Okay, what's your strategy?"

The Mayor sensed correctly that the couple didn't like him. While they wanted the campaign manager job—the commissions on television advertising alone paid extremely well—in fact Willis Snippen and his wife Marge dreaded meeting the Mayor. Certainly they hoped to work for him, but they didn't like him. He had the reputation of a charming rogue, a man who could be captivating and witty, but fellow campaign professionals also described him as highhanded, demanding, never satisfied, never grateful, always critical.

Neither Willis nor wife Marge felt they had to put up with that kind of aggravation. This was a meeting designed to discover if he was going to take their advice.

Bobby Vargas-Watson's reputation preceded him. He was an incumbent candidate forever in trouble of one sort or another. "My hobby is dabbling in scandal," he famously told a reporter trying to nail him to a wall. Consequently his campaign managers found themselves dealing with feuds and outrageous escapades from a Mayor who was positive nothing could truly undermine the hold on voters he'd cultivated over three decades when he was far and away the most popular television news anchor in the Bay Area.

Holding a list of "issues" the campaign would have to face, Willis Snippen pushed the LSU ballcap back on his head. His bony face drooped into a baleful scowl. The list had some real winners. Where to start?

Breakfast came. Willis and Bobby had the corned beef hash with an egg over easy on top, surrounded by hash browns and sourdough toast. Willis figured he'd run it off later.

Marge was no runner. She abstained, but gazed longingly at the sourdough toast and corned beef hash her husband and the Mayor were forking up. Not to mention those calorie bomb Irish Coffees. Both specialties of the house.

"We have issues and possible solutions," Willis Snippen said, putting his fork down, and snapping a sheet of paper in the air. Item one on Snippen's list was a recent potentially explosive scandal. A young prostitute claimed Bobby Vargas-Watson was a customer at a brothel in the Mission district where she was employed. Or so the media reported was "alleged," by "sources."

"We got to come up with a better story about the whorehouse," Willis said in a low voice meant to convey the seriousness of the situation. "I don't think this 'investigation' gambit is going to work."

The Mayor scooped hash into his mouth and slurped his drink. "Why not? I was a reporter in this town for over thirty years."

Marge took a breath and rolled her eyes. "Bobby, let's not waste time with bullshit. You say you were 'investigating' a report of a whorehouse in the Mission. Got it. Maybe you were. But they got an underage girl who works the place."

"So?"

"Our sources say she says she can identify your distinctive penis."

"My johnson? What's distinctive?"

"Yes. Your ... johnson. She says there's a birthmark on the underside."

Bobby burped up a dismissive laugh. "It may surprise you to learn this. I've never seen the underside of my johnson. Who would believe that, anyway?"

"Trust me," Willis joined in. "Our source in the police department says she's quite believable. She says she had it in her mouth."

Bobby Vargas-Watson scrunched his face. "And what are they going to make me do? Whip it out to show she's lying?"

"They made Michael Jackson show it," she said.

"I ain't showing my dick," the Mayor grumped, "and what's more the public isn't going to demand I show my dick."

"Mr. Mayor, the problem is the story fits a pattern," Willis continued. "The pattern is your attitude, which voters see as too fast and loose with your marriage vows." He checked the second item on his list of issues. "Issue two. You are a moth flying to close to a flame named Cass Papadop."

"People like to talk."

"You're right about that. That is the talk. Rumors become fact in a political campaign. We suggest you get out front and vigorously deny it. She's a married woman."

"A lesbian marriage isn't a real marriage," the Mayor muttered.

"It is in San Francisco," Marge said.

"It isn't in the lawbooks."

"Not yet, but it's going to be. That's beside the point. You are a married man, too. You have to stop being cute when asked about your so-called friendship with Papadop. You two worked at the same television station. Just say you are friends and former colleagues. Playing footsie with rumors of an affair isn't doing you any good."

Bobby Vargas-Watson shrugged. "I talk to her on the phone once in a while. Not much of an affair."

"Just come out and say so."

The Mayor grunted, sullen. The advisers had more.

Marge continued. "We need to dial back the wild side. People remember things. At KBAY you took the floor director to dinner to welcome her back from her honeymoon. You parked under a security camera. She went face down in your lap. Unfortunately the security camera was in tip-top working order. The tape leaked. Lots of people say they've seen it."

"Years ago. Years and years ago. Water under the fucking bridge," the Mayor said, again dismissively. "But I wanna get back to the whorehouse bullshit. Shouldn't the fact she's an admitted whore give voters the idea she might be lying?" The Mayor leaned back, his arms wrapped tight around his chest. His body language sullen.

"But she's not, is she?" Marge asked. "The truth tends to come out."

He gave up. "Yeah okay. Let's just say she had my dick in her mouth, if you must know," he sulked. "But people generally assume a whore is a liar. So why should this one get the benefit of the doubt?"

"Doesn't matter if she's lying if lots of people believe it," Willis interjected. "We need something that puts all of this stuff behind us."

Marge picked up the point. "You could call a newser, update the public on your wife's condition. The cancer is bad, not getting better. Let people see your compassionate side, your love and loyalty to your wife. You could let it drop that your wife hasn't been able to lead a normal life. She rarely appears in public, can't cook or do laundry for herself, hasn't had a proper vacation in years."

Here Marge paused for the indelicate part coming next. "You could hint she hasn't been able to have sex, what with her cancer and all. Hearing that people might put two and two together and figure you were just answering the call of nature."

Any port in a storm. Mayor Bobby Vargas-Watson turned to Willis. "That's an interesting thought."

"Of course," Willis said, making a hand gesture that indicated another side to the story. "Blaming the sick wife could make things worse."

Marge wasn't letting it go. "It could go either way. Women voters will get it. Seems counterintuitive but we've got polling that shows they'll feel sympathy for a spouse not being taken care of at home."

Mayor Bobby looked at Willis with a question mark. Willis reddened, caught off guard by an unrehearsed moment. "Marge, really?" he asked.

"Really, hon," she shot back with vehemence. "Women strongly relate to that issue."

"I give up," Willis mumbled as he sank back in his chair.

Bobby Vargas-Watson glanced back and forth between the advisers. "This is starting to feel like a therapy session for you two. I need advice on my situation, not yours."

The television set in the corner distracted the three of them. It was the shooting on the Embarcadero. "Shit. That's Mickey Judge," the Mayor said. "Fucking guy is a magnet for trouble." The television images of the shooting and the chaos that followed held their attention. The campaign advisers needed his attention back.

"The way to handle this is full confession and an appeal for forgiveness," Willis said, shooting a curled lip glare at his wife. "Don't blame your wife. Don't blame anybody but yourself. Seek counseling. Show you've learned a lesson and you will emerge from this embarrassing episode a better man."

Mayor Vargas-Watson turned his eyes from the television to the advisers. "You think she won't use a confession against me?" he asked, referring to his likely opponent in the upcoming election, the sitting District Attorney.

"She's going to use the whole episode against you. Better you have something other than a bullshit story to counter it."

"You honestly think the full monty is the way to go? Just hang it out there. 'Yeah, I was banging a teenage whore, but I've been to counseling and my urge to have sex with a girl in a Catholic schoolgirl uniform has been cured.' You really think that after a grotesque humiliation like that I'll come out ahead?"

Willis bugged his eyes. "Hey. It's California."

Marge sighed and waded in. "You were there. You've said so. It's very chancy denying you had sex with an underage prostitute. She's going to be everywhere telling her story. You're backed into a corner. Of all the ways to weasel out, straight up telling the truth is the one that invites the fewest problems. Bullshit stories spawn unpredictable ugly news."

The Mayor wasn't satisfied. "Spitzer never should have resigned, the pussy."

It wasn't just Spitzer. The road to re-election was littered with the corpses of politicians who had a zipper problem. No getting around that. Marge gave her husband a look that said "Your turn."

The couple had worked this out in advance. If the Mayor resisted a truth strategy the opposite was the only choice left. "Okay, forget the truth," Willis said. "We do have another idea," Willis paused and gave his wife a raised eyebrow that said, should I?

Marge nodded back. "Go ahead."

Willis took a deep breath and plunged ahead. "What if you just bluster your way through it. Say they're lying. They're all lying. The DA is lying. The girl is lying. The whores are lying. Throw mud at everybody. Be outraged. Be angry. Be furious. Say that isn't me on the security tape. Say the tape has been doctored. Charge the DA with using her office to railroad a political opponent. Accuse her of corruption. Go big. Go bold. Don't be afraid to just lie lie lie and point the finger at them. Call them all liars."

Mayor Vargas-Watson guzzled the dregs of his Irish Coffee and held it up for a waitress to see he wanted another.

He glanced back at the window. A homeless guy was the only person peeking in. Actual voters were not in attendance. He lit a cigarette. "That might be the way to go," he nodded. "That crazy bitch needs some mud on her too. I shouldn't be the only one dressed in a shit suit."

Willis winked at his wife. She let out held breath.

"Do we have the gig? Willis asked.

The mayor looked back and forth from husband to wife, from wife to husband. He nodded. "Yes, but I think I need to go even bigger. I need to put all that stuff in the rearview mirror and I think I know how you two can do it."

He glanced back and forth. Both look confused.

"What's the scam?" Marge asked.

"El nombre es Berto."

"What?"

"The name is Berto. Re-branding. I need a new brand."

"You are going to change your name?" Marge marveled.

The Mayor nodded. "Don't be confused. It's not just the name. It's a whole new person. A whole new me," the Mayor waved his cigarette around in a moment of exuberance. "Bobby Vargas-

Watson disappears. Roberto Vargas appears in his place. 'The name is Berto' is the slogan. In English and Spanish."

Willis and Marge Snippen were stricken with simultaneous migraines.

"But it's the same guy. You, the same person," Marge objected "How the hell are we going to pull that off?"

Bobby Vargas-Watson smiled as he stomped out his cigarette on the floor. "That's why you get the big bucks. Figure it out."

16

Cassandra Papadop's silver Audi convertible slid up to the yellow curb in front of KBAY on Golden Gate Avenue. A bus had just pulled away. The air hung heavy with diesel fumes. "You ready?" she asked.

Mickey Judge shrugged. "Sure. What's the worst that can happen?" He watched a squad of pigeons squabble over a crust of bread in the gutter.

"The worst?" She laughed. "You could be fired for the second time in a month."

"Shit," he said, his attention drawn away from the pigeons. "You think?"

She shook her head no. "C'mon. You saved people from every station in town. They're going to give you a parade, baby."

Mick got out of the car, a little unsteady from the booze at that lunch before lunch. "You coming in?"

"Best not," she said. "Remember I need you to run some interference for me over in Fremont. Could be big. Humongous." She winked and flashed that smile.

He watched her speed away, dismissing the Fremont thing, whatever that was. Probably just another Cassie mirage. She seemed to specialize in those.

It was his phone again. This time he recognized his agent's number.

"Holy crap, I can't believe you did that? It's everywhere. You're on TENN and CNN. I'm getting calls—Britain, the BBC, ITV, Sky. Everybody wants to put you on. Can you do interviews?"

"Beats me. Going in to see Saracenetti now. I would think he'd want to make the most of it."

"I'm sure he does. I might be able to get another bump out of him after this."

"I'll call you back after I see him."

"I'm calling him now. He should be sky high. Call me back."

Mick punched off the call. He could see he had a dozen voicemails to check on. Later.

Except for one.

"Jesus, Dad. You scared the shit out of me."

Tammy Judge, his fifteen-year-old daughter.

"I've been calling and calling. Where are you? Are you okay?"

"I'm fine. I had to talk to the police." He left out the drinks in the restaurant basement in North Beach. "Now I have to go in and see the boss."

"Dad, what the fuck? You could have been killed."

"I'm not letting that happen. I'm okay," he repeated.

"I'm coming up right away."

Mick repeated what he said to Grace, his girlfriend. "Let the dust settle. Give it a day or two. I'll call you later."

"You better."

He kicked at the pigeons pecking at gutter garbage, walked into the lobby. The security guard said, "Mr. Saracenetti said newsroom conference room as soon as you walk in."

"Got it," Mick said. He took the stairs down one flight to the basement newsroom.

The newsroom was a bunker. Underground, windowless, packed with desks jammed up against each other. Two glassed-in offices at the near end, for Paul DuFroid, the news director and some goon assistant news director. Plus a cramped conference room.

At the other end of the newsroom the glass-fronted assignment desk was the center of activity. It was where his old friend Danny Fuller ran things. Fuller had two or three helpers behind the glass hunched over computer screens, handling phone calls, an ear on police scanners. Scattered map books mixed with breakfast plates. A big white board with the name of every reporter, a story slug marked by each. Marin Pile Up. East Bay Shooting. Diablo Valley Molest. South Bay Double 187. And so on.

In the middle of the room reporters and writers hunched over keyboards in rows of messy desks, intermittently jumping up, hurrying to the far side of the room where small edit bays spewed squealing tape rewinds and fragments of sound bites.

Camera people stood around on the perimeter waiting to be sent out, sipping coffee, joking around.

When Mick walked in heads turned, and the room fell silent. Even the edit bays went quiet.

Not the greeting he expected. In an instant Mickey got the feeling this might not go well.

To a degree Mick had somehow forgotten, the reporters and writers and show producers were pure San Francisco. LGBTQs in daring fashion, socialists in their scruffy jeans and plaid shirts, activists wearing anti-capitalist buttons, promoters of various causes wearing t-shirts that screamed their politics. A few graybeards who'd been to every street demo since Viet Nam. More young faces as yet unmarked by life but certain in their judgments.

At this moment this collection of faces was openly hostile. He could read the thought bubble in the room as clearly as if it were written in neon. "Murderer," it said.

"Okay, this is wrong," he muttered to himself.

On his right was a conference room. Gathered around the table, leaning in over a speakerphone were Saracenetti, the pear-shaped News Director DuFroid, plus a couple of others Mick didn't recognize, but he assumed were lawyers.

Saracenetti glanced up. Saw Mickey. He made hand motions to shoo everyone out. Mick could read his lips when he spoke into the speakerphone. "I'll get right back to you." He waved Mick into the room.

As the others filed out, Paul DuFroid gave Mick a malevolent glare that said "schmuck."

The room was warm but the atmosphere was frigid.

Mick turned and watched the group go, his expression twisted in confusion. He turned to Saracenetti. "What's up?"

The silver haired boss lowered himself into his chair wearily. "Grab a seat." The room smelled of a mixture of cologne and hair gel and flop sweat. Half empty paper coffee cups left wet rings on the table.

Mick sat down. Brow furrowed, his eyes narrowed on the boss. "I don't like the vibe, Don."

"Your agent is bugging me to book you on television all over the world. Don't do it."

"Okay," Mick said. "Why?"

Saracenetti made kissing lips, but not the good kind. "That was

New York on the line. Corporate lawyers. They got people in Iraq maybe in the line of fire. Worried about injured or dead employees. Then this pops up. They don't need this. We've never had an employee kill anybody."

Mick started to interrupt, but Saracenetti stopped him with a hand in the air. "And nobody ever thought we'd have an employee kill someone on the air."

Mick recoiled "Wait. The guy was going to kill everyone. You realize that, right?"

Don Saracenetti frowned. "They don't know that, actually," he said, nodding at the phone, referring to New York.

"They didn't see the assault rifle?"

"They saw it. But they can't be certain he was going to use it."

That hung in the air like a motionless cloud of smoke. "Are you shitting me?" Mick asked after a moment to gasp a breath, stunned, leaning forward.

"No, I'm not," Saracenetti said wearily. "Now look, we're going to go out there and say you are a hero because you saved at least ten lives. We're going to take that position publicly."

"That's the right thing," Mick nodded but wary more was coming.

Saracenetti held up his hand—don't interrupt. "But the lawyers aren't really sure how that's going to hold up in a court of law."

Mick jerked his head up. "What court of law?"

"I guess you haven't heard. The family of the dead guy has a lawyer. They already announced a lawsuit against you, and me, and his station and the network."

"For what?"

"Millions. I forget how many."

"But for what?"

"Wrongful death. They're claiming their dead son was just going to rob the crews. Had no intention of harming anyone."

"Both guns were loaded. What for?"

"It was to intimidate you to submit and hand over your valuables."

"Not with bullets in the chamber. That's bullshit."

Saracenetti shook his head, gravely serious. "The other stations are running with it. Big. Already on the air with 'Deadly Channel 8, Grim Reaper Channel 8, Trigger Happy Channel 8.' Whatever bar you've been in the last couple hours didn't have a television on, I guess."

Mick felt a migraine coming on. "Wait. You're telling me the managers whose crews I saved are playing along with this bullshit wrongful death?"

Saracenetti nodded, pursed his lips. But said nothing.

Mick waited for a response. None was coming. The boss was thinking.

"So you're telling me you're going to back me up in public, but behind closed doors the knives are out?"

Saracenetti gave up holding back the truth. "That's an overstatement. We just need you to go home until the dust settles."

"Go home? You mean suspended? What the fuck, Don?"

Saracenetti was avoiding eye contact. "Hey look, put yourself in our shoes," he said, coming alive, but defensive. "I don't think there's any instance of a live shooting death on television. And especially not one by a reporter working for the station airing it. We're in uncharted waters here."

"Bullshit uncharted. The charted waters are stick with your guy."

"C'mon. Rod Wings didn't stick with you."

Mick ignored that. It cut too close to the bone. "Especially when your guy did the right thing. What would you be doing now if the punk had got off a few rounds and killed Spike or any of the others in his line of fire?"

"We'd deal with it."

"So what's wrong with dealing with this? At least none of the good guys are dead."

The older man put his hands flat on the table and stood up, an air of resignation. "See that newsroom out there? Bush just launched a war. They have been roused from their far-left slumber. Any idea how many pacifists and vegans and gays and lesbians and polyamorous and meat-is-murder types you got in that newsroom?"

Mick shrugged. "Assume all of them."

"Correct."

"So what?"

"They're already on my ass to fire you."

Mick turned and looked out on the newsroom. No question. The faces turned his way were scowling. "And? Are you?"

"No." Saracenetti paused, then quickly added, "because that would be admitting we're wrong. But I do have to send you home to lay low until this blows over."

"Sounds like a slow-motion firing."

"Not yet. I'm sticking with you. I'm going to have to fight it out.

As far as this place goes, you got balls to the wall camera guys who will back you up a thousand percent, plus a couple reporters, especially the ones with a military background. But the rest of the newsroom might as well be the peace collective crossed with PETA crossed with the youth commie league. Believe me, they think you committed murder. And the murder of a person of color. And you being white? The worst."

"They think shit. So what?"

"Who do you think is leaking all the stuff the other guys are airing?"

"Seriously?" Assassins in his own newsroom.

The Don nodded sheepishly.

Mick stood up, turned toward the newsroom and defiantly returned their hostile stares.

"Fuck them all," he said, turning back to the boss. "They weren't there. They don't know what happened. They're a bunch of pussies."

"We don't use gender slurs around here these days Mickey."

"Fine. A bunch of chickenshit twats. That better?"

"No. Worse."

"Well, fuck 'em."

"Mick just go on home and cool down. Let everybody calm down."

"If you even think of firing me, I'm getting a lawyer myself and suing the bejesus out of this network."

"We've already figured that in."

Mick could feel his heart pounding through his shirt. His face was flushed red. He was sweating. He was furious. "I'll just say this. Don't fuck with me. It will get all kinds of ugly."

"I hope that isn't a threat, Mickey."

"Of course it's a threat. You're betraying me. I don't have to take it."

Don Saracenetti sighed deeply. "Maybe this was all a mistake."

"What?" Mick demanded, wheeling around. "You bring me in, make promises, tell me you like the way I get in over my head and then bail at the first trouble?"

"Never mind. Just go home and chill out."

Mick threw open the door of the conference room and stalked out. He pulled up at the newsroom door, turning back at the faces staring at him. A roomful of angry eyes. The smell of sweat and scrambled eggs and hamburgers and weird sex. Too many piercings, too much pink hair, too many rainbow tattoos. "Hey! I saved lives of your colleagues," he shouted. "And you turn on me? Ingrate cowards!"

The newsroom erupted in screams and shouts. The air filled with wadded up paper and books and pencils and tape boxes flying at him.

"Fuck you all," Mick said as debris clattered against the wall and banged off the conference room glass behind his escape.

Outside the fog was still hanging at the tops of the buildings, but starting to burn off as the sun peeked through. Mick stood on the corner of Hyde and Golden Gate.

Pete DuFroid came through the lobby door. "I'm gonna need your badge," he said, holding his hand out.

"Who says?"

"The lawyers."

Reluctantly Mick pulled the lanyard over his head. "You never did want me in this job, did you?"

The News Director was a plump, misshapen man in a cheap suit. His face was sallow and fleshy, his mouth a thin line above a weak chin. But his eyes danced with delight. "I checked into you. I knew it would come to this. The Don couldn't be convinced, but you did my work for me." He had a smirk on his face.

"I don't get it," Mick said. "What was I supposed to do?"

"Don't go all Rambo and humiliate the station. That would have been a start."

"So let the guy do the gun thing. See if anybody drops and then shoot him?"

Pete DuFroid shrugged. "Who knows? You didn't give him a chance to hurt anyone so we'll never know, will we? Point is, it was a mistake to bring you in, and now you've ushered yourself out the door. Good work."

"Fuck you."

"See? Perfect. Insubordinate too. You're the best. Thanks for firing yourself. Saved me the trouble."

He turned and waddled away.

Mick's phone buzzed. It was Spike. "Fat ass Pete just took my badge. Think I'm fired," he said, without a greeting.

"Shit," Spike said. "Look, the crews are glad you did what you did. They understand."

"Great. But that's not doing me much good at the moment."

"Meantime, heads up. Don't stand around the station," he said.

"The leather crowd is talking about coming out to look for you."

"Who?" Mick said, lighting a cigarette.

"The boys from The End Up." The codpiece and cock ring bar near the old Hall of Justice. Some of the editors and writers were regulars. "They're only tough in a crowd and today they got a crowd."

"Oh Christ," Mick said, immediately lurching north on Hyde Street. "Are those wankers a problem or just posers?"

"Don't hang around to find out. I'll call you later," Spike said and clicked off.

The phone buzzed again. It was agent Johnny again. "You know what? They kinda fired me."

"What?" his agent screamed. "All the world wants you and they fired you?"

"What can I tell you? San Francisco is weird."

"I'm calling Rod Wings. He likes a guy with balls."

"He fired the guy with balls."

"You just grew two more. Things are different."

We'll see, Mick thought. Maybe Agent Jimmy just hasn't caught up to the new reality.

17

Out of range of the reported vigilante posse of long-neck swilling leather boys, Mick sat at the bar in The Gold Dust on Geary Boulevard across the street from the vehicle entrance to the St. Francis Hotel on Union Square. It was the kind of place where the others at the bar not only wouldn't recognize him, they wouldn't even look up at him.

It was his third vodka soda of the day and it wasn't even noon. "Things happening fast," he muttered to himself. In town two weeks and already on the verge of fired again.

How does this happen?

His phone buzzed.

Hoping it was his agent calling back with good news, he glanced at the number. It was the Mayor's office.

His honor's assistant said the Mayor would like to see you, could you come by now?

"Let me check my calendar," Mick said.

"He told me to tell you he knows you got nothing going on," she replied, an undisguised smirk in her voice.

Obviously Mayor already heard about his newsroom blowup. He might still have the juice at KBAY to straighten things up. Mick hotfooted it up Geary to Larkin Street, and made a left through the heart of the Tenderloin. His route took him just east of KBAY, and into the plaza of Civic Center. The library, which had become a day room for the homeless, was on his left. To his right, kitty corner across the plaza, stood City Hall, a domed monument to the grandiosity of San Francisco civic leaders. The monstrosity was wearing a fog cloak.

The mayor's office was up a grand staircase, and then off to the left. Mick's quick steps echoed off the stonework.

His Honor, the Mayor Bobby Vargas-Watson, and Mick had known each other for many years. Vargas-Watson had been San Francisco's most successful television anchorman on Channel 8 for decades. The smoldering Latin look—intense brown eyes, rugged jaw and cleft chin, the jet-black hair that turned a magnificent silver as he aged—it all worked television magic for a very long time. And when the inevitable generational change loomed on the horizon, Bobby Vargas-Watson—"Veedub" his underlings called him behind his back—shocked everyone by announcing his retirement from the air and his candidacy for Mayor at the same news conference. He won the Mayor's office easily.

Mick had worked for Veedub when Mick was starting out. He kept in touch with his old mentor through the years he was away from San Francisco.

Mick learned early on when Veedub called it was smart to cast aside whatever and just jump. Things hadn't changed merely because Mick had been out of town for a few years.

Mick found him lounging in his inside office, the one hidden behind the showpiece office where news briefings and protocol meetings took place. Veedub liked to smoke. Bobby had the tall gilt-edge windows pushed open, his feet up on the radiator watching the flocks of pigeons and people on the plaza in front of City Hall. He blew Parliament cigarette smoke into the fog.

He glanced over at Mick coming through the door, and nodded to a chair. "Make yourself comfortable, buddy." He butted out his cigarette, lifted his feet off their perch. He swiveled around in a high back leather desk chair.

"How'd you learn to shoot like that?"

Mick sat down. "Dad, of course."

Veedub nodded. "Of course. Your Dad."

He frowned. It was his way of being sympathetic. "You know you're toast, don't you?"

Mick returned the frown. "Nice to see you too, Bobby."

"Mayor Bobby to you."

Mick smiled. "Mayor Veedub to me."

"You know I hate that, right?"

"Why? Everybody likes to have a catchy nickname. Ad guys call it branding."

"Matter of fact I'm all in on branding. But Veedub makes me sound like a German mini-bus. Fuck that."

"Fine. Be stubborn."

Bobby gave Mick his famous anchorman stare, the one intended to convey seriousness, authority, and confidence. "You know you're toast, don't you?" he said again.

"You're repeating yourself. But why do you say that?"

"I stay in touch. They can't bring you back even if you're righteous. Can't have somebody on the air who killed somebody on the air. Simple as that."

"We'll see. My dad told me to always keep a lawyer's number memorized."

"You dial back that murder mystery theory of yours?"

Mick shook his head no. "Why should I?"

"Because you're making enemies. Not accepting he killed himself means you suspect a lot of people. Including cops. They don't like that one bit."

"That might explain Bone Hendrix being a dick."

The mayor pointed an index finger to the ceiling. "He's a dick because you're rattling the cage of his boss."

"You mean Ms. Washington? The one with the snitch factory out at the jail?"

Now Bobby shook his head no. "Forget it. She's too slick. You'll never make that stick."

"I got one of the snitches. He tells me how it works. She plants a guy in a cell, he takes the stand. Lies in court. Somebody goes away for a long time. Snitch gets a slack cut."

"Nobody cares. The guy who went away needed to. You're wasting your time."

"I thought you'd be grateful. Your only real political opponent caught in a scandal."

"I'd love for you to find a real scandal. That one is weak."

"Jean Washington may be an empty suit, but she is super-ambitious," Mickey said, passing over the Mayor's gloomy take on his investigation. "Isn't she planning to run against you?"

The Mayor scoffed. "She shouldn't," he said. "The campaign folks say I've got a scandal problem. I figured out what to do."

"What's that."

"I'm rebranding."

Mick scoffed. "What's that? Like New Coke?"

Veedub bristled at the jab. "Don't be juvenile," he said.

"Okay, fine. Rebranding to what?"

"Rebranding as Roberto Vargas. The campaign ads practically write themselves. The name is Berto. El nombre es Berto. A completely new persona."

"You're joking."

Veedub shook his head. "Nope. Go for the Mexicans. I'll get them in huge numbers. I'll get those white techies without much trouble. They all like burritos in the latest Mission hot spot and they don't see Latinos as threatening, like they do blacks."

"So what does she do?" Mick didn't have to say who he meant.

Bobby understood. Jean Washington, the man-eating candidate for anything. "If she's smart she doesn't take me on. Next election she can probably grab a Senate seat. Then sit tight until it's time for a Presidential run. I'll be in the Governor's office and I won't interfere."

"Why not?"

"No point. She can't win the White House. That business of a woman with a wife plays well here but not in the great middle. Believe me," Bobby said, lowering his voice. "But against all best advice she's probably planning to tee up a run for Governor by beating me first. Make me a loser."

"Don't you have a lock on the Mayor's job?"

"Of course," Veedub sniffed. "But you think I really want to run this snake pit? Gay men, gay women, transgenders, poor, rich, mega rich, techies, a few Mexicans, one or two blacks left, but not many." He waved his hands around to encompass the city. "All in all a weird stewpot of every kind of entitled grievance and special interest you can imagine."

"The Chamber of Commerce must love hearing you quoted on that."

Veedub waved him off. "I want to get out of this fucking vortex of insanity. Run statewide where I can just go for the Mexicans and slide right into whatever I want. And what I want is that Governor job."

"Your half Mexican, half white schtick is over?"

Veedub nodded. "No point in the half white bit anymore. Get those Mexicans in L.A. and the Central Valley behind me. I can still live here. Have a state cop driving me up 80 to Sacto …" He pronounced it "Sack Toe." "Sure. That probably would do it."

"And you think Washington wants that too?"

"Bitch probably does. She should run for Attorney General or Senate but her ego says she deserves more power. Running against me for mayor is just her figuring she can knock me out now so she won't have to do it later."

"You think she's that smart?"

"Hell no!" he boomed. "That's the point. She's not smart. Swear to god she'd run for President right now, but her people are telling her she needs to be Governor first."

Mick was confused. Senate, Governor, Attorney General, San Francisco Mayor. Sometimes it felt like the political class was just divvying up the state. Plus the labyrinth of San Francisco politics bored him.

"So, you really do think they're gonna drop me like a hot rock." It was not a question.

Veedub bobbed his head yes. "I told you you're fucked. Get over it."

Wasn't much for Mick to say. Veedub was emphatic. "Hope you're wrong. I'm going to fight it."

Bobby waved him off. "Yeah, whatever, fight on. But meantime you need a job and I got one for you."

Mick laughed. Bobby had come at him several times since he became Mayor, offering the job of press secretary. Even chasing him down in New York. Mick hated the idea, always said no. Politely.

"Mr. Mayor …" he began, but Bobby cut him off.

"Not that PR job. You've said you don't want it a zillion times. This is something more suited to your—how shall I put it—your caring personality."

Mick waited a few moments to see if more was coming. "Yeah,

what?"

Bobby gave Mick his anchorman stare and took a long moment to respond, and when he did, it wasn't about a job. "We got a thing, me and Cass."

Oh shit! There it was. His love life. Mick groaned out loud.

"Try to act like a sensitive human being once in a while, you asshole," Bobby said softly, leveling his stare into Mick's eyes. "We got a thing, a real thing. Like love."

Mick squirmed. He didn't like talking to guys about love.

Bobby went on. "I know what you're thinking. If I'm so in love why did I let her marry that dipshit. I did not, I repeat, did not want her to marry that crazy bitch. But she wouldn't listen. She wanted the notoriety, the opening nights at the symphonies and the operas, the socialite parties in Pacific Heights. That's why she did the gay marriage thing. It was trending." He paused. "Plus, she wanted to stick it to me."

Cringing to hear Bobby Vargas-Watson opening the door to his personal life, Mick tried to end it. "Why stick it to you? She could have done all that with the Mayor," he said.

"Not with the Mayor's terminally ill wife sitting alone at home."

That was a surprise. "I'm sorry to hear that. I didn't know."

Veedub snorted. "Who knows how long she'll last. It's terrible, but her condition has tied my hands."

"How?"

"How would it look for the candidate for Governor divorcing his tragically stricken wife?"

That would be a problem, Mick agreed. "I didn't know that's what you were thinking."

"If it wasn't for that I would have married Cass. But …" he shrugged, "what could I do? Couldn't dump the wife. We haven't gotten along in years, but the political downside would be horrendous. Ask Newt."

Mick was silent. The Mayor's personal life was super-seriously none of his business. "What do you want me to do?"

Veedub took a deep breath. "For starters, I want you to not bed her."

Mick recoiled. He managed to suppress a laugh. "Who?"

"Cass."

"Wait. What?"

"You're back in town. You used to have a thing …"

"Never had a thing ..." Mick interrupted.

"Alright. Nearly had a thing."

Mick didn't deny that. "Nearly" wasn't even quite right, but for this conversation it would do.

"And she's pissed off at me from time to time so it may occur to her that it's an opportunity to take care of unfinished business with you."

"Wouldn't occur to me."

"Why not?"

"After my divorce I don't do crazy anymore."

Veedub let a long sigh slip his lips. "Okay, she's crazy, but I do love her."

He stared at Mick emphasizing the point with a moment of silence. "And when my wife passes—which is just a matter of time—Cass and I are going to be married. So don't fuck that up for me."

How to escape the vortex of Bobby Vargas-Watson's infantile puppy love? Mick hoped one trenchant observation would hasten this to a close. "You're waiting for your wife to pass away, then you're asking Cass to get a lesbian divorce from Washington, and then you two are going to get married? Looks like a three-bank carom shot."

"For starters that lesbian thing isn't a real marriage in California. But, yeah. That's my plan."

"Is it hers?"

"She hasn't committed. But she will."

Mick looked at his old boss and friend trying to figure this out. "Okay then. Congratulations are in order. I promise I won't get in bed with her."

"You promise no sex? In bed. Out of bed. Back seat of a car. Blanket in the woods?"

"None of that. No sex. That good enough?"

The Mayor nodded it was. "Thanks. Appreciate it."

"Right," Mick said. "Now you said you wanted me to do something. What?"

"Yes. That." He lit another cigarette. "I want you to keep an eye on her."

"Who?"

"Cass."

"You just finished telling me to keep my hands off her and now you want me to ... what? Hang out with her?"

"Yeah, pretty much."

"You got cops who can look after her. You don't need me."

Bobby laid his hands on his desk, open, palms up. "I can't use the cops. They leak, they talk to the media, some of them want me gone. That's out."

Mick didn't object. It was probably true. "Why not a private eye?"

"No. I also need someone who knows her, and has personal reasons to stick close to her. That's also you. And don't forget, this is a paying job, and a good paying job at that."

"A city job? You can't do that."

"A campaign job. Tons of money in that slush fund."

That brought Mick back to his situation. He might need money.

"Okay. Keeping an eye on her about what?"

Bobby knocked on the desk like he was gaveling a meeting to order. "For instance, she wants to make big money, really bad."

"Yeah. She said."

"Talked to her this morning. Wanted advice. Some deal where she's supposed to broker the sale of some art thing."

Mick was surprised she had already talked to her boyfriend about that. The call from the contact had only come in this morning, during his fracas on the Embarcadero. "She wants me to go check out a guy in Fremont who says he has something big."

"A guy in Fremont. That's the one. God knows what that could be."

"She didn't say what it was? I figured it was just another of her schemes. I didn't ask."

"No, she probably doesn't really even know yet. But I don't need her getting arrested in some scam just because she's got big money on the brain."

"I already said I'd do that for her. That's not a job. It's a favor."

Mayor Bobby scrunched his face. "No. It's a job. Take it."

"Okay," Mick said to end it. "Fine."

The Mayor nodded thanks, and changed the subject. He stared out the window at the swirling cloud of pigeons. "You know what my biggest electoral problem is?"

"At the moment I'd say it's the brothel story"

"Nothing," he snapped back, waving the problem away with a sweep of his arm through the air. "If I get cornered I'll just say I was drunk and have no memory of any of it. Blacked out. Beats me how I got there. Maybe somebody took me. Maybe the DA sent a cab for me."

"Just walk back the story you were 'investigating'?"

"Sure. Why not?"

"What about the Cass story floating around? You are married."

"People know about Tina's condition."

"Publicly fucking around can't be good."

"It is not publicly fucking around. A few people know, but the media around here knows better than to cross me," he snapped again. "It's just a one outlet story at this point. And even if there was something definitive out there, there's enough people left in this state who like a guy who fucks women. So weirdly, it's a scandal that actually plays in my favor. See?"

"Not really."

"And believe it or not gays like it that I'd carry on with a lesbian. Though she's not," he added quickly. "It's not any of that at all."

Mick's mind was focused on how to straighten out the situation with KBAY instead of the Mayor's problems. But he had to hold up his end of the conversation. "Okay. What?"

Veedub flipped a cig out of the pack on his desk, put it on his lips, lit it, exhaled smoke. "If there is ever a picture of this, I'm fucked." He paused to let the point sink in. He laughed uproariously. "Imagine! I could be caught banging another guy's wife in the back seat of a car on Columbus Avenue, like our late former Mayor, with somebody getting a picture. No problem. But ever catch me smoking a cigarette in public, I'd lose a million votes. That's how fucked up this state is."

Mick had to let a small laugh escape. "I'm aware."

"And you know who's dying to get that picture?" Veedub asked, not noticing Mick's remark. "That half-breed lesbian bitch Jean Washington!"

"Anybody hears you talk like that you'll have big problems, guaranteed."

Veedub threw up his hands. "Keep an eye on Cass for me. It's a job. You'll be on the campaign payroll."

Mick took his checkbook out of his coat pocket, and peeled off a deposit slip. "Put money there. I'll get back to you."

Without saying more, he got up and walked out of Mayor Bobby Vargas-Watson's office.

"Hey wait a second," the mayor called out stopping him at the door.

"What?"

"Do something about your clothes. You got blood and mud all over your pants. You're starting to look homeless." The soon to be rebranded Mayor Roberto Vargas, champion of Mexican voters from Shasta to San Ysidro, swiveled in his chair, exhaling smoke out the open window into the fog.

Mick walked into the park in front of City Hall and sat on a bench. He called for a DeSoto cab on his phone. The dispatcher said ten minutes. Which seemed long. But enough time to grab a quick smoke.

A homeless guy passed pushing a grocery cart overloaded with possessions that looked like trash. He left a trail of malodorous air.

The phone was going to buzz itself out of battery life. It was Jimmy the agent. "Rod's thinking about it."

"Thinking about what?"

"He's thinking maybe he made a mistake."

"Does that mean he'll take me back?"

"Maybe. He's thinking. Did you get along with his wife?"

"Beth loves me."

"Hope so. I'll be back in touch."

He sat on the bench shaking his head. "What a fucked-up business," he said out loud, speaking to only himself.

His phone buzzed. It was Cassie Papadop.

"I know you've had a busy day," she began. "But my guy is getting hinky. Says a family issue. Might not be able to talk for a few days. Can you go over to Fremont and check this thing out for me?"

"Now?"

"Not right this minute. Tomorrow morning will be fine. You'll be free, right?"

Mick was just too tired to resist. "Yeah, I guess."

"Just go check the guy out for me. Look at this thing. I don't want to show my face until I know it's real. You good with that?"

Mick sagged his shoulders. "Okay, give me the name and phone." He got out his reporter's notebook and the phone number she read off.

"His name is Zardari," she said. "Ali Zardari."

"Jesus. What's that?"

"Something from somewhere. I don't know. People from god-knows-where over there in Fremont."

18

Wajahat Zardari's body lay on the medical examiner's table in the Beirut Internal Security Force forensics unit. A single bullet dead center to the back of his head the cause of death.

The middle-aged medical examiner, Dr. Georges Khoury, looked up from his work at the detective standing at his side. Name Vartan Boustani.

"A guy with a single gunshot to the head doesn't usually warrant the attention of a senior Inspector," Dr. Khoury said.

"This one is strange," Inspector Vartan replied. "Very strange. He had a few passports. His name is Shaloub. That was Lebanon. Zardari. That was Pakistan. Something else very unusual. United States. Again, name Zardari. He had passports in all those names."

"Which of the identities is real?"

Boustani shrugged. "Don't know. He probably got the Lebanese passport bribing someone. The Pakistani one might be real, but altered. Changed the birthdate and the picture. The U.S. passport is difficult to counterfeit. The others are relatively easy. So I have to assume the truth is that he was an American."

"Will the embassy track him down?"

Boustani shrugged. "They have their hands full with a war. But we'll see."

"Any chance it's all bullshit and he's Israeli?"

Inspector Boustani shook his head. "No, I don't think so. This is some other kind of mystery man."

"Where was he killed?"

"At the docks. Ticket in his pocket. He was on his way to board a ship. Very early. First light. Evidently he was stopped at a roadblock. Thieves."

"One of them shot him?"

"Yes. Figure it had to be a wounded man. This guy already shot all of them. It seems he got out of his car to finish them off when one of the wounded got off a last shot. We arrived to find six bodies. And we have no idea who he really is or what he was doing."

The doctor was intrigued about the car. "What kind of car?"

"Japanese. An Acura. Or Toyota. Beat to shit something. I'm not sure. Why?"

"I have a little side business. Our salaries here are not so good."

The detective understood. The forensic medical examiner bought and sold used cars to supplement his income. "It's in the impound lot. The usual. The colonel will take a bribe and allow someone to buy it. You know how it works."

The two men went out for a smoke. Wajahat Zardari lay on the table, the hole where his face used to be staring up at the ceiling. Two days later he was buried in a plain box in a grave marked by number 2003-489 in a pauper's cemetery.

Dr. Georges Khoury mentioned the car to a friend, the owner of a popular and successful taverna in the Hamra district. Saadee Habib wanted to see the car. The restaurant owner was looking for a car that wouldn't attract attention. Other men in his economic position liked to show off with expensive luxury cars. Saadee Habib thought ostentation was a mistake that invited kidnaping, armed robbery, and worse. He wanted automobiles that said to the world he was poor.

Saadee Habib was a short man of significant girth. He loved food and indulged himself. He paid Dr. Khoury a small finder's fee and waddled into the office of the Colonel overseeing the impound yard. He paid a bribe of one thousand U.S., plus a purchase price of another thousand U.S.

He had the dingy Toyota Camry towed to the auto body shop of a friend. The bullet hole in the door was patched, a few dents pounded out, the car was painted dark blue. Habib had the worn seats reupholstered. Then he drove his refreshed car to his home, a luxury apartment building overlooking the sparkling waters of Beirut harbor. Saadee Habib was satisfied with his new vehicle, confident he could ride around the rough streets of Beirut unnoticed and secure in the anonymity of a fat man in a plain car.

When he collapsed at his restaurant and died of a heart attack a week later the secret compartment in which Wajahat Zardari hid the antiquity Death in the Reeds had still not been discovered.

Inspector Boustani's caseload of murders soon distracted him. The Zardari passports laid in his inbox, new files piled on top. He didn't inspect Wajahat's car closely, and consequently failed to notice the hidden compartment. The impound yard supervisor was even busier and gave the vehicle no thought. And Saadee Habib hadn't bothered to look closely at the underside because if he laid on the ground to look, he was too fat to get up.

But Ellie Habib, Saadee's son, found it. He arrived from Paris to take care of his father's estate. He sold the apartment, most of the proceeds to the lender. Some left over for himself. He sold the furniture. The art was packed up for shipment. And there was the car. Elie had no idea how long his father had the car, but it appeared to have been painted recently, the interior redone. He thought he should get a good price.

Before he sold the vehicle, he took a close look. When he scooted underneath the vehicle to inspect the muffler he noticed the box welded to the trunk floor. Back topside he searched and found a locking mechanism hidden in the tail light housing that opened a door cut in the floor of the trunk. When the spring-loaded door popped open the carpet bumped up. Pulling the carpet back, he found a smallish silver case inside the compartment.

Ellie Habib figured it was some kind of strange stash that involved his father's gambling. His father kept his life of wagering and card tables secret from his wife while she was alive. He often hid cash from her as well.

When Elie Habib opened the case and found an interesting plaque, he changed his mind. Now he believed his father had secretly spent money on a piece of art he liked. His father did that. And he often hid his acquisitions from his mother until he could think of a propitious moment to reveal the acquisition, often claiming it had been purchased years ago, forgotten until just now.

Ellie Habib had no idea this piece of art had nothing to do with his father at all.

All Ellie Habib knew was that like the other dozen or so pieces of art from his father's collection he would take home to Paris, this small piece would look very nice on the wall of his office. He admired his father's taste in art.

19

A convoy of Marines arrived at the Iraqi Museum in Chevy SUVs, a couple Humvees, and one Mercedes sedan liberated a few days earlier from a Saddam Hussein palace compound.

A Reserve Lt. Colonel dismounted his Humvee. He surveyed the museum grounds, quietly impressed with the monumental

Sumerian style architecture. Reading about the Museum of Iraq didn't do it justice. The Iraq National Museum fairly shouted the word antiquities.

He strode straight into the yawning gates of the Museum, accompanied by armed men. As he headed in he couldn't help but notice a four foot hole in the transept above the arched entrance of a secondary museum structure. "Fucking tankers," he mumbled to himself.

Firing a tank round through the National Museum of Iraq was not going to make his arrival any easier. U.S. forces had already bombed the city, invaded it, captured it, pulled down the statue of Saddam and as an unintended consequence, had given the go sign to local and out-of-country thieves who looted the museum. Which just happened to be the greatest repository of Middle Eastern art in the world. Now here was Bart Trappani coming in to say, hey everybody I'm here now to make everything better. He was not expecting a warm welcome.

Moving through a warren of small offices connected by a labyrinth of hallways, he finally came upon a woman in what appeared to be the Museum manager's office. She sat disconsolately in a swivel desk chair surrounded by people she was assigning the job of straightening out offices of turned-over desks, emptied drawers. Even though she projected determination to make things right her face was the very picture of dismay. In a short walkthrough Bart Trappani had already seen just how daunting her job was.

Bart Trappani knew who she was. She was the Director of the National Museum of Iraq. Her name was Murwah Nawali, an academic holding a PhD in middle eastern history and art from a British university. He knew that she had already estimated the museum losses in the thousands of items. Recovering that many stolen or looted items was at best scary difficult, at worst impossible.

He introduced himself as the officer assigned to assist the Museum staff in recovering looted items. Ms. Nawali was not impressed with the arrival of an American Marine officer.

She laughed in his face. Bitterly. "Now the Americans want to help? Nobody guarded the Museum. An American tank was right there, a hundred yards away while looters ransacked the place. Thousands of ancient objects are missing. Thousands."

The Marine officer frowned. He was square jawed, clean shaven.

His intense stare bored through her. "Cuneiform cylinders?"

She turned away from his gaze, shrugged. "So many there's no count." She wore a hijab and a desolate expression in her eyes. Her world had been ruined by the American invasion.

"We'll get those back. We have reward money."

Then he asked her for a rundown of the most valuable.

She listed fifteen to twenty items. A famous vase about four thousand years old. A stunning set of gold crowns and helmets three thousand years old. A lot of very valuable items she said, "Including Death in the Reeds."

The Marine Colonel let his body sag in his chair. He grimaced. "Unbelievable piece. I saw the other one at the British Museum."

The woman nodded in agreement. "Irreplaceable. An amazing work of art."

"I was hoping they overlooked it."

She shook her head. "I have indications it was the first thing taken."

Lt. Colonel Bart Trappani spoke firmly. "I will find it, and I will return it to your museum. That's a promise."

She frowned. "I hope you have better luck than you've had with your Gardner Museum."

"They haven't put me on that case," Trappani replied. "But I'm on this one."

Bart Trappani had reason to be confident. In civilian life he was an Assistant United States Attorney assigned to the Southern District of New York in Manhattan specializing in art theft and fraud. He put people in prison. His investigations were dogged and his prosecutions meticulous.

He'd studied the classics as an undergrad, before law school. Out of law school he joined the Marines, saw some action in Somalia, then joined the Judge Advocate General's office. In his role as an AUSA he'd taken a special interest in art fraud cases and art counterfeiting cases. Especially the illegal trade in looted antiquities.

Over the next few weeks he made good on his promise to Mrs. Nawali best he could. His team located the precious Sacred Vase of Warka, the world's oldest known stone vessel, one used in mysterious ancient religious rituals.

Mrs. Nawali also had reason to fear that the treasure from the royal tombs of Ur had been stolen. This included the helmet of King

Meskalamdug from 2500 B.C. The helmet weighed over two pounds of solid gold. One sheet hammered into an ornamental war helmet. The intricate details included the hairstyle of the period, complete with stylized human-like ears. Despite fears it was gone forever Trappani's team located it in a flooded basement of the annex to the museum, hidden from thieves by a fortuitously broken sewer main.

Trappani worked tirelessly to recover missing treasures and succeeded to a great extent. About half the ancient items stolen from the museum in the initial invasion turned up, either in response to the reward money he offered, or on tips from Iraqis or from concerned citizens who just walked in with an object they had taken, they said, for safekeeping. Trappani handed out stacks of U.S. dollars in rewards, no questions asked, when an antiquity was returned. His campaign included blanket announcements of rewards on Iraqi television. It worked.

Trappani also dug into the museum personnel records. He interviewed every museum employee. He convinced many it was time to bring back whatever objects they had taken "for safekeeping."

In the course of going through personnel files he ran across the copy of a Pakistani passport. He asked Ms. Nawali, "Who is this Hamid Zardari?"

She sighed. "He was one of the cleaning crew, a janitor."

"Where is he?"

"Gone. Probably back to Pakistan. He was a Balouchi."

"How did he happen to be hired?"

She pursed her lips. "He was a friend of a young man who was in charge of the janitors. Mustafa Hajj. Strange young man."

"How so?"

Mrs. Nawali was a woman of transparent sympathies. "In the west the word for men who are attracted to men?"

"You mean 'gay'?"

"Yes. Gay. I thought he was probably gay. As you know a dangerous thing to be in Iraq. He was found dead. Shot himself. He was in a stolen car. Maybe Zardari had something to do with it. I don't know. But he is gone."

Trappani stared at the picture. Sometimes you couldn't easily age a Middle Eastern man's face. This guy, however, looked to be in his thirties. His hair was close cropped, looking like maybe he had some premature gray. His eyes were intense. His mouth set hard. Trappani couldn't put his finger on it, but the guy seemed faintly military. Was this the guy? And if he was, was he acting on his own? Or was he sent to steal by a sponsor, an individual, or worse, by a government?

"Saddam didn't let just anybody into the country. How did he wind up here?"

She answered carefully. There were still ears everywhere reporting to regime figures embedded in Iraqi life, even in what was turning into a long-term American occupation. "Saddam's people liked Balochis. The mastermind of the attack on New York was a Balochi. I heard this fellow arrived on a freight truck from Jordan. He evidently got the proper paperwork to stay. And the Hajj boy hired him for the cleaning crew."

Trappani cautioned himself to avoid immediate conclusions not founded on evidence. And so far he had nothing in particular on Hamid Zardari, except his connection to the gay young man who killed himself. Odd circumstances which seemed to ping Trappani's radar.

The file was not very helpful. It included the Ministry of the Interior resident and work permit, and a copy of the Pakistani passport. He could have the American Embassy in Islamabad run it through the Pakis. Might turn up something. Might take months considering the Pakis. Hamid Zardari might not have been the thief, but he was a person of interest.

Trappani was curious. "What was he like?"

Nawali's manner was quiet and thoughtful. Her face was framed by her hijab. She tended to purse her lips when she was thinking, considering her answer to a question.

"He was an interesting fellow. Older than his boss by ten years or more. It seemed he'd been around, worldly. And he was fascinated with the art we have in the Museum."

"A janitor who seemed to be educated on the antiquities here?" Trappani asked. He thought that was odd.

Mrs. Nawali nodded yes. "I liked him. He liked to pretend he was uneducated. Stupid, even. But he was intelligent. He knew a lot about the objects we protect here."

"So you think he might have been the thief?"

She shrugged. "I'm of two minds," she said, with a wan smile.

While he dropped the subject with Mrs. Nawali, the name stuck with Trappani. Could this Zardari have been the one to come to the museum to take The Reeds? It seemed like a long shot, but where was this Hamid Zardari? Trappani had no way of knowing. And nothing in the record of the museum gave him any clue as to where Zardari might be found.

Trappani sent an email to his superior asking for a query with Pakistan on the name. He didn't expect much. He went about his work.

As he reached out to Iraqis to return items looted from the Museum he also spoke to friends in the military about his new mission. Word got around and soon a friend in Central Command in Tampa—Cent Com—sent him a note to give him a call.

"I heard about your new gig," Colonel Harley Wiggins told him on the sat phone. "Came across a piece of information that might fit into what you're doing?"

"Shoot," Trappani said, his interest piqued.

Colonel Wiggins had run across a fact few people were aware of. The morning after the barrage of Tomahawk missiles that hit Baghdad kicking off the war, three Russian attack helicopters were given permission to enter what was now U.S. controlled airspace to evacuate Russian nationals.

"Okay," Trappani said. "And?"

"They didn't evacuate anybody. They landed in the parking lot of the Iraq Museum. Our guys thought the Russians lied to them, but there was nothing they could do about it except watch them fly away. We didn't have troops in Baghdad for another couple weeks."

"You're sure they were on the Museum grounds?"

"Absolutely positive. I've seen the sat images."

"Can you send those to me?"

"Will do."

There were thousands of potential suspects in the looting of the Iraq National Museum. Most were nameless Iraqis who might be convinced to return items taken by payment of a reward in American $100 notes. A bunch of Russians on a looting mission might be beyond his reach.

Before he left Iraq about half the objects that had gone missing had been returned. Trappani returned home leaving behind a team and a system to continue to hand out American one-hundred-dollar notes in exchange for looted objects or information leading to a looter.

However the Death in the Reeds plaque remained missing and weighed on Trappani's conscience. It was a stunning piece of ancient art. It was now in the possession of someone who had no right to it.

Justice would not be served until it was returned to the Iraq Museum.

Now he had two possible suspects. The first was the mystery man named Hamid Zardari, the one with the suspicious looking Pakistani passport. But even if the U.S. State Department could pry details loose from Pakistan, other matters at State were considered more important. It would take time.

The second suspect? Russians. He didn't know which Russians in particular, but he knew who would have sent them if in fact the flight of Russian choppers came to steal antiquities. In Trappani's experience that would be Gennady Markov, the spook who had of late become the personal art collector for the Russian President.

Bart Trappani promised himself it was now his mission to track down the mysterious Zardari and the Russian named Markov.

20

Markov was not pleased that Pete Grand busted up Pippy Sampson's gallery and injured his bodyguard. "You really do have to develop a sense of sophistication about these things," he scolded Pete Grand.

"You didn't hire me to play nice."

Markov sighed. "Yes, but all you're going to do is make the little shit angry, and I guarantee he'll try to get back."

So, of course, Pete Grand suspected an ambush as soon as he found the call on his voicemail. Pippy Sampson was too sweet, too accommodating. Pippy's message said they should meet at half past seven in the evening, he had the object in question, and to bring the money, whatever it was Pete's client had agreed to pay.

He said he wanted to meet Pete at an odd place, a public space in the Hackney district of London called Clissold Park.

It all smelled extremely fishy and very amateurish.

Pete's plan was to go to the meeting spot well in advance to check it out. If it looked like it was even remotely legit, he would call Markov and have him bring the money.

But he didn't anticipate that would be the case. His intuition said the diminutive art dealer was still in a hissy fit about being pushed around and he was luring Pete into a trap of some kind.

The meeting spot was the southern tip of Clissold Park, a neighborhood green of no particular distinction. Two hours early, Pete surveyed the location for what might be his greatest danger. He concluded it would be from the rooftop of a nearby four-story apartment block. A sniper would have a clear shot from that point.

Gaining entry to the building was as simple as just walking in. Pete Grand went to the rooftop to wait. From his perch, he could hear the laughter and chatter coming from a nearby pub, and bile rose in his throat. He would much rather be in the warm and inviting pub with a whiskey and a pint.

Then the drizzle began and Pete's anger ratcheted up. Why should he be subjected to the irrational and childish temper of a dwarf art dealer with the ridiculous name Pippy? The situation he found himself in roused his since of injustice, and gave him a splitting headache.

Pete Grand pondered. He thought it couldn't be this easy. Would the midget art dealer really set such an obvious trap? He couldn't be that dumb.

But Grand was surprised to discover that yes, he was that dumb.

After a nearly an hour of waiting, the door to the rooftop creaked open. From his shadowy recess Pete saw a man glance around to see if he was alone. Failing to see Pete tucked in the shadows of an equipment overhang, he hurried to the balustrade. He took a position kneeling out of sight to the street below.

Pete Grand peered out from his hidey hole. He didn't know a lot about guns, but he recognized the weapon the man removed from a backpack case as a sniper rifle. The man snapped open a collapsed stock. He screwed a suppressor to the muzzle of the barrel.

Pete thought the gun was a little much for the shot. It couldn't have been more than a hundred yards, which should have been easy with most any rifle, but maybe this guy did a lot of long-range shooting.

In any case, Pete knew what the man was doing. He was waiting for Pete Grand to show up to meet Pippy Sampson. Only Pippy wouldn't show. Pete would be standing, waiting, a perfect target.

The man sat on the roof, his back to the balustrade, setting up his rifle. He took his coat off, folded it neatly, and placed it such that he could kneel on it, while sighting the rifle over the balustrade. He seemed to know what he was doing. Like he'd done this sort of work before.

In his darkened recess Pete slipped off his shoes. He wanted to approach the shooter without making a sound.

As the appointed hour grew near, the man assumed a kneeling position, the rifle resting on the three-foot solid balustrade. If someone on the street below bothered to glance up the barrel of a rifle would have been clearly in view.

Pete waited for a passing bus. Earlier he noticed they often made quite a racket.

As he heard one of the lumbering vehicles approach, Pete stepped out of his hiding place, walking softly but quickly to his prey.

First, he kicked the rifle over the edge. The man turned to face his attacker. Pete heard the weapon clatter on the street below.

The man was not very big, considerably shorter and weighed considerably less than Pete Grand. The larger man had the advantage; the smaller man could not escape.

Pete picked up the squirming man, one ham size hand squeezing the man's neck, the other gripping his belt. Pete raised him above his head. As the man started to scream, Pete threw him like a sack straight out into the air.

The scream didn't last long. It ended in a crunching thud on the pavement below.

Pete Grand retrieved his shoes, and walked down the stairs and away from the building. A few blocks away he grabbed a cab and ordered the driver to Grafton Street.

He passed Markov's snooty Arts Club, and a store called Victoria Beckham, whatever that was, and emerged from the cab at the Pippy Sampson gallery. Fortunately, a noisy society event was underway. Pete Grand slipped through a tuxedo crowd, made his way inside, and slid his way to the stairs that led to Pippy Sampson's offices.

He met the little twerp coming down to join the party.

Pippy Sampson's eyes widened like saucers. He immediately knew his man Alfie had failed. And perhaps was not living any longer. Pippy was in a miniature black tuxedo, a drink in one hand. He threw the drink at Pete and turned to run back up the stairs.

Pete bounded up the stairs three at a time, and closed the distance with his quarry. They both burst into the second-floor gallery, Pippy heading for his office as fast as he could, his screams for help drowned by the boisterous crowd below, Pete Grand behind him at no more than an arm's distance. At Pippy's office door, Pete picked the little man up with the same two-handed grip he used on the sniper. He banged through the office door with Pippy's face.

"You send someone to kill me, you little shit?" Pete snarled under his breath. He did not expect an answer.

Pippy Sampson's nose was smashed flat and bleeding. The blow against the door stunned the art dealer into dazed mumbling.

Pete Grand wasted no time. He quickstepped across the office holding the art dealer in the air like a doll.

At the window overlooking the gardens, Pete swung the window open with his elbow. He pitched Pippy Sampson through the opening. He was surprised the little shit didn't make a sound all the way down to the pavement. Pete glanced out the window. He saw the bleeding figure splayed on the back patio.

While he was walking back down the stairs, he heard the crowd in the party scream and shout and run to the back. He joined the crowd as it gathered around the broken figure of the art dealer, then edged away.

An hour later Gennady Markov stared at Pete Grand in a seething fury.

"You killed the guy who was supposed to receive the thing the boss wants? What were you thinking? Now how do I track it down?"

Pete sat in a wingback chair in Markov's library surrounded by leather bound volumes Markov never read and expensive paintings Markov seldom bothered to enjoy. He shrugged. "The guy sent someone to kill me. He was never going to call with the goods."

"You don't know that," Markov snarled. He was furious. The one guy he was certain would be contacted about The Reeds was in a morgue and now the subject of a police investigation, along with the gunman splattered on the street in Hackney.

"What's with this fetish of yours? This thing of throwing people off high places?"

"Have you ever thought about how to kill someone?"

"Of course."

"I don't mean who to call to kill someone. I mean being the one to actually do it?"

"You're asking me if I get my hands dirty."

"I'm asking you if you've thought about how to do it so you can't be traced. So the killing doesn't come back on you."

"Get rid of the gun."

"There's still a gun. Falling from an open window isn't a murder weapon."

"What if someone sees you?

"I'm careful about that."

None of this satisfied Markov. "Have you talked to a psychiatrist about this?"

"Of course not. Why would I talk to a psychiatrist? And you said 'fetish.' What does that mean?"

Markov stewed. "We have to get you out," he said after a long silence meant to intimidate Pete Grand, but which failed.

"To where?"

"To the place where we can keep an eye on the next most important person in finding The Reeds."

"Where is that?"

"New York. And this time do not kill the sonofabitch, understand?"

"Just make sure he doesn't try to kill me," Pete Grand said, returning Markov stare with cold eyes. "I don't like people trying to kill me."

21

Mick was in the '93 Honda Accord he bought from a used car lot in the Sunset District. Another beater after his original beater was declared too expensive to fix.

The cantilever section of the Oakland Bay Bridge always gave Mick the yips. A few rusted bolts failed in the '89 earthquake and a couple cars nosed down to the roadbed below. Even with a dramatic example of the state's incompetence to keep motorists safe, most people gave the creaky old bridge no thought.

Safely on the mudflats of the Oakland side, he took the 880 Freeway south, just past the Navy Yard and the Oakland container terminal. The freeway looped around west Oakland and turned true south at about Jack London Square. The 880 corridor is heavily industrial, and all the way south, past the Oakland Airport, past San Leandro and Union City, Mick was pushed from behind and boxed in on the sides by heavy big rigs, spinning wheels at the top of his windows.

He headed for the Irvington section of Fremont to meet Ali Zardari. Ali was nervous about meeting Mick at all, but since Cass said it was okay, he agreed. He told Mick to come to a South Asian restaurant called the Pakwan on Fremont Boulevard. Mick had no intention of eating Pakistani food. He was not adventurous about food.

The restaurant was a converted American fast-food drive-in, a late 60's chain of some sort that was distinctive for the style of the building. Mick forgot what they were called. Another whacky idea for a restaurant, a chain long forgotten, though the buildings remained scattered around the country. It had a spacious parking lot, and an outdoor seating area protected from the wind, rain, and infrequent sun by drop-down canvas and see-through plexi curtains.

"Are you Ali?" Mick asked the only person sitting at the outside tables.

The young man nodded he was, and Mick took a seat. He sized the boy up. Maybe twenty-two, tops. Perhaps younger. Slender. But probably muscular. Dressed American college boy style, plaid shirt, black jeans, hoodie, backpack. Good-looking kid. Handsome face, jet black hair, wary eyes.

"I'm Mickey Judge. Cass wanted me to check out this situation."

The boy nodded. "I watch TV. I know who you are."

Mick gave the kid an impatient look. "So you want to tell me what this is all about?"

The boy was quiet for a few moments. "I don't really," Ali finally confessed. "I wanted to tell Ms. Papadop and I don't really understand why she couldn't come meet me."

Mick grimaced and gestured come on with his hands outstretched, palms up. "She's not going to run across the bay to meet a guy she doesn't know who hacked her computer to get her phone number. You know what the word stalking means?"

Ali's face flushed, embarrassed. "I was not stalking her. I was simply doing an investigation. How to get in touch with her. I haven't tampered with any of her data."

"Yeah, whatever. I'm here for information, not to forgive your hacking. Tell me what you got. She wants to know."

Ali Zardari gulped hard at being treated harshly. "An extremely valuable antiquity is going to be available soon."

"She told me that. What is it?"

Ali swallowed hard again. This guy was annoying. "It's a duplicate of the one held in the British Museum. You can see it in the British Museum catalog. It's item number one two seven four one two."

Mick scribbled down the number. "I obviously don't have a British Museum catalog with me. Tell me what it is."

"You have to look it up for yourself."

Scowling, Mick sat back and stared at the guy. "I figure you're a senior in college, right?"

Ali nodded. "Not college. University."

"Stanford? Right across the bridge?"

Ali nodded again, but he frowned. He didn't like where this was going.

"Let me guess. Computer science?"

Typecast as a South Asian computer nerd, Ali's anger rose in his throat. "Yes. So what? What's that got to do with anything?"

"I think what it's got to do with is you're full of shit," Mick said. "You don't have any rare antiquity. I don't know what your game is with Cass, but she's a friend of mine and I'm not letting you near her. You're a stalker and a creeper and I don't believe you for a second."

Eyes wide in fury, Ali stared at Mick with utter contempt. "I don't know why I'm talking to you anyway. You're the guy who shot somebody on television. You've been fired from your job. You are totally disreputable."

"Good. Our business is done." Mick stood up from his chair. He headed toward the parking lot.

But Ali didn't want him to go, even if he instantly disliked the guy. "Wait. I'll prove to you I'm for real," Ali said, barely controlling his rage. "Just look at this."

He pulled a manila envelope from his backpack, and withdrew the sheet of paper Wajahat sent him.

Mick turned back. He snapped the paper out of Ali's hand.

"This is it," Ali said. "This is proof of what I'm telling you."

"What's this called?"

"Death in the Reeds, a national treasure of a certain country," Ali said, contemptuously. "You see it's resting on a newspaper, look at the date."

Looking closely Mick could make out the date on the USA Today, two weeks earlier.

"Where is this from?"

The boy didn't seem to want to say.

"I have to come back with some information. Where's it from?"

"I shouldn't have to walk you through everything. But I guess I do. There are only two in the world. One in the British Museum. The other in the Iraq National Museum." Ali stopped, looking at Mick as if saying figured it out yet?

"Where is it now? Can she see it?"

"I don't have it yet, but I will soon. She can see it then."

Mick grew annoyed at the cat and mouse game.

"Hold on. Is this something from Iraq? Is this something that was looted at the start of the war?"

"I really can't say any more. Just show her the item and have her get back in touch with me."

Ali got to his feet to leave. He snatched the picture from Mick's hand.

"Hold on," Mick said again.

The boy turned to face Mick, the two men staring hard into each other's eyes.

"If this is war booty, I can promise you it is very, very illegal," Mick said in a soft but serious voice. "You get caught with something like this it's not a big payday anymore, it's federal prison. And probably not some Club Fed like Santa Rita, or Lompoc. Probably some ugly place like Terminal Island. The feds take smuggling looted antiquities very seriously. If that's what you got you should rethink the whole thing. You might not see the light of day till you're in your late forties."

Ali's eyes widened. "Maybe meeting you was a mistake," he said. "Have her call me." And he turned and walked out.

The hell I will, Mick thought.

At the wheel of the Honda, he retraced his route north on the 880 Freeway through Oakland and then west across the Bay Bridge.

Back in San Francisco Cass Papadop was waiting for Mick in the bar at the Big Four, the Huntington Hotel's five-star restaurant.

Mick found a parking spot—amazing!—on the back side of the Pacific Union Club, the 19th century mansion that served as a club for the Robber Barons and their friends. At the door to the Big Four Mick stood outside smoking a cigarette. The California Street cable car rumbled by, bell dinging. Grace Cathedral's spires stuck into the fog like knives. Across the street a tai chi class silently struck poses in Huntington Park. He stepped on the butt and walked into the cool darkness of the classic city bar. The sounds of San Francisco did not penetrate the walls of the Big Four.

Mick was carrying a coffee table book he picked up at a used book store on Post Street on his way to meet her.

"Whatcha got honey buns?" she smiled brightly.

He slid onto a stool next to her and asked the barman for an Absolut and soda. He opened the book and laid it in front of her. "This is the item," he said pointing to the photograph of Death in the Reeds. "Well, not quite. This is one of two in the world. It's at the British Museum. The kid claims to have the other, which is at the Iraq National Museum."

She pinched her lips and arched her eyebrows. "Really?"

"Maybe. He's either lying, which is bad. Or worse, he really has it, or will have it soon."

"Worse?"

"Yeah. Way worse. If the kid has this thing, it's an extremely illegal stolen cultural heritage piece. If he has it, that means someone looted it from the Museum as the war started because before two weeks ago it was definitely in the Iraq National Museum. This is as illegal as illegal gets. You shouldn't get near it. It's years in federal prison."

Cass frowned. "Bad as that?"

"Very bad boogie. Even talking to him about it puts you on the hook for conspiracy. My advice? If he calls again, tell him to lose your number."

She studied the picture. "How old is it?"

"Almost three thousand years."

She ran her fingers over the picture. "Doesn't seem very big."

"About four inches by four inches."

She looked up at him with true curiosity. "How do you know about this thing? You just saw him this morning."

"On the way back I called a guy in New York I know. Name is Irwin Feinstein. I did a story for TENN when he got busted with a shitload of antiquities. He might be the world's foremost expert on these things."

"What did he say?"

"He wanted to hang up on me. Said 'I can't talk about things like that. If it's been stolen,' he said, 'I want nothing to do with it.' He's worried about violating his deal with the feds and getting tossed back in the can."

She nodded, appreciating the man's situation. "Irwin Feinstein?"

"Yeah," Mick said, immediately sorry he mentioned the actual name.

"Did he say what it was worth?"

"Priceless, absolutely priceless," Mick said. "That's why it's so much trouble for anybody either handling it or conspiring to handle it."

"I see," she said in a soft voice, unable to take her eyes off the picture. "Mind if I keep the book?"

"It's yours," Mick said.

"Great. Let's drink."

They clinked glasses. "To staying out of trouble," she said with her bright smile.

"Indeed," Mick agreed.

But he wasn't convinced she was convinced.

22

Billy Norton had to lie to his partner, who also happened to be his superior. He was not real comfortable doing it, but he was already in so deep.

His desk was separated from Bone Hendrix's desk by an eyeball level divider in the detectives' bullpen at the new police headquarters on Third Street. Billy held the phone to his ear, mumbled "uh huh" a couple times, and then said, "Okay be right over."

Bone Hendrix looked up from his computer screen across the divider. "What's up?"

"I hafta go over to the Hall." Meaning the Hall of Justice. "See the deputy DA on the Hunter's Point job." He was referring to the case of an 83-year-old woman murdered by a neighbor high on PCP.

"What about?" Bone asked. His eyebrows drew tight, forming that skeptical V at the top of his face.

"She wants to ask me something about the report."

"What about the report?"

"Beats me. But she says I wrote it, so I'll have to be on the stand and she wants to talk. Said it will be quick."

"Hmmm," Bone said. "Long as you're out, bring back lunch."

"Cool. What do you want?"

"Torpedo Burger, the big one, fries. But make sure they make the fries fresh, and crispy. None of that limp shit."

"Cheese? Onions? Veggies?"

Bone nodded to all that. "Yes, yes, and yes."

"Got it," Billy said. He grabbed his jacket off the back of the chair and headed out.

Billy was a little embarrassed about this episode, but there had been so many others just like it. He wasn't called to confer with a deputy DA on a murder case. He was called to meet the District Attorney, Jean Washington, about a special project she had Billy working on without the knowledge of his partner and superior, Bone Hendrix.

The SFPD Crown Vic sped down Third Street, past all the gleaming new construction that would shock someone who decamped from the city only a few years earlier. Billy was impatient, but there was no way across town without traffic. He took the Fourth Street Bridge across Mission Creek. He turned on Townsend and jammed it west alongside the Cal Train tracks. At Eighth Street he crossed Market Street and dove into Civil Center. The District Attorney's office was at the corner of Polk and McAlister, across the street from City Hall.

San Francisco is only seven miles by seven miles, and Billy's trip across town was even less, but traffic slowed him down. It took him thirty minutes.

He walked into the DA's suite, and nodded to her assistant. "She wants to see me," he said, without breaking stride. He was arriving at Jean Washington's office late, exasperated, and anxious. Bone would be wondering what was taking him so long.

The DA's office was situated in a corner of the building with a view of Civic Center Plaza, which was fast becoming a homeless encampment. Jean Washington was watching the pigeons and the homeless congregate in the plaza.

She turned and leveled her gaze at Billy Norton. "At ease, Inspector," she said, turning away again.

Billy made a face behind her back. At fucking ease indeed!

"Inspector Norton, what do you think makes a good candidate for President?"

Billy frowned. How was he supposed to answer that? "I'm not sure, ma'am"

"Well, I am sure," she said, turning back to him. "Let me educate you. It's likeability. People like someone for their appearance, for instance," she said, drawing an open hand down from her face, over her chest, down until her hand rested against her side. She bared her gleaming white teeth in a forced smile.

"People also like accomplishments, such as holding previous office and excelling at that office. You understand?"

"Yes, I certainly do understand that point, ma'am," Billy said carefully.

"What people don't like in a presidential candidate is any inference, any credible inference, I should say, of wrongdoing in office. You understand that, correct?"

"I do indeed, yes ma'am."

"Do you see how I need to do something about the reporter, Mickey Judge? He is using his position as a reporter to carry out a personal vendetta against me. Which also means he supports our philandering Mayor."

Wonder if she's heard the rumor about the Mayor and her wife Billy thought. "Neither one is good," Billy agreed.

"I need you to get something we can charge him with," she said, glancing back at him. "Any ideas?"

Billy stood in front of her desk, a little confused. "He's already been fired. This shooting has slowed him down a lot. What are you worried about?"

She turned to face him. Jean Washington's eyes telegraphed her mood, whatever it happened to be. Today her mood was determined, focused on vanquishing her opponents. "Did you know I was a Captain in the Army?" she asked.

Surprised, Billy shook his head no. "I didn't know that. What branch?"

"Artillery," she lied. She actually spent only one year in the Army as a rank private before wangling a discharge. She turned back to the window, spinning out her Captain-in-the-Army fantasy. "I often think if I had a mortar right here, I could drop one on KBAY, just to the left over the Earl Warren building. Maybe right into Mickey Judge's office. And I could drop another in the Mayor's office, over there to the right," she pointed at City Hall.

She turned back to Billy, the fantasy concluded, her face in a deadly serious scowl. "I will deal with Vargas-Watson. But I can't afford to take any chances with Mickey Judge. What I need you to do is get Judge out of my hair permanently."

Billy nodded that he got it. "Yes, Ma'am. Understood."

"So," she said slowly, drawing the word out. "Any ideas?"

Put on the spot, Billy resorted to his old standby. "I could go into the snitch pool."

"And do what?"

"Find someone who could testify that Mickey Judge and our victim knew each other and had a beef. Motive for murder."

She nodded approvingly. "That's a start. Anybody in mind?"

Billy nodded he did. "I got in mind a woman over in Chowchilla sitting out five years for drugs. She probably wants some improvement in her situation."

"Do I know about this one?"

Billy shook his head no. "No reason you would. Common whore."

"Can you make sure she wouldn't cave under cross?"

"It's why I suggest her. She's a confirmed liar. Once she commits to a lie, it's her truth."

Jean Washington thought about the situation for a minute, staring out at the foggy Civic Center Plaza. "I need to pull you off the PD. Come over here as a special investigator. Temporary. Until this is done."

"You don't want me working with Bone?"

"No, I don't." She sat down in the enormous executive chair behind the desk. She liked to swivel. "He's a problem. I don't think I can trust him."

He's too honest, Billy thought. She needs someone like me, someone who doesn't mind bending the rules. Okay. But what's in it for me? "So how will you handle this? You call the chief. Borrow me?"

She nodded yes.

"So can you ask her to do something for me in light of the special duty?"

She frowned. "She'll do what I say. What do you want?"

"I want a promotion. To Lieutenant."

Her frown deepened. "That's a big ask. Would that outrank Hendrix?"

He shook his head no. "That's his rank. We would be equals. Probably break us up. I'd get my own Sergeant Inspector partner."

She shrugged. She didn't care. The police chief was a member of the LGBTQ Commission, where Jean Washington sat as chair.

"I'll see what I can do."

With that Billy was dismissed to head out to work on his snitch.

Within the hour Bone Hendrix was called to Chief Peggy Chung's office.

"Billy's been pulled for special duty at the DA's office," she said when Bone sat down.

Hendrix jerked back like he'd been smacked across the forehead. "That explains why he didn't come back with lunch," he thought. "What special duty?" he asked.

Chief Chung shrugged. "She didn't say. She just said she wanted him."

Bone didn't like it. He smelled something wrong. "Am I still working the Judge case?"

The Chief pursed her lips and thought about that. "I guess not. She's working on a grand jury over there, and she wanted Billy on it. I guess you can pick up your other cases."

Bone and Chung had once been partners before she began her rise in the administrative ranks. They knew each other well, and trusted each other. "Something seem off to you?" he asked.

She rolled her eyes and shook her head side to side like a pinball was bouncing around in her skull. It was her "who knows?" expression. "You never know with her. Not so unusual the DA asks to borrow a special investigator for a Grand Jury proceeding."

"But it usually is both partners. This feels like she's cutting me out for some reason."

"Maybe you should thank her. You really want in on this one? Already feels like it's going to be a shit show that has more to do with her political ambition than actual crime."

Bone nodded. The Chief had it about right. "Yeah, okay, you got a point. You gonna put me with a new partner?"

"You want one?"

"Not really. Can I go solo till whenever?"

His old partner laughed at him. "You always preferred solo, so fine. But …" she said, then stopped.

"But … what?"

Peggy Chung leaned forward on her desk to invade her old partner's space for a moment. "But you're off the Judge case. I don't want you getting in her way."

Bone Hendrix held up his big hands in the stop position. "No problem. I didn't want the damn thing in the first place. The guy's a nightmare"

Hendrix left the Chief's office officially glad to be off the case, but positive there was something afoot that was wrong. He didn't mention it to the Chief, but the fact that Billy Norton lied to him raised his suspicions. Billy said the deputy DA wanted to see him about the Hunter's Point murder. But then he went straight to the DA herself and it wasn't about a small-time murder at all. Bone figured he'd keep an eye on things now that nobody was watching over his shoulder.

23

Cass Papadop and Mick said their so-longs at the sidewalk in front of the Big Four. He walked across California Street, and down the alley at the east side of Huntington Park to the Honda behind the Pacific Union Club.

She waited for the valet to bring her Audi. She hung a U-ey on California and drove west. She crossed Van Ness, and goosed the gas heading uphill into lower Pacific Heights. At Divisidero Street she turned right headed to the crest at Broadway. At the top the Golden Gate Bridge and the white caps of the bay stretched before her. She turned into a driveway that formed an S downhill to a smallish mansion. A Porsche and a black Escalade were nosed into a set of double garage doors.

Cass was expected. A sharply dressed elderly man stood at a railing on the landing at the top of a set of stairs of Talavera tile.

Simon Moss called down to her, his voice trilling a laugh. "An old man gets a call from a beautiful young woman his mind immediately leaps to his youth." His relationship with Cass Papadop was jokey and flirty.

"You figured an afternoon delight?" she called back, mounting the staircase.

"These days that's my dread. I spent a lifetime disappointing beautiful women. I vowed to stop."

"No, no, Simon," she gushed. "I'm sure you haven't lost a step." She paused for his wide-eyed expression of delight. "It's not your teenage years I want. It's your ancient expertise that's gets me so hot." She delighted in sexy flirting.

"That I can handle," he smiled for her. "Come in, dear."

Cass Papadop and Simon Moss became friends on the circuit of parties she lately attended, since her marriage to Jean Washington. She liked him immediately because he was on to her: he knew she was not gay and liked to needle her about a straight woman playing the part of a lesbian.

Simon was an art dealer by profession. The one person in the city she could ask if the object proffered by Ali Zardari was real, or if it was not.

Simon Moss ushered her through the door into an airy living room appointed with deep couches, crowded coffee tables, walls hung with beautiful pieces, and windows that looked out on the glistening waters of the bay and the Golden Gate Bridge.

White hair, sagging jowls, baggy eyes, Moss was every bit his 75 years. He was dressed for an elegant and relaxing afternoon. He wore a loose linen shirt the color of a Georgia peach, milk chocolate gabardine slacks and soft Italian slip-on shoes. His face was the fleshy version of a handsome young man midway in his seventies. His eyes were watery but lively, and his smile revealed nicotine-stained teeth. He offered her a drink. She took Chardonnay.

They sat opposite each other, a large coffee table strewn with art books between them. She laid her own on the table open to the page Mick had marked. She slid it across the table.

"Simon, what is that?" she asked, pointing at the plaque.

He leaned forward to inspect the object beneath her finger. "That's called Death in the Reeds, but you knew that. It says so right there," he said pointing at the caption under her finger.

"I'm asking what is it, how valuable is it?"

Simon Moss chuckled. "It's priceless. It's never been for sale. There's another in Iraq, if it hasn't been bombed into oblivion by that wretched Mr. Bush," he said, "Why?"

"I'm curious. What would it be worth if the British Museum suddenly decided to sell it?

Moss laughed heartily. "That would never happen. But I'm sure the Museum has it insured for hundreds of millions, if the directors bothered with insurance at all. They may not. It would be very expensive. Prohibitively, expensive, I would think."

"When you say hundreds of millions," she asked carefully, making certain the add a charming smile, "do you mean lower than five hundred million?" She paused. "Or above?"

Simon Moss shook his head and wrinkled his nose. "I don't think it's a billion, if that's what you're asking." He stopped to consider his answer. "But I wouldn't be surprised if it's worth two, three hundred million. Just supposing you first had the object and second you had a couple potential buyers bidding against each other. Why?"

She flipped the book shut. "Just a game I'm playing with one of our billionaire friends," she said, with a wink. "I just wanted to make sure I knew what I was talking about."

He didn't buy it. "I should add," he said, "a couple things." He held up his index finger. "Number one, the item would have to be authenticated. There are so many fake antiquities floating around, hustled by unscrupulous grifters. You'd have to put the item in front of someone who could say for certain it was real or fake."

"Ever heard of Irwin Feinstein?"

He nodded. "Yes. A true expert, but he was found to have a trove of antiquities which were smuggled out of Italy and Greece and Turkey, and he had to give a huge collection back to the countries they'd come from. I'd say he would be very gun shy about getting involved."

"Anyone else in that caliber?"

"You find experts here and there at universities. In this country. In Italy, I suppose. Maybe in Istanbul. But he's the American expert, despite his embarrassing brush with the law."

Cass took it in, thinking she would have to convince Mr. Feinstein. She would need Ali's piece authenticated. "You said two things. What's number two?"

Moss had almost forgotten he wanted to make a second point. "Oh yes," he said, "Simply that possession of this item would be extremely illegal. Like prison time. Years and years of prison time."

"So I've heard," she laughed.

Cassie got off the subject and they gossiped for a little longer, but she was through with Simon Moss for the moment. By the time she finished her glass of wine she excused herself with profuse thanks, lots of giggling and cheek kissing. She took a long steep driveway down to Vallejo Street, and headed for the Bay.

On Vallejo Street she punched the dial button on her phone. "Ali, it's Cass Papadop." She stopped to let it sink in.

On his end Ali was immediately nervous and barely able to speak.

"Let's meet. Can you come over to the city?"

Ali's mind raced. It was the most beautiful woman he'd ever seen and she wanted to meet. He was thrilled and frightened. "I have to take BART," he said, referring to the Bay Area Rapid Transit train. She said that was fine. She told him to take BART to the Embarcadero station, walk across the Embarcadero to a restaurant called Saltwater. "I'll be at a table by the windows."

In his Fremont bedroom, Ali rustled through his closet. Something presentable to meet the glistening TV lady. He picked a light blue long-sleeve dress shirt with a button-down collar that was only a little wrinkled. He grabbed a green tie, and pulled on the black slacks he wore to see professors. He slipped on a navy blazer, put his Toshiba laptop into a backpack, and headed out. A ten-minute drive in his balky Saturn to the BART station in Fremont. He waited twenty minutes for a train. The trip was another forty minutes. Ali Zardari walked into the restaurant on San Francisco's Embarcadero an hour and a half after hanging up with Cass.

The lunch rush was over. Place virtually empty. Ali Zardari asked for Cass Papadop and was directed up a staircase to a room overlooking the piers to the south, and the Bay Bridge. His ideal woman sat at a window table with a bloody Mary and the Chronicle.

"Ms. Papadop?" he asked nervously.

"You must be Ali," Cassie Papadop snapped on her high wattage smile. "Sit down, good to meet you." She had a nose for a man who fell the minute he saw her. She could tell in an instant the boy was already in love.

He took a seat opposite her, looking out the window to the south, Pier 7 in the foreground.

"Is that the pier where that guy shot that man?" he asked.

Cass turned around. "Yes. It sure is. That's right where it happened."

"Do you know him?"

She smiled. "You could say that."

Ali wondered what that meant. An air of mystery was part of her appeal, but also raised a pang of jealousy. Was that guy who told him he'd go to jail her lover?

"Tell me about yourself?" Cass asked. She could tell he was nervous, and figured she could get him to relax talking about himself.

She was so beautiful, so beguiling in Ali's eyes. And here was this stunning woman asking him about himself. It was intoxicating. So, he jumped in. Ali explained he was a student at Stanford, that he was graduating soon, that he lived in Fremont, that his parents were "business people." Cass assumed they were small retailers, perhaps dealing in ethnic food. Since he didn't say specifically, she let the line of inquiry drop.

Ali was almost giddy with excitement telling this beautiful woman about himself. But he also felt he was not being completely forthcoming if he did not mention the news he'd just received, news that probably meant he might not be able to deliver what he'd promised when he met that guy who said he was her emissary.

"Before we go farther," he said, slipping into a mournful tone. "After I saw your friend I went home and found a letter. It's bad news. Terrible news, actually."

Alarm crossed Cass's face. Had someone beaten her to the object? "What?"

"The man who obtained the object," Ali began, "I got a letter just today that he was killed."

"That's terrible. Who is he?"

Ali didn't want to say it was his brother. But she looked at him with such concern and sympathy his initial hesitation was swept away. "It was my brother, Wajahat." His voice choked.

"Oh my god, that's awful," Cass whispered sympathetically. "How as he killed?"

"I don't know," Ali said. "A letter from the U.S. State Department. My brother had been identified as a man who was killed in Beirut a couple weeks ago. The U.S. got an inquiry from the Beirut authorities. He had a U.S. passport. Fingerprints confirmed. The Army confirmed them. He was a retired American military officer."

Cass was starting to get confused. "Wait. So your brother was retired from, what?"

"The Army."

"Retired from our Army?"

Ali nodded.

"He was killed in Beirut. What was he doing there?"

"He lived there."

Cass nodded. Okay. "And what does he have to do with the object you showed by friend?"

"He was the one who obtained it."

"Let's not play word games," she said. "Is he the one who stole it from the Iraq Museum?"

Ali nodded nervously. He didn't like the word "stole" but there didn't seem to be another choice. "Honestly, I just presume so. All I know for certain is he sent me this picture," he withdrew the picture from his backpack, handing it to her. "Which I took to mean he had it. But then I heard nothing further from him until the letter to my parents informing them he was deceased."

The boy's eyes misted up. Cass clutched his hand with both hers. An electric jolt up his spine at her touch. "How awful for you. How are your parents taking it?"

He shook his head. "I haven't shown them the letter yet."

"Why not?"

"I haven't worked up the nerve. My mother will be devastated."

"I'm so sorry," she said, her hazel eyes damp. "What a terrible thing. Your parents will be crushed."

Ali nodded. She was right. She held on to this hand. He didn't resist.

"What about the object?"

He shook his head. "I don't know. He had it. He was killed. I have no idea."

Cass looked at the handsome boy with her most sincere expression of empathy. It was a sorrowful situation, but what about the object?

He was very attractive. No, he was drop-dead gorgeous. She gave a thought to what he would be like in bed. A delicious thought. But fleeting. Complications could be dangerous. But still....

She saw he obviously loved his brother. She believed it must be true that he was sick at the thought of telling his parents. She wanted The Reeds, but she realized she had to show great sympathy for his situation.

His brother was dead. His parents would be devastated. Whatever. What was important was the simple fact this boy was her only connection to the object that would make her wealthy beyond dreams.

"You have to find it," she said softly.

"What?" Ali asked, startled.

"You have to go to Beirut to bring back your brother's remains anyway, right?"

Ali nodded. "I guess so. I hadn't thought that far yet."

"Have you ever been to Beirut?"

He shook his head no.

"They speak French there, I think. Do you speak French?"

He shook his head no again. "I speak a little Arabic. My parents speak Urdu and Pashto. I'm better at those."

"Arabic will do," she said. "You must go."

Ali stammered. "I suppose so. I hadn't thought about it."

"How else are you going to bring back your brother's remains?"

"I don't know. Maybe they could ship the coffin?"

She shook her head no, emphatically. "Can't do that. You won't even be certain they send back the right box. You must go."

Ali stammered more. "Money. I'm not sure my parents have the money to send me on a trip like that. And I'm sure my father would want to be the one …"

Cass interrupted. "No, no, no. Does your father know about the object?"

"Definitely not," Ali answered. "Wajahat would never tell him about stealing something so valuable. My father would forbid it."

"See? Your father can't go. You must go yourself."

"My father would never let me go," but even as Ali said the words, he remembered he'd secretly sent his father's Pakistani passport to Wajahat. He didn't even know if his father had another; he definitely didn't have a U.S. passport. His mother and father were scheduled for citizenship, but 9/11 put that off track, delayed for a while.

"Don't ask him," Cass said. "Just go. Arrange to fly your brother's casket back, and track down the object. If you're lucky, whatever way he was killed didn't involve stealing it from him." She stopped to think about that. "Of course, if someone did steal it from him, there's probably nothing to be done. But you never know. Maybe it wasn't taken."

Her eyes danced with the possibilities. The death of the man who possessed it was an obstacle, for sure. But it was an obstacle that could be overcome. For a brief moment she thought about going herself, but instantly realized that was impossible. She didn't speak any of the languages, and she'd be lost. Better to have the boy go.

Ali was lost in his own thoughts. She was probably right. He should go. But money. This would cost money. Much more than he had. "I'm not sure how I could manage," he said, his mind reeling.

Cass was doing calculations. Probably around two thousand

dollars for plane tickets for the boy. Maybe a thousand to ship the body back. Another thousand in expenses on the ground. All in, maybe five thousand tops, all contingencies accounted for.

"Okay, don't worry about the money," she said. "I'll take care of it."

"You what?"

"I'll give you the tickets. I'll give you some cash. You go. I'll cover the money."

The boy's mind reeled. "I don't have a passport."

"I can get it rushed through overnight." She knew she could pull strings.

"How?"

"Connections. Comes with TV." She turned serious. "Will you do it?"

"I guess," he said, hesitating. But he was thinking he couldn't turn down the offer if she was putting up the money. "My parents will be so grateful ..."

"I'm happy to do it," she interrupted. "On one condition."

"What's that?"

"You must make an effort to find that plaque. It's very important."

"If professional thieves stole it, there isn't much I can do."

"I bet that isn't what happened. He was killed. He lived in a dangerous neighborhood. I have a feeling the object is floating around somewhere. Just make an effort. If Hezbollah ambushed your brother and took it, that's one thing. But if it's still in his apartment or his car or his bank deposit box, you have to try to find it."

Ali nodded. She was so beautiful.

"Deal?" she asked.

"Sure," Ali said. "Deal."

Cass leaned across the table, flashing her cleavage. She took Ali's face in her hands and kissed him on the lips. "A deal sealed with a kiss," she said. "The best kind of deal."

Ali realized he couldn't stand up just yet. She would see his erection.

24

Billy Norton had an idea for the ideal candidate to link Mickey Judge to Ladarius Rasheed, the black kid who ended up dead in the reporter's heroic shooting on the Embarcadero.

Her name was Dani Charm, born Celeste Johnson. Dani was an occasional porn "actress" and sometimes pole dancer at the Mitchell Brothers' O'Farrell Theater in the City. She'd got herself mixed up in a major drug buy, and was doing five years at the Central California Women's Facility in Chowchilla. It was a three-hour drive.

Billy knew Dani Charm from his assignment to the drug unit before transferring to homicide under Bone Hendrix. He'd done the original interrogation, and he both liked her and felt sorry for her. She was a minding-her-own-business aspiring porn actress, quite happy with the occasional fuck film, while regularly employed dancing nude. Dani Charm got busted when her girlfriend tried to score big with a heavy meth deal.

Dani was gorgeous. A stunning blonde, slim, perky breasts, and a butt like a peach. She had the smile of a school girl and the sexual appetite of a starving pit bull. Like most of the dancers at the Mitchells' theater, she was a lesbian, but didn't mind going through the motions of sex with a guy if the money was good.

Billy remembered the interrogation like it was yesterday. "Most of the guys are gay anyway," she said of her "acting" partners. "But if they can get it up, I can fake it too," she told Billy with a nonchalant shrug. "Life is good when your pussy squirts cash."

The remark stuck in his mind.

Dani went to CCWF two years earlier, and the warden's law enforcement liaison was happy to go over her prison file, including a list of her cellmates. One stood out.

The cellmate was a lucky break. On that information, Billy was sure she could help. And he was positive there was something he could do for her that would induce her to tell a story he needed telling. Everybody in prison needs something.

In a tuxedo black '01 Firebird, four speed with a 5.7 liter V8, a raging firebird and air scoops on the hood, Billy Norton vroomed across the Bay Bridge, headed east on the 580 freeway. At Castro

Valley the road swings directly east, past San Francisco's distant suburbs, through the Altamont Pass into the Central Valley. The landscape changed dramatically as he dropped into the great inland valley: coastal green gave way to the suede hills of dry grassland, and the lush farmland watered by the giant aqueducts from the Shasta Dam far to the north, and the state water project sucking the Sacramento and San Joaquin rivers dry to fill pools in L.A.

He passed by the turnoff to Interstate 5. It would have been faster, but it was boring: Just a long ribbon of concrete that would wind up in L.A. He preferred Highway 99 which would take him south through the valley towns: Modesto, Ripon, Turlock, Merced and finally Chowchilla. It was a pleasant enough jaunt, ripping southbound in the left lane, giving a shit about the CHP. He had a badge.

At Avenue 24 on the south side of Chowchilla, he headed eastbound to the Central California Women's Facility, a sprawling low-rise prison that covered a square mile of farmland.

Three hours and thirty minutes after jumping on the Bay Bridge at 8th Street, Billy Norton sat in a lawyer's conference room at the prison waiting for Dani.

She was led in by a uniformed guard. "You good, or do I have to hang around?"

"I'm good," Billy said. And the guard closed the door as he left, and snapped the lock shut.

Prison strips a person down to what he or she really is. Dani wasn't a blonde any longer. Her pale chestnut hair was cut short, bull dyke style. Her eyebrows were thick. Her lips still had the pout but not the pink. Her eyes were dull blue, the sparkle snuffed out. She looked like it hurt to smile.

"What do you want?" she asked in a beaten voice.

"I come bearing gifts," Billy said, pulling packs of Marlboro Reds from his pockets. "They wouldn't let me bring 'em in the carton, but there's all ten."

"Why thank you," she mumbled, scooping the packs into her lap, and slowly finding pocket space for her score. "So what do you want?"

"What can I do for you? Short of getting you out early, I might be able to get you something you might want or need. Better accommodations, different unit? What you need right now?"

Dani blinked at Billy like she didn't have the energy to jump across the table and claw his eyes out, but she wished she did. "What do you want?" she asked again.

"You had a pal in here who died, right?"

She nodded. "A real bullshit thing. You get sick here, they let you die."

Billy agreed, but didn't really care. It wasn't why he was here. "Yeah. Her name was LaTonya Rasheed right?"

She nodded back. "So?"

"She ever talk about her cousin Ladarius?"

"You want me to say she did?"

"She ever tell you about Ladarius having a problem with a reporter named Mickey Judge back in the City?"

"That what you want me to say?"

"She ever tell you that Ladarius was threatened by that reporter Mickey Judge when he wouldn't cooperate on a story the reporter was working on?"

"That what you want me to say?"

"She ever tell you Ladarius was worried sick this reporter was somehow or another going to get him, Ladarius, killed?"

"She sure did, if that's what you want me to say."

"Before she died were you and Latoya lovers?"

"I cum like a banshee over black girls."

"Before she died, did you and Latoya arrange to have a fellow inmate conduct a marriage ceremony?"

"No. I'm an ordained minister of the Universal Life Church. I was the officiant at our own wedding." She gave him an exhausted smile. "Story getting good enough for you?"

"Getting there. Now did your wife Latoya tell you that Ladarius was getting threatening calls from the reporter Mickey Judge?"

"She complained about it constantly in the month before she died."

"Did she tell you that some of the reporter's calls came while he was still working in New York City before he came back to San Francisco?"

"She sure did. She thought it was weird that a reporter in New York was pressuring her cousin to lie about a story. She was worried sick."

"Did she express any of these fears on her deathbed? Did she make a dying declaration?"

"With her last breath."

"Will you sign a written statement to that effect?"

"Right after you have me moved from the general population to the PHU," she said, referring to the Protective Housing Unit.

Billy pulled a prepared statement from his briefcase, what the lawyers call a proffer. It outlined the testimony Celeste Johnson, aka Dani Charm, would give if called before a Grand Jury. "Just sign it now and I'll have my conversation with the warden."

"I don't like guys fucking me," she said, looking over the paper.

"Yeah, you're gay, I know. But I don't fuck over my grand jury witnesses," Billy said. "You'll get your move."

Reluctantly, she signed.

Billy thanked her, called the guard, and left. He went to the office of Warden Charles Summers and asked the favor of moving his witness Celeste Johnson to the PHU. He showed the warden her signed statement. "She'll need protection if she's giving this testimony, and the SFPD would appreciate your consideration."

Warden Johnson scowled, but he was really in no position to not do as asked. The SFPD could make a lot of noise in the Governor's office.

Billy Norton was back in the Firebird in an hour headed north to Merced. There was a former San Francisco hooker who lived there, ostensibly gone straight. She was a waitress in a truck stop who booked after-hours work. He called ahead. She cleared her calendar. Billy knew well in advance he would be horny as a bull in a herd of heifers after talking to Dani. He'd seen her movies. The waitress and former city hooker would do.

After vigorously refreshing himself in Merced, Billy slept in and ate a hearty breakfast at the truck stop, where his evening partner served him with a two-hundred-dollar smile. Billy called Jean Washington's office and made an appointment for three in the afternoon. He hit the road and roared back to the city, his foot to the floor.

Once across the Bay Bridge, he snaked through city traffic, and double parked in front of the DA's office. An SFPD placard and flashing lights acted as a meter maid deterrent.

He walked into Jean Washington's office and put the signed affidavit on her desk. "Think that'll fly?"

Jean Washington read the paper with rising interest. "I must say, for a straight white boy you have quite an imagination," she said. "Yes, that will do nicely. Take the rest of the day off."

"Thank you," Billy said.

She looked at him like she had him figured. "You stayed overnight on the road?"

"Yeah. Long drive."

"Long drive my ass. Maybe you need to see your healthcare professional."

"Pardon?"

"You got the look of someone all fucked out. I assumed you got a whore somewhere along the way."

They say she's dumb, Billy thought. Maybe not so much.

"I always take a shower in a raincoat."

She snorted. Jean Washington was a germ phobic, an insect phobic, a disease phobic. "Then make sure you don't have any creepy crawlers. I don't want you dropping them off in the office."

25

A journey halfway around the world. Ali had no idea how simple it could be. It didn't seem possible to put that together overnight, but in fact, it was too easy.

A day after Cass Papadop insisted he go to Beirut she pulled up in front of his house in her Audi convertible. He dashed out of the house and practically jumped into her lap. Buzzing with the excitement of the sudden trip, Ali also could not believe his luck. The woman he thought the most beautiful he'd ever seen actually came to his house to pick him up. In her car. With the top down. And the wind in her hair. And those eyes! He was ecstatic.

She had his ticket in one hand, the overnight passport she yanked strings to get through in the other. He was headed to Beirut, Lebanon.

"You ready to do this?" she asked, flashing that smile he loved. She slipped her hand off the automatic transmission shift and laid it on his thigh. Her touch seemed to singe his skin.

"Yes, of course. Absolutely I'm ready," he lied. Ali Zardari was as nervous as he could be. He lied to his parents. Told them he would be away for a few days on a class retreat to Yosemite. He hadn't told them about the letter that came to the house for them, the one informing the Zardari parents their son Wajahat was dead. He'd kept it from them so he could make this trip. It was terrible and he felt sick about that. But he was on a secret mission and Cass Papadop was his partner. He tingled at the thought.

"I've figured out where you need to go," she said, pulling her hand back to the wheel. "It's all in a note tucked into the ticket folder. And good news for you. You're going Business because it was the same as Economy for some reason."

"But expensive?"

"Oh, yes. Six K."

"Six thousand dollars?"

She shrugged. Yeah, a couple times more than she thought at first. "Hey, next day travel. It's expensive, but it's my investment in this project." She smiled at him again. "I'm proud of you Ali. You're going to repatriate your brother, bring him home. And you're going to find that object he died for. It will set your family up for generations. What you're doing is important."

His mind wandered to how they would celebrate when he returned. For a moment he couldn't take his eyes off the place where her seat belt crossed her hips, the V at the top of her legs. The diagonal seat belt crossed between her breasts, nipples poking her red silk shirt. He fixed the images in his mind.

Thirty minutes later she jerked the Audi to a stop in the parking structure at SFO. She walked him in, arm in arm. He could barely breathe. At security she gave him a warm hug, purposely pressing her breasts against his chest. It was true the boy turned her on a little. She gave him a kiss on the cheek that lingered longer than a simple peck, and set his heart racing. "You do good and stay safe. Send me emails on your progress." She kissed him again, and turned to leave, his last look was her swaying hips. A butt that sent blood rushing to his pants.

It was a brutal long journey. Twenty-six hours in all, including a five-hour layover in Paris at CDG, Charles De Gaulle International Airport. He was surprised at the Paris airport named after long dead French President Charles De Gaulle. It was plopped down in farmland, surrounded by green fields. And the gates were in small boxy buildings stuck onto the terminal. Completely unimpressive. The terminal itself was so-so modern, nothing special, and on the sidewalk outside he was surprised to see Africans in tribal dress wrestling huge piles of checked baggage, including actual furniture. "Holy crap," he thought, "they come to Paris with everything but the water buffalo." He had three thousand dollars in cash and an

American Express card in his name. More money than he'd ever had in his life. All from Cass. He took a cab to an airport hotel and slept for three hours. The next leg was on Royal Jordanian, with a stop in Amman for another long layover and then on to Beirut.

From his window seat Beirut rose like a dream, jutting into the sky straight out of an azure blue sea. Ali didn't quite know what to expect, but he was surprised at the high rises packed tightly together, taken aback at the thoroughly modern look. Was Beirut the third world? Or the second? He read about Beirut in an airport travel guide, its history as a crossroads of the Middle East, but from the air it was much more than he expected.

On the ground, it was another story at first. Rafic Hariri International Airport was a modern, impressive structure but a total disaster. He waited two hours in a packed crowd to reach the customs officers. He was cleared after answering a few questions in his limited, but passable Arabic. He declared himself a tourist.

He took a taxi, a newish Mercedes, to the Radison BLU Martinez Hotel near Zaitunay Bay. He was relieved to find the room American style. It was spacious, it came with television and internet, a marble shower, a bidet, a king bed, and little bottles of shampoo. And the rate was cheap. He left his clothes in a pile on the desk chair, crawled into the comfortable bed and slept for six hours.

When he woke up in the morning dark, he showered and dressed in fresh clothes, and sat on the balcony looking at the lights of the city. At six in the morning, room service opened and he had coffee brought up. He logged on to his email and sent off a note to Cass Papadop that he was in Beirut and safe. When he noticed people starting to fill the street in front of the hotel, he went out to look around.

Wide eyed, he walked the streets around the hotel in a daze. It was such a cosmopolitan city. People here could be dropped onto the streets of the Bay Area and no one would notice them as out of place. Women were fashionable in their hairstyles and clothing. Certainly, there were women in full body covering and hijabs, but he was surprised to see them carrying shopping bags from the upscale shops he might find on Union Square in San Francisco. He could hear French and Arabic spoken in a dizzy mix. Many signs over businesses were in English. Coffee Shop. Sandwiches. Wine Bar. Some got English a little sideways. A bar called Kiss Bomb made him snicker. Soldiers in camo and berets stood sentinel in doorways with automatic rifles, but overall, the scene was friendly, calm and entirely relaxed.

Ali walked and walked, making his way to the Corniche. He gazed in at the stunning sea and jagged shoreline. Amazed he was there.

He stopped for lunch at a café where an attractive woman in western dress smoked a hookah at the next table. He had a baguette sandwich with cucumbers, ham and French cheese, along with an Italian beer. Beirut seemed like San Francisco with better weather and strange languages. Bullet pocked buildings here and there. Ancient history. Now a relaxed and carefree air he hadn't expected. He felt completely at home.

Returning to the hotel he found a succession of messages from Cass urging him to report back. She wanted to know if he'd made contact with the police, what he had learned. In response he lied. He said he hadn't felt well after the long journey, a case of jet lag, and he'd spent the day in bed. But he assured her he would get over to the police station the next morning.

The next dawn he was dressed waiting for first light. Eight o'clock came slowly. Made his way to the Wadi Abou Jmil police station near the harbor, as her note had instructed. It was a four-story concrete building with small windows, and a top floor terrace that gave the impression of the private space of a high ranking official. A tangle of wires leading into the building hung from poles on the street. Ali assumed they were power lines, and communications lines, phones, perhaps even internet.

The waiting room stank of stale cigarettes and sweat and the faint hint of urine. Ali waited an hour until a detective named Vartan Boustani emerged and took Ali inside.

There was a language problem, but Ali's rudimentary Arabic and Inspector Boustani's rudimentary English sufficed to convince the detective Ali Zardari was in fact the brother of the murdered Wajahat Zardari. He was in Beirut to claim the body.

Inspector Boustani acknowledged he'd worked the case, but held back any details he might have had. Instead he questioned Ali: did he know what his brother was doing in Beirut, what his activities were? Ali said all he knew was that Wajahat lived here a number of years and loved the life. What was his brother doing with a phony Lebanese passport and an altered Pakistan passport? Ali had no idea.

That didn't exactly satisfy the detective, but the boy seemed to know nothing more so he let it drop. Boustani gave Ali the number of the grave site in the pauper's cemetery, and the name and phone number of a fixer who could help with arrangements to have the body disinterred and prepared for shipping. "It will be complicated," he counseled.

Ali asked about his brother's personal effects. It took half an hour, but one of Boustani's assistants eventually turned up in the office with a small box. It contained Wajahat's wallet, a set of keys, no cash. "Money has a tendency to disappear," the detective said with a resigned sigh.

"What about his car?"

"That was taken to the impound. I'm sure it was sold."

His list of things to do expanding rapidly, Ali went back to the hotel and called the fixer. Mohammad Amir promised to meet Ali in the hotel restaurant later in the day. Ali went through his brother's wallet. He found Wajahat's Lebanon driver's license, which listed an address. He took a taxi to the address.

Mr. Malouf, Wajahat's landlord, had already rented out the small apartment where his brother lived, but he had a cardboard box of unremarkable personal possessions. A quick glance confirmed the antiquity was not in the box.

That left Wajahat's car, which the police report noted was a 1994 Camry. Ali went to the police impound, and after the normal delay while officials determined he was who he said he was, he learned the car was sold to a Mr. Saadee Habib, owner of The Taverna on the Corniche.

Ali took a taxi to the restaurant and a friendly woman who was the manager told him Mr. Habib had died of a heart attack in the restaurant just a few short days after he had purchased Wajahat's Camry. She gave him Mr. Habib's former address.

Another taxi to a building in the Syoufi area where Mr. Habib lived. The spacious apartment was for sale, Ali was shocked at the price: close to a million US. After a few phone calls an agent arrived to show him the unit. The agent was impatient and immediately suspicious the boy was not a serious buyer. But Ali ignored the pressure to hurry and looked around. The walls had not been painted yet, and Ali noticed the outlines of many framed pieces of art. But there were no secret safes, and the cursory look in closets and cabinets produced nothing of interest.

Ali pressed the exasperated agent about what happened to the previous owner's possessions. After much cajoling and a cash fee for his time the real estate agent gave him the name of Mr. Habib's son in Paris. The son was the family member who came to Beirut, closed out the apartment, sold the furniture and presumably the car. He packed up the art for shipment to an address in Paris where he lived.

Another American hundred-dollar note and Ali got the address in Paris and a phone number for the son, a Mr. Elie Habib.

Before Ali could do anything about Elie Habib in Paris, he had to rush back to the hotel to meet the fixer, Mr. Mohammad Amir.

Mr. Amir wore a fez and a rumpled black suit and an expression of extreme fatigue. He had a bushy white moustache, white hair, and jet-black eyebrows. His face was dominated by a prominent nose, deep lines, and heavily lidded eyes. He explained that there would people to pay. The men who would disinter Wajahat's coffin. There would have to be a new coffin purchased because the city buried the unclaimed bodies in cheap wooden boxes unsuitable for shipping. And he would have to pay a shipping agent to handle the transfer of the coffin to the airline, and there were fees to pay in government offices for permits to remove human remains. And he would need a credit card number to pay the airline. He took Ali's Amex number and all but a couple of hundred dollars in Ali's cash.

It was 8 pm when Ali wrapped up his business for the day. He called Cass Papadop from the phone in his hotel room.

San Francisco was ten hours behind Beirut time. Cass Papadop had hardly slept all night worried about how the Ali Project, as she called the Beirut trip, was coming along. Her phone rang at 10 a.m. in San Francisco.

"Oh god, it's good to hear your voice," she enthused. "How are you? How is Beirut? Any progress?"

Mistaking her intense interest in Death in the Reeds for genuine interest in him, the hair on Ali 's arms tingled.

He told her all he'd managed to accomplish in one day, which was quite a lot.

"I'm really pleased," she said, purring in his ear. "You made great progress."

"I have to take some money from the American Express office on your card," he said. "I had to give all my cash to the fixer arranging Wajahat's return."

On her end, she grimaced. This was obviously going to cost more than she planned. But all the more reason to home in on the antiquity.

"I want you to focus on two things," she said. "First, Mr. Habib in Paris, but before that, the car. You have to find who bought the car from the son. That's where it's most likely he had what we're looking for."

"Not a bank box?"

"Didn't you say the police told you he was killed in a carjacking on his way to the port?"

"That's what they believed."

"Then it was in the car. If he was leaving Beirut he wouldn't have left it in safe deposit box."

"You're probably right."

"He was taking a ship somewhere and then flying home. You have to find that car. The piece may still be in it."

Ali was getting a headache. "How can I do that? I have no idea who bought the car off the son."

"But the son does. Call him in Paris. Get a name. Find the guy."

"Then what?"

"Look in the car. Under the seats, in the spare tire compartment in the trunk. Search that car. It may still be there."

They ended the call on a sweet note, Cass Papadop whispering in his ear like he was her boyfriend. But he'd seen a new side of her. Insistent, pushy, almost nagging. But then he thought of her hand on his thigh and he dismissed the doubts. Maybe he was just tired.

He looked at his watch. It was 7:30 p.m. in Paris. Might as well call.

"Mr. Habib? You don't know me. My name is Ali Zardari …"

At the end of a fifteen-minute conversation Ali had the name of a young man in Beirut who bought the car. His name was Yusef something, Eli Habib couldn't remember. But he had a phone number.

In Paris, Eli Habib clicked off his phone, wondering about the odd call. A stocky man with the olive complexion, brown eyes and dark hair of his Lebanese heritage, he mulled what the call could mean. Was it possible the brother of the original owner of the car was looking for the item he found in that metal box welded to the underside of the car?

He glanced up at the piece of art on the wall of his office. Probably not, he thought. His father was the guy with money. His father was the guy who bought art. Why would the owner of a beat-up Camry be driving around with a piece of art in a hidden box? Most likely he was a drug dealer and the box was for dope or cash.

No. The original owner of the Camry wouldn't be carrying a piece of art. His father would. His father was like that.

26

Don Saracenetti refused to see Mick inside the Channel 8 building, but he did insist on a meeting. He left a voicemail: one o'clock in the afternoon at the office of a lawyer named Kitty McManus, whom Mick assumed was a Channel 8 lawyer. He was wrong. She was an attorney Saracenetti had arranged to represent Mick.

Her office was in a building that was once a firehouse, located at the top of the hill above Cole Valley, the unofficial lesbian neighborhood of San Francisco.

When Mick pulled up to the building in his beater Honda he felt a pang of jealousy. It was a mission revival firehouse long ago abandoned by the city, but always a beautiful structure. Tall and stately, it reminded Mick of a square face wearing a hat. The upper story windows seemed like eyes and nose, and at the street level, towering redwood doors swung open like a gaping mouth. The roofline seemed like red Spanish tile hat. Since the city abandoned old Engine 40 at this location, the building endured a series of owners who knew its value but never seemed to have the funds to do a renovation right. Mick's dad frequently pestered him to buy the building, but Mick was working out of town, his money was tied up in living expenses and alimony and he never got around to it.

In the meantime lawyer McManus had evidently jumped on it. And judging by the exterior finishes she evidently had the money to do it right.

Mick rang a bell at a garrison door on the Carmel Street side. He was buzzed in, and entered a long hallway leading to an interior door. On his right, a glass wall, and behind the glass, the garage.

Two cars parked tandem. The vehicle closest to the exit was a Mercedes sedan, black and sleek. The vehicle parked nearest made Mick's heart sink. It was his dream car. A 1968 Shelby Mustang convertible, the 357 with all the Carroll Shelby performance upgrades. Red, white top, red interior. Polished to perfection. "Who is this lawyer?" he wondered.

The door at the far end opened and he was greeted by a dark complected Arab woman with a winning smile and soft, friendly eyes. "Please come in, I'm Kadija, Ms. McManus's assistant."

"The Prophet's favorite wife."

She blushed. "It's nice that you know," she said.

Mick followed her through an outer office and into another office, this one clearly belonging to the boss.

"Miss McManus will be with you in just a moment. She's upstairs in the residence."

"Is the Don here?"

"Who?"

"Mr. Saracenetti."

"Not yet. But he's expected any minute."

The office had a very high ceiling, perhaps 12 feet. On the wall to his right, bookshelves all the way up, each straining under the weight of what looked to Mick to be valuable volumes. A library ladder rolled on rails in the floor.

To his left, the boss' desk, with conference chairs in front, and art that looked like the real thing on the wall behind. Straight ahead were floor to ceiling windows. He gazed out over Cole Valley, off in the distance the University of San Francisco spires, and in the far distance the Golden Gate Bridge.

And upstairs was a residence? Shit. Once again Mick kicked himself. He could have had this building fifteen years ago, and compared to today, he could have had it cheap.

Behind him the door opened and he turned to find Don Saracenetti walking in with an attractive woman he assumed to be Kitty McManus.

"Sorry I'm late," The Don said, coming forward quickly, offering his hand. Mick shook but with no enthusiasm. He thought this meeting was odd, as if they didn't have a relationship that had turned bitter.

Kitty McManus was right behind. She also offered her hand, and Mick felt a bit more vigor in the shake. She was dark-haired with brown eyes, a pert nose and cupid lips. She was wearing a lawyer suit, midnight blue with chalk stripe, tailored tight, and black high heels. She had a slim waist, long legs and inviting cleavage. "I'm Katherine McManus," she said. "Everybody calls me Kitty." She had a quite beguiling smile and a saucy glint in her eye. Mick could feel the sex radiating off her.

"What are we here for?" he asked.

The Don took one of the seats opposite the boss desk; she sat in her massive desk chair, the polished surface of the desk an elegant expanse of dark wood.

"Please sit," she said, gesturing to the second chair placed before her desk.

"I don't get this," Mick said, lowering himself into the chair.

"Stay cool," Saracenetti said. "This is for your own good."

Mick started to recoil, but McManus spotted his reaction and hurried to settle him down.

"You may not think it at the moment, but Don is doing you a favor. Let me explain before you react." She nodded at him with a prim smile that was meant to say she was serious.

"For the moment I'm acting as your attorney in this matter with Channel 8," she said. "You could always dismiss me, but when I explain things, I don't think you will."

Mick pinched his face like a lemon squeeze. "Generally, I prefer to pick my own lawyer."

"Don saw what was coming and he contacted me to represent you," she said. "He is honestly acting in your best interest."

"Maybe I should do openers," Saracenetti said, interrupting her. She shrugged okay, go ahead.

"For a variety of reasons, not the least of which is the shooting, Channel 8 and the network are severing ties with you," he said.

"Firing me," Mick interjected.

"If you prefer," Saracenetti nodded. "Now you know I like you. It's not my decision. It's corporate. They hate you. It's also the newsroom. With the exception of Danny Fuller and most of the shooters, they hate you too." He looked Mick in the eye. "But you probably knew that."

Mick shrugged. Yes, he knew that.

"So in my own private capacity I reached out to Kitty. She's a friend," and the way he said it made Mick immediately suspect more than a friendship. "I knew you were going to need a lawyer."

He paused to let the point sink in.

"I know you're going to sue, and you should. I feel betrayed by the company," he continued, "and I feel hung out to dry, forced to go back on my word to back you up in whatever trouble you stirred up on the station's behalf. Admittedly I didn't think it would be shooting someone to death on air, but all the same …" and he drifted off.

"As long as we're laying our cards on the table," she interrupted, "it's probably my turn." She smiled at him and continued. "You are an interesting client. You were clearly in the right in your actions, no matter the outcome."

Mick was glad to hear that, though he wondered if she was just shining him on. After all, she was a lawyer.

"You have civil litigation looming with the network to compensate you for your contract, and for punitive damages for the network's treatment of you. What you also may not know yet is the District Attorney intends to impanel a Grand Jury looking into the incident with an eye to an indictment." A pause to let it all sink in. "So I am offering my services. Pro bono. That's Latin for 'free.'"

Mick ran his fingers through his hair and shifted in his seat. Should he believe The Don? Should he believe her?

"What do you get out of it?" he asked. He looked her hard in the eye.

She nodded, pursed her lips considering her answer. "Fair question. To be honest, I don't expect you to get more out of the network than two or three years of your contract. Maybe a modest punitive award. You weren't around long enough to logically claim you are owed much more than that. And it's not going to be enough for me to take the usual third, not enough for you to give up the usual third. I know that. Don knows that."

She paused long enough for Mick to interject. "So what do you get out of it?" he repeated.

Kitty McManus was getting to that. "There are all sorts of political offices about to open up as Jean Washington makes her move up the ladder. I'm interested. You are going to be in the news rather consistently for months. Representing you gets me on the air. Maybe daily. That will be my compensation."

"I would be a face-time client?" Mick heard of such arrangements.

She nodded. "Yes."

"Isn't that an in-kind campaign contribution? Like, illegal?" Mick asked Saracenetti.

"I'd deny it outside this room, but yes, we are fudging the rules a little."

The room fell silent as Mick thought things over. This was corrupt as hell, but it was Saracenetti's corruption not Mick's. So what difference did it make to him? "In that case," he said after what seemed like minutes, "I'd like to confer privately with my counsel."

"Good enough," Saracenetti said, rising. "I'll call," he said to Kitty McManus and he walked out.

Mick stood and walked to the other end of the room to look out over the spectacular view. "I think I can see my house from here," he said quietly.

She was at his side. He could feel her heat, smell her musk. She stood close enough to brush his shoulder.

He glanced over at her and she met his eyes.

"I'll represent you well. And you're going to need it."

"How bad is my problem with Bone Hendrix?"

"It isn't him. It's that DA you were trying to bring down. She knew everything you were doing. She's determined to bury you."

Mick grimaced. Maybe he'd been a little too casual about covering his tracks. Now he had the she-wolf on his trail.

He stared off at the view. "You seriously think they can put together a criminal case against me? I honestly can't see it."

"That's what's so dangerous about a Grand Jury. They can indict anybody for anything. She may not get you convicted but she can drag you through the gutter. Ruin your reputation and credibility."

Mick grunted, frowned.

"Cheer up," she said, taking his arm. "That's why I'm here. To make sure you come out of this in good shape."

Naturally Mick wondered if she was a good lawyer. How could he check?

"Are you going to be honest with me?" he asked.

"Always," she replied, holding his stare.

"Are you fucking Don?"

She didn't even blink. "Yes," she said. Then she waited a beat. "But not exclusively." She smiled, like the devil at the bedroom door. "I see you like the view. Can I show you the place?"

She led the way and Mick followed her to the car nest. "The Mustang is fantastic," he said, running his hand over the glossy red paint of the fender.

"It's my play car," she said, taking him arm in arm. "There's nothing like ripping around the city at night with the top down, just for the fun of it."

He confessed. "I like the building a lot. Years ago my father told me I should buy it."

She smiled. "Well then you'll want to see what I've done. Let me show you upstairs."

The residence was where the firemen's barracks and kitchen and group showers used to be. Beautifully redone. The living room looked west, tall windows and comfortable furniture, more of what he called "real art" on the walls. The kitchen was granite and stainless and dark wood. There was a hallway that led to some bedrooms, but she didn't lead him there. "Have a seat, enjoy the view," she said. "I'll be right back."

When she returned from the hallway leading to the bedrooms, she had changed out of her lawyer's suit into a casual dress, a green sleeveless wraparound tied at the waist. The color made her eyes pop.

"I have to show you this." She led him to a narrow spiral staircase. "It used to be the hose tower, where the firemen hung the canvas fire hoses to dry. It's an amazing view."

She had him lead the way. "The best way to avoid tripping," she said, "is just look at the next step. Don't look up." Nonetheless as he ascended the staircase he wondered if she was looking up at his ass.

At the top was a very small room with a stupendous view in every direction. He felt like he could see the Farallon Islands out past the Golden Gate. He could see Hunters Point and Candlestick Park to the southeast. He could see the concrete towers of the financial district, the Bay Bridge, and the Oakland hills. "This might be the best view in the city."

He heard small motors whirring and blinds rolled up slowly from the sills, rising over the windows about three quarters to the top. Light spilled in from the clerestory opening. "That's pretty cool," he remarked, and turned.

She stepped forward and took his hand. "We should shake on our deal," she said. "It's always the best way to conclude a deal. The relationship between lawyer and client is a sacred trust."

Mick didn't notice at first, but she had pressed the end of the sash of her dress between their hands. She looked in his eyes with a naughty sparkle of secret sex. She took a step back, still holding his hand. The sash pulled loose from her dress.

"You like the view?" Her wrap-around dress untied and fell open.

Mick whistled softly. The view was spectacular and so was the body. Her breasts were cupcakes topped with pink nipples, her stomach flat, and the tuft at the top of her legs waxed Brazilian style. "I could tell instantly we would be great together," she said. Mick glanced at the plump cushions on the couch. This is what the crow's nest room was for.

Sex was not what Mick was looking for; however, after the boss suddenly turning on him, now trying to get back in his good graces, screwing Saracenetti's girlfriend would be a satisfying payback.

But he usually heard a cautionary bell go off in his head when a woman came on to him. Perhaps it was paranoia or irrational, but he always suspected women like that were up to something he wouldn't like in the end.

But here he was. There she was. It was certainly tempting. He could certainly imagine those legs wrapped around him. He could imagine those breasts in his face as she rode him on top.

It was tempting.

But he was saved from his impulse.

"Hey hon, you up there?"

It was Saracennetti's voice. He was back.

"Oh shit," she whispered, grinning at him. "His timing absolutely sucks," she said, shaking her head. She quickly tied up her dress. "Yeah, hon, come on up. I'm showing Mickey the view." She grinned at Mick, and whispered, "To be continued."

She pushed a button, quickly opening the blinds.

Saracenetti climbed the spiral staircase huffing. "Oh, you're showing him our love nest," he said. "Got to be careful with this one. I hear he's a seducer."

"Don't be silly. Just showing my client the view. He says he can see his house from here."

Saracenetti gave Mick an up and down appraisal. "Don't get any big ideas, buddy. This is my turf."

Mick shook his head. "Of course not, Don. She's been a perfect lady."

"I wasn't worried about her," he growled. "You're the wild child here."

My god, does he have any idea? Mick asked himself. Appears not.

27

Cass Papadop swiveled in an Eames chair looking out over the twenty-second-story view of the Golden Gate and the bay. She was thinking about how to sell Death in The Reeds.

Two of Silicon Valley's most successful billionaires topped Cass Papadop's list: Bikram "Babu" Chakrabarti, a venture capitalist who hopped from one mega startup to another, amassing a fortune said to be north of $30 billion. She knew him from parties in Pacific Heights. He was also a horrid little man with dreadful halitosis, filthy hands and beady little close-set eyes always fixed on a woman's breasts. Despite his wretched appearance and personality, his billions allowed him to get away with ferocious womanizing, cutting a wide swath through the slim blue-eyed-blonde mothers and daughters of the Bay Area social scene. He specialized in the wives of lesser millionaires.

The unfaithful wives tended to justify rutting him with the hope he would let hubby in on the next multibillion-dollar moon shot.

Chakrabarti was also a collector of art and the proud owner of a museum quality collection.

The second man was also a collector and miserable in his own way. His name was Lawrence "Bunny" Nelson, the founder and CEO and grand poobah of Delphi Integrated Controls, among Bunny's rivals known as "DIC." His company dominated the data processing needs of Fortune 500 customers. He was worth upwards of $80 billion. He never tired of making sure everyone knew it.

Both men would want to know for certain the item Ali was bringing home was the real thing.

Therefore, Cass needed an authenticator. And she remembered that Mickey Judge had mentioned a name. She devised a plan.

It was not hard to find Irwin Feinstein's number.

Irwin was intrigued to get the call. She introduced herself as a television "executive producer and host."

"I'm going to be doing a blockbuster program exposing an art fraudster," she confided. She was going to be interviewing a self-styled "Indiana Jones" type character who discovered an antiquity "which he claims is very ancient and very rare." And Ms. Papadop, would like to fly him, Mr. Feinstein, to San Francisco to do an authentication on camera.

Cass Papadop swung into the role with gusto. In fact, she said, there are only two of these objects in the world known to be authentic, and she was quite certain her target was trying to defraud a naïve buyer. "I fully expect this item to be a fake," she confided in Irwin Feinstein. "This character is entirely disreputable and has been known to pass off fakes in the past. I'd like to catch him on camera."

Irwin Feinstein was a seventy-two-year-old man who had made his fortune in ladies' fashion. He was bald with a wrap of wispy gray hair around the base of his skull. He had a sharp nose, a receding chin, and sleepy eyes parked in deep sockets behind thick glasses. Along with his art collector wife Miriam he was known for a stunning array of antiquities that he was forced to forfeit "in a mix-up with the authorities." Like everyone else in his circle he was not without ego. But in his case ego had been severely injured by his tangle with the law.

"Television?" he asked. "Network or local?"

"A nationally syndicated show called Art Thieves, which is running now as a pilot in San Francisco." There was no such nationally syndicated show.

"Art Thieves?" he asked. He'd never heard of it.

She was expecting the question. "So you're in New York. My production company hasn't chosen a New York affiliate yet," she said, slipping into a confidential tone. "There's a bidding war going on for the Tri-State area, but I'm sure it will be sorted out soon."

"If I were to agree to appear, will the episode be shown in the New York area?"

"Certainly," she said, with all the confidence of a liar who could live her lie as solid gold truth if necessary. "We'll have a New York affiliate in a week or two. This episode will air in about three weeks. In fact, you could very well be the featured player in our New York market debut," she added brightly.

Irwin was intrigued. In his office in a three thousand square foot penthouse on 64th at Lexington, Feinstein mulled the possibility. He and his wife had been thinking about how to engineer a splashy comeback in the highly social world of art collectors. After his disastrous arrest and prosecution for possession of looted antiquities the couple had been in society exile. Irwin's offense was the so-called 'dirty pots' so highly prized by his erstwhile friends.

Yes, they were dug up by tomb robbers in Italy and Greece, they were smuggled through Switzerland's duty-free zones into the hands of restorers and onward to the auction houses in London and New York. Yes, it was illegal, "technically" he always said, but all the people who he thought were friends did it too. He and his wife were devastated when they shunned him after he got caught.

It was a terribly embarrassing episode because it was so stupid. He had a marvelous collection seized by the authorities and only because one piece was placed in an alcove leading to his bathroom, and a picture of that very alcove was featured in a decorating magazine photo essay on his spectacular apartment. An art cop spotted the piece, and the police showed up with a search warrant.

The story was in all the papers, especially the most humiliating aspect: the seizure of almost all of his ancient pieces, the collection that was his calling card in New York and London society circles.

Featured on an important television program might just regain some of his society cachet. A public relations rehabilitation.

Not to mention first class tickets to San Francisco, a few days at the Huntington Hotel on Nob Hill, and visits with his friends in Pacific Heights. No doubt that wonderful Dede Halsey might even arrange a cocktail party for their arrival.

"What is the piece your rogue archaeologist claims he has?"

Cass had to be careful here. She knew this question would come up. She had rehearsed a completely phony response that sounded solid gold.

"He says he uncovered the third of a two-piece set. One of the real pieces is in the British Museum, and the other in the Iraq Museum."

"Oh my god," Fink interrupted. "Your person says he has another Death in the Reeds?"

"Exactly right. You're quite prescient," Cass said. "Of course it's a total joke. In three thousand years only two have ever been found. If there were a third or fourth," and here she interrupted herself, "they are thought to be plaques from a royal throne, right?"

"That's right," Irwin mumbled.

"So, three doesn't make sense. Four maybe, but if you found a third, you would expect a fourth to be nearby, but he says he dug the entire area, and never found a fourth."

"An obvious outlaw," Feinstein said. "I have personally seen both the British Museum piece and the Iraq Museum piece. I would be able to spot the authentic pieces in an instant."

"That means you could spot the fake in an instant?"

"Absolutely," he said, swelling with pride in his expertise. "Although one must be careful. News out of Iraq is the original in the Iraq Museum has been stolen. Taken under cover of the American bombing of Baghdad."

"Has it?" she replied, sounding surprised. "Well, that's a shock. Has it turned up?"

"No, it hasn't," Feinstein said. "In fact, the rather disreputable prosecutor in a case involving my wife and myself is in Baghdad trying to recover items looted from the museum."

"Is he?" she said, genuinely surprised. "That's a coincidence."

"Not really. He thinks he's an art expert. He's not, really. But he thinks so."

"Well, irrelevant to us. We have a counterfeiter we're going to expose."

"Yes," Feinstein said, and with that single word Cass knew the deal was done.

She spent some time going over logistics with him, in very general terms. Yes, she would make travel arrangements. Yes, the Huntington Hotel would be perfect, in fact she would arrange for another room to do the shoot. Yes, she knew Dede Halsey very well, and would be getting in touch with her immediately to let her know the Feinsteins will be in town. Yes, I'll be back in touch in a day or two.

"Perhaps I should involve my public relations person," he said. "Do you know Wilhemina D'Froissart?"

Of course Cass did not. But she assumed it must be one of those New York courtesans who married into the name. None of the actual Froissart family would have a public relations company. "Of course, I do. But let's save Wilhemina for promoting the final product when it debuts nationally in New York. And we wouldn't want word to leak out. My Indiana Jones would bolt if he knew you were going to be present to authenticate the item."

"I see," he said. "I suppose we'll be doing this in secret?'

"Oh yes, highly secret. The element of surprise is what we're going for here."

"Very well," he said. "I'll expect to hear back from you in … what?"

"A day," she said firmly. "Two at the most. This is fantastic. You will be the star of this program, Mr. Feinstein."

Cass hung up with the plan forming in her head. She would trap him into authenticating the true object by bringing him into a room with The Reeds and with tape rolling. Feinstein would be shocked to see it was the real thing. He would realize his legal jeopardy. He would bolt. She would use the tape as evidence of authentication for her buyers. That would kick off the bidding between Chakrabarti and Nelson.

What if Feinstein ran to the authorities? She counted on the likelihood he would not want to be connected in any way for fear his parole would be revoked, and he would be back in that humiliating federal prison.

It may have felt slimy. But it was a plan.

28

The flack for the state prison system was a former reporter Mick had worked with way back when he was at Channel 2 in Sacramento. Kip Hinkel decided he wasn't going any farther up the television ladder and he might as well settle for an easy gig and a nice fat state pension.

"Hey I got you cleared for that interview at Vacaville," he said when Mick picked up the call.

"Holy crap that's fucking fantastic," Mick said. "Those goons up there said it would be months."

"Aren't you working on something to nail Washington to the wall?"

Mick hesitated. It was kinda spooky Hinkel knew.

"C'mon, it's Kip here," he said, sensing Mick's hesitation. "We know things."

"Yeah, Okay, that's what it is."

"Good. Last thing I want is that bitch in the Governor's office. There'd be a person of color standing in my doorway saying 'outa the way white boy.'"

"Okay great. So when can I get up there?"

"You're cleared for day after tomorrow. Friday at 2 pm. Ordinarily I'd be there to show the flag, but this is one of those things I want to pretend I didn't really know about. Routine request, cleared it, had a doctor's appointment, couldn't make it down there to babysit the interview."

"Deniability?"

"Damn straight. 'Oh, did the inmate say that? Gosh, that's unfortunate. I guess we'll know next time not to clear that reporter through.' That's how it'll go."

"Cool, thanks."

Now Mick had a problem. Since he was fired he didn't have a crew.

But the interview was too juicy to pass up. And who knows? Maybe he'd get it all on tape and peddle it across the street. Shove it up Channel 8's ass.

He got Spike on the phone. "You still doing freelance?"

"Weddings, yeah. You getting married?"

"No, but what'll you charge for a one day shoot at Vacaville?"

"Day rate is five hundred, four hundred to you if you buy gas and dinner and drinks after."

Mick did a quick calculation. Save a hundred bucks on the shoot, but lay out two hundred in gas and dinner, so a five-hundred-dollar shoot becomes six hundred. But what the hell. "Okay, pick me up at ten Friday morning. We'll go across the bridge into Marin and take the Black Point cutoff over to 80 and drop into Vacaville."

He could almost hear Spike shaking his head. "Fucking guy always telling the shooter the way to go. See you Friday asshole."

The next day Mick went over to the courthouse to do some research on the trial his witness testified in. His boy was named Orlando Diaz, and he had been teed up for a long stretch in Pelican Bay, the gang supermax way up the coast in a town called Crescent City, Del Norte county. Cold. Fogbound. Gray. Hopeless. A desperate place. Instead, Orlando was able to offer testimony on a fellow named Howard Price. He was known on the street as "Right" Price, a major dealer of meth, heroin, blow, whatever was right. For some reason Jean Washington wanted Right Price in Pelican Bay worse than she wanted Orlando there, so Orlando was given the chance to snitch on Right and do his time in Vacaville instead.

Orlando's public defender was Yamina Ortega. Mick knew her from Sacramento when she worked in the Public Defender office there. He stood around in the marble hallway outside Department 105 in the old Hall of Justice until she came out after the morning arraignments.

"I can't represent you," she said, recognizing him and grinning. "I got enough killers on my plate."

"Hey come on, I got a couple things to talk about. Let's go get something at the food truck."

"I'm surprised you haven't turned up on my new client list." She seemed to be laughing at him. She was a sweet-natured Hispanic woman in her middle thirties. Long dark hair, brown face, puffed up cheeks, lively eyes.

"I want to talk to you about Orlando."

"Diaz? He in trouble again?"

"Minding his own business in Vacaville."

"Then what do you want?"

"I want to know how you got him that deal."

"What deal?"

"The one that kept him out of Pelican Bay. Why was the DA so hot to trot on Right Price?"

She looked at him suspiciously. "You got a wireless mic on you somewhere?"

"No way. This is just talk. Deep background. I'm not even writing anything down."

She looked him over again. The smile disappeared. Her eyes weren't so lively. She pursed her lips. "This is the one case I got something out of a rotten system. Most times I get screwed by it."

"Fine. Let's get a burrito."

They walked out of the Hall onto Howard Street and turned right. Half a block up tucked under a freeway overpass a food truck was pumping out burritos and quesadillas and French-dip beef sandwiches. They sat at a picnic table, each with a foil wrapped burrito and a can of soft drink. Mick had a Diet Coke. She took a Fanta orange.

"Orlando had a hit on him waiting in Pelican Bay," she said. "At least that's what I was told. I needed to save his life, so I went along."

"Who asked you to?"

"Word came through one of the ADA's"—Assistant District Attorney's— "that Right Price needed to go down and if Orlando could offer help he could pick Vacaville or Corcoran."

"Okay so you jump at the deal."

"Not really. I can't tell you how many times my guy is the one who loses in this situation. Out of the blue an inmate appears to testify against my guy, and away he goes, never mind whatever reasonable doubt case I've managed to cobble together."

"The snitch factory."

"Pretty much. I tell my guys to watch out for whoever shows up as a cell mate. But you know an inmate doesn't get to pick who's in the cell with him."

"So how do you deal with it on a regular basis?"

"Look, the first rule of the public defender's office is to recognize who your client is," and here she started to count items on her fingers. "First, stupid. Next, guilty. Last, he's probably confessed. So, most times if he goes away, it's not a complete miscarriage of justice. I'm just trying to minimize how bad the time is going to be."

"If your clients are stupid, guilty and have confessed, why does Washington need to put a snitch in the cell?"

She shrugged. "I've often wondered that myself. I think it's part pure viciousness. You know, slam the guy into the mud. But part is just racking up wins. She runs on that shit, you know. Last campaign was 'more convictions than last three DA's combined.' Maybe you weren't here, but that's how it went."

"I can't believe a cellmate can put somebody away with no other corroboration."

"Happens. Easy-peasy for an indictment. At trial a little trickier but if the inmate is a really good liar jurors can get taken for a ride."

"Prosecutor doesn't have to have more than what could be perjured testimony?"

"Sometimes they have a little more. But shanking a fellow inmate is how life goes in the system. Again, depends on whether the witness proves to be a believable liar."

Mick knew these things. He'd heard it all before. He didn't mention he had an interview booked with Orlando Diaz. She would have stopped it cold.

Friday morning Spike picked him up in a plain white '92 Ford Econoline van. "This looks familiar," Mick said.

"Bought it off the station when they upgraded."

"It's ten years old."

"Runs great."

"We won't break down on the bridge?"

"Hell no." He seemed a little insulted.

Mick didn't care. "Let's see the gear."

Spike opened the back doors. First thing Mick noticed were the steel racks bolted to the driver's side. Tripod, light stands, lights in the racks tied down with bungee cords. On the floor at the back doors a foam-lined box with an ancient video camera. Two more boxes for two also ancient Sony tape decks.

"Is that an Ikegami?" Mick asked about the camera.

Spike smiled. "Late 80s. HL 79. I bought everything the station had. Got half a dozen for parts. Always have one up and running."

"What are those decks?" Mick asked, pointing to two boxy devices, one slightly larger than the other.

Spike waggled his fingers like hocus-pocus. "Go back in your memory bank," he said. "Sony BVU 50. You'll recall that machine is record only. Not capable of playing back. In the next box is a Sony BVU 110. That one can record and more importantly, it can play back. So you record on one, and if you have to make a copy you put the original on the 110 and play it back while recording on the 50. Remember those days?"

Mick felt a long-lost memory migraine coming on. "Those fuckers are from the dawn of time. They gotta be thirty years old."

"So what? A new camcorder runs thirty, forty grand. Got this mess of stuff for five hundred bucks each. Got all the BVU decks. All the spare parts I needed for years."

"You couldn't get ten-year-old camcorders for a few thousand?"

Spike looked sheepish. "Probably, but hey … weddings don't pay all that much. This shit is fine."

Mick realized he must have looked sour because Spike noticed. "Dude I got the edit decks too. You're good."

"You can't even get parts for these things. How am I going to deal with this in a regular modern television edit booth?"

"Don't get nuts on me. We still have old tech in the building for the archive tapes. Don't worry. You'll be good."

Spike slammed the doors, and they jumped in the front and buckled up. Mick shook his head. "I haven't seen these things in years. Maybe the day rate oughta come down."

"You're renting me, not the gear," Spike shot back, dropping the Econoline into drive. "So go fuck yourself."

They drove out Geary Boulevard to 19th Avenue and took it north to hook up with the Golden Gate Bridge. Eucalyptus trees and pines towered over the roadway as they passed into the Presidio and through the MacArthur tunnel. Bridge traffic was inbound at this hour, so they made good time across. After zipping through the Marin tunnel, it was blue skies and light traffic for another half hour to Highway 37. They streaked eastbound along the North Bay marshes, past Sears Point, the gateway to Napa, across Mare Island where the submarine base hides. Connected with Interstate 80. That took half an hour, and it was another half hour to Vacaville State prison.

State prisons don't put a lot of effort into architecture. From the parking lot Vacaville State Prison seems to be a long fence topped with concertina wire, guard towers every few hundred yards, fronting some low-rise buildings.

Mick and Spike waited at the reception center for a staffer to come clear them in. Turned out to be a young woman. "Why isn't Kip here?" she asked, in a grumble.

"Beats me," Mick lied. "Expected he would be."

They were escorted through a series of hallways to a visiting room. It was the worst kind. Cubicles with plexi separating the inmate from the visitor, both parties speaking through grimy telephone handsets.

Spike's solution for tapping into the handset on Mick's side was to switch it out with handset out of his bag that was already wired with a plug for the mic cable.

He set the tripod so the camera lens was almost resting on Mick's right shoulder. Then they waited.

It was the kind of place where you don't make small talk. Too many ears. All they could do was glance around at the linoleum floors, the plastic chairs, the florescent lights, the stained ceiling tiles. Prison.

Half an hour later Orland Diaz slipped onto the stool on the other side and picked up the handset. Spike softly said "we're rolling."

Diaz was one of those guys with face tats. He had the teardrops, meaning he'd killed someone. He had the gang tats on his arms that identified his set. He had a collar of faded blue ink that must have meant something, but Mick had no clue. He had a handsome face, regular features, and penetrating eyes. Mick had no doubt he was a killer.

Mick didn't waste time with Orlando's life story. This wasn't that kind of interview. He started with the meat. "Let's go over again what you told me last time I was here. What was the deal offered you to keep you out of Pelican Bay?"

"Deal was I say what they needed someone to say."

"What was that?"

"Right Price was the guy in the car with the gun and he was doing the shooting."

"How did you know that?"

"I testified I saw it."

"Did you see it?"

"My understanding was if I saw Right Price shoot those dudes I would not have to do my time in Pelican Bay."

"But was your testimony true?"

"I swore it was true."

"But was it true?"

"You want to know if it was a righteous snitch or a bullshit snitch? That right?"

"That's exactly what I want to know. Was it BS testimony?"

What happened next caused freak outs in both San Francisco and Sacramento.

The booth Orlando Diaz occupied was narrow, the walls almost touching his shoulders. Same on Mick's side.

Mick could see inmates passing behind him as they came for their visitation and returned to their cells or the dayroom. Seemed to be a dozen or more in the room, but they passed behind the booth so quickly it was hardly possible to make out a face unless the individual turned to look directly into Orlando's booth.

So when a man stopped briefly behind Orlando facing away, it didn't seem all that unusual. The man was gone in a second or two.

Except Orlando's eyes suddenly bulged, and he jerked forward. Then he seemed about to throw up, except it was blood that gurgled from his lips. He stood and turned to look around at the men behind him. And when he did Mick and Spike could see a shank embedded in his back, just below the shoulder blades. Then Orlando fell forward on his face.

"Shit," Spike said, unsnapping the camera from the tripod. He stood so he could get a good shot through the window, onto the floor where Orlando lay splayed.

On the prisoner side of the visitation room the men stood away. No one was visible from Spike's point of view.

Mick shouted for a guard.

Spike stepped to the next booth to try to see whoever it was who stabbed Orlando. The men crowded into corners where they couldn't be seen and turned their backs.

Screaming started on the visitors' side as people saw the blood pooling on the floor on the prisoners' side.

A claxon sounded along with a deafening bell and doors slammed and staff rushed in.

Spike popped the tape and put in a fresh. "Put this in your belt. They're going to seize the tape in the deck." He handed the tape to Mick.

Mick slipped the tape inside his belt in the small of his back, and pulled his jacket down to cover it.

Spike kept rolling on the scene in the inmate side. Staffers rushed in to give medical aid to Orlando. But it didn't look good.

"I think he's dead," Spike whispered.

"Has to be," Mick said.

It only took a few minutes. The young woman was back. "I have to take you to the warden's office," she said.

Spike and Mick sat in a plain state-issue office for about fifteen minutes when a woman in uniform with a bunch of command stripes walked in appearing very harried.

Her breast plate said Ginger Jones, Acting Warden.

"I need that tape," she said, pointing at the recording deck.

Spike nodded. "Of course." He popped the tape and handed it to her.

"What is this?" she asked, turning the tape over in her hand.

"It's a ¾ inch U-matic. Professional tape. A little on the older side."

"We don't have that here," she said. "I'll have to send it to Sacramento."

"We understand," Mick said.

"Tell me what you heard and saw."

Mick was less than honest about what he heard. He characterized it as a routine interview with an inmate about his gang life. But he could be completely honest with what he saw. "A man stopped behind him very briefly, facing away. He walked away. Then I noticed Orlando react. He jerked forward. His eyes got wide. Then there was blood in his mouth. Then he stood and we could see the shank."

She asked Spike if he had anything to add. Spike saw the same thing.

She was nervous. The acting warden needed this like a hole in the head.

But soon she'd heard enough, and they were escorted out.

On the parking lot Spike unlocked the van and put the Ikegami and the BVU 50 in their respective boxes. "Should we make a dub?"

"Give it to her?"

Spike nodded.

"That would probably be the right thing to do," Mick said. "Since we're pulling some shit on her."

They stood at the back of the van for ten minutes while Spike ran off a copy. He played the original back on the BVU 110, recording over to the BVU 50. Not just old school but very old school. Mick insisted Spike copy only the part of the stabbing. "I don't want to give her the interview. It would be on Jean Washington's desk in the morning."

Mick walked the tape into the reception room and handed it to a staffer behind the desk. "This is for Warden Jones." He taped a note to the tape box. "You'll need this. Sorry for the trouble," it read.

He and Spike stopped at the Nut Tree, ordered steaks and settled in for the first of several drinks.

"Ever seen anything like that before?" Spike asked after he drained his first drink.

"Jesus," Mick said. "No. I was in Somalia and saw a guy shot, but it was a good twenty yards away. Never anything like that."

Mick signaled the waitress for another round. Spike stared off, thinking. "I hope I don't have fucking dreams about that. Trouble enough sleeping."

"Maybe just bang the hell out of Whiskey," Mick said. Julie "Whiskey" Sour was Spike's longtime girlfriend.

He snorted. "If this image pops into my mind the noodle goes limp."

Half hour later—the time it took to drive to Sacramento with the tape—Kip Hinkle called. "Jesus, what'd you do?"

"Dude, I hadn't even got to the hard-core questions. I was still in the prelims."

"I assume you bootlegged the good stuff out and made a dub in the van?"

Mick saw no point in trying to bullshit the guy. He'd probably done the same thing a few times. "Of course. I didn't want the good stuff seized. But I did you the courtesy of making a dub."

Kip Hinkel grunted. "Yeah, thanks for that."

"Was this an ordinary prison stabbing or our girl?"

"Beats me," the prison flack said. "Could be both I suppose. But I need to get out of the way now. You investigating the next Governor, a guy ratting on her gets killed? I need to clear the area and fast."

"What are you doing with that tape?"

He laughed. "It'll never see the light of day, you kidding? We're putting out a statement that an inmate was stabbed and we're investigating. End of story."

Mick nodded. He figured. "You know his lawyer will want a real investigation."

"She can want all day long. Her guy will still be dead."

"But eventually you'll have to give up the tape."

"Maybe, but my story is I never looked at it."

Mick exhaled loudly. "Shitty deal, man. Never seen anything like it."

There was silence on the other end long enough to let that observation drop. "What are you doing with yours?" Kip asked, meaning the tape.

"Goes in the bank," Mick said. "It will make air someday, but not today."

"It's pretty hot day-of news," Kip said. He didn't believe Mick wouldn't rush back to air it.

"I've been suspended. I'm not giving anything to those guys." Another round of drinks arrived. Mick took a long pull before continuing. "Look I'm going ahead with the story. When this investigation of your girl is wrapped and I have everything nailed down it might get me back on the air and employed again. This video is golden. It will make the series Emmy material. So, I'm not blowing it off with a one-day story that nobody will care about in a week."

"Just give me a heads up when you're going to air."

"You got it."

When he cut the call off Mick turned to his buddy. "You think it's possible Jean Washington ordered the hit?"

Spike shrugged. "Beats me. But I do think she knows you're trying to take her down. You can't show up at a state prison to interview somebody who has something on her without her knowing. So depends on whether you think she's totally badass."

Totally badass, Mick thought. Of course she is.

"Maybe you should watch your back a little more carefully," Spike added.

Their steaks arrived, and Mick ordered another drink. "I'm driving," Spike said to the waitress. "Coffee."

"You know it never fails to amaze me how we plan shit, and arrange things, and have it all figured out, and then bam! We get hit with something we never expected. Shit just comes out of the blue and knocks us on our ass."

"Remember Bob Johnston?" Spike asked.

"The old camera guy back in the film days?"

"That's the one. We'd be sitting around trying to figure out a story for the day and he'd say 'there's a fuse burning somewhere,' and he was always right."

They clinked glasses, but it was not a celebration.

The next day Yamina Ortega called. "What the fuck?" she demanded. "You get my client killed?"

The conversation didn't go well. "I hadn't even really started the interview."

"But you were asking him about the deal Jean Washington gave him. That was dangerous and you knew it."

"How does anybody know who I'm investigating?"

"Don't pull that shit on me. If you're talking snitches, you're targeting the DA."

"You think the DA had him killed?"

"Oh for chrissakes," she said. Mick could practically hear her fuming on the other end.

"Don't ever come around again," she said, abruptly cutting off the call.

29

Ali Zardari walked out of his Beirut hotel and immediately spotted Vartan Boustani's bald head and black glasses in a car half a block down in front of an outdoor lunch spot.

He jumped into a taxi and watched the Nissan pull into traffic five cars behind. He told the driver to go to the National Museum on Pierre Gemayel and paid him. "It's very important you go all the way there," he said. "Can I trust you?"

The driver took the American one-hundred-dollar bill. "As you wish."

As the taxi slowed to make the next turn, Ali slipped out on the passenger side. He hid in the shadow of the entrance to a small bazaar. He watched Vartan Boustani's Nissan round the corner and follow the taxi as it drove away toward the museum. He hoped.

Half an hour later Ali stood in a parking lot across from the Corniche waiting for the guy Yusef. The white caps on the blue sea sparkled. Rich people in fancy motor boats speed by. Sailboats heeled hard, rails clipping wave tops. Stiff breeze.

Ali thought about the years his brother enjoyed this beautiful life, and he wished he could have been here with him. But his brother was so much older. It was only recently that Ali was old enough to travel to a place like this, and there was never the money.

He noticed a blue Camry enter the lot, moving slowly, the driver clearly looking for a spot. It was the guy Yusef. Ali got him to come by telling him a crazy story on the phone. "I was trying to buy that car when the guy sold it to you. Would you consider selling it? I'd pay more than you paid."

The guy was an Arab, a born trader. Of course, he'd come if a profit was possible.

The guy got out of the car. He was in jeans and a shirt unbuttoned halfway down his chest. Yusef was about Ali's age and he looked like he was a similar guy: Ali pegged him as a computer sciences student. After introductions, they tried to talk but Ali's skeletal Arabic made things difficult. Ali walked around the car looking it over. "Nice paint," he said.

"Guy tells new," Yusef said in messy English.

Ali poked around under the seats. Nothing. He tried the glove box. Nothing. He opened the trunk, found nothing in the wheel wells or the spare tire compartment. He crawled under the car and spotted the box immediately. "What's this?" he asked.

Yusef had no idea what he was talking about. He looked underneath and shrugged.

Ali felt around in the trunk and found a cable leading to one of the tail light compartments. He yanked the cable and a lid popped open. The box was empty.

"There was nothing in here when you bought the car?"

Yusef looked mystified. "Never see it."

Right then and there Ali made up his mind that Elie Habib had found the object and taken it home with him to Paris.

Yusef was confused and disappointed that his would-be buyer suddenly dropped the whole idea of buying the car. The young man was looking forward to a profit.

Back at the hotel Ali called Cass in San Francisco, again beguiled to hear her voice, and anxious to impress her.

"An officer from the Beirut police followed me."

Cass was alarmed. "Why?"

Ali shrugged, as if she could see him through the phone. "I think they want to know what Wajahat was doing here."

"Did you lose the detective?"

"Of course."

"How?"

Pride swelled his chest. "It was simple."

"Really?"

"Yes," he said, with authority. He let it stand. It was enough that she thought he was clever. Details would only open the possibility of doubt or criticism. Better to get on to the good news.

"There was a box that carried the plaque welded to the underside of the car."

"You're sure?"

"I'm positive. It was similar dimensions."

"Okay," she said. "So?"

"I don't think it's here in Beirut. The guys who killed Wajahat," and here his throat caught. He'd been trying to keep Wajahat's murder out of mind. "They were all dead themselves. So they didn't take it. I'm positive none of those ignoramuses at the impound lot found it. It's not in the car now. So that leaves Elie Habib in Paris. He might be the one who found it and took it with him."

"You want to go to Paris?"

Again, Ali's pride puffed up. She was asking his advice. He was starting to feel like the man. "If we want the thing I think I have to."

Counting his original plane fare, the hotel and repatriating the brother's body, Cass figured she was already in about eight thousand dollars, not to mention whatever it was going to cost to bring Irwin Feinstein and his wife to San Francisco for the authentication. But that was later. Right now she could re-book Ali's ticket, pay the change fee for the leg to Paris and maybe be in just a couple thousand more. "Okay, let's do it," she said. "I'll text you your new flight number."

While he waited Ali got on his laptop and scoured the Paris phone book. He found an Elie Habib in a suburb called Saint Cloud, just west of Paris central. It matched the address the real estate agent had given him.

The next morning when he took a taxi to the airport he noticed Boustani's Nissan followed. Ali ignored the detective.

Boustani watched as Ali paid the driver and entered the terminal. Ali pretended not to have seen him. No point in taunting him.

The Middle East Airlines flight was packed. Ali found himself in coach and silently cursed Cass for cheaping out on him. Back at CDG, he hurried through customs to the street. He jumped in a taxi and headed for a hotel Cass Papadop booked for him in Saint Cloud.

The hotel was a few short blocks from the Habib apartment building at 140 Rue Royale. Fortunately, there was a tabac and café directly across the street. Ali set himself up at a table and kept an eye on the apartment house.

He was pleasantly surprised at Saint Cloud. It was a lovely suburb. The buildings in the neighborhood tended to be four or five stories, a mix of older structures that seemed to be postcard Parisian and newer boxy buildings of concrete and glass, which Ali disapproved of. The Habib apartment building seemed small. The mail box indicated six apartments, two on each floor. The Habib unit was 301 on the third floor.

Watching carefully Ali spotted a young woman in the window of what had to be the Habib apartment. She was fair skinned, with strawberry blonde hair, and freckles. Then he got lucky. She emerged from the building with three others, evidently her brother and mother and father. The father clearly was Lebanese, and the son took after him. The mother was a French white woman, the daughter taking after her. They seemed like a pleasant family, talkative, argumentative in what Ali assumed was the French way, but not bickering. And the Habib family sat in the very same café a few tables away.

Now Ali had eyes on each individual in the family. He called Cass, waking her, five in the morning her time. "I'm four tables away from the guy and his family," he said in a low voice the moment she answered. "I see his wife and his son and daughter. Now I know what they look like."

Half a world away Cass sat up in bed, and slapped herself awake. Her voice was morning groggy and deep. Ali imagined she slept nude.

"Okay so you know what to do, right?" she said, kicking off the sheets, stretching her naked body.

"I figure out when they're out of the house for a few hours and I break in," he said.

"How are you going to do that?"

"Try to use a credit card, or a screwdriver. The way I've seen on TV, I guess."

"Just watch them for a day or two to be sure of their patterns. Make sure you know they're out of the house for a while. You don't want them walking in on you."

Now he was going to try his hand at burglary. He thought he ought to get something for that. He was feeling a little cocky and bold. "If it's in that apartment, we got it. I'm right there," he said.

"Yes, you are Ali. You have done fantastic."

He thought he'd push it a little. He laughed. "And when I walk through your door with this thing, you're going to …" He let his voice trail off, the statement not quite finished.

Cass knew what he was saying. The boy was being flirty. He needed a little incentive. Sure, she'd play along. "Oh, when you walk through the door," her voice coming alive, "I'm going to throw you flat on your back," she said, in her morning gurgle.

She could hear him gasp. "Eat your Wheaties, boy, you're going to need your strength," she whispered in a purr drenched in possibilities.

That pretty much did it for Ali. He started this trip as a nervous boy. Now he was a globetrotting man on a mission to win the woman of his dreams.

The next two days he watched the Habib family's daily routine. It was Tuesday and Wednesday, work and school days. The mother left the house early, both days by 7:30 a.m. Then Elie Habib pulled out of the parking structure an hour later in an older model VW Golf. Then both the boy and the girl left for school, book bags slung over their shoulders. He placed their ages as high school, the boy nearing the end, the girl in the early years.

Day two was the same as day one. On day three he made his move.

That was when disaster struck.

He was walking out of the hotel, the backpack with his laptop over one shoulder when he was astonished to see his Beirut nemesis.

The little sad sack named Vartan Boustani sat in the hotel lobby reading the Paris Match.

Ali felt an electric shock at the sight.

What to do?

He walked to the street acting as if he had not seen the detective, his mind racing.

Best to confront him? Or better to ignore him?

The last thing he wanted to do was ask Cass's advice. Boustani was his mess. He had to clean it up himself somehow.

He walked toward the Seine. Without looking, he knew the detective was following.

Did Boustani know he was surveilling the Habib apartment? Had he led the detective to the doorstep of the prize his brother had worked so hard to secure? He felt sick to his stomach and his mind spun on an axis of fear.

In a daze he kept on, afraid to look behind. He passed a Harley-Davidson dealership, an unexpected and incongruous sight that left him feeling even more dislocated.

But the bridge at Place Georges Clemenceau gave him hope. Across the river the gardens of the Museum Albert Kahn. At a glance he could see the gardens gave him a chance to lose the detective. If he played it right.

Though it was a beautiful setting for a relaxing stroll Ali could not enjoy the gardens. Instead, he walked through the manicured grounds frantically scanning for a place to duck out of sight and lose the man he was certain was trailing.

At a postcard setting of massive drooping willow trees a quaint bridge painted red arched across a shallow pond. Ali stood at the center of the bridge and dared a glance around.

There. Back along the path he caught a glimpse of something through the foliage. A bald head. Black frame glasses.

Okay. The man was there, Ali thought. Now lose him.

Ali resumed his stroll across the bridge. Once he was certain he was out of sight of the man following, he slipped off the path into the thick cover of trees and shrubbery. He knelt in the green and waited.

Soon the detective came hurrying along, trying to catch up and keep his prey in sight. He had lost Ali back in Beirut by lagging too far behind.

Ali waited until the detective disappeared along the path. He emerged from his hiding place and headed back the way he came at a near run.

His mind was racing. He had to get into that apartment. Find the object. Then go directly to the airport. It was imperative to get out now. His reservation to San Francisco was the next day, and he had to assume Boustani had that information.

Back at the Habib building Ali stood in the shadows of a doorway and surveyed the situation. No sign of Boustani. The street was quiet. He took a few deep breaths. Calmed his jittery hand.

It was time to make his move.

He figured it was too dangerous to attempt to enter the building through the main door. He could try to get other residents to buzz him in, but who knows? There could be cameras. He also rejected the idea of lurking until someone exited the building and slip in through the closing door. He watched and noticed the door swung closed and click-locked too quickly.

He decided on the basement parking. Less chance to be seen getting through the door to the parking spaces.

A Mercedes exited the parking area. Ali slipped under the door as it was closing. He found the elevator in a vestibule.

He took the elevator to the third floor. He could smell morning cooking in the hall and voices coming from the other apartment.

He went to unit 301, and tried the door. Maybe they leave it open, but of course … no.

Ali didn't know how to pick a lock, but he had seen a breaking and entering incident on television. He had picked up a long, heavy flat head screwdriver at a hardware store the day before.

He slipped the head of the screwdriver in the crack of the door jamb and leveraged it to the left, putting all his weight behind it. The door jamb compressed by an inch. The door popped open.

Ali crept inside, keeping a peeled eye for a camera. He didn't really think there would be one, but it was his first concern. A visual scan convinced him there weren't security cams. He proceeded into the living room. Two couches, a coffee table, a flatscreen TV on the wall. Bookcases. Framed paintings leaning against a wall. Stuff from Beirut, he assumed. Some art on the walls but not what he was looking for. He didn't bother with the teenagers' bedrooms, instead going right to the adults' bedroom. Nothing.

There was a fourth bedroom, an office. Desk, computer, printer, travel posters on the walls.

And right there on the wall behind the computer screen leaning against stacked volumes in a book case was the very thing he came for.

Ali took it in his hands. Death in the Reeds, the real object. He gazed at it for a few seconds, hardly believing it was really in his grip.

"Admire this later," he thought. "Gotta go."

Ali Zardari was out the door, down the stairs, and out on the street in a minute. He walked until he saw a taxi. He flagged it down.

"CDG," he said to the driver.

He scanned the streets as the driver pulled away. They passed his hotel. There was a suitcase and some clothes upstairs in his room. No matter. He didn't need it.

He slumped down in the back seat: there was Vartan Boustani walking back into the hotel.

Sharmouta! he cursed in Arabic. Will this guy follow me to San Francisco? Paris was one thing, but all the way back to the U.S.?

No way, he thought.

He punched redial on his phone. When she answered, he said, "Oh my god, I got it. I got it."

"You have it? Are you shitting me?"

"I have it in my hand right now."

"The real thing? Ivory, jewels?"

"I swear it's the real thing."

"I'm looking at the book. You see little rubies mounted in the reeds?"

"Yes."

"You see the lion on top of the boy, one paw holding the boy's neck?"

"Yes."

"The jaws on the boy's neck?"

"Yes. It's the real thing."

There was a pause on the other end.

"Hello?" Ali said.

Another slight pause, followed by an exhale. "Oh my god. Popped a panty creamer," Cass said, in a juddering whisper. "Baby, you're the best. The absolute fucking best,"

She called in another change to his ticket. Another thousand dollars.

Vartan Boustani realized the next day the rabbit had escaped. There was nothing for him to do but return to Beirut. He had to humiliate himself to his boss in the private suite on the fourth floor. He had blown scarce department funds on a longshot trip to Paris to follow a young American and returned home empty handed.

He was docked a week's pay and put in uniform for a month.

Vartan Boustani spent that month writing parking tickets and settling endless street squabbles

He seethed but he was helpless.

30

The flight from Heathrow to JFK was routine. Except for Pete Grand. He was in business class, stretched out, aggressively taking up space, making his seat mate extremely uncomfortable, gobbling up the meal, throwing down the drinks, his shoes slipped off, his socks stinking up the row.

He grabbed a cab to his hotel, depressed by the dreary neighborhoods of Queens. Owing to some traffic blockage on the parkway the driver chose surface streets, snaking through the threadbare borough of New York. Small shops, dejected houses, pockmarked roads, beaten down people. The diorama of the downtrodden of New York put him in a foul mood.

Plus it seemed to take forever. The sight of the approaching Midtown Tunnel was a welcome relief. Just a couple dozen blocks to his hotel.

At the Fitzgerald Hotel on Lexington he grumped his way up the elevator to his room, and pulled a black suit out of his bag to send off with the bellman for pressing. He purposely undertipped the bellman to see if he could get a rise out of the man. The fact the guy didn't make a peep annoyed him even more.

He flopped on the bed and drifted off in a fitful nap. Dreams bothered him. Anxiety filled nonsensical trips through familiar landscapes populated by the ignorant half-starving desperate people of his youth. Often he wondered why his dreams weren't more pleasant. After all, he'd escaped his personal dystopia. He travelled first class. He wore nice clothes. His bank account featured comas and zeroes. He may have been a thug, but he was a success.

He woke an hour later not the least refreshed. Dreams that came on during naps always had the effect of darkening an already bleak mood.

Pete stepped into the shower for a long soak. Dripping wet he ignored persistent knocking at the door. When he emerged from the bathroom toweled off, shaved and hair combed he found the suit was back, hanging on the inside of the door.

Pete Grand knew what was bothering him. He wanted to tell Gennady Markov to shove it up his ass. His erstwhile employer had been angry with him for tossing the two guys from high places in London. Pete much preferred that method of killing a man, as he tried to explain to Markov. As long as there weren't witnesses who saw him coming or going, it was fool proof. He was big enough to manhandle just about anybody. Fingerprints weren't an issue. A bloody knife or a gun weren't an issue. And he knew damn well it didn't bother Gennady Markov that two men died. The fucker killed people on a regular basis. Instead, Gennady said he was upset his plans to locate The Reeds were impeded by the death of the art dealer. Big fucking deal, Pete said. The little shit wasn't going to cooperate anyway.

But Markov was paranoid about Bart Trappani. The prosecutor was making inquiries to locate Markov, plus the Russian was afraid the two deaths would come back on him. He immediately cleared out of London for his dacha outside Moscow. Pete Grand was sent to New York to see Irwin Feinstein without so much as a thank you. Pete Grand risked his life for the sonofabitch and all he did was complain. And bug out at the first blip.

That little shit on the rooftop was planning to shoot him and the other little shit put him up to it. What was a guy to do?

Dressed and presentable, Pete Grand went down to the lobby bar and tossed down a couple vodkas to put him in the mood for meeting Feinstein.

The art guy's place was straight up Lexington seven blocks at 64th Street. Pete walked uptown surveying the New York of people who have money. Gyms. Wine shops. Restaurants. Ladies' fashions. Shoe stores. Furniture stores. Art framers.

Better than Queens.

He grunted at the protesting doorman at 133 64th Street, and took the elevator to the 11th floor. Two penthouses on that floor. He knocked on the door to #2.

It was a black maid who answered the door. Pete pushed by and parked himself in the foyer. "Irwin wants to see me," he said, knowing full well Feinstein had no idea who he was or that he would be coming. He handed the woman his card.

A few short minutes later Irwin Feinstein emerged from beyond the foyer with a confused look on his face. "Mr. Grand, you upset George downstairs. He's supposed to call up to announce guests."

Pete Grand shrugged. It didn't appear to Feinstein that he was much concerned about breaking house rules. "I'm sorry I can't place the name. Do I know you?"

Pete had been ordered to be on his best behavior with Irwin. But he could see into the interior of the spacious apartment and the windows beckoned. So high up. Eleven whole stories down to the New York City pavement. Tempting.

"Mr. Feinstein, Mr. Gennady Markov sent me to see you. I have some business to discuss."

Irwin recognized that name immediately. "Gennady. From The Hermitage. Very important fellow, come to my office Mr. Grand."

He led the way through the spacious apartment, first passing an ostentatious display of expensive furnishings in a living room, then down a hall that seemed like it might end at a bedroom or two, but the first room along the way was a library-office.

The art collector offered Pete a chair, and he took his place behind the desk.

Pete Grand was accustomed to these kinds of rooms: dark wood, green walls, art in gilt frames, shelves of important-looking books, dim lighting. Gennady Markov had one that was very similar. Pete was not particularly impressed.

"How is Gennady?"

"The usual," Pete said, dismissing the inquiry with an empty response. "He sent me to speak to you about a piece called Death in the Reeds. Do you know it?"

Feinstein was surprised. It was the second time the same piece had come up in just a few days. "I know both of them. The one in the British Museum and the one in the Iraq Museum."

"The Iraq one has been stolen."

Feinstein nodded, a sad expression on his face. "So I've heard. A tragedy."

"Gennady has an interest."

The older man knew what that meant. He knew who Gennady Markov's boss was. "I see," he said. "But Gennady knows I've been taken out of the game by the federal authorities. I doubt I'll be contacted by whoever has it."

"He wanted me to ask you who might be. I need to get in touch with the dealers who might be contacted by the seller."

"Pippy Sampson in London would have been the first on my list," Feinstein said, "but he appears to have committed suicide. Have no idea why. He was on top of the world."

"Sometimes it's a long fall from the top of the world." An almost imperceptible smirk crossed Pete Grand's face.

"Indeed," Feinstein said. He was growing a little uncomfortable with Pete Grand. The man was so big, the scar on his face was hard to look at, and he seemed to give off an air of menace Feinstein hadn't noticed at first. Might be good to move the man along.

"I'll make a list of the people I think are at the top of the dealer game," he said, extracting a sheet of stationary from a desk drawer. He began writing names, and consulting a leatherbound book for addresses, phone numbers.

"Oddly enough," he offered, while scribbling, "I got a call about a fake Reeds just a few days ago."

"Fake? What fake?" Grand asked, his interest come alive.

A little startled by his tone, Irwin Feinstein looked up from his list. "I'm sure it's nothing. A television producer in San Francisco called asking me to participate in her program. She said a person claimed to have The Reeds, and she wanted to expose the man as a fraud. She was certain whatever the man had was phony. She asked me to fly out to confirm it is a fake. I told her I could assure her on the spot whatever this person has, it's a fake."

Pete Grand thought the coincidence was too much. "How could you be certain it was a fake without looking at it?"

Irwin's gaze swiveled around the room as if the answer were as obvious as the books and the art and the furniture. "I'm absolutely positive whatever this charlatan is passing off as The Reeds is not the real thing." He handed Pete the list he'd completed. "What are the chances the object looted in Baghdad already turns up in San Francisco? Zero, I'd say."

Pete stared at the collector without reaching for the list. "There are lots of billionaires in San Francisco."

"I suppose so. Lots of billionaires in New York. And in London and Tokyo and Hong Kong too."

The answer didn't satisfy Pete Grand. He took the list, glanced it over, handed it back. "Add the name and phone number of the woman in San Francisco."

Irwin Feinstein laughed nervously. "I suppose I should ask her first. She said her project was in the confidential phase."

Pete Grand's face darkened and his hand continued to hold the list out for the collector to take back. "Just add the name and phone number. I'll keep her little fucking secret."

The nervous smile on Irwin Feinstein's face evaporated. He hesitated taking the list back.

"I said I'd keep her fucking secret," Pete repeated, in a hiss. "Just give me the name."

Pete Grand was thinking about the windows in the living room. He could pitch this little old man straight through that glass like he was flicking dust off his shoulder. But that asshole Markov made him promise not to.

Damn him.

After his guest left, Irwin remembered. A reporter called about The Reeds too. That pushy man who worked for the cable channel. TENN. Did a story about the Feds seizing his collection. People all over the world saw it.

"What a shithead," he thought.

31

The midnight blue '84 Mustang sounded like a fat man clearing his throat, a low rumble that said get out of my way. Mick backed it out of the garage at his father's place headed for the airport to pick up Grace Russell. It was her first visit since he'd left New York; they were going to see if they could pick up where they left off when things were good.

The long way seemed right. He had time.

He steered the Mustang onto Fulton Boulevard headed west along Golden Gate Park. At Mick's end the park peaks on a hill, bordered by a stone wall, a rise of green grass, stands of pines and eucalyptus trees. On the right the typical mix of San Francisco apartment houses: here and there a Victorian converted into a unit downstairs with another upstairs. Followed by a large apartment building with bay windows. Followed by a Chinese Box, which was once upon a time a Victorian, torn down, replaced by a square structure of zero architectural interest. As a generality these buildings were owned by legal arrivals from Taiwan and built by illegal arrivals from Ireland.

In the numbered avenues the road flattened out. On the park side the stone wall faded away, and a pedestrian could walk in across a narrow lawn onto foot paths through the trees. On the right side, here and there a block of single-family houses, stately structures with garage parking, driveways, and small lawns or gardens in front.

A fog bank hung over the beach in the distance, threatening to roll in and swallow the city.

Park Presidio Boulevard follows a sweeping S turn through Golden Gate Park and spills out on city streets at 19th Avenue. He jammed the gas uphill through the Sunset District to connect with Interstate 280 south to the airport.

This was the way to go for people who live west of Mt. Sutro in what San Franciscans called The Avenues. The route snakes around the back side of the city, and heads south to the airport on the ridge of hills that separates the south bay from the Pacific Ocean.

Definitely the long way but it gave him time to think. Time to think about Grace Russell. They had been off and on for eight years, ever since the end of the OJ trial. That was a long time for a relationship to not encounter a full commitment or a permanent break. But there was neither. They never got so far as a wedding, and they never so annoyed each other that there was a final breakup. But there was occasionally what felt like downtime in the relationship, particularly when distance was a factor, like when he was in New York.

Even when they'd been physically separated he couldn't shake the thought of her. And now that he was back on the West Coast, he suggested—and she agreed—that a weekend would be a good way to see what's what.

Plus there was that heartwarming burst of sympathy when he got involved in that shooting on the Embarcadero. He was moved that she grabbed the phone and called. He later checked. There were ten calls from her before he answered one.

Not that she was the only one who called on the day of the shooting. Other people came out of the woodwork too. David Stork called. That was good. He said the video of Mick defending his colleagues got Rod Wings rethinking the way he blew Mick up. David said Rod probably would need some time to hose down Elana Constantine. She was still an implacable enemy.

But all that was out of mind now. He was excited to see Gracie

Russell again.

At SFO he parked the Mustang in the one-hour zone in the parking structure and walked across a pedestrian bridge into Southwest's Terminal 1.

He waited outside security leaning up against a railing set against the windows. At what seemed like the right time a stream of travelers emerged from the "Do Not Enter" door. Dressed as if they'd come from L.A. Her Burbank flight.

Gracie came through the door looking to Mick like a million-dollar bill. He stepped forward to fold her into his arms. "I missed you," he whispered into her chestnut hair.

"I missed you too but you're the same old asshole," she said with a smile in her voice.

He held her out his arms extended. She never seemed to age. She still had that way of smiling with her eyes.

She was dressed in jeans and a sleeveless blouse, and slip-on shoes with a slight heel. "Why is it always so cold here?" she asked looking past him outside. Fog was draped over the San Bruno hills, seeming about to tumble down on the airport.

"It's a beautiful day, let's go," he said, picking up her bag.

They drove back to his house. His dad's house, actually. She'd never seen it before.

"This is nice," she said, pleasantly surprised. She glanced around at his living room, the leather couch, the wingback side chairs, the throw rug, the dark coffee table, the lamps, the framed art leaning against the walls. "We'll have to do something about this," she said. "Not terrible, but very guy."

"Feel free."

Mick called a cab. "We'll go to Scoma's for lunch." While they waited for the cab he put his dad's car away.

Scoma's is a sand dab and crab house on Fish Alley at Fisherman's Wharf, a favorite of celebrities and Forty-Niner stars. They had a nice lunch, then walked over to the Buena Vista for an Irish Coffee that stretched into two. Then they took another cab back to the house and spent the afternoon in the bedroom doing what bedrooms are for, and talking.

"I never thought of you as a killer," she said softly, running an index finger down the center of his chest to his belly button.

"Me either," he said, cupping her butt cheeks in both hands. A perfect fit.

They talked and napped and talked some more. It was a big lunch and neither was hungry when dinner time arrived, so they walked over to Geary Boulevard and sat in an Irish bar for a couple beers.

Then they walked back and got back in bed. It was like they had never been apart for the last few months. Neither wanted to talk about why the interruption happened. At least not yet. They slept soundly until eight the next morning when his phone was buzzing again.

"It's Kitty McManus," the voice said.

Mick winced. He didn't want to talk to her, but he answered the phone without thinking.

"Can you drop by? We have some important business to discuss."

"How important?"

"How important is it that you may be indicted soon?"

"Give me a couple hours."

He explained he had to drop in at his lawyer's for a quick meeting. "I'll go have the meeting, and then come pick you up and we'll head out for Healdsburg. Do some wineries."

"No, I'll just go with you. We can leave directly after. Save us some time."

She insisted.

They arrived at the former firehouse above Cole Valley half an hour earlier than Mick predicted. Kadija buzzed them in and they were escorted to Kitty McManus' office. Mick thought there was a little surprise in Kadija's demeanor, surprise at seeing Gracie with Mick.

Kitty McManus was also surprised, but covered it well. She introduced herself to Grace, and cocked an eye at her. "Do I know you?"

"Not that I know of," she said. Mick noticed Gracie icing up. He could almost feel her bristling. The smile in her eyes vanished.

The meeting turned out to be about very little having to do with a potential indictment. Kitty McManus said there was indeed a Grand Jury looking into the shooting, but she had no idea so far what exactly the DA had in mind.

She also had news that Saracenetti got word from New York that Mick was just suspended, not fired yet. So he would remain on the payroll for now.

"What's that mean?" Mick asked. Back on the payroll? He hadn't checked his bank account lately. He immediately wondered if

Veedub really was putting money in his account.

"He says it means he's heard you are following a story you were working when still actively on the staff, and he's claiming rights. He insists it's Channel 8's property and you should not feel you are free to shop it around."

That alarmed Mick. Who might have told him about the Orlando Diaz murder? Would Spike? He doubted it, but it was definitely a phone call for later.

They left as soon as courtesy allowed a quick wrap-up. Grace asked what was the story Channel 8 was claiming. Mick reluctantly told her about the Orlando Diaz murder that happened before his very eyes. She wanted to see the tape. They drove back to Mick's house and he showed her his VHS copy. Gracie was horrified. "How does this stuff happen to you and nobody else?" she asked.

"Luck, I guess," he replied, with a laugh.

"You think it's lucky you kill someone one day and two weeks later you witness another killing? That's not luck. That's some weird alignment of the stars, and you ought to be concerned about it."

She seemed to be more bothered about it all than he expected.

"What's wrong?" he asked. "Something is bugging you. It's not that tape."

She pursed her lips, and swirled the wine in her glass. "You're right," she said.

"Okay, what?"

She still seemed hesitant. "That lawyer. How did you get that lawyer?"

"Saracenetti arranged it. I think he's banging her. Trying to do her a favor. Evidently she is looking to run for some office, and wants some face-time on television. If she reps me, she gets on TV."

Gracie nodded as if she figured something like that. She sipped her wine.

"It's illegal as hell," he added. "Violates FCC rules and election law. Just by the way."

"I know her," she said.

Uh oh. "Really? You said you didn't."

"I didn't want to remind her."

"Okay. So tell me." A twist was coming. He could feel it.

She took a deep breath. "She was a rookie lawyer in L.A., DA's office. First job. Downtown in the Criminal Courthouse. The building where I work. It's a small town. Everybody knows everything. I saw her in action. You said she was bedding the boss?"

"Yes."

"Well, that figures. She beds everybody. She was bedding two or three lawyers in that building at any one time. She juggled them like she was a circus act. Do this one, do that one, move on and do another one. Then start all over and do some new ones. She was indiscriminate. Take her to dinner, she bangs you. Take her for a drive to the beach, she bangs you."

"Jesus. So everybody knew?"

"Maybe not everyone. But she talked a lot in the ladies' room and did not cover her tracks. Didn't care who knew. At one point she was doing both the DA, who was her boss, and a county supervisor, her boss' boss. It was a huge scandal."

"Compulsive sex?"

"A lot more calculating that it appears. Sure, some of those guys were just for sport, I guess. But she aimed at guys who had power, and the sex meant she had something on them. Something they wouldn't like to become known."

"Blackmail?"

"She expected a call back. She expected a favor if she asked. And if the guy tried to ghost her she could make him pay."

"How?"

"She went to a wedding and she managed to screw the groom before the bride had a chance."

Mick grimaced. "How?"

"She got him to show her the honeymoon suite. Same hotel as the reception. It's that wraparound dress. Belt comes off, nothing underneath. Ready for sex."

Mick tried to keep from blushing. "That's bold."

"That's all it takes. She invents new ways to bed guys, and you know what?"

"What?"

"She's aiming to fuck you too."

He shook his head no. "Look, I didn't know all that, but she set off my alarms. I can promise you that ain't happening."

"Better not, buddy. That better not happen."

Mick gave her a kiss. "Count on it. Not happening."

She gave him a stormy look, pursed her lips, and nodded. "Good," she said.

"By the way," Mick said, "how did you find out about the groom at the wedding?"

Grace Russell's eyes squeezed tight. "From the wife. A friend. She got sloshed over lunch and told me everything. When her husband didn't follow through with a favor your lawyer asked, word got back to the wife."

"What happened at the reception?"

"Yup. Your lawyer made sure to tell someone she knew would tell the wife."

"So the wife knew she was being played?"

"Yes. She knew McManus was taking revenge. Punishing her husband. But in the end she couldn't get over the image of her husband cheating on her within minutes of their wedding vows. She divorced him. Took everything the court would let her. He was pretty much ruined for a decade."

"Holy crap."

"Be thee hereby warned," she said.

Mick thought about that moment of temptation. When it would have been good to give Saracenetti's girlfriend the bone. Saved from myself when he showed up. What was that Saracenetti said about me, Mick thought, "You don't mind getting in over your head?"

Actually, Mick thought, I do mind.

32

Bone Hendrix got a call from Chowchilla. The warden there was a friend from years back. After listening for a couple minutes, he drove across town and knocked on Mick's door at the house on Paramount Terrace.

Mick and Grace were in the kitchen making a dinner of angel hair pomodoro and a salad. Mick glanced out the kitchen window and saw the SFPD Crown Vic.

"Shit. It's Bone Hendrix."

"Who's he?"

"The cop trying to run my ass into jail."

She laughed, gave him a pout. "That's not nice."

"No, it's not."

Buzzer buzzed. Mick went to the door. They both eyed each other. Mick spoke first. "Inspector Hendrix, what's up?"

Bone offered a handshake, which Mick found unusual, but he took it. "This is Inspector Nick Judge's house. The old man did right by you. Nice place."

"Thanks. What's up?"

"Can I come in?"

Mick didn't see any reason why not, though he wasn't exactly comfortable with it. After all, this was a hostile cop trying to jam him into a trial at the least, and maybe jail. "Should I have my lawyer here?"

Bone snorted a derisive laugh. "For starters you need to fire that ho."

Grace was at Mick's elbow. She liked what she heard. "Bring the gentleman in, Mick. He seems very perceptive."

She reached out to shake Bone's hand. "I'm Grace Russell."

"Bonaparte Hendrix. People call me Bone."

Mick brought Hendrix into the living room, offered him a seat. "Where's your shadow?" he asked, meaning Billy Norton.

"Special assignment," Bone said with a shrug, as if it didn't matter. "I kinda like working solo."

Mick understood. His dad used to say that too. "So you here to take me downtown again, Inspector?"

Bone shook his head. "Naww." He looked around the room approvingly. "Nice place, real nice." He looked Mick in the eye. "Got a beer?"

That surprised Mick. "So this isn't official?"

Bone shook his head again. "I was never here."

"Okay then, a beer it is."

Mick set three Anchor Steams on the coffee table, along with tumblers.

The three sat looking at each other. Mick and Grace on the couch together, Bone in a wingback.

Bone took a long sip of the beer, smacked his lips. "Local beer is the best," he said.

Mick was very confused. "So what's up, Inspector?" he asked for the third time.

"Like I said, I was never here. Whatever you tell me isn't on the record. I'm just curious about some things."

"You sure about that?"

"Positive. Word of honor."

Mick didn't know what to think. He knew cops tricking suspects was completely legal, but Bone seemed sincere. Grace nodded 'go ahead', so he decided to take a chance. "Okay. Like what?"

"You said you didn't know Ladarius Rasheed." The young man Mick killed at the Embarcadero.

Mick nodded. "I really don't. Never saw the guy before."

"So it would surprise you if the DA made a case that you did know Ladarius Rasheed and you and Rasheed had a serious beef?"

"I'd be shocked. You have to know somebody to have a beef, don't you?"

Bone shook his head no. "Not necessarily. People shoot each other over a road rage incident and never knew each other."

"Okay I got that. But I never had any contact with the guy."

"You know a stripper from the Mitchell Brothers named Dani Charm?"

Red rose in Mick's face. "Dani Charm? That sounds like a porn star."

"Real name Celeste Johnson. Porn star, hooker, pole dancer. She got it all."

"Bone, look, I don't hang at the Mitchell's, never did. And besides I heard those girls are all lesbians, and my contacts with lesbians are very few."

"You mean aside from your friend Cass."

"She's a lesbian in name only. Everybody knows that."

"What?" Grace asked. "What's that mean?"

"I'll explain later," Mick said to her. Back to Bone. "What you driving at?"

"So if a former nude dancer at the Mitchell's were to show up before the Grand Jury to testify that you and Ladarius Rasheed knew each other and you had a hostile relationship, you'd be surprised."

"I'd be blown away. I don't know either of those people."

"When was the last time you were at the Mitchell Brothers?"

Mick shook his head thinking. "Fifteen years ago? Something like that."

"Just hanging out?"

"No. Some event."

"Their Christmas party?"

"Probably. Something like that. Every politician except Feinstein was there. Some big party they were having for newsies and city officials, place was packed."

Bone nodded. "Interesting. Dani Charm was ten years old."

"What's going on?"

Bone Hendrix took another long pull on his beer, draining it. "I have to go. Nice chatting with you. Appreciate the beer."

"You're not going to tell me what's going on?"

"Official business. Someday we'll have another beer and I may be able to go into it then."

Bone shook Grace's hand again. "Very nice to meet you, young lady. Please try to keep your friend here out of trouble. He needs the help." His manner was courtly and cordial.

"One more thing," he said turning back to Mick. "I'm sorry we got off on the wrong foot. I know you think your dad didn't kill himself. I think you're wrong, but I'll keep it in mind. If anything comes up, I promise to run it down."

Surprised, Mick took it as a sincere promise. "Thanks. I appreciate that."

Bone started to go, but stopped again. "One more thing," he said again.

"Yes?"

"I'm aware of what happened at Vacaville. Not my case, but curious. What were you talking to Orlando about?"

"You know Orlando?"

"Of course. He was one of ours."

Mick sucked in a breath. "Well, I was talking to him about how he managed to not get sent to Pelican Bay."

"This would be your 'snitch factory' theory about the DA?"

"Yes."

"And you saw him murdered?"

"It's on tape. But I can't show you that tape."

"I don't want to see it. I've seen lots of guys killed. But just for the record that interview was essentially about our District Attorney?"

Mick hesitated. "Yeah. I'm looking into the DA, but I haven't got to the point where I can say positively she's guilty of what I suspect."

Bone Hendrix took it in with an entirely non-committal dog face, his big floppy jowls and dead eyes not giving anything away.

"I'll see you around," he said to Mick.

And he left.

"That guy is as mean as a junkyard dog," Mick said, a couple minutes after closing the door, waiting to hear the door slam on the Crown Vic. "That little episode was totally out of character."

"Why?"

"He's usually brutal with me. That was weird."

Grace looked him in the eye. "You don't know Dani Charm?"

"No. Never heard of her. No idea."

"And you don't know Ladarius Rasheed?"

"Other than shooting him, no."

"And you can't figure out what's going on?"

Mick frowned. "Sure. The DA is trying to make a case that I know Ladarius Rasheed and had a reason to want to kill him. And evidently this Dani Charm is willing to say she knows that's true. And it's probably because the DA can smell I'm on her trail."

"Precisely," Grace nodded. "And what else?"

"You tell me."

"Remember I work in a court house."

"Yes. I remember."

"That's a cop who knows that people are getting ready to lie in front a Grand Jury and he doesn't like it. You got a cop investigating someone, maybe another cop, and judging by that last exchange maybe investigating the DA as well. That's what's going on."

Billy Norton might be hooked up with Jean Washington, Mick thought, because Bone came alone. Maybe Bone is on to them. "That would be good."

"He also said you should fire that lawyer. I agree with him."

"You mean fire that 'ho'?"

"Exactly."

Mick gave her a guilty kiss on the forehead. "I'll get right on that."

"And who is that lesbian who's not?"

"Oh, right. Cass. Have I mentioned her before?"

Grace furrowed her forehead and narrowed her eyes. "You have not."

Mick sighed. "I guess it always seemed too complicated for a phone conversation."

"I'm right here. You can start now."

There was no putting it off any longer. Mick took a deep breath. "Her name is Cassandra Papadopoulos. TV name Cass Papadop."

He stopped. "This might take a while. You sure you want the tale right now?"

"I'm positive. Get on with it."

"Okay." And Mick started at the beginning. "I met Cass twenty years ago …"

33

Bart Trappani's return to his position as an Assistant United States Attorney for the Southern District of New York was a mixed blessing. He'd been in Iraq for weeks, away from his family, and he missed his real work. But he was also wracked with guilt for getting out and leaving his team to finish the job. Not to mention the nagging question of Death in the Reeds.

Trappani handled a variety of cases for the Unites States government, but his passion was art fraud, art counterfeiting, and art theft. In his office on the second floor of the Silvio J. Mollo building at 1 St. Andrews Place in lower Manhattan he kept high resolution photo copies of all the works of art that had been stolen in recent years and were still missing.

Holding a place of prominence pinned to a cork bulletin board in the midst of so many other missing treasures was Death in the Reeds, the piece Bart Trappani ruefully referred to as "another one that got away."

Bart Trappani usually got lunch from a to-go place, a sandwich from Pret A Manger down in the square. Lunch at his desk gave him time to stare at the Reeds and think.

The name Irwin Feinstein was on his mind. He'd put Irwin under house arrest, and seized his entire collection of illegally obtained antiquities just a few years earlier. Irwin hated Trappani, but the only reason he was not sitting in a cell or day room in Danbury, Connecticut or Allenwood, Pennsylvania was Bart Trappani. The prosecutor needed Irwin as a reliable source, and holding "remand" to a federal facility over his head kept Irwin cooperative.

The rogue art collector grudgingly agreed to meet Trappani, but asked that the meet occur somewhere other than his home. "My wife still hates you," he explained. "And I can promise she will make our meeting ugly if it's here."

At times like this Bart Trappani regretted not putting Miriam Feinstein away. She certainly deserved it. Trappani was positive she was the driving force behind the acquisition of the illegal pieces. Her husband gallantly took the fall.

They met across Lexington from Irwin Feinstein's building at Callahan's Steak House. Bart Trappani loved the place and might have gone there for dinner anyway. Set in a narrow building, the restaurant bar was up front at the door, toward the back four black channel-quilted vinyl booths on each side, and a row of four tables between, all dressed in red tablecloths, white napkins and paper place mats. The place was old school, a throwback to 1952, and the only change in fifty-one years was the prices.

Trappani was parked in a booth having a gin and tonic when Irwin Feinstein slipped in. "You know it's kind of embarrassing meeting you here. This is my neighborhood place. When people see you, they'll think I'm in trouble again."

"Nonsense," Trappani smiled. "We'll have an entirely friendly meeting and appear to be just like everyone else here. Matt Lauer is over there with Bill Bratton. Nobody pays attention, and nobody would say anything. It's why I like the place."

Irwin smiled but it was forced, grim. "Fine. It's a friendly dinner. I'm getting the steak."

"I'm buying. Get whatever."

The owner and waitress, Mo Roarke, took their orders with a hurried "you guys ready?" and set down Irwin's first drink and Bart's second.

"So what do you want?"

Trappani played with the straw in his drink, and grimaced. "I need an honest answer."

Irwin Feinstein nodded. "As always. I don't hold anything back."

"Okay then. What have you heard about Death in the Reeds?"

"Other than the fact it was it was stolen in Baghdad? Nothing." His voice trailed off.

Trappani sensed there was more. "But … what?"

"Well, you are the fourth person who has asked me about it in the last week, which I think is a little strange."

"Who were the others?"

Irwin Feinstein started with a sigh, like he was weary of retelling the story. "First a television producer wanting me to act as an authenticator in a trap she was setting for a fraudster, who claimed to have it. But she was positive he was trying to sell a fake. She asked me to fly to San Francisco for that."

"Okay, and the other others?"

"A big scary man came to my apartment. Barged in, actually. Asked if I had heard of the piece coming up for sale. I told him what I'm telling you. No, I haven't heard about it coming to market.

Regrettably, I mentioned the television thing."

"Tell me about the man."

"Six five, I'd guess," he said, raising his hand above his head. "Guessing two hundred fifty pounds. Very big man. A huge scar running from just under his left eye to his jawline. Nasty looking thing. Very abrupt. Oh, and he said he was representing Gennady Markov."

Now Bart Trappani sat up and focused. "Markov works for the Russian President, his personal art collector, right?"

"That's what people say. I don't know that for a fact."

I do, Trappani thought to himself. He'd long believed much of what went missing around the world wound up in the possession of the Russian President. And that would explain the report he got from his friend at Cent Com that Russian Federation helicopters were cleared through American airspace over Baghdad the first night of the bombing campaign.

"You said there were four."

"I almost forgot one. A week ago that annoying reporter from TENN called asking what I knew about The Reeds. I told him it was jail bait and I hung up."

Trappani knew who he meant. Mickey Judge. Was at TENN. Something happened. "Did he say where he was?"

"San Francisco."

Two calls from San Francisco. Couldn't be coincidence. "We're going to need to go over to your apartment and get those names. Miriam can just stare daggers at me."

Mo arrived with their steaks. They both asked for another drink.

Irwin waited until she walked away. "As a matter of fact, anticipating you might be asking about The Reeds, I prepared a note with both names and phone numbers." He pulled a folded piece of stationary from his inside jacket pocket.

Bart Trappani opened the note. Cass Papadop and Peter Grand, and phone numbers. The reporter wasn't on the list. No matter. He'd find him.

"And you told this Peter Grand about her?"

"Yes I did," Irwin Fink said, sheepishly. "When he heard what she had called about he demanded her name and number."

Bart Trappani thought about the information from Irwin through dinner. After they parted he stood on Lexington Avenue in front of Callahan's and made a couple phone calls.

He learned the Brits had put out a request to pick up Pete Grand, suspected of two gruesome deaths in London. He evidently had a predilection for throwing people to their death from buildings. He was known to have flown from Heathrow to JFK before the London police got a BOLO on him. With another call to another FBI office he also learned that a Peter Grand had boarded a flight from Newark to San Francisco.

"Holy shit," he thought. "That woman is in danger."

He booked himself aboard the first flight from JFK to SFO the next morning.

He didn't give much thought to the reporter being in danger too.

34

The Saint Francis Yacht Club sits on a spit of land jutting into the windswept San Francisco Bay. From the bar Mick had a stunning view of The Golden Gate Bridge, the site of a long-abandoned airstrip called Crissy Field, the Civil War era Fort Point, the Marin headlands and casting his gaze eastward, to Angel Island and Alcatraz. And, of course, a full view of the bay itself.

An oozing blanket of fog was pouring over the towers of the bridge into the bay, a breeze kicking up whitecaps. The ferries to Marin splashed through the swells. It was seven in the morning. Mickey Judge was warming his hands around a cup of hot black coffee, perched on a bar stool enjoying the view when Cass Papadop snuck up behind him and startled him with a jab to his side. "Don't look so gloomy," she warned. "You'll ruin my reputation here."

Recoiling from her foolishness, his coffee still steaming, he took a sip and gave her a suspicious side eye. "What's your reputation?"

"Fun." She grinned impishly. "Always with fun people. You look like you don't belong."

"I don't belong," Mick said, glancing around at the people and the furnishings that meant money. "They only let me in because I threw your name around."

"See? Don't ruin my reputation."

"Okay, right," he said. "What's this emergency all about?"

She brushed back her wind rustled bronze hair, and signaled for a coffee of her own, pointing at Mick's cup. "A bit of Frangelico, too," she added to the bartender.

At tables scattered around the bar white haired men read the Chronicle and the Wall Street Journal, sipped coffee and kept a wary eye on CNBC on the bar TV.

Cass settled her rear end on the stool and checked her makeup with a compact mirror she fished out of her purse.

"Dude, I need a big favor," she said in a soft, conspiratorial voice.

"How big?"

"Seven hours."

Mick winced. "In your world seven is nine, maybe ten. The whole damn day. What's it all about?"

"I have to meet a plane and I don't have time to do this, so I'm asking you. Pretty please. Please go do this errand for me."

"What takes seven hours? Or nine?"

"I need you to go to Big Sur."

Mick's face sagged. "Fergawdsakes. That's at least three hours down …"

"Two hours forty-five. I've done it," she interrupted. "I like to go to the Ventana Inn sometimes."

Something in the way she said "I like to go" made him think it was one of the places she saved for a sex getaway.

He gave her his peeved look and continued. "And three hours back. Plus you're figuring an hour there, but whatever this is will probably take two."

Disgusted being asked to blow an entire day, he pictured the drive. Down the 280 to Silicon Valley, take that miserable climb on Highway 17 over the mountain to Santa Cruz. Then a long boring haul farther south across the Gilroy flats to Moss Landing, then Fort Ord, finally into Monterey. After that, press on farther to Big Sur. An honest-to-god haul. "I figure stop for gas, take a piss, get lunch, add another couple of hours. What's this all about?"

She gave him the babycakes look. Slightly pouty, eyes softening, frowny forehead. "I need you to go see Babu Chakrabarti for me."

Mick reacted sharply. "That asshole? What are you doing with him? He should be in jail. Beating up women is a crime in the U.S. even for a dickhead Hindu billionaire."

Cass nodded. "I know, I know, I know. I won't be in a room alone with him, I know."

"So the answer is no. No interest in seeing Babu Chakrabarti, the slime. What a prick. Bush should deport him."

"Bush is trying," she said. "And Babu might get kicked out soon. But I need to get something straight with him before he gets the boot."

The late call the previous evening rang in his ears. Bobby Vargas-Watson urging him "Stick with her. God only knows what she's up to. Don't let her go rogue on me."

"Not okay, but let's hear it. What's your deal with slimeball?"

Cass took a deep breath and a long pull on her coffee Frangelico. "Look, he really wants that thing I was telling you about, the antiquity?"

Almost spitting out his coffee, Mick recoiled. "That illegal as shit deal? You're still chasing that?"

"Honest, I wasn't," she lied. "But he's a major collector. Major. Long story about how he connected me to the thing, but he called. Maybe he talked to Simon Moss."

"Who?"

"My art dealer friend. I asked him to confirm what you told me." She nodded up and down. "And he did confirm just what you said."

"You think he told slimeball about you?"

"I guess. I just need to find out what he's willing to pay. He wouldn't discuss it on the phone."

"Why would he talk to me?" Mick asked, incredulous she was still pursuing when he told her to back off and she seemed to have agreed. "I hate the little Hindu prick. He can go fuck himself."

Cass got very serious. "We're talking about a two hundred, maybe three-hundred-million-dollar deal here. The commission is twenty, thirty million. I need to know if he's real."

Mick looked into her eyes hard. He could see she was dead serious, and she wasn't going to just let it go with a lecture from him. He made up his mind in an instant. He had to make certain Babu Chakrabarti wouldn't touch this deal under any circumstances. He would make the trip to kill the deal. It wasn't just a favor to Bobby Vargas-Watson. It was what he had to do to protect a reckless friend who was getting in way over her head.

"Where is he?"

"The Post Ranch in Big Sur."

"I better get going," Mick said, sliding off his stool and heading for the door.

But he stopped short, and turned back to her.

"Why is it you can't go, again?"

Cass Papadop's "tell" when she was lying was a flicker in the eye. But this time the twinge was caused by the actual truth. "I have to pick up a friend at the airport. Very important I be there."

Mick spotted the telltale tic, but had no idea what it was about.

35

What Mickey Judge did not know was that Pete Grand had a massive head start. While Mick was meeting with Cass, Pete Grand was already sitting down for a breakfast meeting with Babu Chakrabarti at the Sierra Mar restaurant at the Post Ranch Inn in Big Sur.

Pete Grand had landed at SFO the previous afternoon and immediately got a call from Gennady Markov. He was instructed to go directly to Big Sur to meet a man Markov knew well, who claimed to have The Reeds and was willing to make a deal with Markov quickly.

Pete Grand fully expected to be handed the piece, at which point he would drive back to SFO and return to New York immediately.

But the entire exercise had not gone well. By the time he got the rental car and headed south, it was starting to get dark. Driving the twisting switch backs on Highway 17 over the Santa Cruz Mountains in the dark was miserable, and that wasn't the end of it. From Monterey to Big Sur along a narrow coastal road, focusing on whatever his headlights illuminated left him with an agonizing headache. He got into Big Sur and found The Ventana Inn about midnight, hungry and exhausted. Any chance of getting something to eat had long passed, and he spent a fitful night growing angrier each hour he jerked awake in the dark.

At quarter to seven in the morning Pete Grand was already at a table at the meeting place, the Sierra Mar restaurant. While waiting for a server, he looked out over the cloudbank that crowded against the lip of the cliffside, obscuring any glimpse of the ocean below.

The place was empty, save for one couple two tables over. Evidently the vacationers who would later jam the restaurant didn't tend to have early breakfast meetings.

A waiter appeared. "How far down is that?" Pete asked pointing to the white, puffy blanket of clouds.

"Long way, man. It might be three hundred feet," the gender-obscure server said. "Maybe more. That's what people say. It's a long way down, and the rocks are brutal," he said with a shiver. "Surf crashes night and day. Just looking over the side gives me the creeps."

Pete looked the waiter over. A man bun. Tats in Chinese characters. Some kind of piercing through his lip. Another disgusting degenerate as far as Pete was concerned. He ordered a pot of black coffee. "Plus a cheese and onion omelet with a side of bacon, hash browns, and sourdough toast," he rattled off.

The man bun slumped his shoulders. "I'm sorry sir, the chef does not prepare American ordinaire," the waiter said, handing Pete a menu with a foppish wave of his thin arm.

Pete took an instant dislike. There was just something about this boy-girl waiter that made Pete want to throw him. He glanced over at the balustrade separating the dining area from the long drop to the ocean.

Pete eyed the menu then back to the balustrade and the fogbank that stretched to the distance. So many temptations in life.

"Sir, may I suggest the crepes stuffed with seafood? Or the quiche with seafood? The crepes are handmade by the chef and the seafood is excellent as you would expect. Considering where we are."

"Your cook doesn't know how to make an omelet? Your cook doesn't know how to fry bacon? You don't have sourdough bread?"

The waiter, thin, feminine, tattooed, pierced, made a sucking lemons expression. "The chef is world famous. His dishes are world famous."

"I want eggs, bacon, hash browns, sourdough toast. Tell him."

That uncomfortable encounter was a prelude. Then Babu Chakrabarti showed up, and Pete immediately confirmed a suspicion he held the entire torturous drive down from SFO: this was a man who represented everything he hated.

First, Chakrabarti was a red dot Hindu Indian, and Pete hated Indians. They were everywhere in Europe and Pete couldn't understand why they just didn't stay in India with all the rest of them.

Second, he was small, the kind of small that imparts a sense of invulnerability. "Punch me, you will kill me and spend the rest of your life in prison." And Pete hated small men for that. They were annoying and full of themselves.

Third, Babu spoke with the lilting Indian accent Pete absolutely despised.

Fourth, he was a billionaire and Pete hated the smug condescension that came with several billion dollars.

And lastly, the loathsome waiter returned with a breakfast of quiche something that was about the size of a cocktail napkin while Pete was looking for something that would overflow the plate.

He was already in a terrible mood when Babu Chakrabarti looked him in the eye and asked if he was Gennady Markov's "boy."

"Excuse me?" Pete asked, setting his fork back on the table and folding his hands together to restrain himself.

"It's a simple question," Babu said, settling himself back in his seat, and giving Pete a condescending glance. "Are you his go-fer, as the Americans call it, the guy who picks things up for the boss?" Chakrabarti smiled as he slowly spoke the words, making certain the insult was taken for what it was.

"Maybe we should just get down to business," Pete said, trying to keep a lid on his temper. "I am here to take possession of the object Mr. Markov is purchasing from you. Do you have it with you?"

Chakrabarti laughed, blasting Pete with his nasty curry breath. "Of course I didn't bring it to breakfast." He used a napkin to wipe his thin moustache smooth. He played with a fork, dinging it on a coffee cup absentmindedly, oblivious to the annoying sound. "Why am I seeing you instead of Gennady?"

Pete Grand lowered his head to Chakrabarti's level, and stared into the man's eyes with a hard gaze. "Let's not play games. You called Markov. You said you had the object. You two came up with a price and a method to transfer funds. I am here to secure the object. Where is it?"

Babu made a wrinkly nose and shook his head. "It might be here today. You might have to spend another night."

Pete Grand sat back and gave the little man a murderous stare. "I need to get something straight. Do you have the object or not?"

"Well, I don't have it at this instant. But I will have it later."

"How much later?"

Babu shrugged. "I don't know exactly. It's coming in from Paris. My contact will phone me sometime today."

"You told Markov you had it."

"I'm sure Gennady misunderstood. I told him I am securing the object."

"Markov wouldn't have sent me down here on this drive from hell if you didn't have it. You told him you had it."

Babu shrugged. "I may have left him that impression, but no matter now. You're here. You can wait. I will have it later."

Pete picked up the nasty little plate with the obnoxious little quiche thing, and set it on the adjacent table. He glanced back at the table with the only other guests in the restaurant.

"Excuse me," he addressed the couple. "Would you mind taking some air for a moment? I need a very private moment with my friend here."

The man looked over at Pete and cocked his head. "We're almost done with our breakfast. We'll leave you to your privacy in a moment."

"Madame, perhaps I should speak to you," Pete said, turning to the woman. "Perhaps you might persuade your husband it would be best to do as I ask."

The couple looked to be in their fifties. The woman was well past the age of senseless defiance.

"Excuse us," she said, rising. "Devon, let's take a walk as the gentleman suggests." She turned back to Pete. "Let's say we come back for a second cup of coffee in fifteen minutes or so? Will that suffice?"

"I hope you won't mind if I pick up your tab."

"Decent of you," she said, with icy sarcasm. And they left for a stroll along the cliffside path.

"What the hell was that all about?" Babu asked with a sneer.

Pete turned away from the couple as they glided out the door in unmistakable haste. His attention back on Chakrabarti, he leaned forward, elbows on the table. "I read up on you. Aren't you the little prick who beats up his girlfriends and then buys his way out of jail?"

Chakrabarti's expression changed instantly. Glowering, he spat his words at Pete. "Go-fer boys don't talk to me like that," he said, pulling his phone out of his pocket. "Let's get Gennady on the line and get your ass fired and sent back to whatever eastern European shithole you crawled out of."

Pete watched him pull his phone from a jacket pocket. He snatched it out of Babu's hand like a gecko snaps a fly out of the air.

"Hey," Babu objected. "Don't be an ass. Give it back."

Pete flipped it open and punched the contact list. It looked like this was the little shithead's main phone. "So when the call comes in, I will be the one answering," he said.

"You can't do that, you overfed bull. Hand it back."

Pete shook his head. "I don't think so. I don't need you to get hold of the object. I just need your phone."

"I'll have you flogged for this."

"No, I don't think so," Pete said, standing. "Do you know why I don't give a shit?"

"Because you're just a hired thug."

"You should watch your mouth."

"It's you who needs to watch his mouth."

Pete towered over the small man like the town lynching oak. "Is that so?"

He grabbed Chakrabarti by the collar, yanking him to his feet. "Maybe it's time for your breath to cease fouling the air."

Stunned and suddenly afraid, Babu sputtered something more or less like English.

Whatever it was, Pete ignored it.

"I sometimes like to throw people from great heights," Pete hissed into the little man's face. "Just to hear the thud when they hit the ground. But I've changed my mind in your case. I want to look into your eyes as you realize it's over."

Babu's eyes bulged as Pete lifted him off his feet by his neck and squeezed hard.

"Much more personal this way, Babu." He pronounced the name Ba-booo.

The little man flailed his arms and legs in the air. His eyes strained at their sockets.

Chakrabarti tried to make a sound but nothing would come out. Not even a muffled cry. "Try for a breath," Pete whispered in his face. His grip strangled the slightest wisp of air. "Keep trying."

Pete Grand's intention was to squeeze the Indian's windpipe shut, but holding him off his feet by his neck changed things. Inadvertently Pete broke Babu's spine at the base of his skull. Pete Grand actually heard the neck snap.

"Well, shit," Pete mumbled. "A neck like a chicken."

The little man's flailing ceased. He hung limp in Pete Grand's grasp, his death mask set forever in agonized pleading.

"You're a miserable little prick and I really don't like being insulted by miserable little pricks," Pete added to the deceased's face.

Babu's head lolled to one side. Pete Grand lifted him higher and put the small man's chest to his ear. No heartbeat.

"Too quick," Pete muttered. "Thought you'd last a little longer."

Old ways die hard with Pete Grand. The long fall called. He walked to the balustrade and stood Babu on the edge on dead legs. He tested the body. Could it stand? No. Not even a second? Definitely not.

He let loose his grip.

Out on the walking path Devon Johnston and his wife were whispering to each other about the threatening man they'd left behind. They were thinking maybe they shouldn't bother to return.

Melinda Johnston suddenly let out a scream. Her husband turned just in time to catch a glimpse of something tumbling down the cliffside into the fog.

"Oh my god," she said. "That was the little man. He just went down."

Inside the restaurant Pete Grand put a hundred-dollar bill on his table and another on the Johnston's table.

Slipping Babu's phone into his pocket, Pete walked toward the door. Just then the waiter returned to the dining patio.

"My tablemate ran off," Pete said as he passed. "Don't know what got into him."

Mickey Judge arrived at the Post Ranch Inn to find massed law enforcement and search and rescue vehicles, and dozens of uniformed men and women standing around waiting for something.

His SFPD press pass got him a Monterey County deputy who was acting as the Public Information Officer.

"What ya got?" Mick asked.

"Not quite sure. Waiting for the fog to burn off so the chopper can get down there. Evidently a body."

"Somebody fall?"

"Maybe jumped. Big guy and little guy at breakfast. Customers at next table say the big guy asked them to leave. Then they saw the little guy fall over the edge. It's a long way down."

"Survivable?"

The PIO shook his head no. "It's a slope and it has brush in some places, but the body could be all the way down in the rocks. And who knows? The surf could have pulled him out to sea. Anything's possible."

"I need to phone it in. Got a name on the vic?"

"No, not yet," the deputy said, but there was a hesitation in his voice that Mick had heard plenty of times before. A verbal cue that says "ask another."

"People around here know him?"

The PIO nodded. "We're hearing that. Might be an obnoxious little billionaire prick nobody around here likes."

On a hunch Mick asked, "Babu Chakrabarti?"

The deputy laughed. "Well, he is an obnoxious little billionaire prick nobody around here likes much. That I can confirm, but please don't quote me."

"But is it him?"

"Look, same old deal. Can't speculate on the ID until we recover the body and I can't officially confirm anything, but yeah, that's what we're hearing."

"Was he with somebody?"

"Yeah. A big guy. Witness said maybe six feet five."

"Did the big guy throw him overboard?"

The deputy shrugged. "Might be something like that. Who knows? No witness to what happened."

"Did you get video? Anyone get eyes on the car he was driving?"

The deputy wagged his head no. "So far nothing. The restaurant has rich Silicon Valley guests who don't like dining under security cameras. The security cameras outside don't cover the parking lot. Haven't found anyone yet who saw the vehicle."

Mick didn't wait around for the body to be recovered. He hustled back onto the highway, back to the city. He had a sudden jolt that maybe the big man who killed Chakrabarti was after the same thing Cass wanted. Maybe she was in danger.

36

The Audi idled at the curb in front of SFO's International Terminal 1. Cass Papadop had already been chased off by the parking cops twice. But she was back again, keeping an anxious eye on the passenger exit. Ali Zardari should be walking out any moment. They had spoken by cell phone while he stood in line at customs. Face to face with the customs agent next.

Her phone buzzed. Anticipating it was Ali, she hit the talk button and blurted out, "Did you get through?"

On the other end of the call Mick pinched his face, wondering what she was talking about. "Yeah I got through. I got far enough to learn your guy is dead."

Cass, confused for a moment, soon quickly realized it was Mick on the line not Ali.

"What? Who's dead?"

"It looks like Babu Chakrabarti. Your boy."

"Wait. What happened?"

"Not really sure, but the cop said it appeared he was in the patio dining area with a big guy. And the big guy might have pitched him over the side. It's three hundred feet to the surf."

"Holy shit."

"Yes, holy shit. I think you might be in trouble."

"Trouble? Me? How?"

"Because maybe the guy who tossed Chakrabarti was after the same thing you were after. Against my best advice, by the way."

Cass was super-confused now. And not quite believing what she was hearing. "Are you sure Babu is dead?"

"Not a thousand percent. But the cops there think the guy who went over the side was him. They said the restaurant staff knew him. Say it was him."

"But no body?"

"Not when I left."

"Well fuck I'm just going to call. You're not even sure it's him."

"There's a big guy on the loose. Six five they said. Picked that little prick up like the sack of shit he is and threw him into the cloud bank."

"Fuck. I'm calling. Bye."

Cass punched the call off, and scrolled through her contacts. She punched up Babu's number and hit dial. The phone rang several times and a strange voice picked up.

"Hi I need to reach Babu. Is he there?"

"He's indisposed. But I can take a message for him."

There was something in the voice. A faintly Italian accent. A malevolent tone that raised her suspicions.

"Are you the six five guy?" she asked.

"People say that about me," the voice said.

Cass hung up. She didn't like this one bit.

She glanced up and saw Ali emerging from the International Terminal. He looked beat down, exhausted, dragging, but he lit up when he saw her.

Whatever misgivings she had about Mick's report and the phone call to Babu's number, she let slip to the back of her mind as the handsome young Ali tossed his backpack into the back seat and slid into the seat beside her.

Cass stared at him trying to control the electric surge in her chest. He smiled at her, but said nothing, waiting for her to speak.

"Did you do what I told you?"

He nodded. "I put it in my shirt pocket."

"And did they check your shirt pocket?"

He shook his head no. "I said I was traveling to recover my brother's remains who died in a car accident in Beirut. The officer asked me questions and let me through."

She felt like she couldn't breathe. "So … you have it?"

He patted his chest, the shirt pocket, nodded. Then he broke into a huge smile. "I have it."

Cass felt a huge welling up of relief. "Oh god, let me see."

Ali reached beneath his sweater, and pulled the object from his shirt pocket. He held it flat in his hand, offering it to her.

Cass took Death in the Reeds in her hands as if it was a holy object. She looked at it closely, running her fingers over the figure of the lioness, over the figure of the boy, over the reeds in the background. "Exquisite," she said softly. "Just exquisite."

Rising before her eyes was a new bank statement, one that featured a line of eight figures. She shivered at the thought she might have an orgasm on the spot.

She opened the driver's door. "You drive. I want to hold this."

Ali went around and got in the driver's seat.

Cass was oblivious to the trip into the city. She held The Reeds in her lap and just stared at it, enraptured. It was the most beautiful thing she'd ever seen that wasn't a young man with a rippling chest and washboard abs.

When he got off the freeway at 6th street, Ali didn't know where to go. "Take this all the way across Market to Taylor and then up the hill."

They pulled into the parking lot at her apartment building, 999 Green Street.

Clutching the object to her breast, they took the elevator to the 22nd floor. Her apartment had the red door. "I thought you lived at the DA's house," Ali asked, cautiously. He was flummoxed about her gay marriage. He didn't understand. Didn't quite believe it.

"I never got rid of my own place. Sometimes you need to have a place to escape."

She placed The Reeds on the dining table and stood over it looking at it as if it were a message directly from three thousand years in the past. "It's just amazing," she said again and again.

Ali stood beside her, not quite knowing what to do. In his eyes she was still the most beautiful woman he'd ever seen. He couldn't believe he drove her car. He couldn't believe he was in her apartment, her own secret hideaway.

She looked up at him and shook her head. "I can't believe you pulled it off," she said softly. "It's just fucking amazing."

He felt his face reddening. On top of everything else she was amazed by him. He didn't know what to say.

But he didn't have a chance to dream up anything to say. She took him in her arms and kissed him full on the mouth. He held her pressed against him. She could feel his erection.

She sighed as she put her hand on his pants. "So here we are," she said with an intimate grin and a soft voice. "Let's put this to good use," she said.

She took his hand and led him to the bedroom.

Cass didn't bed the boy simply as a thank you. Though there certainly was an element of gratitude. Possession of the multimillion-dollar meal ticket also aroused her, and the boy was handsome and strong and had that wonderful youthful male attribute of quick recovery time. She made good use of his stamina.

Later, when she had exhausted his body and her interest, Cass told him it was time for him to go home and tell his parents what happened to his brother. She suggested he leave The Reeds with her until he finished with his mother and father, and could take the train back.

She gave him cab fare and called a DeSoto cab to take him to the Bart station.

Ali was in such a daze he didn't notice she was putting him on a train and keeping the object his brother gave up his life to possess.

When he was gone she pondered what to do with it to keep it safe. She did a mental inventory of the places she had access to and which would be inherently safe. It didn't take long to realize the perfect place.

Jean Washington's house.

Might as well be Fort Knox. Behind gates. Security. Cops.

Mickey's warnings about the mystery man somehow stuck in her mind even while she ignored his more urgent warnings against possessing the antiquity. What if the guy did kill Babu? What if Mick was right? What if that big guy was really after The Reeds? What if she was struck by bad luck and he caught up with her while she was on her way back to Jean Washington's house? Bad to be holding it.

She considered FedEx. Bubble wrap the hell out of The Reeds, send it to herself at Jean Washington's house.

Upside? "She'll just throw it in my room and forget it," she said to herself.

Downside? Maybe a touch too reckless to trust the yawning maw of the worldwide delivery service to swallow the precious antiquity and spit it up in the right place.

She remembered the Channel 8 messenger service. "Of course. Paul Donder," she said to herself. He ran the messenger service, and was kind of a friend. She had him deliver stuff for her all the time. He appreciated her billing. She punched the speed dial on her phone. "Paul, I need a favor."

Fifteen minutes later a rainbow-hair motorcycle driver was at the security desk. She signed the messenger form, giving the delivery address as Jean Washington's house in Presidio Terrace and the "from" line as the Planet Fitness on Divisidero.

Death in the Reeds was wrapped in Spandex workout pants in her gym bag.

"Now she really will just throw it in my room," she said to herself. She insisted on a copy of the receipt.

37

Dani Charm waited patiently in a holding cell for the arrival of her ride to San Francisco to testify before the Grand Jury. She expected a prison bus, so she was pleasantly surprised to see Inspector Bill Norton.

"You're coming with me," he said, handing her a bag. "There's some presentable clothes, some make up, a brush and I don't know what all. You can change and get yourself ready and we'll go." He seemed abrupt and put out.

She was left alone. She found a nice pair of black pants, stockings, black shoes that were actually her size and weren't too ugly, a plain white shirt-blouse with buttons up the front, and a black jacket. It was all more or less her size, and when she dressed and glanced herself over she thought it was not bad. There was a makeup compact and a tube of subdued lipstick. And a brush and a can of hair spray.

When she called for the guard, she thought she might look pretty good. There was no mirror in the holding cell so it was just a guess.

Billy Norton put cuffs on her and walked her out, making a quick stop at check-in to sign the paperwork that he was taking custody of the prisoner.

They were travelling in his personal car. She wasn't quite sure what it was except it was macho and cop. Billy Norton popped the cuffs off. "You'll be more comfortable. I want you rested and ready to testify, and it's a long drive." He smiled, but she thought it was quite insincere.

Dani stared out the window as they headed north on Highway 99, the main line up and down the valley before Interstate 5 opened. The road was worn, the towns they passed through were depressing, the day was hot, the roadside acacias and eucalyptus covered in light brown dust.

She didn't much like this cop, but he had followed through and got her in the PHU, which made life easier. And he took the cuffs off, which was nice of him. She hated to do it but she was going to embarrass the fuck out of him by escaping. But hey, that's what a prisoner is supposed to do. If given a half a chance, she would damn well take it.

They stopped for something to eat in Manteca at an older roadside restaurant and filling station. Dani asked the cop if she could go to the ladies' room. He followed her down a hallway, knocked on the ladies' room door and called out a warning. "Police, I need you to vacate. A prisoner needs the bathroom."

A voice came back. "Fuck you. I'll get out of here when I'm damn good and ready."

Dani looked at him with her well-practiced sweet expression. "I really gotta pee."

Billy grimaced. Shouted through the door. "Just cover up. We're coming in."

He turned back to Dani. "Okay," he grabbed her by the shoulders, his hands gripping tight, just short of pain. "This is how it's gonna work. The escape from the bathroom is the oldest trick in crime shows. It's like, expected."

He waved his index finger back and forth. "But no. That shit ain't happening here. We're both going in. You go in the stall and do your thing. I'll be outside the stall with this crime fighting device stuck in the door so you can't lock me out." He took a wedge-shaped rubber doorstop out of his jacket pocket, waved it in her face.

"You pee. Pull your panties and pants up and I'll open the door and we'll leave."

She hated this prick. She gave him her bored go-fuck-yourself look.

"Got it?" he asked.

She nodded.

Inside the stall she sat on the toilet and surveyed her situation. She could see the cop's boots under the door. Ridiculous pointy things you mostly see on Mexican farm workers, she thought. He was leaning against the door. The rubbery doorstop was pressed flat from his weight.

Above the stall door a horizontal bar ran the length of the four stalls, stabilizing the partitions. That got her thinking.

On the other side of the door Billy Norton squeezed his eyes into a threatening stare at the woman who emerged from a nearby stall. "Just wash your hands and get the fuck out," he said.

"You're an asshole. I'm calling the cops."

"Save your breath. I am a cop."

The woman doused her hands and snapped a paper towel from the dispenser. "Well, in that case just go fuck yourself," she said.

"Move along," Billy said dismissively.

Inside the stall Dani Charm was starting to hatch an idea. She stood up from the toilet, hitched her pants. Then she carefully climbed onto the toilet seat, mindful to place her rubber sole shoes solidly on the porcelain edge. She focused on the horizontal bar above the door. She'd worked the pole. She knew how swinging worked.

Now she leaned forward and grasped the bar over the stall door with both hands.

Outside Billy Norton was facing the sinks and the mirrors. He noticed Dani's fists gripping the horizontal bar. "Hey, what the fuck?"

At that moment Dani swung forward off the toilet, gripping the horizontal bar, aiming her swinging feet squarely at the stall door. She struck the door with her full weight and kicked forward as hard as she could.

Billy was caught wide eyed. No time to defend himself.

The door smashed off its hinges, and the horizontal bar collapsed under her weight. She flew forward flat on her back, and flat on the door as the door crashed into Billy Norton and threw him into the sinks.

Billy's head banged the edge of the sink counter. His front teeth popped out and his nose smashed flat and bloody. The cop went out like a finger snap.

Dani found herself lying on her back completely horizontal staring at the stall door on top of the cop.

He wasn't moving.

She got to her feet. She didn't wait to see if he was going to get up. She cleared out.

Dani Charm walked out of the ladies' room and headed for the outside door. Straight ahead were four big rigs at the diesel pumps. She walked by each one picking out her ride.

The black man at the wheel looked over in surprise as Dani climbed up into the seat beside him.

She picked the black guy because she thought they were always thinking about their dick and they loved white girls. The promise of a blow job would get her anywhere she wanted to go.

"Where you headed?" she asked with her little girl smile.

"Vegas," the black man said. "And the name is Carl."

She reached for his crotch with her prison white hand. "Perfect. You drive and I'll make you feel good."

Billy Norton gathered his senses and pushed the broken stall door off. "Fuck," he muttered. "Fuck fuck fuck." He touched his head and looked at his hand. Blood. "Fuck fuck fuck."

Billy stumbled out of the ladies' room and hurried to the outside door. The bright sunlight made his eyes squeeze tight.

"Fuck me," he thought as he ran across the lot swiveling his head left to right, back right to lift. No sign of Dani. Worse, a tanker rig and a car carrier pulled away from the pumps in quick succession and Billy realized she could be in a big rig and gone already.

Bleeding, groggy and super pissed off he called 911. "Escaped prisoner," he said. He identified himself with his SFPD star number and demanded CHP officers be dispatched north and south looking for a big rig with a blond girl in the passenger seat. A Be On the Lookout, aka a BOLO. Escaped prisoner.

After he got the BOLO out Billy realized pretty soon people were going to want to know how this happened. Billy threw up in a garbage can next to the fuel pumps.

One officer in particular did in fact pass Carl's truck but there was no blond girl to be seen. That was because Dani Charm was face down in Carl's lap paying for her escape ride.

38

Bart Trappani was not a San Francisco kind of guy. He arrived at SFO annoyed at everything he encountered.

As a Marine Lt. Colonel and an Assistant U.S. Attorney, he thought of himself as squared away, but tolerant of different people and different ways. But San Francisco stood out as weird. People at the airport put him off. Women seemed either undernourished vegan waifs or gym-hardened predator IT execs. Men seemed soft and entirely too compliant. And riding into the city he was horrified by the rampant homelessness which appeared to be completely unchecked by the city government. The place was beautiful but it gave him the creeps.

He arrived at the Mark Hopkins Hotel in a cab. Wind almost blasted the cab door off its hinges. He noticed the flagpole three hundred forty feet above at the famous Top of The Mark struggling against the wind. The American flag snapped and shuddered.

In his room he called SFPD chief Peggy Chung first thing. They spoke when he boarded in Newark about Pete Grand.

"We may have a problem with your guy who tossed two people off high places," she said without a greeting. "Somebody just threw a body off a very high cliff down in Big Sur. Seems the victim was strangled before being tossed. Sheriff there called. Said keep an eye out. Might be headed this way."

"Got a description?"

"Big. Very big. Tall. Witness said very strong. Witness said he could have picked up this guy like he was lifting a coffee cup."

"Sounds like Peter Grand," Trappani said, with a groan. "Your people should know he might still carry his old Italian passport under the name Pietro Granatelli."

Trappani rubbed his forehead trying to think quicker than Pete Grand. His lead from Irwin Feinstein said Grand would be looking for a Cass Papadop, but what was the guy in Big Sur all about?

"You know a woman named Cass Papadop?"

"Of course," Peggy Chung said. "She's married to the DA. Jean Washington, a super up and coming politician. Probably be governor. People talking about her as Presidential material."

Something in Chung's voice alerted Trappani. It was the admiring tone at the mention of Jean Washington's name. Guess the Chief was gay. And evidently so was the DA. But a gay black woman for President? What were these people smoking?

"She's part of the reason I'm here," Trappani said. "Papadop may be in danger. I think Pete Grand might be looking for her."

Peggy Chung said she would send over her best man.

Meanwhile at that moment Billy Norton was pacing the floor in the home office of the District Attorney Jean Washington, trying to cobble up an explanation for his broken nose and missing front teeth and why he didn't deliver a witness to the Grand Jury as he had promised. A humiliating situation. How could he let a pole dancer and porn player and part-time hooker escape?

His boss swiveled ominously in her desk chair. Billy Norton recognized she was about to pounce. She listened as he paced back and forth, squinty eyed and disbelieving. How could Dani Charm, a five-foot one-inch woman, manage to overpower a much bigger and stronger cop? He had no answer.

Jean Washington had no sympathy for his injury. She wanted an indictment to dirty up Mickey Judge, to obliterate his credibility. "It doesn't help getting a true bill out of these folks if I drag them in for testimony, make them miss work, and then send them home because my detective got his ass kicked and lost the witness." Her gray eyes focused on Billy like the intensity of her stare might somehow improve the situation.

"I got cops all over the state watching for her. Plus the Vegas PD and Portland and Seattle."

A soft knock at the door interrupted. "Come," Jean Washington called out.

Cass Papadop opened the door slightly, struck her head in. "Sorry to bother you, but did a messenger bring my gym bag by?"

Jean Washington gave her an insincere smile. "No, dear. Haven't seen it."

"It's very important," Cass said as she closed the door.

"All gym bag deliveries are important," the DA mumbled as she watched the door close.

"What are you going to do about Dani Charm?" she continued to Billy Norton. "That little bitch on the loose is a serious fuck up."

Billy knew exactly what she meant. The real reason for his humiliation. Dani Charm now knew something about Billy and maybe even the DA that would be a real mess if revealed: the promise of benefits in exchange for false testimony. He took a deep breath. "We'll get her back to Chowchilla. Just a matter of time."

Washington gave him a disgusted look and rolled her eyes to the ceiling.

"How many days can you stall before we have to give up on finding her and just go get another one?" Billy continued.

"You got another one?"

"We got dozens. You know that. They'll say whatever for a carton of cigarettes and a PHU bed."

Jean caught a glimpse of her reflection in the windows that looked out on her super-wealthy neighbors. She couldn't help but notice how beautiful her long thin neck was, how elegant her jawline, how regal her aquiline nose, how luscious her coffee skin. Beauty had always worked well for her. And now she had added a certain dignity suitable to the nation's highest office. She would be the most attractive person to ever occupy the Oval Office, Kennedy included.

But there was work to be done. She sighed. This was an onerous duty she did not want to be bothered with, but which circumstances required she must. "Let's go over the list."

Billy Norton sat at the chair in front of her desk. "We have a Tenderloin drug dealer doing five years in Corcoran …"

Billy Norton continued with a list of names and possible ways each could blacken the reputation of Mickey Judge. Jean Washington let her mind wander. She should be taking meetings on a US/Russia Summit. On the state of the nation's economy. On her re-election. But here she was selecting the next loser to prop up for a Grand Jury appearance to make sure anything a troublesome, grimy reporter made public would be dismissed as unreliable.

What a waste of my talent, she marveled.

Three and a half miles away, at about the same moment, Bone Hendrix sat down on a scarlet couch in the lobby at the Mark Hopkins waiting for a Fed from New York to pop out of the elevator.

Trappani appeared almost instantly. Bone wearily raised himself back up, annoyed the guy didn't give him a bit more time on that excellent couch. They didn't say much to each other except for handshake and introduction. They were in Bone's Crown Vic headed west on California Street in less than a minute.

"You know this Papadop woman?" Trappani asked.

"Everybody does," Bone said, jerking his head back like it was the strangest question. "She's on TV. Plus married to the DA. Regular gal about town."

Bone flashed his badge at the Presidio Terrace gate and the guard waved him through. He wheeled the Crown Vic to the right and stopped in front of a huge house that seemed to mouth the word money.

"This is where the DA lives?" Trappani said, marveling at the house and its neighbors. "Public service pays a lot better out here than it does in the east."

Bone snorted. "She made a pile in Silicon Valley before politics. The DA gig is her first elected office. Everybody says she's going for Governor next."

"And she lives here with her wife, this Cassie Papadop?" Trappani was still mystified by the whole thing.

Bone nodded yes. "Story I hear is they have separate suites. It's really a marriage for show. One is gay, the other isn't. Both want to be in the papers and invited to the right parties, so they became the city's most famous and popular couple."

"Which one is gay?"

"That would be our District Attorney."

"So this Cass Papadop is not?"

"That's the story. Cops say she's sharing intimate moments with the Mayor. And he's the jealous type."

Trappani nodded but didn't say what he was really thinking: what a bunch of freaks in this town.

Trappani picked up a gym bag on the porch in front of the door. Bone gave him a side eye. Trappani shrugged an explanation. "It's got her name on it. Somebody could run off with it."

"In Presidio Terrace?" Bone asked. "You must be kidding." He rang the bell.

The prosecutor from New York turned around to inspect the neighborhood. Across the street was a massive storybook house, with a sloping roofline of thick shingles meant to give the impression of a thatched roof. Fat columns supported the gabled entrance. Next to it was a towering red brick Edwardian with white corner accents and window casings, a chimney stack with four pipes, and a fenced roof that gave the impression of a widow's walk.

"Cabbage palms," Trappani remarked.

"What, the palm trees?"

"I was in Iraq. Every kind of palm tree known to man."

Bone grunted. Palm tree expert. "Sales brochures in early 1900s promised whites only."

"Keep out blacks," Trappani nodded. "We got those too."

"Blacks didn't have a hope in hell in the first place," Bone said. "This place was meant to keep out rich Chinese."

Bone rang the bell again. Almost immediately the door swung open and Bone found himself staring into the face of his partner, Bill Norton. "What the hell are you doing here?" Bone blurted out. "And what happened to your face?"

"Sorry boss, business," Billy said, reddening. "Whattaya need?"

"I'm gonna need an explanation for this later," Bone growled, "but right now this is Bart Trappani, a U.S. Attorney out of New York."

Billy had a look on his face like he was about to say "So?" Like it made no difference at all who this U.S. Attorney was.

Trappani sensed something was afoot but he didn't want to get sidetracked. "We need to see Cass Papadop. She here?"

The door swung open wider as Billy stepped back. "Come on in. I'll run upstairs and holler for her."

The two men stepped into a marble floor foyer, dark wood walls with framed paintings of San Francisco scenes. A round center table was topped with a crystal vase sprouting white gladiolas.

Trappani looked up. "That's four grand," he said, in a soft voice.

"What?"

"Louis Comfort Tiffany ceiling lamp. Four at least. Could be ten for all I know."

Bone huffed. He was still smoldering about Billy.

A sliding door with etched glass insets rolled open and Jean Washington stepped out. She was dressed in a gray green pants suit, with a white silk shirt beneath the jacket. She held her head high, glancing over the two men with an expression that said, you two are in the wrong place.

"Inspector Hendrix. What up?"

Trappani stepped forward. "District Attorney Washington, I'm Bart Trappani, Assistant US Attorney out of the Southern District of New York."

Washington glanced down at the gym bag in his hand and frowned. A fucking gym bag? She shot a scolding look at Hendrix. "You might have called ahead Inspector."

Trappani jumped in. "Ms. Washington, we didn't expect to find you home. I'm here to see Cassandra Papadopoulos."

Jean Washington arched an eyebrow again, turning her attention to Trappani. "As you might have heard, Ms. Papadop and I are married. I think you can tell me what this is about."

"Frankly, it's about her safety, and since you two are in the same house, your safety as well."

"My safety? How?"

At that moment Cass came skittering down the staircase at the end of the foyer. "What's going on, Jean?"

Washington turned to her, and nodded toward Hendrix and Trappani. "These men say they're here about your safety. What have you been doing?"

"Nothing," Cass said with a nervous laugh. "What's this about?" she asked the two men.

Trappani took the lead, introducing himself. "I have been searching for an antiquity stolen from Baghdad for quite a while now. I understand you've heard of it. Death in the Reeds."

Cass felt an upwelling of dread. What were the Feds doing here asking about The Reeds?

"By the way this gym bag was at the door," Trappani said, handing her the bag. "It has your name on it."

A jolt zinged Cass's body. Oh shit, she thought. This guy is after the thing he's handing me.

"Let's go in my office," Jean Washington said.

Once the door rolled closed Cass jumped in first. "I don't understand. What has this thing got to do with me?"

"I have information you were planning to bring an expert to San Francisco who could confirm or deny an item presented to you was the authentic Death in the Reeds. Is that true?"

"Jesus, Cass, what the fuck are you doing?" Jean Washington muttered.

"It's just a TV show," Cass said to her wife, dismissively. Then turned to Trappani. "What's this got to do with my safety?"

"There is a man who is trying to track down the antiquity. So far he's killed two people in London, and one here in California. I'm afraid he might be looking for you."

Oh shit, Cass thought. That guy with Babu's phone.

"Who did he kill here?" Jean Washington interrupted.

"A Bikram Chakrabarti. Threw him over a cliff in Big Sur."

"Babu?" Cass blurted out. "Babu is really dead?" Shit. That's what Mick said.

"Very," Trappani said. "And we've lost track of the killer. I'm afraid he is looking for you."

"Why?"

"Probably because he thinks you have the antiquity. He works for a Russian who has been assigned to obtain the antiquity."

"For who?" Cass asked, her mind reeling.

Trappani shrugged. "A Russian agent who has carte blanche could only be working for one person."

Jean Washington interrupted. "You think this killer is after Cass? Seriously?"

Trappani just bobbed his head up and down—yes.

Washington turned to Cass. "You need to go."

"What?" Cass reacted, surprised.

"You need to go. Go into hiding."

"When?"

"Now."

"Now? Why?"

"I can't have that guy coming around here after you."

Cass's mouth dropped open. "You're kicking me out?"

Washington scoffed. "Don't be a drama queen. You just need to go into hiding until this man"—she pointed to Trappani—"finds this maniac."

Cass's temper rose. "Wait. What the fuck?" Cass almost forgot Trappani and Hendrix and Norton were still in the room. "Are you forgetting we're married? For better or worse?"

"This is worse than worse."

"You have police protecting you and there's a guard at the gate. Aren't I safest here?"

"You may be," Jean said, "but I am not safest if you are here. You need to decamp immediately. Someplace you can't be found."

Cass was stunned into silence.

Trappani was startled and uncomfortable. The District Attorney threw her "wife" out of the house without a moment's hesitation.

Bone and Billy weren't surprised in the slightest.

Jean Washington sensed the vibe. She looked around at the men. "What?" she said.

Billy Norton shook his head. "Nothing, boss," lisping from the missing teeth.

Bone Hendrix stared at his shoes.

Bart Trappani glanced around. The others obviously knew something he didn't.

Cass was starting to blink back tears when she caught herself, and let anger take over. "I have to get going," she said, furious. "This looks like the end of the road."

She bolted from the room.

Trappani waited a moment, then jumped up to follow her. In the foyer he called after her as she started up the staircase. "Please take this," he said, handing her his card. "If you cannot quickly come up with a safe place that is secret, call me and I'll get you into protective custody. In fact, just call me later. Let me assess your accommodations, for your security."

She took the card. Shoved it in her pocket. "Yeah. Thanks."

"Seriously, call me."

Inside Jean Washington's office, she addressed Billy. "Get on the horn with the chief. I'm going to need a car and a couple officers here 24/7."

Billy nodded okay.

Washington thought of something else. "Another thing. I need you to get something to the Chronicle and the TV people. Say something about Cass Papadop has been the subject of a serious threat to her safety. She's moved out of her marital home and gone into seclusion for her security. We need to let that killer know she's not here."

The three men looked at each other. Chagrin on Billy's face.

"You're a piece of work," Bone mumbled, rising to his feet.

"What's your problem? California's future head of state needs to be protected." she hissed back.

"'Head of state!'" Bone mocked. "You one cold-hearted bitch," he said, giving her his hard stare. He turned to walk to the foyer. "Let's go find this maniac," he said to Trappani. "This place will be a fortress within the hour. But right now it gives me the willies."

"You're going to regret that disrespect," she said to his back.

"Yeah, whatever," Bone said without turning back to her.

Upstairs, Cass was throwing a few things into a fashion duffle bag.

She picked up her phone and punched in a number.

Mick answered with a yes and a question mark.

"Mick it's Cass."

"I know."

"You still doing that investigation of wifey?"

"Sure am. Why?"

"I'm ready to talk."

"Start now."

"Okay, you know that bullshit investigation of my wife you've been obsessing about?"

Mick rolled his eyes. "Yeah, obviously."

"Well, lucky you. It's all true."

"I'm listening."

Cass confirmed for Mick that DA Washington routinely used false cellmate testimony, bought and paid for with leniency, to convict targets she wanted convicted no matter what.

In the hallway, Jean Washington approached Cass's door. She intended to calm Cass down. She stopped when she heard Cass's voice on the phone. She listened for a moment, her anger rising.

The door flew open.

Face to face, Cass and Jean startled each other.

"You sneaking around listening to me?" Cass accused, dropping the phone to her side.

"You sneaking around telling lies about me?" Jean Washington pointed at Cass, her hand shaking with rage.

"Whatever I say about you won't be lies," Cass hissed.

"Better watch your mouth," Jean Washington threatened.

"My divorce lawyer will be in touch," Cass said, throwing the door closed.

Jean Washington turned away and hurried downstairs, her fury rising with every step.

"What was that?" Mick asked. He'd heard the entire exchange.

"I thought I heard that bitch in the hall. Sure enough. She practically had her ear pressed to the door."

"You better get out of there. If she knows you're talking to me about her, no telling what she'll do."

"She's not going to fuck with me. I know too much."

"But that's exactly the problem."

"I'm not worried about her. Besides, I'm getting out of here now."

"You don't need extra people who want to do you harm. We need to get you into a hidey hole."

"God, you're such a paranoid. I'll be fine."

She hung up with a "Gotta go."

Mick pushed the gas pedal to the floor. The Babu mission for Cass left him terribly out of position. He had to get back to the city fast.

Back at the Washington house, the DA was frantic.

Billy Norton had an icepack over the bridge of his nose when the boss found him in the kitchen.

"I need you to call Channel 3."

"I just did."

"You need to call again."

The detective held the icepack in his hand and stared at the DA waiting. "Okay, and?"

"Tell that little bitch reporter you got more. Tell her Cass is checking herself into a rehab center."

"That true?"

"What difference does it make? Tell her it's for treatment for cocaine addiction. Tell her Papadop has been hallucinating. Babbling. Insane. Out of her mind."

"That true?"

"I hate repeating myself. What difference does it make? Just do it."

Billy North put the ice pack back over his nose. "I'll get right on that."

"I don't mean later. I mean now."

Billy let his disgust show. "Yes sir," he said, emphasizing "sir."

Upstairs in her suite, Cass finished throwing things into a bag to clear out.

Unfinished business. She looked at the gym bag on the floor. What to do with this?

If Mick was right, she needed to stash it somewhere the big guy could not get to it. Even though she was going to be persona non grata in the Washington house, she decided she could always weasel her way back in to fetch the bag. So, the best thing was leave it in Jean Washington's SFPD guarded home.

But where? Glancing around the room, she dismissed all the usual spots. Closets, the mattress, bathroom cabinets … all out.

Then she had a thought.

She listened at the door. Voices from downstairs. Jean and that bloody-nose cop.

Cass walked down to Jean Washington's bedroom suite. She eased open the door.

This would be the perfect hiding place. Deep in that shoe closet with Jean Washington's gym clothes. The ones she never wore except for photo shoots.

The Reeds would be safe there.

39

At San Francisco City Hall, Mayor Robert Vargas-Watson interrupted his meeting with Willis and Marge Snippen. He got up from his chair and walked closer to his TV to make sure he was hearing this right. In mounting horror, he watched a news anchor reading a shocking story about the Mayor's semi-secret girlfriend, Cass Papadop.

Willis and Marge were feeding the Mayor sheets of paper on his polling numbers, which showed worrisome slippage. Willis stopped mid-sentence.

The Channel 3 anchor seemed to delight in the story: rival Channel 8's star personality Cassandra Papadop "is reported to have vacated the home she shares with her wife, District Attorney Jean Washington. Channel 3 has learned that she has, in the words of the DA herself, 'gone into hiding.' Reached by Channel 3, District Attorney Washington said she has no explanation as to why her wife needs to go into hiding."

"This is good for you," Marge offered.

"I agree," Willis joined in. "Your name hasn't come up. This is good."

The Mayor shot them a shut the fuck up glance.

A soundbite of Jean Washington filled the screen. "My wife is headstrong and sometimes given to curious behavior. We'll just have to wait to see how this episode shakes out."

The anchor also reported Papadop may be under drug rehabilitation care as "she has been in the grip of substance abuse and is reported to have fallen into a hallucinatory state."

"Drugs?" Veedub asked the television. "Says that lying bitch."

"As long as nobody mentions your name, you're golden," Marge offered.

Veedub knew the derogatory information had to come from the DA herself. He had seen Jean Washington betray people before, but still it was bracing that the latest victim of her backstabbing was her so called "wife." The Mayor could read between the lines. It appeared this gay marriage was over.

On that narrow point Veedub agreed with his political managers. Overall, it was good for him that the gay marriage was on the rocks, though he still wasn't ready to divorce his terminally ill wife.

"The way you play this is don't," Willis said. "Just stay out of it."

"A hundred percent. If your name never comes up you win," Marge agreed.

Veedub shook his head. "You realize you're talking about the woman I love," he snarled at them.

"Pretend you hardly know her."

"Sympathies for the city's first couple. Best play at the moment. Best."

Veedub quickly grew angry. He was enraged that Mickey Judge wasn't on top of this. "Why am I seeing this on TV? What the hell am I paying the guy for?" he muttered to himself. In seconds he was standing behind his desk barking into his phone at Mickey Judge.

"It's all over the air. Cass Papadop in hiding. What the fuck is she in hiding for? And what's this shit about drugs?"

The Mayor's call caught Mick in his Honda beater coming up the Bayshore Freeway out of Santa Clara. Headed back to the city. He'd just got off with Cass. She was promising to tell what she knew about Jean Washington. This was a delicate moment.

"Drugs? Who said that?"

"Probably that bitch wife. Who else? What about the hiding? What's that?"

"I think I know why. Any idea where she would go?"

Veedub lit a cigarette and exhaled smoke out the open window. "Look, you gotta tell me if she's in real trouble because I'm afraid she wouldn't go anywhere. She'd just hole up in that apartment and pretend there's nothing wrong."

"Which apartment?" Mick couldn't believe she would go where anybody could find her.

"You haven't been to her place? Where are you fucking her?"

"That would be best," Willis whispered to Marge. "Somebody else fucking her."

"Couldn't ask for anything better," Marge whispered back.

Mick rolled his eyes. "I'm not fucking her." Veedub—the insecure teenager.

Veedub ignored Mick's denial. Even if he weren't screwing his girlfriend, it could be someone else. The only person he was sure Cass Papadop wasn't having sex with was her wife. As for men, he could never really be sure. She was impetuous, she tended to snap decisions, especially about lovers. He knew because he was one of her sudden decisions. "Go check out her place. She's not answering her phone."

Marge and Willis frowned at each other. "Not good," Willis muttered.

"Is there a way we can spin this?" she whispered.

"How?" Willis whispered back.

"Humbled by love," she said. "Make a play for sympathy."

Veedub pointed at them and drew a finger across his throat. "Shut up."

"Who shut up?" Mick asked.

"Not you," Veedub said into the phone. "Tell me what you know."

Mick didn't want to tell Veedub about Pete Grand. The way the Mayor was freaking out, no telling what he'd do. "Okay, just let me check it out. Can you get the cops to put somebody at her place just in case?"

"No, no. I don't want gossipy cops involved."

Marge and Willis nodded. Yes. No gossipy cops.

"You just go there. If she's there, just get her out and go somewhere she can't be found. The foothills. Napa. Vegas. I don't care. Just somewhere. And then tell me where she is and tell her to answer my damn calls."

Mick wanted off the phone. "Okay, I'll look into it." He wasn't terribly concerned about Cass's safety … yet. Even though Pete Grand was ahead of him he would have to locate Cass, and that probably would take a little time. Mick hoped.

As for Jean Washington, he assumed the principal threat from her was just a PR campaign to impugn Cass's character and credibility. He figured she wouldn't dare pose a threat to Cass's safety.

Veedub snapped his phone shut.

"You need to stay far far away from this," Willis said.

"Like starting right now," his wife added.

Just get out of here and work on my rebranding." Veedub pointed to the door. "Don't fuck that up."

It took Mick another half hour to barrel into the city and skid to a stop in front of the tall concrete apartment building known by its address, 999 Green.

He strode into the lobby and immediately confronted a security guard behind a desk. "There's a ruckus going on just outside. You may want to call a cop." He wanted to avoid going through the front desk routine: the guy calling upstairs to see if the guest could proceed.

The man peered out the windows. "Just to the left," Mick said. The guard rose and walked to the front door. Mick slipped into an elevator and hit 22.

He walked down a long gray carpeted hallway and rang the bell at 2204. He could see the peep hole darken, and then the door flew open. "Can you believe the bitch threw me out?" Cass Papadop demanded. "Come in. I'm in hiding," she said, making air quotes with her fingers. "Or I'm in drug rehab. Channel 3 can't decide which."

Mick followed her in, past an open kitchen, into a living room with a stunning view of the bay and the Golden Gate Bridge.

"You can see Japan from here," he remarked.

"It's so fucking great," she said. "I almost forgot how great. Glad to be out of that freak show house. And I'm glad to be home. Have a seat," she said waving her arm at the couch.

She plopped down in an Eames chair. She was dressed in jeans, a blue silk sleeveless blouse, and blue leather ankle boots. Her hair was wild and windblown, her brow was furrowed, her lips set in a pout. Cassie Papadop was angry. Hurt.

"So you're ready to tell me things about the DA?" Mick asked.

"I couldn't fucking believe it. Cop tells her some guy is after me and she turns to me and says get out."

Mick noticed she entirely ignored his question. Still hesitant to tell on the wife.

"Evidently she's telling reporters you're a drug addict. Walking around spewing shit about you."

"Bitch," Cass mumbled. "Nothing too low."

"She actually said get out?"

"She said, 'you need to go into hiding.' Same thing."

"Veedub says it's all over the air …"

"The bitch," she repeated. A pause. "Wait. You talked to Bobby?"

"He ordered me to check up on you."

She shook her head. "He's getting to be too much."

That was something Mick didn't want to get into. "So let's talk more about the wife." Mick pressed.

She gave him a weary look. "I can tell you plenty. But can it wait? I'm still rattled." She held out a shaky hand. "See?"

"Okay," Mick said. "Later."

She was drinking. Mick noticed the bottle of Absolut, and poured himself one. He dumped a few ice cubes in.

"Where you going?"

She gave him an annoyed look. "Right here. Why should I go anywhere?"

That was a very bad idea in Mick's view. "I was just down in Big Sur. Guy threw your pal Babu down a five-hundred-foot cliff."

"The cliff isn't five hundred feet," she interrupted with a dismissive wave.

"Whatever. It's certain death. And seems it's his thing. Same guy killed a couple people in London a week ago. He's looking for that thing you were angling for."

She waved him off again, disgusted. "For starters, I'm totally over that," she lied without a second thought, which Mick recognized as a total lie. "Secondly, do you have any idea how many people want to kill Babu Chakrabarti? Only dozens of investors, particularly a few he cleaned out. Not to mention those husbands whose wives he was buggering. Could be anybody."

Mick shook his head no. "Bullshit. Whoever this guy is, he's serious. He's on the trail of that antiquity and you've already put it out there you have some angle on it. He'll come to get you, too."

"Oh, don't be so dramatic. I don't have any such thing. Number two, how's he going to find me? This place isn't on my driver's license, I'm not the official renter, my aunt is, and it's not listed in the phone book. Plus not that many people know I have a place here."

"You're full of crap. You had the Chronicle in here a couple years ago doing a story on your remodel. I saw it online from New York."

"It was my aunt's remodel. And that was years ago."

"There's a new thing called Google."

"Google schmoogle. Some knuckle-dragger has no idea how to use that."

Mick rolled his eyes. "Why are you fighting me? Just get your ass up, grab that bag," he said, pointing to the bag she'd thrown on the floor, "and let's go. We'll park you in a motel up in Gold Country. Unfindable."

She recoiled at the idea. "Fuck you. I don't need to run off to some bug-infested motel room."

"Do I have to remind you that your wife now knows you've turned on her? No telling what she'll do. Come on, let's go."

"She can't do anything to me except lie about me. Besides, I got lots of friends in Pacific Heights who will loan me a suite or a guest house."

Mick picked up her phone from the coffee table and tossed it into her lap. "Start calling."

"Calling who?"

"You just said you have friends who will let you hide out. Start calling. I'll sit here until you find someone and then I'll take you over."

"Fuck you, Mickey. This is no way to treat me. I'm your friend. I'm the one person at Channel 8 who's sticking with you, and you treat me like a baby? Kiss my ass."

"It's because you are the one person sticking with me that I'm insisting you go hide someplace. If he spots your car he'll ram it, get in your bleeding face, and demand the thing. You resist, he'll kill you. This guy is serious."

"Oh, fuck off. How's the guy going to spot my car on the street?"

"I don't know," Mick shot back. "He seems to be pretty good finding people."

She waved him off. "If I'm the one who knows where it is—why would he kill me?"

"Ask Babu and the art dealer in London. Oh wait. You can't. They both could have turned the thing over to him. But they're dead."

She refused to take the threat seriously. "Get out," she said in a level voice. "I don't need babysitting."

The door chimes rang.

They both shot the other an alarmed look. Now Cass betrayed her fears. Her face sank and she muttered, "Shit."

Mick rose and walked to the door. Passing by the kitchen, he reached for the knife block and took the biggest blade by the handle. He peered through the peep hole.

"Holy shit," he said, turning back to her. "It's the kid."

He opened the door, startling Ali Zardari. "What are you doing here?" he demanded.

Ali recoiled, taking a step back. "What are you doing here?" he responded. Then he pushed his way past Mick and hurried down the hall to the living room.

"What's he doing here?" Mick demanded of Cass.

She didn't answer, but Mick saw the look on her face: the expression of a woman who has given into temptation and now would rather the guy didn't show up.

"Oh, for chrissakes Cass," Mick said, disgusted. "You didn't."

"Shut up," Cass mumbled.

"What's he doing here?" Ali demanded again, pointing at Mick. "Is he your lover, too?"

Mick rolled his eyes. Too. There it is. She was balling the boy.

"I can't believe it," Mick muttered, shaking his head.

"I can't believe it either," Ali shouted.

Cass had enough. "You both have to get out of here," she said, standing. "This is my place and I'm feeling way too crowded. Both of you—leave."

Ali's macho cratered. He hesitated, the look of a sick puppy crossing his face. He thought he had the lover he'd always dreamed of. Now another guy. Now she ordered him out. "We have business to discuss," he whispered.

"I know. We'll talk later. Just go."

Still, he hesitated. "Just go," she repeated.

Ali started for the door, slowly.

"You too, Mick. I need some space."

Mickey was resigned. "This is nauseating," he said to her directly, looking for an explanation. It was clear to him she'd bedded the boy, for what reason he could only imagine. He stared at the kid again. True, the boy was handsome, good shape. About twenty-two. There was something about young men controlling women couldn't resist, he supposed. But still. How could you, Cass? Mick was confounded. He opened the door for the boy. "Go."

Ali went through the door, but reluctantly.

Mick turned back to Cass. "You don't have much time. Find a place or I'll find one for you."

"Just get out," she said, not wanting to look him in the eye.

Mick and Ali rode down in the elevator together. Neither wanted to speak to the other, but it was considerably more uncomfortable for Ali than Mick. "Did you get hold of that antiquity?" Mick asked. The boy just glared at the floor.

Ali bolted from the building. Couldn't get away from Mick fast enough. Mick watched him marching south on Jones Street, head down, arms swinging, backpack bouncing, probably headed for a BART station for a train back to Fremontistan.

At the corner of Jones and Green the Honda was nosed into a spot against the curb—the hill was too steep to allow parallel parking—and Mick sat staring out at Alcatraz, wondering if somehow the little shit Ali had managed to get his hands on the antiquity, and if that was the reason she bedded the boy. Or did she just decide to take a romp? Hard to tell.

His phone buzzed. He answered. "Kitty McManus here," the voice said. "We need to meet. Where are you"

Last thing Mick wanted to do was meet up with the lawyer. He'd been meaning to dump her as his attorney. Maybe this was the perfect opportunity, even though he didn't have time.

"What about?"

"Channel 8. You dodged a bullet on the Grand Jury for the moment. Appears the DA bungled something, the jurors are back in civilian life but only for the moment, I'm sure. But the Channel 8 business is starting to heat up. Where are you?'

"North Beach," he said, feeling he should be vague.

"Good. Let's meet at the Washbag. About forty-five minutes. We can grab a bite and I'll lay this out."

The Washington Square Bar and Grill—the Washbag—was right down the hill. "Okay, forty-five minutes." The place was as good as any to fire her face to face.

After cutting off the call Mick punched in the Mayor's number. "She's in her apartment. Angry. Won't leave. You really do have to send a cop over to sit and watch."

"Watch for what?" Veedub was annoyed. He was beginning to see the outlines of what he didn't know.

"The cops surely know," Mick said. "There's a BOLO from

Monterey County on a guy who killed another guy down there. He could be why wifey wanted Cass out, and why she should be hiding. But I can tell you she doesn't seem to be in the mood to go anywhere."

"Well, fuck," Bobby hissed. "Why would a killer be after her?"

Mick ran over what he thought he could tell the Mayor. "She got mixed up with that guy from Fremontistan who was promising he'd soon have a very valuable antiquity. She got stars in her eyes about big money. The guy in Monterey is after the same piece and evidently killed someone down there over the thing."

"What's the thing?"

"Something stolen from the Iraq National Museum."

"What the fuck? Is that true?"

Mick exhaled a long breath. "I don't know Bobby. I honestly don't know anything for absolute one hundred percent certain. And she doesn't want to talk about it."

"Fuck."

"Just get the cops to send a car over, keep an eye out for the guy. I'm not sure of his name. But the cops know. He's very big, six five or so. Very strong. Picked a man up and tossed him over a cliff in Big Sur. But they should know about him."

"Fuck."

"You keep saying that. I can hang here for about half an hour, then I gotta go meet with the lawyer."

"That Kitty McManus?"

Slightly embarrassed Mick mumbled "yeah."

"A total lynx. Your dick will fall off."

Great, thought Mick. Even the Mayor knows. "Just get somebody over. I'll come back later and get her. She has to go someplace where no one can find her."

"Okay, the chief will have a car there in half an hour."

Mick didn't have the heart to tell him his girlfriend was sweating up the sheets with a boy who could do it three times an hour.

He drove down into North Beach to Washington Square and took a table to wait for his nymphomaniac lawyer.

40

The spy from the Russian consulate on Green Street in the Cow Hollow district assigned to track Pete Grand reported in to Gennady Markov and the FSB Colonel was not pleased. He learned there was already a Be On The Lookout, a BOLO, for Pete Grand, owing to the apparent murder of a Silicon Valley billionaire in Big Sur California.

"I didn't have to take being disrespected when I was poking around for dirty pots in Etruscan graves and I certainly don't have to take it now," Pete snarled into the phone. "The little shit looked down his Hindu nose at me."

"I ask again. What's this thing about throwing people off high places?" Markov asked.

On his end Pete shrugged. "Not this time. He had trouble breathing. I pick the man up, he couldn't get a breath. He stumbles over the edge. What can I do?"

"Stop picking them up," Markov sighed.

"Okay, fine. But I need an address. You got people for that."

"Who?"

"That Papadop woman. I think she has the thing."

Pete Grand was driving a Hertz car on San Francisco's Embarcadero, doing little more than killing time until he got a good address on Cass Papadop.

"Relax for a few," Markov said. "I'll get back to you."

Pete grunted into the phone and punched the end button.

A sunny day on the Embarcadero, blue skies, puffy white clouds and a bracing breeze. Crowds of strollers, joggers, young parents with babies, jammed the sidewalks. Traffic snarled the roadway. Not Pete Grand's kind of place. He turned left on Broadway, and made his way uphill until he came to the Condor Club on the corner of Columbus Avenue. Pete Grand's one hobby was pornography, and he vaguely remembered something called The Condor Club was the first topless bar in the country. This might be it. It looked like a strip club. The sign featured a cartoonish woman with exposed breasts and red lights on the nipples. He rounded the corner onto Columbus Avenue looking for a parking place. None to be had.

He kept driving. Passing a park, he noticed a bar and grill, decided to stop there for a drink. Wait for Markov's call back.

He parked the car in a yellow zone. Sign said buses only. Fuck 'em, he thought.

Pete Grand walked into the Washington Square Bar and Grill and took a stool at the bar.

To his left, two tables from the end of the bar sat Mickey Judge waiting for Kitty McManus to arrive.

41

Mickey Judge punched off his phone, ending a short conversation with Mayor Veedub. The Mayor's questions came in a flood. What's going on? What's she mixed up in? Who else is involved? Has she taken leave of her senses? Is that drug thing real? The Mayor was an overflowing bucket of paranoia and legitimate fears about the love of his life. Mick had to talk him off the ledge, and promise he had things in hand.

None of it was quite true, but he had to get Veedub out of his hair. He had his back to the bar and his eye on the door. His jaw dropped ever so slightly at the sight of Kitty McManus walking in on Don Saracenetti's arm.

Bringing the boyfriend for a meeting with a client you tried to bed the first time you met him? The woman was nothing if not bold.

She spotted Mick first, and led the Don by the arm to the table. Mick stood and shook hands with Don, though not warmly, and he allowed her to lightly buss his cheek.

Kitty McManus fussed with the seating, finally arranging herself between the two men.

Mick noticed her ring finger and blinked. "So, what's this?"

She held out her left hand, the third finger sporting a four-carat rock. "We're engaged," she announced proudly. Saracenetti nodded. He already looked trapped.

"You're blushing, honey," she teased him. Her right hand was on Mick's thigh.

"Well, yes we're engaged," Saracenetti said. "We've been playing house long enough. Time to get legal!" he said with a nervous laugh.

She let her hand wander higher on Mick's thigh. He scooted his chair back a couple inches.

"Is that why you called me here?" Mick asked, trying not to let his annoyance show too much. She gave his knee a squeeze and withdrew her hand.

"Not exactly, but kinda related," she said. "It's not all domestic bliss with Don and me. I've actually been working on him," and here she gave him a little smile, "to call off the dogs, and bring you back to your rightful place as the investigative reporter for Channel 8." She waited for Mick to react.

He just stared back at her.

"And he has convinced New York it wasn't your fault, and you saved the lives of your colleagues, so the network has agreed to let you return."

Mick looked over at Don, who offered a stiff smile. "I think it all worked out for the best," he said, nodding, but without discernable enthusiasm.

"Seriously?" Mick asked. He scooched forward to get eye contact and a truthful answer from Don.

"Yes, yes, yes, very seriously," Kitty answered. Her hand was back on Mick's thigh. "Don really went to bat for you."

Don nodded ruefully.

"He did indeed," she continued. "He got the network legal department to allow me to broker a modest settlement with the family of Ladarius Rasheed. Plus he had a big newsroom meeting yesterday. He argued to the staff that you had done the right thing, you had saved lives, and while it was unfortunate that the young man died, he did have a loaded semi-automatic assault rifle which he very likely would have used to kill or maim upwards of ten people." She looked over at her husband to be and squeezed Mick's thigh. "I was so proud of him."

Mick looked at Don and realized the guy would not only be cuckolded every day of the week, he was completely pussy whipped.

"Did you get me more money?" he asked Kitty while staring at Saracenetti. The Don looked beaten, nodded up and down ever so slightly.

"You are now the highest paid street reporter on the West Coast. Higher than anybody in L.A. even," she beamed.

Mick turned his eyes back to her. "And the DA's Grand Jury investigation?"

"Another lawyer, a colleague," she began, and the way she said it Mick just knew she was banging that guy too, "told me the DA had the Grand Jury blow up on her because the detective on the case let a witness escape while he was bringing her in to testify against you. So it appears that thing is on hold."

"Until they get someone else they can bribe or pressure to say what they want."

She nodded. "Probably. Seems to work that way."

Don scuffed his chair as he stood. "Gotta hit the head," he said as he turned toward the men's room. "Please excuse me." He bumped into a big guy on a stool as he went, mumbling "excuse me" again.

She watched him go and then turned back to Mick with a gleam in her eye, and her hand back high on his thigh. "He's a dear," she said.

"You were going to screw me the day before he asked you to marry him?"

"No, I was ready to screw you the day before I asked him to marry me." She laughed. "That's different."

Mick sat back and blew a deep exhale. "Does he know?"

She shook her head. "No, no. Doesn't suspect." Now she smiled wide again. Hand wandering his leg under the table. "If he did, we couldn't do it, but he doesn't. So we can." She seemed overly pleased with herself to have worked out this revolting arrangement.

The idea of having sex with her repulsed him. "Are you moving in with him?"

"Oh yes," she chirped brightly, as if she hadn't just been propositioning him again. "He has a wonderful house in Sea Cliff. I have big renovation plans."

"You're keeping your firehouse place?"

"Certainly. That's the office." She flashed a sly grin again.

Wow, Mick thought, law office with playpen upstairs. How convenient.

What did I get myself into?

A big man at the bar slid off a stool and headed to the door, his phone against his ear. He brushed the back of Mick's chair as he lumbered by.

Don returned to the table.

Kitty McManus now excused herself to go to the ladies' room.

Saracenetti watched her go and when he was sure she was out of earshot he turned back to Mick. "I know what you did," he said softly, with a malevolent stare over the top of his reading glasses.

Shit! "What?"

"I know you took advantage of her. Tried to seduce her.

Unbelievable you would do such a grotesque thing the very day you met her. Were you trying to humiliate me? Rub my nose in it? Young stud moves in on the older guy's girl? I know I said I admired your willingness to get in over your head, but that was too much." He was hissing the words out between his teeth. "Just too much."

Mick held his tongue. His eyes about to pop out of their sockets. He couldn't decide what to do. Tell the prospective groom his soon-to-be wife was a raging harlot who dropped her clothes the second Don was out the door? That didn't seem like a good option. So he pursed his lips and waited.

"So," Don continued after a long pause, elongating the word, "I'm not going to let this ruin my life. If I ever get a chance to fuck your girlfriend I'm going to jump on it, believe me. But in the meantime, I'm going to put this behind me and go on with life."

Mick bobbed his head up and down approvingly, staring at his hands. Still quiet, waiting. Finally, it seemed Don had said what he was going to say. "You still want me to come back?"

Saracenetti waited to answer that one. A long thirty seconds. "Yes, and I want that kick-ass story you're sitting on. I want it on the air pronto."

"Which one?"

"I know you have video of a murder at Vacaville prison. I want it on the air." His mouth was set in a steely grimace. "Not going to pixilate it or obscure it in any way. I want that murder on the air."

"You know that's part of the story of Jean Washington's corrupt DA's office, right?" Mick asked carefully.

"Yeah, my star's wife. Fuck that. We're not accusing a possible Presidential candidate of murder. Forget it. You don't have to go into that. You were interviewing a gang member in prison and he was killed before your very eyes."

Mick held his tongue again. That certainly was not how he intended to do the story, but this was an uncomfortable moment. Excruciating, actually.

"By the way," Saracenetti said quickly, seeing his wife-to-be coming, "that will never happen again. Right?"

"Oh absolutely. Right." Why do powerful men keep asking me to not have sex with their girlfriends? Mick asked himself.

"Your word?"

"My word."

Kitty McManus sat back down in a flutter of chatter. She'd run into a friend back there. Talk, talk, talk.

Mick tuned out.

This lunch was torture.

They ordered things. She chattered.

Mick was mulling. The Don wanted Mick to turn the Vacaville thing into a story all on its own, without bringing the DA into it. But most important, "Don, how do you know about that?"

Saracenetti took a slug of his drink and wrinkled his nose like he couldn't believe he was asked that question. "Kip Hinkle used to work for me when I was News Director in Sacramento. He called me to say I should bring you back, that you were sitting on a big story," he said as if Mick should have figured it out in an instant. His Rueben sandwich arrived. Kitty had a fruit salad. Mick's burger suddenly looked to him entirely inedible.

The lunch seemed to take forever. All Mick could think about was calling Rod Wings and begging him to take him back. The scene in San Francisco was so fucked up.

About the time the check was to arrive, Mick's phone buzzed and he saw it was Spike.

"What's up?" he asked, hoping it was something that would get him out of there fast.

"It's Cass. Looks like she jumped."

"What?"

"Jumped."

"How bad?"

"She's dead."

Gape-mouthed, Mick hesitated for a moment. "Where?"

"999 Green."

Mick snapped the flip phone shut. "Gotta go," he said, knocking his chair over as he stood.

Saracenetti and Kitty McManus stared as Mick fled to his car.

"Now what?" Saracenetti wondered aloud.

Kitty McManus fastened her eyes on Mick's butt as he ran out the door. She shrugged. "Who knows with that one …"

42

Swerving around slow-moving cars and buses, Mick flew up Union Street.

Dead? Could Cass Papadop really be dead? Would she have jumped, killed herself? No way. It had to be the big guy. Or maybe the boy wonder who was so crushed when she put him back on the shelf? Or maybe the bitch DA who knew Cass was ready to talk.

A few blocks up the hill he turned left on Jones, climbing an even steeper grade to the top at Green Street, the towering 999 Green casting a long shadow all the way down the hill. At the top he had to steal a spot using half a yellow zone. He found Spike pulling his sticks from the van. He was the only newsperson on the scene. Sirens were closing from a distance. "Where is she?"

"On top of that car over there," he pointed. "I got a still." He handed Mick his Canon pocket camera.

The picture was heartbreaking. Cass was face-up, looking at the sky, a distant almost serene look on her face. Her hair was windblown, her arms and legs casually extended as if she had flopped onto a bed. The roof of the car was caved in.

"Jesus, poor Cass," Mick muttered. "She wouldn't listen."

"Listen to what?"

Mick ignored Spike's question. "No cop around when you got here?"

Spike shook his head no. "Not a one. I heard the call on the scanner. Over at Ina Coolbrith Park getting weather shots." A small park with one of the best views of the city. "I was here in a minute. You can hear them coming now."

The cops blew it off, Mick thought.

Unless the Mayor didn't call them.

"Stand by," Mick said as he hurried away. He crossed the street and pushed through a small crowd gathering around the stoved-in car. There she was, splayed across the crushed roof of the car. Her eyes were not moving, dead still, gazing to the sky. He reached out and touched her cheek. No twitch. No response.

She was dead.

Papadop dead! He turned away. He did not want to look any longer.

Cops were arriving. Mick stepped back from the crowd and looked around for the guy in the blue blazer and striped tie, the desk guy in the lobby. The guy was at the curb with a phone to his ear.

Mick walked away slowly as cops streamed past him, shouting for the spectators to back away.

He slipped into the garage without being noticed. He made his way through the parked cars keeping an eye out for a security guard or a cop, anybody who might spot him and run him off. He stepped into an elevator and hit twenty-two with his elbow. Leave no fingerprints.

The elevator seemed to take forever, and when the doors slowly slid open he hurried down the hallway to find Cass's door wide open. Inside was a mess. Overturned Eames chair, couch on its back, scattered broken glass and personal things on the floor. Curtains billowing out the open sliding door to the lanai.

Mick snapped a few pictures with Spike's Sure Shot. He stayed away from the window and made sure he didn't touch anything. He spotted her phone on the floor. Using his shirt tail, he flipped it open, punched last dial. Two calls in quick succession. Jean Washington and the Mayor's office. So she finally talked to Bobby.

He thought of taking it, but quickly dismissed the idea. Grabbing the phone would be tampering with evidence and in his frantic mind he couldn't quickly think of a way to weasel out of something as serious as that.

But he did spot something else on the floor that looked interesting. A wadded-up paper. He smoothed it out. A messenger receipt. The paper was torn, looked like it'd been stepped on and ripped into pieces. The "to" line was interesting: Jean Washington's house. The "from" line a gym on Divisidero Street. He glanced around for the other part of the paper that might contain a notation on what the item was. Spotted nothing. He decided he'd chance taking it.

He pocketed the paper. Figure it out later. He took a few more pictures, though he wasn't quite sure why. He certainly didn't want the police to know he'd been in the crime scene. He hurried out.

Now a different problem. He was afraid of running into cops in the elevator coming up, so he passed the elevator bank, and skittered into the stairwell. Twenty-two floors are a lot, but he made it to the basement garage fairly quickly.

Outside a crowd had gathered, police cars and ambulances were stopped at crazy angles in the intersection. Uniformed officers stretched out crime scene tape. He made his way over to Spike. "Anybody else coming?"

"You kidding? Everybody. The old rule that we don't cover suicides is out. It's all hands on deck."

"Good." Mick punched the number of the assignment desk into his phone, it rang once and a man's voice came on: "Desk."

The shithead news director Pete DuFroid was at the desk, sticking his nose into the Danny Fuller's business. "Pete, bad news. Don hired me back. I'm taking Spike, I got the inside story. Save me room at the top of the show."

"Fuck off, Mickey."

"I have the story of why she was murdered. Don't make me call Don."

"Murder? It's a suicide. She jumped."

"She did not jump," Mick replied emphatically. "She was pushed, and I've got the story why. I told you, don't make me call Don. Save me a slot at the top."

Mick hung up. "You got a sat truck?" he asked Spike.

"No. Microwave van. But as long as I can see Sutro, we're good." Sutro Tower was the city's prime repeater tower for bouncing a microwave shot into the station. "Where we going?"

"Fremont."

"No problem from there."

It was a little tricky getting to the Bay Bridge because of the lights, but Spike pressed and they blew through some yellows and luckily caught a lot of greens.

When they made it on to the Bay Bridge, Mick called Bone Hendrix.

"You aren't fooling yourself into believing she jumped, are you?" he asked when the homicide Inspector answered.

There was a long silence. Then Bone answered. "No, of course not. I got a suspect in mind."

"He's first on my list too. And don't forget the bitch DA."

"She is stupid but not that stupid."

"I wouldn't be so sure," Mick said. "Her political career is on the bubble."

"There's always a silver lining," Bone mumbled.

"But there's another possibility and even if my guy didn't actually do it, you still want to talk to him."

"I'm listening. Who?"

"I'm calling to tell you to expect my call. I'm tracking him down now and when I have him cornered, I'll call you."

"We're the police. We do that much better. Who is he?"

"Inspector Hendrix, I'm still a reporter. As soon as I get him on tape, I'll call. It's a promise."

Mick got the Zardari address and phone number from 411. When someone picked up the phone he could hear crying and wailing in the background. A deep male voice said hello and asked who's calling.

Mick hung up. It was enough to know that Ali was home.

Spike ripped through the tunnel on Yerba Buena Island, flying across the cantilever section of the bridge, and floored it headed south on the 880 Freeway, the both of them praying they wouldn't be spotted by the CHP.

They pulled up in front of the Zardari house in thirty-five minutes, ten minutes shaved from what it would take a law-abiding driver. The Zardari family lived in a beige tract home on a residential street that could have been dropped down in any American suburb. It had a two-car garage, a small lawn in the front with a withered tree set in a circle of white stone. It looked like it might have four bedrooms, the front door recessed along a concrete walkway beside the garage.

"What's the plan?" Spike asked.

"Can't take a chance they barricade. Let's go in hot," Mick said. Spike shouldered his Panasonic DVC camcorder with the Frezi light clamped to the post topside. Mick carried a wireless stick mic and a spare Anton Bauer battery.

The door was answered by a man Mick took to be Ali's father. The older man was handsome like his boy, the primary difference was the added years and pounds and swooshes of gray in the hair and beard. He looked like an aging Omar Sharif. But of course the elder Zardari didn't want Mick in the house, didn't want him speaking to his son. It's always that way.

"I just lost one son. Now what does Channel 8 want with the only son I have left?" The sound of inconsolable sobbing wafted from somewhere in the dark recesses of the house.

Mick decided to drop the hammer. "Mr. Zardari my condolences for your lost son. But your son Ali is going to be a suspect in a murder case. The best thing he can do for himself right now is talk to me, get his story out to the public before the police make him out as a killer. If god forbid he's arrested I promise I'll have a lawyer waiting at the courthouse to bail him out."

"Arrested?" the older man's voice registered true shock. "For what?"

"A famous woman named Cass Papadop is dead. She was pushed off a high balcony. Your son was involved with her. He was in that apartment an hour before she was murdered. I know it's true because I was there, too. The police will be here soon. He must talk to me now or you might never see him again except in prison." Mick didn't hesitate to stretch the truth when needed.

Hamid Zardari, the rotund halal grocer, clearly sampled the foods he sold. Sweat appeared on his brow. Now he was frightened. "The neighbors are watching. Come in."

Mick double-checked the power switch on the hand mic with the Channel 8 cube. Spike had the camera on his shoulder. No time for tripods and lights. This was going to be down and dirty. Mick glanced at his cameraman with a wag of the eyebrows and Spike nodded back. It meant he was rolling. As soon as they were in the living room, Spike let the camera wander in the direction of the mantlepiece, crowded with family pictures.

Mrs. Zardari emerged from a back room. An attractive middle-aged woman, she was dressed Pakistani style, a long maroon shirt dress that came to below her knees, with trouser pants tight at the ankles. She went straight for her husband and hooked her arm in his.

If it had been up to the Zardari parents, nothing would have happened for Mick and Spike, but the sobbing from somewhere deep in the house seemed to settle down, and momentarily a red-eyed handsome boy emerged from a darkened hallway.

"Ali, it's Mickey. Come talk to me."

Ali pushed between his parents, ignoring Spike and the camera, ignoring the mic in Mickey's hand. "What happened? How did this happen?" he demanded.

"I hate to break this news to you but I am positive she was murdered."

His eyes welled up. "Murdered? Why?"

"The antiquity."

Ali's hands gripped the sides of his face. "Oh my god, no. Not that."

"Yes," Mick said, nodding. "The antiquity is the reason three other people have already been murdered. Police are looking for a mystery man. Three people murdered from London to San Francisco. All because they had something to do with Death in the Reeds."

"Is my son in danger?" he elder Zardari asked.

"Could be," Mick replied before turning again to Ali. "Where is it?"

Ali didn't want to answer. Mick had to push. "This is serious now, where is it?"

"Tell him, Ali," his father said.

Ali relented under his father's authority. "I left it with Miss Papadop."

"What she was going to do with it?"

"She said she would put it somewhere safe until we chose a buyer. It's worth millions and millions."

The messenger receipt leapt to mind. "Did she say she was going to send it somewhere?"

"She didn't say."

"Let's go back. How did you get the antiquity?"

Ali put his hands to his face, covering his eyes, and shaking his head. "I went to Beirut to find my brother. I tracked it from there to Paris. I went to Paris. I took it from the wall of the man who had it. I brought it home."

"You broke into a home in Paris?"

Ali just nodded yes.

"Who took it from the Iraq Museum?"

"My brother."

"Where is he?"

"He was killed in Beirut."

Ali's mother suppressed a sob. Behind Ali both Mick and Spike could see Ali's parents' eyes grow wide. Most of this they were hearing for the first time.

"Were you and Cass lovers?"

Now it was Ali's turn to break down in choking tears. When he regained control, he nodded. "Yes. I loved her. I think she loved me."

Mick doubted that, but let the boy have his fantasy.

"How did she get involved?"

He sniffled back his tears and straightened up. "I called her. I said I had a very valuable object coming into my possession and she could make a lot of money if she could help me sell it."

"Do you know who she tried to interest?"

"I know there was an Indian guy in Silicon Valley. A disreputable fellow, but rich."

"Babu Chakrabarti?"

"Yes. Him. I guess."

Now Mick decided it was time to turn the corner. "Do you realize you might be a suspect in Cass Papadop's murder?"

Ali's eyes widened. His mouth opened, but words would not come. At first. Then there was a gusher. "No, no, no. I loved her. I wouldn't harm her. Who says I am a suspect? That's slander. That's libel. That's a damnable lie."

"Where were you today at about noon?"

"I was here."

Hamid Zardari interrupted again. "Tell the truth, Ali."

"Okay, I was driving home. I got here about half an hour ago.

"There it is. You could be a suspect."

"Why?"

"Timing. You could have been at her apartment. That's opportunity. Motive? You were lovers and she broke it off."

"She didn't break up with me."

"I was there Ali. She sent you away. You were angry."

"No, I understood. She wanted to be alone. She told you to get out, too."

"That's true, but I wasn't in her bed. You were."

"I loved her. And she loved me. She was the one who led me to her room. I didn't force myself on her."

Barely audible, in the background Ali's father blurted out, "a kufr?" and groaned. He and his wife held each other tighter.

"You also might be a suspect because she took the Reeds from you."

Again, Ali's eyes widened and he shook his head vigorously left and right. "No, not true. She did not."

"Where is it? Do you have it?"

"She said she would put it somewhere safe."

"Did she tell you where?"

Now his eyes gave away the realization that she had blinded him with sex and bamboozled the prize out of his hands. "No, she didn't."

"If you had to find it to turn it over to the authorities. Could you find it?"

The answer was painfully long coming. "I don't know where it is."

"So she stole it from you."

"No. She said she would keep it safe."

"But you don't know where."

He shook his head no.

"Are you willing to tell the police everything you know?"

"Of course he will," Hamid Zardari interrupted. "My son is honest."

"Will you Ali?"

The boy nodded, and whispered, "Yes."

On Mick's glance back and a nod, Spike stepped back for a wide shot of Mick and Ali and Ali's parents. Mick knew it was his turn to talk so the editors would have set-up shots. Spike quickly stepped behind the parents and got a shot over their shoulders of Mick listening, a cutaway shot for editing soundbites together.

Mick thanked Ali for doing the interview. "Better sit tight. An Inspector Hendrix from the SFPD will be here shortly to speak to you."

"Should I take my son to meet Inspector Hendrix?" Hamid asked.

"It would probably be a good idea. Shows he has nothing to hide."

"Should we call a lawyer?" Hamid asked.

"Do you have a lawyer?"

Hamid shook his head no.

"Try this one." He regretted doing it, but he handed Hamid Kitty McManus' card. "She will meet you at the Hall of Justice. A lawyer should be with Ali when Inspector Hendrix interviews him."

Back outside at the van Spike started feeding in tape. The producer of the Six was screaming over the radio for Mick to call in.

Mick had to call Bone Hendrix first.

"His name is Ali Zardari. This is his parents' phone number," he said, reading off the number. "The father is going to drive him over to meet you at the Hall."

"When are they coming?"

"My guy is getting a shot of them driving away now."

"Got a license plate?"

Mick read back the plate number. He heard Bone cover the phone with his hand but could still hear him tell someone to get the CHP to track the car.

In a minute he came back on the line. "Are you telling me I should watch television so I'm prepared?"

"Probably a good idea," Mick said. "I don't intend to hold anything back."

With one exception: the torn messenger receipt.

43

Don Saracenetti called after the live shot. "You got the kid to puke his guts. Hard stuff to watch. But nobody could look away. Kick ass. I'm glad I brought you back, but I still don't trust you. Just keep delivering and you can keep your job."

"Jesus Don, shouldn't you say something about Cass? The poor girl is dead?"

"I have plenty to say about her. Just not to you."

Well, fuck you, Mick thought as he snapped his phone shut. Cass Papadop was dead. It was a shocking and sobering reality. And just so damn sad.

His phone buzzed. It was Saracenetti again. "Oh, and thanks for sending Ali to Kitty. I do appreciate that. But I still don't like you. Did I say that? I guess I did. The good news for you is that some people in the newsroom like you again. Some. Not all."

The loathsome Pete DuFroid called to tell him to get back to the shop. The 11 pm producer wanted him on set with the anchors to redo his story and a debrief.

Bone Hendrix called. He wanted to meet after the show. He had questions.

Mick was certain Ali hadn't killed Cass. He was almost certain it was the big guy, whatever his name was. He agreed to meet with Bone and some guy from New York because he needed the big guy's name, and Bone needed something from him—he wasn't sure what—so maybe there was a trade to be worked out.

The 11 pm hit was largely a redo of the down and dirty interview with Ali. His confession that he and Cass hooked up might embarrass Jean Washington and humiliate Bobby Vargas-Watson but they would just have to deal. It was a crucial part of the story.

At midnight Bone Hendrix, Bart Trappani and Mick were seated at a table in the basement of a restaurant in North Beach. Prosciutto hams hung above their heads. New York Italian Bart Trappani felt quite at home.

"I'm not telling you who my number one suspect is, because

that's police business, but you already figured out who it is," Bone said as their drinks arrived.

"I just need his name."

Bone and Trappani exchanged glances and Trappani shrugged.

"Can you keep it off the air for now?" Trappani asked.

"Sure." Mick actually didn't think he'd keep that promise.

"Pete Grand is what he goes by. His real name is evidently Pietro Granatelli," Bone said. "But we still need a way to confirm it's him if he makes contact. So far his name isn't out there for hoaxers to use."

Okay. Made sense. Mick was determined to find the guy and he had the same reason as Hendrix for keeping the name to himself. For now.

"He's an Italian tomboroli, a grave robber," Trappani said. "Antiquity laws have put those guys out of business, so he had to turn to his natural ability, which is hurting people." Trappani appeared to be a squared-away Marine. He had the high and tight haircut. He was in shape. His tie was always in place. His shirt never came untucked. He sipped a drink and could stretch it out for a couple hours without finishing.

"Is he after The Reeds for someone?"

Trappani pinched his face tight. "I shouldn't say, but it's probably Russians."

Some oil oligarch or maybe Putin, Mick thought. Doesn't matter right at the moment.

"What's the deal with throwing people off cliffs?" Mick asked.

"It's his fetish. Cliffs, windows, high buildings," Bone said. "He loves it, evidently."

Trappani jumped in. "Look, I'm here to retrieve the antiquity and return it to the Iraq Museum where it belongs," he said to Mick. "You guys got a murder case. Bless you. Find the guy. But I need to get my hands on the antiquity. Did she tell you where it is?"

The way he posed the question, Mick didn't have to lie. "No, she didn't. She didn't even really admit she had it. Ali is the one who confirmed she had it because he gave it to her."

"What did he say she did with it?"

"Just what you heard on the air. Put it somewhere safe is all he said."

Trappani was stymied. It was looking like the hiding place died with Cass Papadop.

"Meanwhile, I want the killer. Pete Grand," Bone Hendrix said.

"Me too. He might be the guy who killed my friend."

"Were you one of her boyfriends?" Bone asked, sneaking the question in, looking for a telltale reaction.

"No." But he didn't bring up the Mayor, Bobby Watson-Vargas. He knew he'd have to talk to Veedub soon.

"Have you eliminated the DA?"

Bone recoiled. "As a murder suspect?"

Mick related the confrontation he overheard on the phone between Cass and the DA.

"That's one crazy bitch but she can't be stupid enough to kill," Bone said.

"Even threatened with the end of her political career?"

Bone shrugged dismissively.

"Cass told me she was ready to talk. The DA plays rough."

"If you mean that Vacaville murder, that's a stretch," Bone scoffed. "Let's just concentrate on the big guy."

Mick wasn't so sure it was too much to suspect Jean Washington. But he let it go for now. "Did you pull Ali's travel records?" Mick asked Bone.

Trappani spoke up. "The Feds did that. He travelled to Beirut, and then to Paris and then here."

"I pulled Papadop's credit card records. She paid for it all," Bone added. "She was up to her eyeballs in obtaining a protected antiquity. If she were alive Bart would have to arrest her."

"Any more on how the thing was stolen in the first place?"

Trappani answered that one. "We're tracking it down but Ali's late brother, Wajahat Zardari may be the guy who pulled it off." Mick nodded. He knew that part.

"Appears he got into Iraq," Trappani continued. "Used his dad's passport. Weaseled his way into a job at the Museum. Jacked the object. Ran to Lebanon. Got killed in Beirut."

Mick nodded. Didn't know that stuff. Useful.

Bone and Trappani were together on one point. They had squeezed out of Mick all they were going to get that was useful, and now they wanted him out of their hair.

"I'm solving a murder," said Bone, "so please butt out."

"I'm recovering an antiquity. I need you to stay out of the way," added Trappani.

Two men with badges brushing him back. Trappani shook his hand. "Sorry about your friend," he said, meaning Cass.

A thought popped into his head. "Just curious," Mick said to Trappani. "Did you ever meet her?"

"I did," Trappani said, nodding. "Quite an attractive young woman. We went to the DA's house to question her. I actually handed her a gym bag that was on the porch. Had her name on it."

"Funny," Mick said. "Don't usually leave your gym clothes on the porch."

Trappani shrugged. "Had a tag. Messenger service."

Mick smiled, and nodded. Nothing more to say at the moment. The torn receipt in his pocket told Mick they could want him to go away, but he was still in the game.

Back on the street, Bone and Trappani wheeled off in Bone's SFPD Crown Vic. Mick checked his voicemail. Veedub had left several messages.

Mick called him back.

The Mayor was a blubbering mess. In between waves of sobbing grief, he asked Mick "did you really have to include the fact she was involved with that kid?"

Involved, Mick thought. Guess banging was too rough for Veedub. "He was in love. Explains why he did everything he did."

"The only saving grace is you left me out of it," Veedub groused.

"You really weren't in it."

"Don't rub it in." He asked about any suspects. "Think that bitch could have done it?"

"Doesn't seem like it," Mick lied. No point in stirring the Mayor up more than he was already.

Veedub told Mick he was personally making funeral arrangements for Thursday, two days off. He asked Mick if it was true he had pictures of the body.

"I still have Spike's camera and yes there are a couple pictures of the body," Mick answered, truthfully.

"You'll destroy those, won't you?"

"Sure," Mick said. He had to say he would. But he wasn't so sure. The pictures were no use to him or Spike. They would never be shown. There was no point in keeping them. Same with the signs of a struggle in her apartment. Mick couldn't show those on the air because it would indicate he'd been in the apartment before the cops arrived. That would lead to endless trouble. But still. Once the pictures were gone there was no getting them back. "No problem, I'll erase them," he said. But he didn't mean it.

"Thank you. One more thing."

"What?"

"Will you speak at the funeral?"

"Me? A eulogy? Shouldn't you do that?"

"What? That'd be as good as admitting the affair? I can't. Please do it."

"Okay."

What would he say? A beloved woman got involved in illegal smuggling of a priceless antiquity and paid with her life?

No. Best leave that for the news.

44

Mick's plan was to use himself as bait.

The mysterious Pete Grand was lurking somewhere around San Francisco trying to locate the multimillion-dollar antiquity. From the day Cass died he would have known—from Mick's television report—that Ali Zardari no longer had possession of the object, nor did he know what Cass did with it. Typical of Pete Grand that his impetuous urge to hurl a person from great heights actually made it impossible to reach his goal. Seemed he'd killed the one person who knew where Death in the Reeds was.

Mick had to chalk that up to the big guy's uncontrollable volatility. Or just plain stupidity.

The big guy didn't know where to find the object behind all his murders.

But Mick knew. Now it was just a matter of making certain Pete Grand knew that Mick knew. Then Pete Grand would come to Mick.

His return to the Channel 8 newsroom wasn't a huge welcome, by any means. But the days of heaving garbage and tape boxes at his head were over. Mick sat in an edit booth just off the newsroom with an editor reworking tape for the day-after package.

Other people were working on the Cass obituary, somebody else was doing the piece that rounded up tearful testimonials from the city's famous faces, but the crime story—who killed her—that was Mick's.

The tape editor was a late twenties butch lesbian named Sally Pepper. She went by Sal. Sounded more masculine. She wore her red hair in a mop on top of buzz cut sides, she had a nose ring, nipple piercings you could see through her tank top, and tats of various designs on her arms running up her neck to just below her ears. "I never really liked her," she said to Mick as they sat down to go over the tape. "Faking gay is offensive."

"You glad she's dead?"

Pepper reacted with a scowl. "Of course not. Just wish the born straight would stay out of my space."

"Fair enough," Mick said. There was not much good that comes out of a hostile relationship in the close confines of an edit booth. Better to get along.

They pulled some bites from the Ali interview that hadn't been used the night before. Spike went to the library for close shots of Death in the Reeds. A writer accompanied Spike to get a bite from the head of the Asian Art Museum on the importance of the piece. "A priceless antiquity may be lost for a second time. Tragic," he said.

The script was in the computer. Don Saracenetti had seen it and offered neither compliments nor objections. Same with Pete DuFroid. It felt like a standard follow up. Mostly rehash.

The assignment editor, Danny Fuller, dropped by the edit booth to needle Mick.

"Doesn't it feel great to completely own a story?"

Mick grinned. "Sure does."

"The other guys are eating dust. Either ignoring the story, pretending it doesn't exist, or trying to catch up and always a day behind."

"Always keep your boot on the neck of the competition," Mick said.

KBAY was wallowing in the giant ratings that came along with an explosive and exclusive story. DuFroid could hate him, Saracenetti could waver on him, but the sales department was stacking cash.

It was huge and wholly owned by Mickey Judge and KBAY.

Fuller lingered at the door. "What's the surprise going to be?"

Mick snorted. "Why do you think there's a surprise?"

"I saw the script. Pure vanilla. Straight tell. Completely not you. What are you saving to puke up live when they can't stop you?" Danny was a skinny guy with lanky black hair that always seemed to be demanding a thorough shampoo. The mischievous glint in his eyes were a mirror image of his personality.

"Danny, you are a wise man. But if I was planning something like that and if I told you …" he paused. "Then you would feel obligated to tell dickhead and the boss and that would spoil all the fun."

"So where should I put a camera?"

Mick thought about that for a moment. "You could put one in the newsroom to get some tape of Pete blasting out of his office screaming. But that wouldn't do much good because you could never use it."

"No. That wouldn't make air. And whoever leaked it would get fired."

"Yeah, so that's out." Mick thought about it a little more. "Better. Put a crew outside. Get Bone Hendrix screeching to a stop in his Crown Vic. He'll storm into the lobby. Then you could have the crew actually escort him downstairs, rolling the whole way, of course. And you might even get great stuff of him grabbing me by the neck and squeezing until I turn purple."

"Don't tease me."

"That will happen."

Danny Fuller grinned. "Now you're talking. Done deal."

Then he disappeared.

A couple of the reporters stopped by to say "great job" and "way to go" and such. But there were others who kept their distance, who didn't like the sudden return and instant ascendancy of a guy they thought they'd gotten rid of.

Even the anchors were a little leery of him. Gary Wisdom—oddly, his real name—a former Cal quarterback, was the lead anchor at 11pm, along with Colleen McGilvray, both gorgeous specimens of their genders. They welcomed him to the set with formality dialed down to chill. Mick sat to Coleen's left, the lead anchor stud on her right.

The news opened with high drama, of course. "Tragedy struck close to home for the Channel 8 news family," Wisdom announced with the somber air of a funeral director. First up was the obituary, a combination of explainer on her death ("She may have jumped,") and a round-up of her life and career, her "wife" figuring prominently with a full two minutes of sound bites from DA Washington, the self-proclaimed "love of Cass's life."

That was followed by a long package of reactions from the city's prominent people, Mayor Veedub, county supervisors, the society figures from Pacific Heights, Senator Feinstein, Governor Brown, and even players from the Giants, and Forty-Niners.

Finally it was time for Mick and the investigation into Cass

Papadop's murder.

The anchor lead described a manhunt for the prime suspect, an exceptionally large and vicious foreign-born brute who had allegedly killed three people in search of a stolen antiquity before he was suspected of killing Cass Papadop.

After the anchor handoff, the first words Mick spoke was breaking his promise to Bone Hendrix: Mick identified the suspect as Peter Grand of London, "unarmed but dangerous."

Mick threw to his package on the roll cue … "Pete Grand is here and he's stalking the antiquity."

While the package was running, Mick slipped a note to the beautiful Colleen McGilvray: "Ask me if I know where Death in the Reeds is."

Coming out of the package Gary Wisdom asked Mick about the search for the suspect. Mike kept the answer short. He wanted Colleen to have time for a question.

And she did.

"So Mick, after all your reporting on this story, do you know where the antiquity is?"

"I do," Mick said. "I'm absolutely positive I know where it is."

"Where?"

"I can't say yet because we're still investigating how to retrieve it, but I do know its location."

"Okay," she said brightly, "more to come on this amazing and tragic story."

As he predicted Pete DuFroid came flying out of his office screaming for somebody to get that sonofabitch Mickey Judge down here right now!

And as predicted the crew waiting on the sidewalk got a good shot of Bone Hendrix' Crown Vic skidding to a stop and Bone hopping out with another guy in tow. The crew followed them into the lobby, opened the elevator door and offered no objection when the two men jumped in the elevator.

And as predicted there was excellent tape of Bone Hendrix grabbing Mick by the lapels and demanding to know the location of the antiquity that had cost so many lives.

And really awesome video of Mick refusing to tell.

Mick knew exactly where The Reeds was. And he had a good reason to not reveal what he knew just yet. That's because he knew Pete Grand would be coming after him next. Which was the plan.

45

Mick was able to weasel out of the interrogation by Trappani and Bone because of the funeral. Trappani was livid. He wanted the Reeds now. Bone was sure Mick was full of shit. "He has no clue where that thing is."

True to his word Veedub staged an over-the-top show for Cass's funeral. And at his suggestion—an order, really—Channel 8 carried it live.

Under stunning blue skies—always a rarity in fogbound Colma, San Francisco's cemetery suburb—black clad masses assembled in grieving silence, whispering greetings. A one-stop funeral home, chapel and gravesite at Cypress Lawn in Colma. Cass's Greek parents would have preferred the Greek Orthodox church on Green Street—just five blocks from 999 Green—and the Greek Orthodox cemetery in Colma, but both were too small to properly host the mourners.

Cass Papadop always drew a crowd of A-listers. The grieving widow, Jean Washington, stunning in a black form-fitting dress, seated next to the Governor. They were parked in the row of pews directly across the aisle from the forty-strong Papadopolous family—Veedub had them jammed into a black limo caravan streaming down I-80 from Sacramento. The roster of Pacific Heights swells arrived in a swarm of black cars. The congressional delegation sat alongside Veedub in the second-row pew opposite the family and a rogue's gallery of Silicon Valley billionaires. An array of floral grotesquerie lined up in a hallucinogenic pastel forest. The casket was mahogany polished to a mirror finish with sparkling brass and emphatically closed. In place of an open casket, a glossed-up portrait of Cass in her glorious prime stood on an easel front and center.

An Eastern Orthodox priest led prayers and readings from the gospels. Her nieces read a poem. Jean Washington daubed tears as she gasped phony sobs over the love of her life. Don Saracenetti said a few lines about her star-power and her millions of loyal fans. Veedub rose to say he was too broken up to say much about his longtime colleague. He said he asked Mickey Judge to stand in for him.

Many in the gathering wondered why Mickey Judge was giving a eulogy. He'd been her friend two decades earlier. But he'd been gone a long time and only recently arrived back. Worst of all he was the guy who revealed her secrets on the air. People thought it was weird.

After the reception, Mick walked to his car parked under a stand of pine trees. A note was under the windshield wiper.

So you want me? Terrible mistake. If you have the guts, tomorrow at noon. Rodin. Come alone or I don't show. Pete Grand invited him to a face-to-face at the Rodin statue The Thinker at the Palace of the Legion of Honor.

"Gotcha," Mick said to himself.

But he had to stop and think about the location. At Lands End, the far reaches of the Richmond District where the houses are west of the Golden Gate Bridge on a point of land looking back at the entrance to the Bay and the Bridge. On a Monday the Legion of Honor Museum was closed. Chances were good few people would be around. But there were always hikers, and a public golf course was nearby. Mick could count on a few witnesses.

However, it was a location fraught with danger. The shoreline was rugged, some spots having cliffs with two-hundred-foot drops to the water or the rocks below. It would not be difficult for Pete Grand to pick a lonely spot to toss Mick over an edge.

What to do to stay safe?

Back at the station Mick went searching for Spike. At the assignment desk Danny Fuller was still in his funeral suit, entirely out of place in the glass cage of frantic and looney assignment editors. He checked the board and said Spike had radioed he'd be back from the funeral shortly.

"I'm going to need him tomorrow."

"More fun?" Danny asked with an impish grin.

"May be close to wrapping this thing up."

"Okay, he's off the board for tomorrow, but the shows will want to know what you got."

"When I know, they'll know."

Saracenetti ran into him in the stairwell. "That was some bullshit stunt you pulled yesterday. Bone says you lied."

"About what?"

"Knowing where the damn thing is."

"I know where it is. No lie."

"You're obligated to turn it over."

"Patience."

"Patience bullshit. I said you have a way of getting in over your head but you are totally outdoing yourself." He started to walk away, then turned on his heel. "And by the way, I want that Vacaville murder tape on the air as soon as this Cass thing settles down." Something more came to him. "And no sneaking in live bullshit about the DA."

He stalked off without an adios. Mick reminded himself yet again to call Rod Wings as soon as he wrapped this story.

Mick pulled Spike out of his truck and hustled him over to his small office behind the Studio Grill. He had barely moved in when Saracenetti benched him after the Embarcadero shooting. There was a phone, a computer, a printer, a desk and two chairs. Next to the printer two coffee cups with green fuzz covering month old black coffee.

"Here's the scenario. He wants me to show up at the Rodin statue tomorrow at noon."

"He wants you to tell him where the thing is?"

"I assume."

"Are you going to tell him?"

"No."

"Then why would you meet him? That's a place where he could shove you down a cliff and you'd probably die. I thought you were done being stupid."

Mick pondered an answer. Spike was right in a certain sense. Pete Grand was a killer. Mick would be taking a terrible chance meeting the killer at a place of maximum danger. What was the point exactly?

"I want to ask him if he killed Cass."

Spike jerked his head back in surprise. "Wait. Aren't we sure he killed her?"

"Not really. We just assume it because of this thing he has about throwing people over the side."

"Do you think he'd confess to you?"

"Yeah, I do. I think he's proud of the people he's tossed. I bet he'd say right away he did it … if he did it."

Spike shook his head. "You're out of your mind. This is a terrible chance to take for virtually no upside. What are you going to do if he says he didn't? Go on the air and say 'I personally interrogated the alleged killer and I believe him when he says he did not kill Cass Papadop.' That's pretty fucking lame if you ask me."

Mick looked his friend in the eye. "I think I owe it to her."

Spike shook his head no. "Facing her killer at the spot he's picked out which just happens to be a perfect place to do to you what he's done to, what? Three other people?"

"He won't push me over a cliff. He needs me to get what he wants. And I'm the only person on the planet who knows where it is."

"Oh? Then why did he kill Cass? She knew where it is."

"That's the issue, isn't it? I'm not entirely sure he did kill Cass, and that's precisely the reason I can't be sure."

"So what're you going to do? Take his word for it?"

Mick shrugged. "So how do I do this safely?"

Spike looked over the situation and shook his head no again. "Meeting him alone is asking for it."

"So what do you suggest?"

Spike shrugged. "To me there's no choice but just come out there rolling and see what happens."

"You and your camera right out in the open?"

"Yeah. Why not? What's he going to do? Throw us both over?"

Mick rejected the idea. "I can't put you in that position. He might very well throw both of us over." Mick rocked his head back and forth. "I'm going to have to do this alone."

"Dude, that makes no sense whatsoever. First, all alone you're in danger. Second, if we don't have video, it might as well never have happened."

They sat staring at each other, each looking for an answer.

"Maybe you're right," Mick said. "I should just no show. He'll figure out another way to contact me. He has to. I'm the one who knows where the thing is."

On the walk back across the street to the station Spike watched his old friend, and he could almost see the wheels turning.

He didn't believe for a second that Mick would forgo the meet. Of course he would go.

"Dude, I can see what you're thinking. What good does it do to go out and face this guy alone? You can't arrest him. You can't interview him. He can do plenty of bad stuff to you. What's the point?"

"Who says I'm going?"

"I can see it on your face. You're telling me you won't but I know you will."

"You're wrong. I'm going to skip it. He'll come at me another way."

They parted at the corner of Golden Gate and Hyde. Spike went into the station. Mick headed for his car.

Everything about Mick's body language and his denial told Spike that his friend was lying.

Spike went straight to Danny Fuller and took him into an edit booth. Danny listened carefully. "Where's the meet?"

"Mick said the Rodin, tomorrow. Noon."

"The video is gold. Absolute gold. Can we get the shot?"

"You want me to sneak out there and stake him out? What happens if the goon sees me?"

Danny frowned. "Yeah, this is tricky. We need to get permission for this. Above my pay grade."

They both marched out of the edit booth and went to see News Director DuFroid.

He listened. "The Don has to okay this."

They all rode the elevator together to Saracenetti's office.

"Mick has a meet with Cass's killer?" Saracenetti boomed. "That's huge. How do we get pictures?"

They cooked up a plan. Spike would hide in a rent van and get a shot of the meet up.

"What if Mick is in danger?" Spike asked. He was feeling maybe he shouldn't have said where and when the meet was to happen. "It's both pointless and taking a big chance."

"Who knows what's on Mickey Judge's mind?" Saracenetti scoffed. "In a public place like the Palace of the Legion of Honor that thug doesn't dare do anything."

Saracenetti glanced around at the frowning faces of his underlings and shook his head. "He'll be fine. And we'll be the only outfit on earth that has a picture of the guy. This is huge. Huge!"

46

There was plenty of reason to be fearful meeting a killer. Especially a killer who would demand to know the location of the Reeds and more especially because there was no way Mick was going to tell him.

Mick decided to go armed. It was a total violation of a reporter's ethical standards, but this was not a time to worry about such niceties.

Before the meeting at the Rodin, he spent the evening in a storage unit at a Public Storage facility on Third Street near Police Headquarters. He had rented the place when his dad died because he couldn't quite bring himself to get rid of his father's things.

The storage unit was depressing. His dad's personal possessions, boxed, labeled, and stashed. Every time he saw the charge on his Amex bill he wondered why he didn't just close it up. But here he was, shifting boxes around looking for particular things that might just save his life. He searched through his father's stuff until he located what he needed.

It took an hour but he found three items he was looking for. First, his dad's snub nose .38 special. Mick decided he would carry that in his jacket. But his father always cautioned if you were carrying a gun you needed to carry a back-up. To that purpose his father had a special pair of black dress boots, which he wore on the job. Inside the uppers of the right boot was a pocket where his dad kept an emergency weapon. The weapon was small. Actually, very small. It was a five-shot mini-revolver called the Sidewinder that fired .22 Magnum ammunition. Smaller than his hand, the gun fit nicely in the pocket of the boot.

Along with the .38, the boots, and the Sidewinder, he found boxes of the ammunition he needed.

He sat on some boxes and pulled on the boots. His feet were just a bit bigger than his dad's. The boots were tight, but he didn't plan on walking far and the gun was there if he needed it.

The next morning Mick rolled out of bed and noticed a dreary fog-bound day out his window. Figuring there would be wind and fog at the Rodin statue, Mick pulled on a set of thermals, and thin socks. He wore light running pants over the thermals, and a hoodie sweat shirt. He pulled the boots on with a bit of a struggle.

He slung on a leather bomber jacket and checked his guns. Both loaded and ready.

He showed at the meeting spot forty-five minutes early. Mick parked near the Rodin statue, and scanned the parking lot, the start of the hiking trail. He didn't see Pete Grand. He failed to realize a plain Jane rent-van at the side of the Museum was the hiding spot for Spike and his camera. He leaned against the pedestal with his cup of coffee to wait.

The meet time was noon. After forty-five minutes, the coffee was gone and still no Pete Grand.

Suddenly Mick realized what few cars were in the lot had all pulled away. One minute there are people and cars, the next minute they vanish. Vehicles and people would reappear but for an instant he was alone. The only vehicle was that unoccupied delivery van at the side of the Museum. He glanced around, saw no hikers or wandering tourists. It was one of those rare occasions in a city where a person could find himself alone for a few fleeting moments.

And at that moment a tall figured stepped out of a Eucalyptus stand and motioned him over. It was Pete Grand.

Mick walked across the parking lot slowly, sizing up the big man.

The scar across his face multiplied the menace of Pete Grand's size and bulging strength. His eyes squeezed to slits focusing on Mick.

At about fifteen feet Pete Grand's hand emerged from his jacket pocket holding a gun. Mick froze. He cursed himself for not being ready with his own weapon.

"Stop there," Pete said. He stepped forward holding the gun pointed at Mick's chest. For a couple of moments Mick couldn't take his eyes off the nasty hole at the end of the barrel. "Where's your gun?" Pete asked.

"Who says I have a gun?"

"Don't play games. You'd be stupid to come without one. Where is it?"

There was no choice. Mick remembered the Westerns he watched as a kid. The bad guy had the drop on him.

"Jacket pocket, left side."

Pete moved close enough Mick could smell his body odor. The guy hadn't taken a shower in a day or two. He reached into Mick's pocket and pulled out the .38. "Cop gun. Who's the cop?"

"My dad."

"Is he hiding here somewhere," Pete asked glancing around.

"No. He's dead."

"Anybody else follow you out there?"

"No."

Pete put Mick's gun in his left jacket pocket and held the other in the opposite pocket.

"You're the little shit who has my prize," he said.

Mick shook his head no. "I don't have it. But I know where it is."

He grunted disapproval. "The last guy bullshitting me about that took a long fall."

"I've heard that about you."

Pete stared at Mick for a long moment, then nodded his head to the right. "Let's walk."

"Where?"

"That way," Pete said, pointing.

Mick felt fear rising in his throat, like bile. Pete Grand was directing him across the fairway of one of the links of the Lincoln Park golf course. Straight ahead were the cliffs of Lands End.

And it only took a few steps to realize his father's boots were tighter than he expected. He would have to ignore the pain in his toes.

"Where we going?"

"Just keep walking."

They walked and walked and walked until they came out of Lincoln Park on El Camino Del Mar, the street that winds through a wealthy neighborhood called Sea Cliff.

"Where we going?" Mick asked again. His feet were killing him.

"Keep going."

Mick thought about flagging down a passing car, or running into an open garage. But Pete Grand was thinking ahead of him.

"If you try to run, I shoot you," he said, seeming to anticipate Mick's thoughts. "And if you do something stupid like calling for help from someone passing by? You know I kill the both of you, right?"

"Shoot innocent people?"

"Of course. It'll be your fault."

Mick thought about the gun. It looked like a modern weapon, maybe a Glock or a Sig Sauer. Probably had a clip holding more than a dozen rounds. Yes, he could kill a lot of people.

"I thought you threw people. What's with the gun?"

"A man should be flexible. Can't always do things the way you'd like to."

When they emerged from Sea Cliff onto Lincoln Blvd. and headed north, uphill, Mick had a sudden and frightful realization.

They were on their way to the Golden Gate Bridge.

Mick's mind raced. He hadn't planned on this. The son of a bitch isn't going to shoot me. He's going to toss me.

47

Spike was in a panic. He called Danny Fuller. "I lost him."

"Fuck. Where'd you last see him?"

"Mick and the big guy walked across the 8th fairway at Lincoln Park Golf Course. They got on the cliff trail. I couldn't follow in the van."

Danny Fuller was in his chair at the KBAY assignment desk flipping through a Thomas Brothers map book.

"So did they go to the left or the right?" Left would take them toward the Sutro Baths and the Cliff House. To the right would take them through Sea Cliff. But either way there were scary cliffs that claimed lives every year.

"They talked for a few moments," Spike said. "I couldn't tell for sure in the viewfinder but I think that guy had a gun. Kinda looked like it."

"Where are you now?"

"The Palace parking lot."

"Any cars?"

"A few. Museum's closed."

"Hang there. I'm getting the chopper up. He can set down in the parking lot."

"You'll catch hell."

"I know. Just hang."

"Better call Bone Hendrix. This doesn't look good."

"You make that call. I'll get the chopper."

"Jesus, Danny. I don't have his number."

"Just call the PIO. Whoever it is today can get to him."

It took twenty minutes to get Bone Hendrix on the phone.

By that time Mick and Pete Grand were on the bridge approach. And Mick's feet felt like big blisters about to pop.

48

Along the trudge from Sea Cliff, downhill to Baker Beach and back uphill to the Bridge, Pete spoke two words. Repeatedly: "Keep walking."

When they passed through the crowd of bus tourists at the Joseph Strauss statue, Pete kept a big hand on Mick's shoulder, like they were old pals out for a stroll. The other hand was tucked in a pocket holding the gun.

"Far enough." At the Golden Gate Bridge midspan Pete told Mick to stop. At that point the 7500-foot suspension cables dip to their lowest level, about seven feet off the bridge roadway.

There was a yellow call box attached to a light pole, and a small blue sign with white lettering: Crisis Counseling. The consequences of jumping from this bridge are fatal and tragic. There is hope.

The Golden Gate Bridge is held up by massive suspension cables three feet in diameter, made up of twenty-seven thousand individual wires wrapped tightly in more wire and covered in a protective coating of International Orange paint. From those massive cables hang two hundred and fifty steel ropes two inches thick which hold up the road deck.

Mick took stock of his situation. From the top of the handrail to the bottom of the massive suspension cable there was an opening of about four feet. Mick instantly realized that this opening gave the killer plenty of room to shove a person through. He quickly calculated that if this happened there was a small chance he might grab the pickets of the railing and hold on. But for a really strong killer—Pete Grand's reputation—there was also the possibility of him actually throwing his victim over the suspension cable. In which case there was no chance Mickey could grab something to save himself. It was the thin breezy air all the way to certain death.

People dressed in sweaters and ski jackets streamed by. "This is good," Pete said. "Let's enjoy the view." He leaned up against the railing like a man resting on his stroll.

It was a hot day in the Central Valley a hundred miles east. That rising hot air draws in cool air from the ocean. Fog and wind were blasting through the gate. The gusts whipped Mick's hair. Two hundred twenty feet below, the tidewaters roared under the bridge in a fierce chop. He shivered in his leather jacket, more from the gasping drop than the cold.

"See your situation?" Pete asked. "You should look down and think."

Mick looked over the edge. The killer wanted him to focus on the deadly waters. But Mick noticed eighteen inches of steel roadbed protruding from under the hand railing. He wondered if it was enough to save him.

Bridge walkers brushed by them. Mick summoned a shaky defiance. "As long as these tourists keep coming by, I think I'm okay."

Pete Grand sneered. "There will be a break," he said, looking to the north and south. "The crowd isn't continuous."

He refocused on Mick. "You tell me what I want to know. If you don't," he jerked a thumb toward the long fall. "Over you go. "

Mick shook his head. "Stupid plan. You'll get caught. You'll be in San Quentin Prison right over there," Mick pointed across the bay.

The big man nodded as if he expected Mick to say something like that. Pete ran his hand over his facial scar. "People see my face and they are frightened. Most people assume this scar isn't from an accident in the kitchen or a childhood wreck on a bicycle."

"Is it?"

He shook his head no. "It's from a fight, of course. But people shouldn't assume that. It could be anything. The point is, the scar gives people an excuse to assume I'm just a stupid thug."

"It's a fair assumption."

"See? You think so too," Pete's eyes lit up as he got to his point. "But think about this. If I was the clumsy, knuckle-dragging ape you take me for, how come I do what I do and walk away? People are upset and they want to know how come the bad guy doing the bad things isn't caught? And yet … I'm still out and about to do more bad things."

Mick shook his head. "So far you've just been lucky."

Pete Grand smiled. "I've been doing this a long time. Nobody is that lucky."

"You think you can outsmart everybody?"

Pete shrugged. "It's true sometimes I let my temper get the best of me. I seize an opportunity and might appear to be hasty. Rash. But most times I think things through and plan. To make certain I'm not in one of your prisons."

He nodded at Mick as if to say get it?

"So what's your plan here?"

Pete leaned over the railing and looked down at the deadly water. "You tell me where the object is. And then we keep walking over to the Marin side. We get in my car. We drive wherever, we retrieve the object. I let you go and I disappear. Just like always."

"I don't believe you'd just let me go."

"Believe what you want. You asked what's the plan. That's it."

Seemed far more likely to Mick the big man would just kill him once he had the Reeds. "And if I don't?"

Pete nodded. "That's why I brought you here. I wanted you to see the long way down. It should make you think. But if you're too thick to comprehend, then yes … I make you fly. And I walk away. Just another tourist on the bridge."

"You're an unusual looking guy. People will ID you."

"If anybody sees us when you go over," Pete Grand said, "they'll look at you going down. They always do. I'll walk away quietly while they're all screaming. I'll be gone. A ghost. Vanished in the fog." He laughed softly. "You think I'm a big dumb asshole. But maybe you've noticed I do what I do and disappear. I'm better at staying ahead of cops than you give me credit for."

Mick shivered. "Eventually you'll make a mistake."

"But not now. I want to know where the object is. This is your time to tell me."

Mick shook his head no. "I'm not telling your where it is."

Pete grunted his disapproval. "Keep an eye on the tourists. When you see we're alone for a minute or so you better tell me immediately or over you go."

Mick shook his head no again. "I don't believe you. What's the point of killing me? I'm the only one who knows where it is."

"That's an issue, isn't it?" Pete Grand mused. "It's hard to explain, but fortunately for me my client is a very patient man. If I don't get the object now, it will turn up eventually. And I will go retrieve it. The principle here is I can't let an insignificant little reporter defy me, stand in my way, and get away with it. The next guy has to know what happens."

"You're assuming if you don't get it now, you will later. It might be lost a long, long time."

Pete shook his head no. "Nothing stays lost forever."

Traffic was whizzing by at high speed, wheels on the roadbed zinging. The fog was streaming over the bridge deck. Mick glanced toward the Marin side. There was a break coming in the marching column of shivering and giddy bridge walkers.

"The point is this," Pete continued, pointing at the water below. "I want you to look down at this long drop. I read that a body will reach a speed of 75 miles an hour. Very painful impact. If you're lucky you die right away. If you're unlucky you're in agony for a few minutes until you drown."

Mick looked over the side. Pete was right. The fast-moving choppy water looked vicious. And nothing between him and the abyss but that eighteen inches of extra roadbed.

Mick noticed the break in groups of bridge walkers had arrived. It was time to do something to save himself.

"I don't have my pack. Got a smoke?"

Pete Grand shook his head. "Mooch," he said, handing Mick a pack of Marlboro Reds and a Zippo lighter.

Mick's grip slipped and he dropped the pack at his feet. "Sorry," he said, leaning down to pick it up. He grabbed the cigarettes with his left hand, and his right hand slipped inside his right boot. He came up with the Sidewinder. The gun was small, so small it fit between the palm of his hand and his index finger.

Pete Grand let an expression of surprise cross his face for just a moment. Then he laughed and held up his hands. "Oh, you have a little gun?" he sneered.

"It's big enough."

Pete's gun was in his pocket. He knew better than to reach for it now. "That thing probably doesn't even make a noise. You sure it can hurt somebody?" He ducked his head back and forth, mocking Mickey's tiny gun.

"I'm sure."

Pete made a frowny face. "Maybe you miss. Maybe you learn to fly."

"Maybe you live, maybe you don't."

They stared at each other, each sizing up his chances.

In the impasse Pete let himself have a thoughtful moment. "I know why I wanted to see you," Pete said. "I still don't understand why you wanted to see me."

"That's easy. Did you kill Cass Papadop?" Mick asked.

Pete smirked. "Oh, that. You reporters are reckless sometimes. I could sue you for claiming I'm good for a crime I didn't commit."

"Please do. Sue me."

Pete waved him off. "But to answer to your question. No. I didn't kill her. Why do you think it was me?"

"The way she died. You killed three others throwing them off high places."

A boyish grin blossomed on the frightening face. "There's something about throwing a man into thin air that just feels good.

Don't know why. I'm told I must see a shrink about that."

"So you threw Cass?"

Pete raised his hand to stop Mick. "Doesn't make sense I should toss her. She could tell me how to find what I'm looking for."

"Now you're the one not making sense," Mick rejected the denial. It was worth nothing. "You wouldn't kill her because she could tell you where to find the Reeds, but you'd toss me? I'm the only living person who knows where it is."

Pete Grand took a second to light a cigarette, staring at Mick. He exhaled a swirling stream of smoke to the fog. "Yeah. It's a bit of a contradiction. I'm a complicated guy."

"Why should I believe you didn't kill Cass?"

"Why should I bother telling you anything? I don't care what you think."

"I'm the one with the gun. Maybe I just shoot you for her."

Pete Grand fish-eyed Mick. "I didn't kill your girlfriend."

Mick shook his head. "I don't believe you."

"So don't. I don't care. But I still want what I want. Where is the Reeds?"

"Forget it."

"Don't push your luck," Pete snorted. "Where is it?"

"I won't be telling you that."

"If you don't, you better flap your wings."

"You're not going to touch me." Mick leveled the gun at Pete's chest. "I'm leaving now." He took a step back.

Pete laughed and stepped forward, matching Mick. "You scaring me with that midget gun?" He bobbed and weaved. "Can you pull off a head shot? I doubt it."

Traffic had been streaming by in both directions in a constant whoosh of speed. But now nothing. Quiet. Both men noticed. The roadway was empty.

Pete Grand craned his neck to see behind him. In the distance on the Marin side traffic was stopped by CHP cars with flashing lights. Behind Mick traffic was stopped in the same manner on the San Francisco side.

Both men turned to the sound of a helicopter rising from below their view, turning as it churned the air. Spike was in the open door with his camera.

"You set a trap?" Pete asked, genuinely surprised.

Mick shook his head no. "Not me, but I'm glad somebody did."

They stared at each other, each deciding what to do now. "It's over, you're done," Mick shouted over the rotor wash.

Pete Grand swiveled his head left and right, sizing up his situation. The mask of reasonableness dropped. When cornered Pete was still a man ruled by anger, by temper on a short fuse. He seethed with corked-up rage.

Then he exploded. He lunged at Mick, grabbing him by the lapels of the jacket with both hands. "Gotcha!" he hissed into Mick's face.

Mick recoiled from the monster's breath, but he was caught. He pressed the gun into the big man's chest and pulled the trigger. One shot seemed to do nothing.

"You miserable prick, if I go down, you go down," Pete Grand snarled.

Mick pulled the trigger four more times. He saw some blood at Pete's shoulder and a bit more on his right arm. But it didn't slow Pete down.

Pete Grand had Mick in his massive hands. Mick struggled to break free, but he felt his feet leave the ground.

In the Channel 8 newsroom Saracenetti, Fuller and DuFroid all yelled "Fuck" in unison as they helplessly watched the live pictures of Mick lifted in the air.

In New York Rod Wings leaned forward over his desk watching the live shot that popped up on TENN's air. The screen carried a lower third: Breaking News! San Francisco.

"Holy crap," Wings muttered to himself. "That's my guy."

In the life and death struggle on the bridge Mick flailed the empty pistol at the beast's head, drawing a little blood, and he banged his other fist on Pete's skull. To little if any effect. Mick felt himself turning in the air parallel to the roadway, the suspension cable in his peripheral vision. A terrible panicked feeling he was going airborne swept over him.

But Mick could feel the man's arms quaver. Perhaps he'd wounded him enough after all. Still, the giant had the strength to push Mick through the opening between the railing and the suspension cable.

Mick went over the side.

His knee struck something, and he grabbed for it. The steel rail that protruded from the road deck a foot and a half. Evidently the giant didn't have enough strength to propel Mick into thin air. Instead, he thudded onto an outcropping of steel, just enough for Mick to cling to. One leg dangling over the edge, he sprawled flat and seized the steel rope that held the roadbed.

He felt a big hand punching at his back, trying to dislodge him. Below white fog surged toward Alcatraz. Below that the deathly maw of rushing tide, an angry, furious chop.

Mick looked down and his heart sank. He clamped onto the pickets of the hand railing.

Mick looked up. Pete Grand was leaning over the railing, his big arms punching and pushing at Mick's back, his face contorted in rage. Both men were desperate. Mick pulled his dangling leg up on the thin ledge. He let loose with one hand. He reached for Pete Grand's swinging arm, caught it, gripped tight, and yanked.

It was shockingly easy. In his fury to push Mick over the edge the big man heaved most of his weight over the top of the hand railing.

When Mick jerked the arm hard Pete Grand tumbled over the railing.

Mick caught a fleeting image of the big man falling past him.

But Pete wasn't done. His big hands latched on to Mick's belt and hips, jerking Mick back over the side.

In the KBAY newsroom all eyes were on the monitors. Gasps and "oh-shit" and "fuck" and "oh my god" rose from the transfixed crowd. Saracenetti's eyes widened like saucers, his hand over his mouth. Danny Fuller winced and slapped his forehead.

In New York Dave Stork got up from his desk and walked up to the monitor. "Hang on buddy," he muttered.

In the studio Martha Molloy calmly told the viewers. "We believe one of those two men is our former colleague Mickey Judge."

In L.A. Grace Russell stood in her kitchen stunned at the picture of television. "For god's sakes Mick," she mumbled.

In San Diego Tammy Judge's eyes bugged at the television. "Mom, come see this," she shouted.

On the bridge two men were on the jagged edge of death. Mick had two hands welded tight to the pickets of the railing.

The huge Pete Grand was dangling, holding onto Mick for his life.

Mick shook his legs and kicked furiously. He felt the big man's grip slip from his hips to his legs.

The big man's weight slipped on the slick material of Mick's pants. Mick felt the light jogging pants sliding over his butt, down his legs. Cold air hit his thermals. Television viewers saw Pete Grand desperately hanging on to Mick's pants, the pants slipping down.

Then the hands were clinging to Mick's boots.

Mick glanced down. The big man was twisting in the onrushing wind, suspended by a thread over the fog. His murderous eyes wide and fixed on Mick, his face contorted in desperation. And terror.

With the bridge traffic halted the ocean rushing in on the tide seemed like the roar of a jet. Mick's hands ached but he willed his grip on the balustrade tighter. The steel ledge cut into his chest. His hands ached and slipped. He squeezed even tighter.

His dad's boots came loose.

He felt the weight release.

He glanced back and saw Pete falling, waving his arms as if that might help. The big man disappeared into the fog bank.

Mick redoubled his tight grip on the steel rope. He swung one leg, and then the other back on the ledge.

Then he felt hands grabbing his collar and his legs. He felt the hands pulling him up. In a moment he was back on the safe side of the railing, lying on the concrete face down, the welcoming cold surface against his cheek.

Mick rolled over. He looked up at the four CHP officers who pulled him up. He turned to one side and saw Bone Hendrix bounding from an SFPD cruiser. He looked to the right. Through the pickets of the balustrade, he could see Spike in the open door of the Channel 8 chopper, the camera pointing at him. He sat up trying to catch his breath. His heart was pounding so hard he thought he could feel it pushing against his shirt. CHP cruisers stopped at odd angles, lights flashing, doors flung open. Four officers standing over him, breathing heavy, grinning.

"You having a heart attack?" Bone asked, pulling Mick to his feet.

Mick shook his head, gasping for breath. "Don't think so."

"You are a dumb shit, but I couldn't let you drown," Bone said.

No shoes. Socks gone. Bare feet. Thermals for pants. It wasn't his best look. He gave a halfhearted thumbs-up in Spike's direction. For the newsroom. And the viewers. He surprised himself with the random thought they'd be on the edge of their seats.

The CHP officers who pulled him over the railing stood back, giving him breathing room. "You guys saved me. Thank you."

Both hands on his shoulders, Bone steadied him on his feet. "Any injuries?"

Feeling weak, Mick managed to get out a few words. "Banged my knee."

"Come on. Get in the car. We have to get out of here and let traffic through. People hate traffic jams."

"Thanks again," Mick said to the officers. "I thought he had me."

Bone glanced down at the Sidewinder lying on the walkway. "You know it's illegal for you to possess that gun?"

Mick bent down, picked up the gun, looked it over. He flicked it over the side. "What gun?"

49

Bone told the cop at the wheel to head for Torpedo Pier between Fort Point and Crissy Field. When they arrived, the Channel 8 chopper set down, let Spike jump out and lifted off again. Trappani was waiting for them in a U.S. government car. He and Bone and Mick and Spike walked to the end of the pier. They waited twenty minutes in the wind watching the Coast Guard boat tossing in the swells under the bridge. Mick was freezing in bare feet and thermals. Bone gave him rubber flood boots from his PD cruiser. Mick slipped his icy feet into the boots and smoked a cigarette. Bone lit a cigar. Trappani quietly disapproved.

"Your boss is a reckless asshole," Bone said exhaling smoke.

"Sounds right. What'd he do?"

"Decided to get pictures of Pete Grand rather than call the cops to grab him. Douche."

"Wasn't my idea."

"No. You were reckless and stupid."

Mick didn't argue. He probably was stupid.

They watched the Coasties. They'd been turning circles looking for the body. Now they were stopped.

"They pulling the body on board?"

"I'm sure."

"He's dead?"

"You're an idiot," Bone answered. The Coast Guard boat headed toward them.

"I know," Mick said.

Spike was on the phone with the station. Mick could hear him directing a news car to pick them up at the Torpedo pier parking lot.

"You actually realize how idiotic it was to use yourself as bait?"

Mick nodded. "Hanging over the edge that was hard to ignore."

Shivering in the biting wind Bart Trappani was chomping at the bit. "Look, glad you're alive, but I don't want the antiquity disappearing on me. Where is it?"

"Safe as a girl in church," Mick said, wrapping his arms around his chest against the wind. "But you may need a search warrant."

"We can do that. Name and address."

"Jean Washington, 32 Presidio Terrace."

"Oh shit," Bone groaned. "We gotta stir that hornet's nest?"

"It's there. I'm sure she has no idea," Mick said. "Cass hid it there."

"Do you know exactly where?" Bone asked. "The judge will want to know."

Mick shook his head no. "Remember that bag you handed to Cass?" he asked Trappani.

"Don't fucking tell me," Trappani groaned.

"I'm positive. I found a torn messenger receipt that showed Cass sent something day before she died."

"Where did you find that?" Bone demanded, immediately suspicious.

"In her apartment," Mick said. "I ran up there right after she fell."

"You fucker," Bone snapped.

"I'll get a Federal magistrate to swear out a warrant," Trappani said, punching numbers into his phone. "I'm the one who has to take possession."

"What are we going to do? Shake down the whole house?" Bone asked Mick.

"Probably. It's in there somewhere."

"Wait," Trappani interrupted, snapping his phone shut. "I'm going to ask a Federal judge to give me a search warrant of the District Attorney's home on your hunch?"

Mick shrugged. "Might be easier if you just asked her if you can search the place. It's not her fault Cass hid it there."

Trappani and Bone swiveled their heads looking at each other. "Let's do it that way," Trappani said. "Just so we're not at war with her."

"Unless she's a suspect," Mick said.

"You still not done with that?" Bone groused.

The Coast Guard boat pulled up parallel to the end of Torpedo Pier. A tarp covered the body. Two crewmen pulled the tarp back. Bone confirmed the identification. "That's him unless prints come back saying it's not."

"Check that out," Mick groaned. "A Kevlar vest."

Bone nodded yes. "You might have hit it once or twice."

The Coasties told Bone to send the coroner wagon to Sausalito, their base, and they shoved off.

The wind blowing in was enough to stiffen a flag like a board. "I'm glad we got the guy," Bone said. "He killed some people. London looking for him, Monterey County wanted him. But I got bad news for you."

"What's that?"

"Grand didn't kill Cass Papadop."

Mick's face slumped. His suspicion was true.

"How do you know?"

"He was at the PD impound yard bailing out his car."

"You positive?"

Bone nodded. "Got towed from a Washington Square bus stop. Got a credit card charge showing he had a drink in the Washbag. Went out, found his car gone. He was in a cab to the impound yard when she went over the balcony."

The image of a big man brushing against the back of his chair at the Washbag flashed in Mick's memory. His heart sank. That was the moment someone was pushing Cass off her balcony.

Mick's mind raced. Then who?

Bone continued. "He's got an alibi from the SFPD. Doesn't get much more solid than that."

Everybody split up. Bone commandeered a black and white. Trappani was in a Fed car with an FBI driver. Mick and Spike got in a Channel 8 news car. Mick called the desk to say they'd need a transmission van at Presidio Terrace.

The unmarked news car slipped through the gate behind the black and white carrying Bone and Trappani's fed car. Mick was leaning against the van smoking a cigarette when Jean Washington's black Suburban lurched to a stop in the gated neighborhood. She was not happy to see him.

She didn't say a word, but she stopped and inspected him up and down. "I'm a little underdressed," he said as she shook her head at his oversize rubber boots, thermals and jacket. She smirked. Turned away.

Her driver, Billy Norton, gave Mick a toothless snarl. He followed his boss in.

The sun was out. Mick closed his eyes and warmed like a lizard.

About an hour later Trappani emerged with the gym bag under his arm. He was wearing latex gloves.

"Hey Bart. I led you to it. Least you can do is show me."

Trappani glanced at Bone, who gave him an almost imperceptible nod.

Trappani pulled the object from the bag and unwrapped the gym pants Cass used to protect it.

Mick said, "Describe it for us, please."

The object lay in Trappani's open two hands. Spike leaned in, his lens a foot and a half above it. "Created about 850 B.C., making it twenty-eight hundred years old more or less. Carved from ivory, probably by Phoenician artisans, who lived in what we now call Lebanon. The rendering of the two figures is exquisite, the lion's paw holding the boy down, its jaws sunk into the boy's neck. It is one of the most important treasures of the Iraq National Museum and it belongs to the people of Iraq. It will be returned."

He wrapped the object in Cass' gym clothes again, slipped it into the gym bag and walked to the idling U.S. Government car. Spike turned and followed him, rolling until his car pulled away.

Bone stopped to answer questions. He scowled and grunted answers in monotone. "It's a good thing Pete Grand is no longer terrorizing and killing people. But he was not the killer of Cass Papadop. That case is still open."

Mick swung by his house. Got some dry clothes, socks, shoes. There was a lot of news for Mick to cover that night. His confrontation with Pete Grand on the bridge. The struggle in which he could have fallen to his death. The fact that the man who threw people from high places died in a fall from a very high place. The recovery of the antiquity that led to the death of Cass Papadop and three others. And of course, the news that the killer of Cass Papadop was still unknown and at large.

It was a big day for Mickey Judge.

Don Saracenetti met him coming off the set after his seven-minute report. "Repeating myself. I said I admired you for being willing to get in over your head, but don't ever, ever go this far again."

Mick smiled. "I don't intend to."

"I mean it. I'll have to fire you again if you do."

Mick caught a cab home. He needed a drink.

Grace called. "You asshole. I almost had a heart attack."

"Book a flight and I'll make it up to you."

The call was interrupted by another call. He saw it was his daughter. "Just book a flight, I gotta talk to Tam."

"Dad this is getting old," his daughter said, scolding. But he could tell there were tears in her eyes.

"I'm not dying honey. I have to embarrass you at your wedding."

They chatted during his ride home. She was shopping for shoes. Did he like Vans? It was weird but endearing. He left her laughing.

He needed to put a call in to Rod Wings to make sure his former boss saw the day's events. But that could wait until tomorrow.

Next on his list: he had to think over the most important question: who killed Cass Papadop?

50

Wajahat Zardari's funeral at Cedar Lawn Cemetery in Fremont rolled out late. Mick was surprised at the delay. Evidently it takes days to get a body through customs. The Zardari family and friends gathered at graveside. Ali stood with his parents, tall and handsome and grieving.

Mick watched from a tree line. He slipped away without bothering Ali. It was not the right time.

The next afternoon he drove over to Fremont, knocked on the Zardari door. Ali answered. "Let's go for a ride."

The young man nodded. "Sure," he said.

"I thought we'd get something to eat," Mick said. They drove away from the house.

"Let's find a bar," Ali said softly. "I think I'd like a drink."

"Oh right. You still facing charges over the antiquity?"

Ali nodded. "Miss Kitty says she can get me out of it. I meet with her tomorrow."

Mick kept his mouth shut.

A Tiki bar on Fremont Boulevard seemed good enough. They sat in a bamboo booth. The handsome boy ran his eyes over the drink menu. "What's a Mai Tai?" Ali asked.

"You don't drink much, do you?"

"I can't think of the last time," he smiled. Sheepish. "Maybe high school."

"Don't drink that Mai Tai shit," Mick said. "You'll be kneeling at the toilet from the sweet stuff. If you're going to drink, make it one kind of alcohol with club soda or water."

"What should I have?"

"So you really never drink?"

The handsome boy shook his head no.

"We'll have two Absolut and sodas," Mick told the waitress. "And bring us some pu-pu's."

They talked about his brother. "How did your brother wind up in the Middle East?"

"He joined the Army to become more American. He was at language school because he already spoke Urdu and some Arabic. They were teaching him French when the Gulf War broke out and he went."

"Why didn't he come home?"

"When he was released from the Army he went back to Cyprus. Then to Beirut. He loved it there. He made it sound so fantastical." A dreamy expression came over the boy. "Every time he came home he told me stories. I wanted to go too."

Mick asked how mother and father were taking it. "They are sad, of course, but Wajahat was a wanderer. I don't think my dad was terribly surprised. He knows what the Middle East is like."

It was time Mick got to the point. "Who knew you and Cass were having sex?"

He laughed ruefully. "That's such a funny expression. 'Having sex.' It's like the sex is something you can have, like lunch. We were making love." His eyes welled up. "I loved her." He looked Mick in the eye. "I really did."

"Did you tell anybody?"

He shook his emphatically. No.

"Did she?"

He shrugged. "She might have. She told me she'd been in an affair with a married guy, and she was breaking it off."

"And did she break it off?"

He shrugged again. "I think so. I guess it's a hard thing to do. She seemed upset and distracted that day. I assumed she had a talk with him."

The call log on her flip phone. The Mayor's number.

They picked at the pu-pu plate and each had another drink. Mick was not surprised the boy was wobbly when they left.

"Best if you just go to your room and take a nap," Mick said when he pulled the car to a stop in front of his house. The boy shuffled up the walkway to the front door.

An hour up the 880 to the Bay Bridge and across the bay to Civic Center. City Hall loomed. Mick walked up the sweeping marble staircase slowly. He wasn't anxious to confront Bobby Vargas-Watson. But he had to.

The Mayor was in his usual place, feet up on the radiator, the gilt-edged window thrown open, smoking, staring off into space.

He swiveled around in his chair startled. His secretary followed Mick through the door, objecting that she tried, but she couldn't stop him. He waved her off. "It's alright."

Mick plopped in a chair. Bobby threw him the pack of Parliaments, and slid a lighter across the desk. "That was quite a show you put on. How's it feel to come back from the dead?"

"You knew before I reported it on the air. She told you she was having an affair with the boy. She was dumping you."

Bobby furrowed his brow, took a deep breath and a long exhale. "This is true," he said, nodding.

"And you were angry."

"This is also true." He continued nodding.

"And you two had a fight. You knocked over the chair and flipped over the couch and the coffee table, breaking things, making a mess."

"How would you know?"

"I was there. Surprised we didn't meet at the elevator."

Veedub said nothing. He stared at Mick. Pursed lips set in determination. Eyes sad.

"And you followed her out to the balcony."

The eyes squeezed tighter.

"And you pushed her. She went over the railing. Did you even reach out to grab her?"

Veedub shook his head slowly. "I would never answer that question."

"Why?"

He took a long minute to search himself for an answer. It came slowly. "I was jealous. Angry. Hurt. I loved her, but she never really loved me." He sighed and spun in his chair slowly. "The young boy was too much. You know how I worried you were going to be next. I took your word for it that you wouldn't. I didn't see this kid coming. Shocked me. Absolutely shocked me."

They were quiet.

"What are you going to do?"

"I was hoping that big guy would be the suspect. I was hoping he would die in a police shootout. Your caper on the bridge gave me hope."

"Trouble is Bone found out where he was at the time. Couldn't have been him."

Veedub nodded. Yes, he understood. "There was the DA. She had gobs of motive."

"But it wasn't the DA. It was you."

Bobby Vargas-Watson shrugged. "I still like her for it."

"Good luck with that. I figure everything points to you."

"We'll see."

"So what are you going to do?" Mick asked again.

The former heartthrob anchor and present-day Mayor seemed to abandon placing blame elsewhere. "I'm going to raise Melvin Belli from the dead." He laughed at his own joke, weird, a bit giddy. "Actually, I got the best defense lawyer I could. I'm going to present myself to Inspector Hendrix. I'm going to say it was a terrible accident. I had no intention that she die. I had no hand in her death. I was present when she lost her balance. I was there when she fell. I've been in shock ever since."

"That's your story? She fell?"

Veedub nodded. "She was threatening to jump if I didn't calm down. She lost her balance and fell. That's my story."

Mick felt like it was his third funeral in a week. "You'll never be governor."

The mayor shook his head slowly. "Don't be so sure. It's California. This is the home of strange and terrible things that really do happen."

A sad smile on his face.

Jean Washington's mean eyes came to mind. "She'll beat you over the head with this. Her wife, after all."

Veedub agreed. "She'll try. But Cass's affair with that boy might embarrass her."

They were quiet for a bit. Mick thought his defense was tragically thin. She fell? A long shot selling that to a jury.

"You know I'm going to report this."

"When?"

"When you going to see Bone?"

He shrugged. "Tomorrow morning."

"You already have a lawyer?"

"Yeah. Kitty."

"Jesus. Not you too."

"Sometimes I can't resist temptation. Don't tell Don."

"She's just trying to get something on you."

Veedup scoffed. "Any idea how many women think they have something on me?"

Mick shook his head.

"I'll break it at 11."

"Asshole" he said under his breath. "Can't give a guy a break."

"You killed Cass!"

"It was an accident."

"You said yourself you were furious with jealousy. The apartment was torn up. Looked like you were in a rage."

Veedub lit another cigarette. Gave Mick an evil eye. "We'll see." He let an optimistic moment take him. "Maybe there won't be a trial."

"Dreamer," Mick scoffed. "She's still the DA. She'll be delighted to put you in prison."

"You going to play this big?"

"Of course. Primary suspect tries to kill me, while my old friend and one-time boss is the real killer. Shocker. The headlines will be screaming tomorrow morning. The New York Times and The Washington Post will pick it up. You'll make the network news." He stopped. "Big," he added.

"Better not say I'm the killer. It was an accident."

"Right. I'll be sure to note that."

Mick left the Mayor's office. He slogged his way across the Civic Center Plaza, and up the short rise on Hyde Street to Golden Gate Avenue.

The newsroom was sparsely populated. The 6 pm crew had cleared out. The 11 pm writers and producers were still gobbling take-out dinners, horsing around. Paul Jockey was the 11 pm show producer. "I got your lead," Mick said.

Paul was in his late forties, bad acne, thinning hair, blotchy eastern European skin, icy eyes. "Can you beat a triple homicide in Marin with kick-ass stringer video?"

"Hang on," Mick said. He sat down at a computer and began to write. In five minutes he was done. He hit the "file" button and it went into the script que. "The slug is Papadop Killer," he said to Paul Jockey.

The producer stared at the screen. Widening eyes. "Do the Don and Pete know?"

Mick shrugged. "Not from me."

"I have to call. Better put some makeup and comb your hair. And tie your tie."

51

Mick dumped the harlot lawyer, Kitty McManus. It was all too weird. His excuse—not that he needed one—was she was representing the Mayor. Mick might be called as a witness against Veedub. She said she understood. "But maybe we should get together. The DA is still planning to bring the Grand Jury back. You should get my insights to pass along to your new lawyer."

There was always a bed in her voice. "Sure. We'll schedule something," Mick promised, with no intention of following through.

It had been a tough few days. Mick holed up at home. Sunny afternoon. He plopped on the back deck with a six-pack of Anchor Steam and a pizza. A good time to talk. He buzzed Grace Russell.

"You owe me a sit down and a long explanation of what happened."

"No problem. I've pretty much told everything to the world."

"The channels down here carried all your adventures. But I think I should get a personal telling. You left a lot out last time we talked."

"I just had to keep some stuff to myself until it was time."

"If we were married they couldn't make me testify against you."

"That's true," he said with a laugh.

"Mick—watching TV—I thought I would die."

"Over it now?"

She ignored his question. "Proud of yourself?"

She liked to needle.

"A little, yeah. As long as I'm impressing you, I guess I'm happy."

"That's sweet." Her attitude softened. "I have some news for you."

"I don't know if I can stand more news. What?"

"A girl who goes by the stage name Dani Charm was picked up

in Pacoima. A brothel complex of three double-wides. Scuzzy as shit."

Mick gasped. "Where is she?"

"Lynwood. The women's jail."

"I'll be at your door in five hours."

The '84 Mustang needed a run anyway. A bag of clothes, the left-over pizza, his dad's thermos of black coffee. The Mustang rumbled through the streets. Stoplights annoyed Mick. He got on I-80 at the 8th and Bryant onramp and opened it up.

The fastest route from San Francisco to Los Angeles is the Bay Bridge to I-580 to I-5. The first leg to the I-5 junction is supposed to take an hour and twenty minutes. Mick did it in an hour. From that point to Grace Russell's house in Tarzana is supposed to take four and a half hours. Mick made it in three hours forty-five minutes. The west side of the San Joaquin Valley was one long blur of green fields and suede hills. Mick glued his eyes on the rearview. If any vehicle was gaining on him, it had to be CHP. He lucked out. No problems. He knocked on Grace's door half an hour earlier than predicted.

"You are dangerous," she said. She threw her arms around him. They kissed like teenagers.

He kicked the door closed. He heaved her into his arms and dropped her on the bed. They got to know each other's bodies again.

The next morning at eight o'clock sharp he called Kip Hinkle in Sacramento. "She's your prisoner. Clear me into Lynnwood to do an interview." No point in bringing up that little betrayal to The Don.

"What's the story?"

"She's going to nail Jean Washington."

"When can you be there?"

"Ten o'clock. I'll be gone by ten thirty."

Danny Fuller pressured the L.A. O & O desk to pop loose a one-man band. They met at the Century Regional Detention Facility in Lynnwood. Kip Hinkle's juice got Mick and the photog into a dayroom. A guard in L.A. Sheriff's Department greenish khaki escorted Dani in.

She liked the idea of being on TV. She fussed with her hair.

"What do you want to know?"

"How was it you were on your way to testify before a Grand Jury in San Francisco?"

"Oh. That," she said, a smile creeping across her face. "You want to fuck with that cop?"

"I want to know what happened."

She began to talk. By the end Billy Norton was doomed.

Tape in hand, Mick headed up I-5 again. This time he diverted at Chowchilla to the Central California Women's facility, the state prison.

Warden Summer confirmed that Billy Norton visited the prison to take a statement from Dani Charm. "He kind of pressured me to move her to the PHU because of her cooperation," he said. Mick scribbled down his quote.

"This is mopping up," Mick told Danny Fuller on the phone. "Just a dirty cop working for a dirty DA."

"By the way," Fuller said. "The Don saw the Vacaville tape. He said we can't use it. Too graphic."

"He's been raggin' my ass to get that tape on the air," Mick objected.

"Yeah, but then he saw it. Also said no way you got a connection between the DA and the killing. So it's dead. He locked it up in his office."

Mick just shook his head. What was the point? He had a copy of the tape at home.

It would just have to be unfinished business. For now.

The 6 pm show slotted him as the lead.

He made it to Golden Gate and Hyde barely in time. He stood over an editor's shoulder. They pulled two bites of Dani Charm revealing the corrupt scheme of Billy Norton. Mick jumped on a computer and whipped out a script. A nice lady patted his face down with makeup that gave him a slight tan. She brushed his hair. He cinched his tie as he walked onto the set.

The story didn't name Jean Washington. It didn't have to. Billy Norton was on the griddle. He would take care of Jean Washington.

Bone called him after the show. "I've been waiting for this moment. Can you give me that tape or do I have to get a warrant?"

"I'm just guessing the station lawyers will want a warrant. But I have a copy. Meet me for a drink. I might lose it at the bar."

They met at the Big Four in the Huntington Hotel. Bone flashed his badge and asked for a booth in the dining room. They picked at bar snacks and pounded down drinks.

Bone was happy to take Billy down. He felt he'd been betrayed.

"What will it take for him to puke on Washington?" Mick asked.

Bone shook his head. "Not much more than the threat of prison. He'll fold."

A week later Jean Washington held a news conference to announce she was stepping down for 'health reasons.' The Oval Office dream was as good as dead right then and there.

Mick would like to have pinned the Vacaville shanking on her. Bone said forget it. "The guy who did it got shanked himself a week later. Whatever reason he had died with him."

Mick thought okay for now. But you never know. Sometimes things take a while to surface.

But the upside? The threat of a prosecution against Mickey Judge for the death of Ladarious Rasheed ended with a thud.

As for Bobby Vargas-Watson he was charged with murder. He had to give up the Mayor's office, of course. He appeared for arraignment in an orange jumpsuit, pleaded not guilty. His trial would take months, but in a jailhouse interview with Channel 3 he claimed he was still a candidate for governor and would swing into the campaign as soon as his acquittal came down.

52

To decompress from the drama—and to make up for keeping them out of the loop for so long—Mick took Grace and Tam to New York on a vacation. Bought first class tickets on United Airlines. Rooms at The Essex House. Stroll Fifth Avenue. Peek in at St. Patrick's. See the museums. See a show or two. Go down to World Trade and get angry over the pile of wreckage.

Mick also had an appointment with Rod Wings at The Empire News Network. Rod took his call. "As long as I'm in town I'd like to come by and say hello," Mick said.

Mick went to the TENN building alone. Grace and Tam had tickets for a matinee. Before the meeting Mick did a hit on the midmorning show about the Reeds story and the shocking end.

The video at the bridge with Pete Grand hanging from his legs had been playing and replaying on national news for a week after the event. His old friends at TENN gave it all one more go. "Since you're in town," his friend David Stork said, "let's get you on the air." He was booked on Martha Molloy's show, and she gushed over having him on the set again.

After the hit on Martha's show, he went up to the second floor for the meeting with Rod Wings. "My God, man, hanging off that bridge you almost gave me a heart attack," the founder of the network said in greeting. The fat man was great, as always. If Mick wanted to come back, he'd make a place for him. "You sure got a set of balls." Rod urged him to think about it.

The war was on the television, but Mick no longer felt the urge. He was flattered to have the offer and he tried to show it. But in the back of his mind he thought he'd probably stick around in San Francisco for a while. Grace and Tam were good reasons.

The ebullient mood didn't last.

The roof caved in for Mickey Judge as they sat in the corner couch arrangement overlooking on 6th Avenue. "I'd have to hose down Elaine to bring you back," Wings said. "No easy thing. She doesn't seem to have forgiveness in her DNA."

As if on cue, a soft knock at the door and the large figure of Elaine Constantine breezed in. The pants suit was funeral black. Her eyes focused on Rod as if Mick didn't exist. She flopped a fresh copy of the New York Post on the coffee table.

"Thought you should see this," she said. She wheeled to go without waiting for a response.

The newspaper headline was what they called The Wood, typeface rarely used because it was so large it seems to scream. FAKE! it read. With a picture of Death in the Reeds.

In shock Mick glanced up. Elaine Constantine was stopped at the door, staring back at him. "Nice going, champ. Got scooped on your own story."

With that she was gone.

Rod grimaced. "Man, oh man, she do hate you," he said, shaking his head. Focusing on the newspaper. "Uh oh," Rod said, picking up the paper. He scanned the opening graf. "Turns out the antiquity returned to Iraq has been declared a copy, not the original piece stolen at the start of the war," Rod read out loud. "That's big," he whistled.

Mick stared at the paper in Wings' hands feeling as if he'd been hammered between the eyes.

Rod passed the paper over to Mick. "Well, she was right. Scooped on your own story." He whistled again. "Now you have some follow-up to do," he added.

Fake? A replica? Not the original? Mick's mind stumbled. "Thanks for your time, Rod," Mick said, jumping to his feet.

Rushing through the TENN hallways Mick's face burned in embarrassment. Beat on his own story. That hurt. Worse, the Beast delivered the blow. How could it be true? How did this happen? "My fault," he mumbled to himself. "My fault." How did I get beat?

Because he let down his guard. Because he took some time off. Because he set the story aside for his girlfriend and daughter. Beat.

Maybe because he was not skeptical enough about the authenticity of the object when it was recovered.

"Shit shit shit," he muttered to himself.

On the street, he jumped in a cab. Downtown to the Fed building. Bart Trappani gave security the okay to bring him up.

Mick felt nauseous. "Bart, tell me this is bullshit."

Trappani was his squared-away self. A Marine Colonel sitting in a prosecutor's chair. He grimaced, shook his head no.

"It looked good at first."

The pace of Mick's heart ticked up. "At first?"

Trappani shrugged. "The piece is gorgeous. Far as I was concerned it was the real thing. At the museum they were ecstatic it was coming home."

"What happened?" Mick scowled.

Trappani pursed his lips, his mouth turned down in a prosecutor frown. "I took it to Irwin Feinstein before I sent it back. He said he couldn't be certain, but he suspected a replica."

"Suspected?" An electric jolt of hope zinged through Mick. "Maybe he was wrong?"

Trappani shook his head no. "I was obligated to return it no matter what he thought. I sent it off to Baghdad. Word came back a day or two ago. They were reluctant to admit it publicly but they agreed with Irwin. I guess they got over their reluctance," he said nodding toward the copy of the Post on his desk.

"Two days ago? You didn't call me?"

Shaking his head, Trappani frowned. "I don't call reporters."

Mick dropped it. He let down his guard and got burned. Can't blame anybody but himself.

Mick's phone was buzzing in his pocket. He glanced at the screen. The KBAY assignment desk. Evidently, the New York Post story had made its way west.

He dropped the phone back in his pocket. He'd call back shortly.

He was flummoxed. How could this be? The replica story didn't make sense. "The piece we recovered was stolen from the Baghdad Museum. True or not?"

"True. We think," Trappani said.

"Okay, we think. But how could there have been a replica in the Baghdad Museum?"

Trappani pursed his lips and thought about an answer. "The only explanation that makes any sense," he began slowly. "is the replica replaced the original some time ago. Death in the Reeds might have been stolen before the start of the war. Maybe way before. Anybody's guess when."

"When do you think?"

Trappani shrugged. "No idea. None at all."

"Are you convinced the Iraqis are telling the truth?"

"About what?"

"Maybe they made the replica. Maybe the Museum in Iraq made it to protect the original."

Trappani shrugged again. "Possible, I guess. They're not admitting to anything. All I know is the authentic Death in the Reeds is still loose somewhere. At least officially."

In the wind. Again.

Mick asked if Ali Zardari could be prosecuted under the antiquity law for possession of a fake antiquity. Trappani wasn't amused.

A voicemail from Saracenetti. "What a pig fuck. Get on the air and dig us out of this hole." Pete DuFroid seemed to be delighted, even personally booking a story slugged "Mickey Judge Mea Culpa" on all the shows, starting at noon.

The rest of day he had opened each hit with an embarrassing admission. "I got burned." He explained he followed the story as a reporter should. "The fact the central figure in the story—the Reeds itself—turned out not to be what Wajahat and Ali Zardari thought it was, what Peter Grand thought it was, what Cass Papadop thought it was … that is stunning news."

Mickey Judge begged off KBAY'S 11 o'clock news. "It's two in the morning here." So his last live shot on the story for Channel 8 was from the network's Times Square studio that evening at 9 pm Eastern, 6 pm Pacific.

"Bottom line," he concluded, "it's personally a blow, of course, and I am embarrassed to belatedly learn the whole saga was about a fake. But much worse than my personal regret, the entire tragic series of events including the death of our colleague Cass Papadop was completely senseless. It was over a fake, a counterfeit. That's a terrible fact, and I'm so sorry for her."

He paused. Then he ended his report. "The whereabouts of the real object, the genuine Death in the Reeds is at this point unknown."

He signed off. "Mickey Judge, Channel 8 News, in New York City."

Grace and Tam sat in the studio to watch the last report. "It's not your fault, Dad," Tam consoled him.

"I know it's not," he said. "But it feels like it."

He needed cheering up. "Your friend David did us a favor," Grace said. "Let's get out of here."

David Stork had arranged a table for three at Rao's, the city's best Italian restaurant. Stork set it up through a friend who had a friend who had a table on permanent basis. That's how it works at Rao's. Grace and Tam were blown away by the marinara, the meatballs and the seafood salad. And the cheesecake. Along with the other happy diners they sang "My Girl" with owner Frank Pellegrino, a Rao's tradition.

It was a fun evening, even for Mick. For an hour or two he was able to forget the wreckage left in the wake of a story that was a ratings bonanza, but ultimately became hollowed out by the senselessness of so much grief over an object that was not real.

He regretted that wreckage. People died. "But how were you to know it was a fake?" Grace asked in the cab headed back to the hotel. She noticed he had sunk back into a funk after the fun dinner. "Whether the thing was real or not, you followed the story. You broke the case and you broke the news. And it was an enormous hit. You said so yourself. The ratings were the station's biggest ever. You have nothing to be ashamed of."

But he was ashamed. "I should have been more suspicious," he said.

The New York City vacation over, they rode in a cab to JFK, filed onto the American Airlines 777 and took their seats for the flight to SFO. Grace and Tam sat together in first class chatting. They seemed to get along better than his daughter got along with her mother. That was a win.

Mick sat across the aisle with a sense of dread. He didn't want to get fired again. He didn't want to have to take Rod up on his offer, if the offer was still on the table. His agent said don't worry, you have a contract with KBAY. But Mick knew all that meant was KBAY would have to pay him. They wouldn't necessarily have to let him keep the job. The suits in New York would probably be the deciders.

Was he going to be fired again?

Was he going to have to be defiant, pretend he didn't care?

He was wracked with worry. He was apprehensive. He was shamed. He was exhausted.

But he needn't have been concerned.

Turned out Grace was right. Ratings counted more than anything. And Mickey Judge had brought home a boatload. Saracenetti was a sudden hero at the network HQ in New York as the accountants toted up the billing. DuFroid was told in no uncertain terms he was to keep his hatred for Mickey to himself.

The newsroom regulars seemed to still be basking in the glow of their time at the center of the news universe. Buzz counted and in this case the buzz was favorable.

"Welcome home," Saracenetti gruffed as he passed Mick in the stairway to the newsroom.

DuFroid walked by without a word.

The newsroom broke into a gracious golf clap as he walked in.

To his great relief Mickey Judge still had a job.

He had to keep his relief to himself.

He was a guy who was not supposed to care if he got fired or not.

But he did care.

THE END

Over four decades **John Gibson** was a television news reporter, a network news correspondent, a cable news anchor and a radio talk show host. He lives in Texas. *OJ's Knife* was his first novel, also published by Stark House Press. He previously published non fiction titles *The War On Christmas, Hating America,* and *How the Left Swiftboated America.*

RENDERING BY KEN LUNDY

Made in the USA
Middletown, DE
16 September 2022